'It requires both thought and generosity to write plausibly about the gulf between age and youth, but Cartwright has the trick of it. This is a book that it is going to last'   *Scotland on Sunday*

'A powerful story of five characters caught up in events beyond their control – his most powerful yet'   *Woman and Home*

'If the world were a fair place then the new Justin Cartwright would be up there with the new Rushdie or Amis. It may be that he's not flavour of the month because his is a quiet voice, composed and deeply elegiac. It's put to stunning effect in *The Promise of Happiness*, a devastating portrayal of a shattered family'   *Arena*

'A subtle, sensitive and highly involving piece'   *Big Issue*

'An unflinching but generous portrait of modern family life'
Hephzibah Anderson, *Daily Mail*

'*The Promise of Happiness* is an elegant book, stuffed full … his true genius lies in the painfully familiar characters he's created. You'll recognize them all, at first with a shiver. But with Cartwright's prose to guide you, by the end you'll have grown to love them'   *Zembla*

'Another beautifully written book from Cartwright … Switching between characters, the author picks out the details that separate generations: language, manners, possessions. He succeeds in portraying love in all its forms in this most accomplished tale'   *Good Book Guide*

'Hugely enjoyable … a sorrowful portrait of a rapidly changing England'   *Sunday Times*

'*The Promise of Happiness* favours a broad canvas and the sort of robust, technically dazzling realist writing we've come to associate with American 'family novels' like *The Corrections* and, especially, Philip Roth's magisterial elegy for innocence *American Pastoral* ... With its devastating breadth of empathy, *The Promise of Happiness* is even better than *White Lightening*'   *Time Out*

'Cartwright gradually reveals a family struggling with conflicting feelings'   *Waterstone's Books Quarterly*

'Hilarious, despairing, rapier-sharp'   *Publishers Weekly*

'Like Jonathan Franzen, with whom he has been compared, Cartwright writes pitch-perfect dialog, inhabits his female characters as fully as he does the male, and glares unflinchingly at contemporary life. He knowingly delineates the darkest traits of decent people; the vain, petty, and hateful things most people say only to themselves. His characters are nonetheless endearing and his intricate, nuanced portrayals of family relationships astoundingly good'   *Library Journal*

'Cartwright has been gaining a formidable literary reputation,

al
is
il

h

a
d
es
st

y
ss
ss
ss
e
s

d
r

s
,
s
n
y

'The pleasure of Cartwright's writing lies in its deft observation. It is a richly enjoyable addition to a growingly impressive oeuvre'
Financial Times

'A novel that will strike a chord with anyone who has ever pondered the invisible hoops that bind families together'
Mail on Sunday Books of the Year

'His flowing back and forth across the generation divide covers swaths of emotional terrain, many passages bearing such a surfeit of wisdom and resonance that one wants immediately to clip them out and stick them on the wall' *The Times*

'One of Cartwright's greatest strengths as a novelist – and he is a traditional novelist of the highest order – is his ability to present us with characters who are lifelike and convincing ... This is a novel very much of our time and for our time ... I doubt if there is a better English novelist of his generation' *Scotsman*

'Love and pain are rarely far apart in *The Promise of Happiness* by Justin Cartwright ... a multi-layered and moving analysis of family dynamics' *InStyle*

'Cartwright is a brilliant stylist of the emotions – classic, yet contemporary. *****' *Eve*

'Cartwright is beautifully in tune with the minutiae of hope, disappointment and curious love affairs within all the family histories in this excellent, enveloping novel – and his emotional intelligence is a joy to read' *Metro*

'A touching, beautifully observed novel written with precision and sympathy' *Spectator*

THE PROMISE
OF HAPPINESS

Justin Cartwright

BLOOMSBURY
LONDON · BERLIN · NEW YORK

Quoted material from: John Betjeman, *Summoned by Bells*, John Murray, 1960;
Bernard Williams, *Morality: an Introduction to Ethics*, Cambridge, 1976, and
Truth and Truthfulness, Princeton University Press, 2002; John Updike,
The Early Stories, 1953–1975, Hamish Hamilton, 2004

First published in 2004 by Bloomsbury
This paperback edition published 2010

Bloomsbury Publishing Plc, 36 Soho Square, London W1D 3QY

A CIP catalogue record for this book is available from the British Library

ISBN 978 1 4088 0707 1

10 9 8 7 6 5 4 3 2 1

Typeset by Hewer Text UK Ltd, Edinburgh
Printed in Great Britain by Clays Ltd, St Ives plc

Bloomsbury Publishing, London, New York and Berlin

www.bloomsbury.com/justincartwright

FSC
Mixed Sources
Product group from well-managed
forests and other controlled sources
Cert no. SGS-COC-2061
www.fsc.org
© 1996 Forest Stewardship Council

For Penny

I am the family face;
Flesh perishes, I live on,
Projecting trait and trace
Through times anon
And leaping from place to place
Over oblivion.

Thomas Hardy

When has happiness ever been the
subject of fiction?

John Updike

Prologue

A man of sixty-eight is standing on a Cornish beach, peeing on small molluscs.

A woman of sixty-four is trying to fillet a mackerel in a low, dark kitchen in a lime-washed and slate-roofed house.

A girl of twenty-three is standing on the set of a commercial in a studio in Shepperton, near London.

A man of twenty-eight is hiring a car from Alamo Rentals, in Buffalo-Niagara, New York State.

A woman of thirty-two is sitting on her bed, her things packed, in the Federal Correctional Facility, Loon Lake, New York State.

These are all the Judds, previously of London N1, now scattered, but, like leaves caught in a vortex of wind, about to be gathered up.

Chapter One

Charles Judd has walked on the beach almost every day for the last four years. When it is cold – it's early spring, but freezing – he needs to pee more often than is natural. Away from the house, where Daphne is heroically trying to cook something fishy from Rick Stein's cookbook, he often pees in the open. There's nobody around, and it reassures him that when he's out of the house he can pee freely. There's none of that gush of youth, of course, and he has to be careful of the wind direction, but still he feels calmed. When he was a young man, peeing imperiously into the urinals at Fox and Jewell, he used to direct a strong stream at the cigarette butts or the blue cakes of deodorant that lay on little rubber mats. This deodorant had an unnatural glitter, and released an unnatural smell of pine. Why do deodorants smell worse than the odours they are disguising? Minicab drivers in London always make their cars stink of resin, issuing from little Christmas-tree things swinging from the rear-view mirror. When he used to send the company car to be washed, he told the fleet manager, Arnie Prince, to ask them not to wipe it down or spray it with Fruits of the Forest or Bavarian Conifer or whatever it was. But it always came back stinking: *What canyer do, Mr Judd, they're Nigerians. I'll try sending a runner wif a cleft stick next time.* Arnie Prince was a card.

At this time of year at the beach the scents are deeply marine. The air itself is loaded with fishiness and iodine and dislocated mussels. He sees a fishing boat coming in over Doom Bar, trailed by freeloading seagulls. The sight still stirs him: that the basics of fishing haven't changed; that the fish lie in the boxes lustrous and dying; that the fishermen throw nets over the side. But he knows that the sight of the dumpy little boats coming up the Camel Estuary doesn't stir him quite as deeply as it used to when they first came down here. He tries to imagine the last breath he will take and the last view he will take in. (Although you don't 'take in' views in the way he had once imagined: science has shown that the brain assembles the images according to its own plan and that you have no control.)

No, his last view is not going to be of *The Maid of Padstow* or *The Cornish Princess* butting up the estuary. He is trying to avoid these thoughts, which suggest the death of hope. He remembers with a pang the last uninhibited fuck he had with a young woman – she was a trainee at Fox and Jewel – and for a few weeks they had fucked blithely in the office after hours. He was so happy, and so was she.

'You love this, don't you?' he said.

'Yes, with you.'

'Come on, you love it anyway.'

'It's true, I love fucking,' she said, 'but I've got a steady boyfriend, you know.'

He knew. That was twenty-three years ago. He walks up the path through the dunes across the tenth hole of the golf course, towards the church, which had once been buried in sand. A squall is coming in off the estuary and he shelters under the lychgate. The church still has a half-excavated look, as though they had dug it out of the advancing sand dunes only sufficiently to let the congregation in the door and some light in the windows. He goes to church occasionally, because Daphne is on the flower roster and helps with fund-raising. He once took charge of a donkey at the church fête. The donkey took off at a fast, determined scuttle and he had run along beside it holding on to a screaming child. When the donkey tried to duck under a barrier he had pulled the child off just in time. Daphne was horrified: *God, you're useless. You're embarrassing. All you were asked to do was lead a donkey and you turn it into a Wild West drama*. It was true that he had tried to liven things up by making the donkey trot, but the bony, dusty, fundamentalist, biblical creature took umbrage. (People don't use phrases like 'take umbrage' any more.) The child's parents had taken umbrage too: *You fucking near killed her, you wanker*, said a short, pot-bellied man in a West Country accent. No good protesting, because it was true that anything could have happened if he hadn't just managed to snatch the child off the donkey's back before it ducked under the barrier. Donkeys are intractable, highly unsuitable for children. Jesus rode a donkey. Appropriate transport for a humble man. And maybe Jesus didn't try to make it trot. Last spring they were going to Jerusalem on a Holy Land tour with Cox and Kings, but the situation in Israel had deteriorated. They got the deposit back. Perhaps they would go when things calmed down.

As he stands under the lychgate he sees the little boat battling its way towards Bray Hill, following the channel, which at low tide is nothing more than the river bed, a dark thread in the water, a bit like the thread they take out of the lobsters from the fish market. In the beginning they used to congratulate themselves: *Look, we're eating lobster once or twice a week*. Some foods seem to confer status on the consumers, the way salmon did before it was farmed. Now salmon is cheap, slimy, and strangely mutant. And now they only have lobster when visitors come.

The rain is moving on; it goes in curtains, drawn along the estuary. There is a connection between all this water – the estuary, the scudding rain, the boat sending up a small frothy bow-wave – and his bladder. There's no one about. As he pees he reads the gravestone:

John Betjeman
1906–1984

He doesn't like the fancy-curlicued, arty script of the headstone. It seems to him to contain volumes of smugness; of taste; of self-congratulation. He walks across the thirteenth fairway, minutely faceted by the rain. You have to hit a pretty good shot to get up in two. Although he was flattered to be given membership so quickly – *fast track* – he has been staying away from the clubhouse itself since Ju-Ju was arrested.

Their house, Curlew's End – 'Which end?' said Clem – stands between the golf course and a lane that leads down to the bay. It is double-storeyed, white-pebble-dashed and slate-roofed, built in 1928 for holiday-makers. The garden is half rabbit pasture, which he mows sitting on a Hayter 13/40 tractor mower. He never told Daphne that it cost nearly two thousand pounds not including the optional disk which prevents crankshaft buckling. He has become quite adept at zipping around the meadow, the two-stroke Stratton engine hammering away, until he stops to empty the rear grass collector. Over by the hydrangeas – the only flowers that truly love life by the sea – he has a compost heap. It is protected by a dry-stone wall and some yew trees, which lean away from the wind. They don't bend at all and yet they appear to be fastidious, trying to distance themselves from something unpleasant. In this way they are very English, he thinks.

But then so am I, and increasingly ridiculous.

The compost is used in the more sheltered part of the garden behind the house, where they have a proper lawn and some flowers, presided over – patronised even – by more hydrangeas. Here he tries to enrich the sandy, thyme-bound soil. As he mows in summer he inhales the scents of grass and thyme voluptuously. The Hayter has six settings and cuts this lawn – the proper lawn – very close. But he has lost his early enthusiasm for jumping on to the driving seat and he has allowed the first rule of lawn-mowing, *little but often*, to lapse. The rabbits help by nibbling assiduously. At first he had tried to control them, but they live in a bramble jungle between Curlew's End and the golf course, so thick and impenetrable that he began to see them as the Vietcong of this little set-up. He concentrates now on keeping them away from the flowers and the shrubs, using netting that makes the garden look like a small concentration camp. The mower is in the garage for the winter.

I must get another dog. The last one – a dachshund – fell over a cliff in full cry.

Now he can see the light in the kitchen and the outline of Daphne moving about. He pauses to watch her and in that instant he sees not only her but himself yoked in ghostly outline to her.

By what paths have we arrived here, beside the sea?

As she pauses to catch Rick Stein's drift, her head bowed for a moment, her self – her thickening body, which is beginning, like the yew trees, to take on a defensive posture – is stalled for a moment. He can't see her face – she is silhouetted – but he knows that she will be frowning fiercely at the page. She hates cooking, but she resolved to master it when they moved here. She felt that she should make a pact with seafood – crabs, lobsters, sea bass, mussels et cetera. It would indicate her commitment to the new life on the seashore, to an active retirement. He has never used the word 'retirement'. To her this cooking could be evidence of a new closeness between them. Maybe she thinks they are living off the land in some way, he a hunter-gatherer, she tending the flame. To him, retirement sounds like the first word of his epitaph: retired, withdrawn from life, in preparation for the long sleep to come, the retreat back into the inorganic world, under a few feet of thyme-infused turf, like Betjeman. Like Betj.

As he looks at Daphne, now chopping something, he sees for a moment Ju-Ju. It is unfair on Daphne that Ju-Ju is taller and more graceful, but still there's something in the quick positive move-ment of Daphne's head that reminds him painfully of Ju-Ju. Once Daphne said to him, 'She's the love of your life.' And he said, 'It's just fathers and daughters,' dismissively. But it was true that he loved Ju-Ju, and it was a physical passion. Sometimes when he was lonely he longed to sleep next to her as he had done when she was a child, although he had never allowed himself to think of her having sex with anyone, least of all himself.

Coming down here, leaving London, was a mistake. And yet whenever he goes to London he sees something repulsive: on the tube with Charlie, he saw opposite them a boy and a girl, with studs in their lips and tongues and ears, kissing. The girl –

probably a drug addict – looked about twelve; she was wearing mittens of rainbow colours and her pale, paper-thin skin was sooted around the eyes. (He can remember chimney sweeps and the smell of soot.) As these children kissed, smiling narcotically, he thought of those magnets he had had at school, which produced a sort of metallic skating between sheets of paper, or made a haystack out of paper clips. Their tongues might become stuck together. Charlie, ever sensitive, said, 'It's nothing, Dad, it's nothing,' when he had sighed, probably loudly. What did he mean? And this is something he has realised about families, that they have idealised expectations of each other. On the one hand more allowances are made, but also more is demanded. There seems to me a sort of Koranic law inside the family, no matter what chaos and madness and laxity rules outside the house. Charlie was really trying to say, 'Lighten up, Dad, you don't want to look like a cunt.' Other members of the family want you to look good, because they share your flesh and blood. And it is true that we all have unrealistic expectations of our family: for example, he often wanted Daphne to be wittier and taller and more graceful because that was what he aspired to himself. At Fox and Jewell he had always been seen as urbane, with a light touch. The clients liked him.

Now Daphne catches sight of him and waves. He opens the gate, the one that leads from the Vietcong maquis and the golf course, and crosses the lawn. Even after rain it is firm. In London the lawn was sodden and heavy. Their house looked over a patch of grass at a Victorian church that was always weeping, like those saints in Ireland, salts and dead rainwater. At the back door, which has its own lean-to atrium for tools and coats and sticks – where the deceased dog's lead still hangs – he removes his coat. It's a National Trust fleece, unobtrusively decorated with an acorn motif. He shakes the coat once, and then changes into his indoor shoes.

'You've still got that hat on.'

'Oh yes. What are you cooking?'

'Rick Stein's mackerel with gooseberry sauce.'

'Sounds good.'

'I'm struggling.'

Four mackerel corpses lie on a board. Neither of them likes mackerel – oily, dark fish with tough raincoat skin – but Daphne feels obliged to buy them once in a while because they are plentiful, cheap and, so all the cookbooks say, nutritious, full of life-giving oils and omega fats. Perhaps she worries about his brain cells.

'You have to remove the backbone and then sort of dust them with flour before lightly pan-frying them.'

'Do you want me to help?'

'Please. It says how to fillet them on page twenty-one, but . . .

He looks at the recipe. The picture shows the fish lying neatly on a plate, crisp, decorated with a small, casually composed salad of rocket, with a glistening mound of gooseberry sauce and a generous – not too refined – lemon wedge next to it.

'I couldn't get gooseberries but luckily we have a jar of lingonberries that we got in Sweden.'

'That was six years ago.'

'Do you think they will have gone off?'

'Everything goes off.'

He sharpens the knives and cuts off the heads and tries to remove the backbone. The flesh of the mackerel is bloody. When he finally pulls the backbone free, what's left of the fish looks like a swab from an operating theatre.

Daphne has opened the lingonberry sauce.

'It's a little crystallised around the top, but deep down it looks all right.'

'Fine. Let's have diced mackerel chunks with crystallised lingonberries and while we are at it why don't we see if we can find those Italian artichokes in oil which we have been keeping since 1979 for a special occasion. We'll just throw them casually around the plate, *à la* Rick –'

'Charles. Please don't.'

He stares at her. His head is full, bulging from the inside against the walls.

'Daphne, do you mind if I bin these fishy remains?'

'You're not cross, are you?'

'No, why should I be? Shall we forget about mackerel for ever? We don't like them and they make the place stink.'

He slides the mackerel off the board and into the bin, and then he scrubs the board.

'Charlie rang. He's in Buffalo.'

'Buffalo. Home of the Buffalo Bills.'

'He said that they are going to take a few days in New York to get her things sorted out.'

He takes his hat off, but as he does so he realises that it will be impregnated with fish oil, which, however healthful, will for ever remain in the fibres of the tweed to remind him of the day they forsook mackerel and his daughter was let out of prison.

'How was your walk?'

'It was fine. Rained a bit, but I took shelter.'

Now they are standing in the kitchen, across the scrubbed table, a jar of encrusted lingonberry sauce separating them, but they both know there is a lot more, a sort of barely controllable turbulence.

'What shall we eat?'

'I could go to the fish and chips on my way back.'

'All right.'

'Chips?'

'Small portion.'

'OK. I'm off.'

'Take your time. I'm on flowers.'

He puts his scented hat back on and goes out into the vestibule. She can hear him fiddling about, looking for the keys, tying his shoes, sighing, before the door opens. For a moment she can hear seagulls. It's like one of those radio shows they used to listen to as children, with comic sound effects when the doors opened. She was once told that they used coconut shells for the horses' hooves. The clip clop, clip clop was in fact just half-coconuts banged down on a paving slab at the BBC.

The mackerel are in the pedal bin and liable, as Charles said, to stink the place up, so she fastens the plastic bag and takes it outside to the real bin. Then she goes out of the front, down the lane – in summer a mass of cars wrestling politely – heading for the bay, and down towards the path to the church. She never goes out the back way through the brambles and across the golf course on her own. Charles will be on his way to the pub at Chapel Amble. For two years now he hasn't gone to a pub around here. He can't bear the thought that everyone knows Ju-Ju is in jail. It's killing him. She went to the medium-security prison at Otisville twice and Loon Lake once: Charles didn't go at all. He won't discuss it, beyond saying, 'I can't do it.' It's killing him. His walks have become longer. He's liable to go out at any time. She's suggested another dog, perhaps something with more sense, like a Labrador. He's always been a person who kept a lot back. In thirty-six years of marriage she's never felt she knew him through and through. When Ju-Ju turned twenty-one she told her about the letter he had written her. He had never mentioned it. She begged Ju-Ju to show it to her: it was a wonderful letter, fifteen pages long, unmistakably a love letter. 'Fathers and daughters,' said Ju-Ju by way of explanation, and she saw that they shared a Masonic code. But that doesn't explain his relative indifference to Sophie.

The lane closes in just before the turn-off to St Enodoc. It's wet and dark. Marriage is a strange thing. She takes comfort in this phrase, which many people use. Coming here has brought them closer, whatever Charles thinks. He believes that in some ways marriage has diminished him. As she crosses the fairway, she sees that the church, up above to the left, has a light on. She came to love the place when the children were small and they first came here on holiday. She went with the children to Betjeman readings and moth hunts on Bray Hill. She once tried to explain to Charles: I feel I belong here. Balls, he said. But he loved it too. He loved the coast path and the estuary. He used to swim, until one day Charlie had had to save him. He had suddenly panicked. It was a year after the take-over of Fox and Jewell, and six months after he was manoeuvred off the management committee. When Charlie came down the two of them would swim out and round the buoy with a bell on it. They had left it late that day and the tide was turning. Afterwards Charles had gone to bed for a few hours, shocked and cold, and humiliated that a skinny boy – Charlie was only eighteen then – had held his arm and calmed him down.

The financial pages had described the take-over as a merger, but really Brown, Kaplan and Desoto had simply gobbled up Fox and Jewell. Charles had to share a secretary and the partners' dining room, panelled with dull portraits, was used strictly for new business. He had been fond of his secretaries. Although they had never discussed it, she knew that he had nearly drowned because of the new management committee.

John Betjeman's association with the place has left a kind of patina, not visible to all. But it coats the village and the lane with warmth and order. Some of the bigger houses, more sheltered than theirs, have a look that – she thinks – only comes with centuries of what her mother called breeding. Although she tries hard, she knows that she doesn't quite have the ability *to make a house a home*. Her mother often used that phrase and it irritated her, but now she is using it, albeit mutely. They lived in a succession of Army houses so that there was always the sense that it was pointless to put down roots, another of her mother's excuses. Now she is trying to put down roots, but her children are scattered and her husband is distracted. At first he tackled the garden and practised his golf enthusiastically while she was taking cooking lessons at Rick Stein's in Padstow. She enjoyed taking the ferry over every morning but she wasn't any good at the cooking. The mackerel dish she tried to prepare looked pretty simple. There is something deeply alien about fish, whatever the cookbooks and pundits say. And the uglier, bonier and more unpleasant their habits, the more we are supposed to like them.

As she walks towards the church, up the path that also leads to the tenth tee, the light is going. Out on the estuary the sea is smudged, as though the silver polish has just been applied and it is waiting for a final rub with a soft cloth. Which it won't be getting. There is still some light in the sky, low over towards the railway bridge, and it is this which makes the light from inside the windows of the church so pale. There's also a stained-glass window, which from here is opaque. She likes this puritan plainness. She goes through the lychgate, down the gravelled path, and to the porch where the flowers stand in a plastic bucket. At this time of year they have to phone Bodmin and they are delivered. You take what you can get. She brings them in.

The church is cold but it will be warmed up for Sunday service. She unlocks the vestry and finds the vases and the hedgehog things that hold the flowers. She is quite good at flowers. In spring and summer they have great armfuls of cornflowers and daffodils, lilies and roses from people's gardens. When she was asked by Frances to come in on the flower roster she rushed back to Islington to Stella Stevens for advice: simple but abundant is her credo now, more demanding on her than the Nicene Creed. With these flowers – some greenhouse carnations, some long-stemmed red roses, and some South African foliage – it is going to be difficult to be lavish. The foliage is coppery and leathery to the touch. But it gives off an exotic scent all of its own as she snips and chops. She likes a small arrangement for the altar and something more generous in front of the pulpit, to suggest that this parish appreciates the visits of the vicar. Charles – predictably – can't stand him. He says that the vicar's little sermons are banal if not actually meaningless. But Charles also understands that it is important to keep up something ancient as a sort of talisman against what is happening in the world. Sometimes if the wind is strong they feel as if they have gone to sea in the good ship *Enodoc*.

The vicar asked her if she wanted him to say a word about Ju-Ju's release on Sunday, and she said, *Better not, Charles hasn't quite come to terms with it. Will you ask him? All right, but I know he won't agree.*

The vicar believes in witness, but Charles doesn't. She hasn't asked him. Also, she thinks that maybe it's quite exciting, quite contemporary, for the vicar to be able to pass on the church's blessing to a sinner. You don't get many clear-cut sins down here.

As she gathers up the flower stalks and puts them in a plastic supermarket bag and carries her flower arrangement out over the cold flagstones to the altar, and as she fiddles with it a little while, she tries to contain her deep unease. For more than two years it hasn't left her, day or night. Perhaps it would have been a good idea for them to stand, hand in hand, to pray for Ju-Ju – to bear witness to something, to anything. It is not as though Charles has an alternative, more worldly, plan. He is asphyxiating himself. He has his own hands around his throat. *He is in denial*, the vicar said. For a moment she smiles as she imagines trying to tell him that he is in denial. Charles thinks you lose some of your soul if you use phrases like that, or talk about a learning experience or healing or counselling. But the fact is they are both in need of all of these.

She places the second vase on the flagstones near the pulpit and it looks pretty good, the russet foliage studded with red roses. Sophie thinks her father is a stick-in-the-mud: *Like what's so important about the old way of saying things? Language is always changing. You should chill, Dad.* As she tweaks the aromatic foliage – symmetrical but not static is the effect she is after – she thinks that if Charles is prised from the wreckage he might sink.

She looks at her watch. Charlie has promised to ring as soon as he has Ju-Ju safely in his hire car. She puts the unused bits of twine and florist's wire and secateurs away and locks the vestry.

'Anyone there? Daphne?'

'Just locking up.'

'Oh those are beautiful, Daphne.'

'Thank you.'

Frances Cooper is wearing a broad-brimmed Australian rain hat and a long Barbour raincoat.

'Raining again.'

Daphne has been thinking of praying for a moment. For Frances the church has very little to do with God; it's more a shrine to Englishness: flowers, history, familiar – if meaningless – hymns, your own kneeler and a sort of bracing draughtiness, long out of favour.

'Daphne, how's Charles?'

'He's fine. Or was when I last saw him half an hour ago. Why?'

'No. I saw him earlier. I just wondered.'

'He's very concerned. Obviously. It's not rocket science to work that out. But with Juliet coming home soon' (she can't quite bring herself to say 'released') 'he's trying to cope.'

'I can't imagine what it's like.'

'It's been hard for us. Ju-Ju, Juliet, was really dumped in it. She's had to carry the can for others. That's the bit that Charles can't bear.'

Daphne knows that this is not strictly true, but over the past two years she has almost convinced herself that Richie was solely to blame.

'I wanted to ask you all over, and a few friends, to dinner, when the time is right. Do you think Charles will agree? And Juliet?'

'It's so kind of you. Charles may not like the idea immediately, but let's give it a week or two after Ju-Ju gets here. Frances, I'm really touched.'

They embrace in front of the altar, in front of her little arrangement of pinks in the Waterford crystal vase. Frances squeezes her firmly against her waxed coat. She's a solid woman. They are both quite solid, filled with middle-aged substances of mysterious origin.

'Shall we walk back together?'

'I just wanted to say a prayer.'

'Oh righty-ho. I'll be off. We're going to an avant-garde play in Exeter that Pip has produced with her group. I've got to get into something less rustic. Obviously. Will you lock?'

Frances sets off, carrying away the postcard takings, which rely heavily on the proximity of John Betjeman's remains and the charming story of the sand dunes that once engulfed the place: in order to keep the church sanctified, the vicar had to climb down through a hole in the roof once a month. So the story goes.

Daphne sinks carefully to her knees, no resting her bottom on the edge of the pew, and prays. She doesn't believe anyone is listening, of course, but she thinks that God encompasses everything that we are and that includes the hand-stitched kneelers and the wind and the squalls on the sea which are also peppering the windows and Ju-Ju waiting in her cell. Her prayers are like the stitches in the kneelers, contributing in a small way to a bigger design. She doesn't pray for anything specific. That would be presumptuous. Instead she recites the Lord's Prayer almost silently. *Our Father which art in heaven, Hallowed be thy Name, Thy kingdom come, Thy will be done, in earth as it is in heaven. Give us this day our daily bread; And forgive us our trespasses, As we forgive them that trespass against us; And lead us not into temptation, But deliver us from evil. For thine is the kingdom, the power, and the glory, For ever and ever. Amen.* She whispers the words *forgive us our trespasses, As we forgive them that trespass against us* more boldly. She is thinking of Ju-Ju, but also of Charles. She kneels for perhaps another minute so that her seriousness and silence will allow the prayer to percolate outwards. She rises from the floor. She has to move one knee and push hard with her arms to get herself upright.

Charles once said to her, We've come to live in a bloody pantomime: the beardy vicar, the fat woman (Frances) with the lesbian daughter (Pip), the fishermen who hate our guts, Rick Stein dreaming up more silly ways to fry fish, the ghost of Betjeman stalking about in plus fours, the lethal donkey derby, the obese children on the beach, the ruckus about the lady golf captain's parking spot. It was funny, but he wasn't laughing.

She turns off the lights, closes the heavy doors of the church, locks them and walks down to the fairway. What Charles seems to have forgotten is that he said the same sort of thing about their life in London: the management committee with its idiot proclamations; the traffic full of murderous yobbos in vans, the dog-poo in the streets, the mad people on the underground. And schools. Thank God that period of their lives is over: schools and tests and places at universities, the middle-class English steeplechase, which so enraged Charles. He wrote countless letters and demanded frequent meetings with teachers. Only Ju-Ju took it all in her stride, never a stumble from St Paul's to Oxford to the Courtauld.

As she crosses the fairway, startling a few rabbits, she remembers Charles saying that Ju-Ju was their *National Velvet*.

Nobody ever mentions that film now, but for me it is still one of the great films of all time. I must have been seven or eight when I saw it first. I dreamed of winning a horse in a raffle. A horse called Pie, because it was a piebald.

In the film it was changed to a bay, and some of the scenes were filmed on Pebble Beach in California. Charlie fell at the first fence and Sophie came off near the finish. It is childish to think in horsey terms, but she doesn't mind. She wants her life to be simpler, so infantilism, if that's what it is, is fine. Her happiest times were with her pony when Daddy was instructing at Sandhurst. It was the longest they ever stayed anywhere, nearly three years. The most glamorous thing she had ever seen was the commanding officer riding his grey up the steps at the Sovereign's Parade. She hasn't been near a horse since she was fourteen, yet she knew as soon as Charles hit it that the donkey was going to run away that day. You have a feeling for horses, which apparently includes donkeys.

She lays the table in the dining room, even though it's just fish and chips from the Codfather in St Minver. She opens a bottle of Australian Chardonnay and pours herself a glass. They have both drunk more over the last few years. It doesn't actually make her sleep better, but it helps her get to sleep. Later she wakes and then it's difficult to get back to sleep. She and Charles no longer share a room. He sleeps in a smaller room, once called the guest room, although the only guests have been casual friends of Charlie and Sophie, often drunk or unexpected. These children can sleep anywhere and make no plans. In London Charlie would go off to parties and reappear two or even three days later. For a while Charles thought Charlie might be gay:

He never has a girlfriend.
He's only twenty, Charles.
I know, but all his friends have.
Will you be cross if he is?
Of course I won't be cross, but I will worry about him.

Two years ago, Charlie had found the beautiful Ana, and he and Ana, despite a short break-up, are together again. She has another glass of Chardonnay. She tries to imagine Ju-Ju's feelings as she is released. The new prison, a low-security prison south of Buffalo, looks like an office park. There will be no heavy doors opening – church doors – to release her. Perhaps she will walk out anonymously, like one of the office staff, to Charlie's waiting car. Charlie has a kind of serenity that she and Charles lack. She knows the reason: a stable and loving home. Charles would have said, *Pass the sickbag* if she had ever claimed such a thing.

I have always tried to be there – as they say – for the children, just as my parents had never been there. The children have been my life's work. And it seems that is not over: Ju-Ju is coming home.

There's a deep silence in the house. When they first came to live here she thought of herself as living out on the fringes of a map. Now she sees herself at the centre of her own world. The map has changed, so that it's London which is remote and unreal. When Charles goes up to his committee meetings, mostly charitable things, he usually comes back looking startled, even confused. His hair, always so thick, returns from London lank and lifeless. Its grey colour, she thinks, is taking on a nicotine stain, like old curtains or pub fittings. At moments he looks seedy and defenceless. That day when he nearly drowned, as she helped him into his bed, she noticed for the first time that veins were appearing on his calves and that he had back fat.

Of course my own thighs are dimpled and, in a certain light, stencilled with blue.

The phone rings. Her heart lurches dangerously.

'No, darling. Charlie's not picking her up till ten, our time. No. I'll ring you right away. Charlie says they are going to New York for a few days to sort out her things in store, and sort out the flat. The co-op. Where are you now? It's half-past seven. Don't work too hard, darling. And eat. Speak later.'

Sophie is always working, and she is much too thin. It seems very poorly organised: they stand about all day and then start work at about four in the afternoon. But still, commercials pay well. Last week she worked for one hundred hours and made over a thousand pounds in overtime. She sees the lights of the car cutting across the rabbit pasture. And then she hears Charles opening the door. She goes to help him with the fish and chips, which are exhaling the scents of the fryer. These are the smells of a different and older world of plain food, believed, wrongly it seems, to have been wholesome and perhaps patriotic, because it hadn't been mucked about with. *A smell of deep fry haunts the shore*, as Betj put it, his nostrils twitching.

'Sophie rang.'

'Oh yes.'

'She wondered if we had heard, but I told her that Charlie was going to ring back. How was your drink?'

'It was fine. I talked to a chap who has something to do with the dome thing, with plants. What's it called?'

'The Eden Project.'

'That's the one. How's Sophie?'

'Busy. As usual. I've opened some Chardonnay, do you want a glass?'

'Yes please.'

She pours him a glass, puts out the plates, and then she unwraps the fish and chips. He is standing near the stove.

'Charles, there's only one cod here.'

'I definitely ordered two. Definitely. Six pounds and eighty pence.'

He reaches into his pocket to inspect the change, but he can't find it.

'You have it. I'll have a sandwich,' she says.

'No, you have it. I'm not hungry, I ate a lot of nuts. I'll just have the chips.'

'We'll divide it and I will get a few tomatoes.'

'You have it.'

'Look, I'll just cut it in half like this. It's a big one.'

'I don't fucking well want it.'

He gets up from the table and catches his thigh and hobbles

towards the living room, which in daylight has a view all the way down to the bay, and he turns on the television. She sits looking at the fish. She's divided it quite neatly. The batter is strangely crisp and bubbly and there is a large gap between it and the fish. The flesh is grey, with an indigo stain where the skin has been removed. Now she can't eat, as though all fish, even this unreformed, solid cod, are reproaching her. She begins to cry. She knows that Charles will appear soon and she tries to stop herself.

'I'm sorry, darling,' he says from the doorway. 'I'm a silly old cunt. Let's just picnic on what we've got. All right? I'm a little tight too. The dome chappie insisted on buying me a large Jack Daniels, which is from Tennessee.'

He sits down; the fish is fine, and with the chips and a few small, cold, hard tomatoes, more than enough. But they have both failed in their own fashion, in the fish department.

Chapter Two

S ophie's job is to look after the clients and also to act as a go-between. The director won't talk directly to clients when he is working. In fact he is famous for his lack of compromise. Sometimes he says to her, *Ask them if they want it done quickly or if they want it done right.* Of course she doesn't put it like that. She says, *He is very busy at the moment, but he has taken on board your suggestion.* And then she gets them another drink or – if she knows they are up for it – she can offer them some cocaine in the production office. She takes some herself: it's the only way she can keep going although it makes her cheeks lightly dimpled like the skin of a lemon or like the heat rashes she used to get on Daymer Bay.

These three clients are Italian. They stand or sit in a gently drifting miasma of cigarette smoke, which is emphasised by the darkness of the studio against the bright lights of the set. They want to be involved, but their ebullience and loquaciousness find no echo in the director. She feels guilty, but then why should she? They knew what they were getting when they hired Dan. Dan enters a sort of trance, lost in the world of lighting and effects. He stares at the monitor for painfully silent minutes, sometimes twisting his long, dark, but greying, hair. In his head there is an image of how it should look, and his particular contribution to advertising is his ability to recreate what is in his head, using live action with effects. Effects are mysterious and even religious.

Today they are trying to make an Alfa Romeo look like a

dolphin. Sophie can't see it yet, because all they have is a car on rollers, against a blue screen. But sixty-five technicians, and three clients, are waiting for Dan. He and the cameraman, Adrian, have been lighting the stationary car for six hours. The camera is mounted on an arm, which in turn is mounted on a dolly and the dolly runs on rails. They haven't even started to rehearse the camera movements, which will all be controlled by a computer, so that each pass of the camera will be identical. Dan specialises in this kind of thing, which is known as motion control. So far as Sophie understands it, Dan will match the camera moves on the car with the camera moves on dolphins. The pictures will be combined digitally and placed on an ocean background, so that the dolphins, with their wonderful streamlined adaptation, will turn into Alfa Romeos. Also dolphins are known for their sensitivity and intelligence, which the ad agency believes is a plus. But there are days of work ahead.

'Dan, what can I tell them? They are restless.'

'Give them some toot. Take them out for dinner. I dunno. We're going to be here all night.'

One of the Italians, Aldo, the art director, is looking closely at the car as if he has seen something distasteful.

'*Sporca. Un po' sporca, guarda qui.*'

'Ee says, eetsa dirty 'ere,' says the copywriter, a girl of about Sophie's age.

'I thought 'e was saying it's a pig,' says Dan to Sophie. 'Porco's a pig, innit? Pork. Porco. Apple sauce. You like?'

A props man with an array of cloths and sprays and polishes attached to a belt around his waist, so that he has a harlequin aspect, rushes forward. He and Aldo cock their heads, bend their knees and locate the problem, a slight flare caused by a piece of diffusing paper coming loose on one of the lights – to be technical, as Sophie sometimes has to be – a 2k Dado, museum quality.

One of the electricians, under the direction of his gaffer, puts down his copy of the *Sun* and climbs a ladder. He adjusts a clamp and covers a corner of the paper with some tape.

'Ow's that, guv?'

'Hokay,' says Aldo.

'Guv?'

'Fine,' says Dan.

The electrician comes down the ladder.

'Soph.'

'Yes.'

'Soph, tell our Woppo friend not to speak to my technicians.'

'I can't do that, Dan. They're only trying to be helpful.'

'Tell them or piss off and I'll do it myself.'

'Jesus, Dan.'

She takes Ornella Illuminati, the copywriter, by the arm. She's the linguist in the party. She has multiple piercings going all the way up her ears. Sophie's small ring in her nose is eclipsed. She has noticed that Continentals often come to London dressed up, as if they are going to a whacky carnival. Ornella is wearing a kilt, heavy knee socks with candy stripes and her hair is short and waxy. Her eyes are very wide open, so that you feel there is a danger of seeing into the eye sockets, like those glimpses of backstage you sometimes get from the cheap seats at the theatre. She leads Ornella to the production office.

'Dan offers you some cocaine,' she says. 'Do you want it?'

'I like-a very much.'

Ornella does a line; Sophie takes very little.

'Tank you, Dan,' says Ornella, giggling. 'Dan is a geenioos.'

'Yes,' says Sophie. 'He is clever. He asks me to say, please don't speak to the technicians. The crew. Speak to me and I will speak to Dan.'

'No problem. We talka too much. Italian people no can keep silence. Dan ees geenioos.'

Ornella kisses Sophie, and puts her arms around her. Sophie is happy that there isn't going to be a scene so soon, on day one of the dolphin transubstantiation, and she hugs Ornella. But then Ornella kisses her on the mouth and tries to insert her tongue between Sophie's lips.

'Ornella, no. Whoa. Like, sorry, I don't do . . .'

But Ornella is laughing. She touches Sophie's front with two hands and makes a cartoon noise, like a horn, *wah-wah*.

'No problem. You gotta nice leetle teeties.'

'Thanks.'

They both laugh. There are no hard feelings. When they emerge on to the studio floor some time later, they are, as people say, giggling like schoolchildren.

Ornella speaks to her colleagues. Sophie is pleased to see that they don't seem to mind at all. Perhaps they see this reprimand as an acknowledgement of their Italian-ness, their essential human-ity, stretching back to Petrarch, and perhaps beyond into the mists of antiquity, which she has never fully penetrated. Or perhaps Ornella has told them the welcome news that there is plenty of cocaine in the production office. Sophie hears the word *cokehye-na*, which is the way they pronounce it.

The camera is now moving, step by step, as they program the computer. The rollers under the car are moving too, so that the wheels are giving off highlights as they rotate. Dan is about to adjudicate on just how fast they should turn. For a long moment Sophie too watches the wheels. When she rang her mother earlier, she was confused by the time difference between London and New York. Ju-Ju, apparently, won't be coming out for another couple of hours. She wanted to speak to her father, who loves Ju-Ju best of all, but he was out.

Eat, you must eat, Mum said. She knew, of course, that her mother was really trying to say that she was concerned: Each day I worry about you. There is an air of desperation about her parents these days. Dad is always out walking briskly on the headland, Mum is trying, for the fourth or fifth time, to learn to cook. And Dad is not able to talk about Ju-Ju at all. He is in complete denial. When she rang she wanted to ask him how he felt now: she wanted to be assured that the weight that has been crushing him has been lifted, that he is happy again. Charlie once said to her, *Dad doesn't want to be happy, Soph. There are some people who don't believe in the promise of happiness.* Charlie has become a bit of a philosopher.

It may be true. But it's worrying the way Dad has closed himself off. If she had told him about Ornella – the little misunderstanding, the bits of metal in her ears, the madness of making a car look like a dolphin – he would be pained and maybe even angry. He's changed; when she was thrown out of St Paul's he had simply laughed: *It's only school and only mediocrities do well at school. Let's go and have lunch.* That was eight years ago, when the world was young. A lot of parents at St Paul's were sort of semi-famous from television or journalism or politics, but even though he was just an accountant her friends had thought he was cool. And he was – until he was fired and they went to live in Cornwall and Ju-Ju was banged up. When he was last in London they met up for coffee in Fortnum's – his idea – and there was a sort of fear and truculence about him. Even his hair – his thick, tousled Ted Hughes hair – was limp and soiled. The bit that long years of training had caused to flow backwards and then downwards behind his ears – pretty advanced for an accountant – was now the texture of . . . She struggles to think of what the texture is; it seems important to be precise, but she can't quite get it. The coke has made her feel warm, right into the cavities of her head.

Now the camera is moving smoothly down the track and the wheels of the Alfa Romeo Spyder are throwing off flashes of light and everyone is happier. It's like a plane delayed: sitting at the airport we are filled with a sort of heaviness, which lifts as soon as the plane moves. We are a restless species. For all the tedium and delays, she loves these moments in studios when things begin to happen. The camera is rising and falling now, to add to their happiness, and the three Italians are sitting looking at their own monitor set up well out of Dan's eye-line. Once you are in a studio and the heavy doors close and the lights are up, you are in a wonderful, artificial world. Anything can be created in here, including cars that become dolphins. It's costing four hundred and fifty thousand to turn those cars into dolphins. Dan's fee is forty-six thousand, and a share of the mark-up, which will be at least another twenty. There are girls from St Paul's with starred A levels and first-class degrees who don't earn that in two or three years. In fact some of her girlfriends are still doing unpaid work experience on newspapers and radio stations. Some are teaching English in the jungle, and e-mailing about the hallucinatory effects of Lariam. Others are doing very well – parent-speak for making loads of money – in law and even in pop music. Reward seems to be scattered in a random fashion in this new-old country. Dan spends his money on things: cars, clothes, furniture, DVDs. He's interested in things. Things to him have qualities and essences which she cannot always see.

Ju-Ju is interested in things, but what she sees in things is not her own image, burnished, but evidence of human striving for the impossible. She said to Sophie once, *You can see everything from rock painting to Michelangelo as an attempt to express the ideal*. Ju-Ju speaks about art with great naturalness. Sophie has tried to remember her voice over the last few years. When she was asked to leave St Paul's, the headmistress told her that it was only because of Juliet that she had been given so many chances: *I believe that you are not as different from her as your record here would suggest. But you will have to go away and work these things out for yourself. We have, reluctantly, given up. Goodbye, my girl, goodbye. I'm going to miss you.*

She didn't mention the drugs. Her study was large, and decorated with prints of Somerville College and a very spindly geranium by the window. Although she had tried to humanise it with pictures of her children and some of the school's best art, her study was unmistakably a high court. Here, above all the restless seething girl/woman longing and fear, she sat in final judgement. The headmistress probably knew that Sophie was helpless. For a while Sophie blamed Ju-Ju, although Ju-Ju was already at the Courtauld and their paths hadn't crossed at St Paul's. While Ju-Ju was striving for the ideal, Sophie was taking marijuana with a boy called Timmy, who was teaching her about sex. She was learning avidly. She would set out from home and often never arrive at school. Her excuses became more and more desperate. She saw her classmates, in that last, terrible term, drifting away from her. The process was like the one described in the science books, continents moving inexorably apart. A gulf had opened and she found herself on the wrong tectonic plate. She could never get back; it had a kind of awful, elemental inevitability. Why couldn't she stop the drift? In her heart she knew that Timmy was a useless wastrel. He wore a tight-fitting knitted ski hat, and carried a guitar wherever he went. He was planning to be something in rock music. His body was very white, curiously bony and soft at the same time. They smoked a lot of marijuana. Then Timmy suggested she sell some to her schoolmates. For a term or so, it had made her feel streetwise and cool, but right from the beginning she knew it was a disastrous mistake. The girls around her knew it too, even as they bought small amounts of dope for the weekend.

Why, darling, why? How could you do this to us? Her mother turned it into a personal drama, of course. Sophie's words to her tutor, said in front of the whole class, *Oh for fuck's sake, it's only weed*, were widely quoted in all the expensive London day schools. Even her mother knew what she had said.

'The thing that really upsets me is that Ju-Ju really made something of her time there.'

'And I fucked up. Is that it?'

'I can't bring myself to say what you did.'

'Leave her, Daphne, it's all over now. Ju-Ju wasn't a paragon, as you know.'

'Charles, I know that all children make mistakes; Mrs Le Maître couldn't have been nicer or more understanding. But Sophie seemed to want to drag us all into the muck.'

'Let's not exaggerate. Just ring MPW and get her enrolled. Bye-bye, darling, you will be fine. I had better get down to the old bean counters.'

He used to walk up to the Angel and take the tube to the City. She and her mother were left in the house that mid-afternoon. It was unbearable. The emptiness pressed on them both. And soon afterwards, Dad was fired. Of course it wasn't called that. He was offered an early-retirement package as a result of rationalisation, following the merger. He took legal action, and lost disastrously. And from that moment his human essences began to dribble away.

In his account, the firm of Fox and Jewell, medium-sized, highly respected for its integrity, had been taken over by cowboys; some of its most respected and senior people had been forced to walk the plank a few years from retirement. It all happened so quickly, so ruthlessly, that his years of drudgery, his quiet progress up the ladder, the endless meetings, the golf tournaments, the Twickenham debentures, the money put away for school fees, the heavyweight dark suits, the laced shoes, the appearance of dependability and honesty – the whole fucking shooting match – now appeared to have been a protracted and cruel joke played on him. Sophie saw that his life, everything that had gone before, was now subject to painful revision. She knew that it was hard for him to accept what had happened. He told Mum that Simon Simpson-Gore had made a corrupt deal with Brown, Kaplan and Desoto to get rid of most of the partners after the merger. Simon Simpson-Gore, who is Charlie's godfather, now has a vineyard in Burgundy, a villa in Antibes, and a house in Palm Springs. He collects Russian Impressionist paintings, which he confidently believes are the next big thing, although once he was happy enough to hang his first wife's cheerful water-colours of sea birds and boats in Aldeburgh on his narrow Islington walls.

And it was Simpson-Gore's affidavit that suggested that over the previous three years Charles Judd's clients were increasingly reluctant to entrust their accounts to him, and he, Simpson-Gore, no doubt out of misplaced loyalty, had to write to many of the clients – copy letters attached – promising to take over responsibility for them personally, in order to keep the accounts. Far from being effectively dismissed, as Mr Judd had claimed, he was offered an overly generous settlement.

Mr Judd had surrendered. The judge ordered Mr Judd to pay Brown, Kaplan, Desoto and Jewell's costs, as well as his own. They sold up in Islington and moved to Cornwall. All this her mother has told her, and sometimes she has heard them arguing about it, endlessly going over what happened, and his lack of prudence. Her mother thinks there is something unstable and unreliable about her father. She calls it a destructive streak. Even when he was pretending to be an accountant, he despised the people around him, and they knew it. Sophie wonders if her mother thinks she has inherited this lack of staying power. Mum believes strongly in genetic bequests.

The Italians are drinking Nescafé out of plastic cups, fastidiously. Coffee is, of course, their subject of special expertise. Ornella says they are hungry. They would like the dinner. And the cokehyena? Yes, very nice. Sophie goes to tell the location caterer, who says she can have it ready in twenty minutes. They have ordered Indian food, because Italians commonly believe that London has the best Indian food in Europe. You can't find good Indian food in Milan: *Non esiste.* Dan will be eating sashimi. He is detoxing (apart from the odd line of coke), something he does every month for two days, and he believes that sashimi is about as natural as it gets; although the problem is, he says, that it makes your shit smell like otter droppings: *That's all part of the game, though. What can you do? I should think our ancestors stunk like fuck.*

'Dan, are you ready to eat? We're going to eat.'

'Go for it. I want to get the Spyder done. The first set-up anyway, then I'll break.'

'How's it going?'

'Slow.'

'Like normal slow or like disastrous slow?'

'Like normal slow. Don't panic. Not yet anyways.'

He turns back to the monitor. She often wonders what it is he is aiming for, or how he acquires this certainty about the way it should look. The Italians have provided their cars and their script and their money, but Dan has taken possession. Only he can turn the Alfa Romeo Spyder and the Alfa Romeo T Spark Lusso into sentient mammals.

It's a Thursday night. Mum's been doing the flowers in the church. Dad has been walking on the headland.

And I have been giving an Italian lesbian cokehyena. Different strokes for different folks, as Dan says.

She can smell the Indian food warming up. Its aroma penetrates the studio by some alchemy, even though the studio has thick, sound-proofed walls.

Spraint. She happens to know it comes from the Old French, *espraindre*, to squeeze out. Squeezings, rather than droppings. She's interested in words. She sees in words what Ju-Ju sees in beautiful objects, the work of humanity, at least the imprint of humanity. Or the squeezings of humanity. She's come to realise that films are not for her. If she's ever going to express herself, it won't be through film but through language. With film you have a mediator between you and expression.

I don't want that. I want to get on with it directly.

It's been forming in her. She never talks about it. And she hasn't told anybody, not even Charlie, that she has applied for university this October.

The Italians – senses chemically enhanced – are very appreciative of the food. It's bog-standard Indian – rogan josh, chicken tikka masala and so on – but they are determined to believe it's wonderful. They point out the dishes they have just eaten to their colleagues: *Incredibile! Questo è molto, molto interessante, una cosa esotica! Mi piace molto!* She doesn't speak Italian, but it's easy to get the idea. She's not hungry. She's nervous. She leaves them, pointing at her phone, and goes to the production office to wait for Charlie's call. She begins to cry. The production office looks on to a car park.

People think of England as historical, green, thatched, I don't know what all, but this is England too: a car park full of pointless little four-wheel drives with alloy wheels and shiny cars with spoilers and behind them a blank brick building, an alleyway full of rubbish, two giant bins overflowing, a sodium light, not so much illuminating as staining the area around.

Then she sees it: This is the colour Daddy's hair is taking on, the precise colour of despair.

Dan comes in.

'Is me sashimi ready?'

'They're just warming it up now.'

'Very funny. Today's the day your sister comes out of the slammer, right?'

'It is.'

'Is that why you are crying? You should be happy.'

'I am happy, Dan. In a way. How's it going?'

'Slowly slowly catchee monkey. How are the Eyeties?'

'They think you are a geenioos.'

'Not far wrong. They were saying in the paper that everyone wants her story.'

'Whose story?'

'Your sister's.'

'Were they?'

'Yes, in the *Mail* anyway. I'm going to eat. You OK?'

'I'll be fine.'

'I'll be fine. Why do women say I'll be fine? I'll talk to the wops while you're recovering. Keep your chin up.'

'Thanks, Dan. I'll be along as soon as I hear from my bro.'

She sits hunched.

Oh Ju-Ju.

Chapter Three

'I shouldn't really be letting you have a car at all, never mind an upgrade.'

'Why's that?' Charlie asks.

'Well, back in 1813, you people like burned our town to the ground, that's all.'

'I'm sorry about that. If I could have done anything to stop them I would have. You were British then yourself, probably.'

He points at her name badge, which reads: *Bethany Smith*.

'No, I'm a real Heinz mutt, German, Dutch, Irish. We were called Schmidt until World War Two. OK, Mr Judd, you're all set. Where are you heading?'

'Loon Lake.'

'Loon Lake? There's nothing much down there, only the Federal pen.'

'That's where I'm going.'

'OK.'

She says OK as if she has heard something significant, perhaps even suspicious. The OK suggests that the lightness of the earlier part of the conversation, her professional charm, might have been inappropriate. Her hair is firmly held in ringlets, which all move together in formation when her head turns; there is a moment's delay as the rear of the paillasse catches up with the vanguard.

'You're all set now. When you get to JFK be sure and go to the rental return, not to the terminal buildings. And leave plenty of time.'

'Thanks.'

'No problem.'

This season's cars are rounded and softened, so that the car park appears to be full of igloos. He scrapes the snow off the windscreen of the Chevrolet Cavalier with a little rake left on the driver's seat. He clears the rear windscreen and pushes and pulls the excess snow away. The air is very cold, but the sun is sharp and bright. As he leaves the airport he has the feeling that he has joined the American mainstream. In America once you are in your own car and under way, you have entered the landscape and become a part of it. American landscape is dynamic; it is a moving show; it passes the windows of cars in procession, as though it has been subjugated just for that purpose. Or – he thinks – it is like back projection in old movies, unfurling in an artificial but pleasing fashion. In a way it's like American life: comforting, flattering and strangely unreal, as though you have entered not just a familiar landscape, but a film you have seen many times. As a matter of fact he has driven the seventy miles to Loon Lake twice before since they moved Ju-Ju here from Otisville.

As he leaves Buffalo-Niagara he remembers Ju-Ju in her unfamiliar low-security prison garb, which looked like orange-coloured doctor's scrubs. The visitors' room at Loon Lake was arranged around a courtyard, with seating areas like a Starbuck's inside and with benches made of slabs of stone outside. Coffee and muffins were available. No guards were visible, although he knew that they were being watched on TV monitors. The women held at Loon Lake seem to have no men. Only mothers or sisters visit them, some with small, stunned children. There is a play area for these children, which includes a tank full of red-and-white plastic balls. Children enter it by way of a ladder and a slide and they duck beneath the surface.

Charlie, now that Ana is pregnant, is beginning to look at children with interest, almost as if he has just noticed a race of pygmies living among us.

Family. Ju-Ju's main worry, back in the summer five months

ago, had been for the family. Particularly Dad. She said, 'Thank God I don't have children. At least that's something.'

But the fact that Dad had not come to see her once in seventeen months worked on her mind.

'Why hasn't he come, Charlie?'

'I don't think he could handle it. He's cracking up.'

'Because of me?'

'No, it started back when Fox and Jewell kicked him out.'

'I wanted him to come and see me.'

'I think he was afraid he would break down. I found it tough enough seeing you the first time in Otisville. He couldn't even bear to hear about it. When I told him they brought you in in manacles, there were tears in his eyes. He got up and walked into the garden, with that smelly little dog. Which is deceased.'

'Oh Jesus, Charlie.'

'It'll be over soon.'

But he knows that it will never be over. Mum thinks that there can be some sort of resolution – the vicar has used the word 'closure' and she has adopted it – if they can all get together in Cornwall. She needs to see them gathered as if this manifestation of family, shoulder to shoulder, will itself prove something. She is trying to put the clock back. She hasn't said it, but he guesses she wants them to go to the church together:

> *The modest windows palely glazed with green*
> *The smooth slate floor, the rounded wooden roof,*
> *The Norman arch, the cable moulded font –*
> *All have a humble and West Country look.*

They will adopt a humble West Country look.

The Chevy is swishing steadily along. A huge truck, aluminium panels and fairground lights – folk art – passes him. She wants them – four and a half atheists – to go to church for closure. They won't be going to St Enodoc to ask forgiveness for Ju-Ju or to call down vengeance on Richie, but to creep back into the fabric of life. The cool silence of St Enodoc is a sort of Narnia, which will show them the way. No, it will never be over: all of them are related to Juliet, who was jailed for selling a stolen window. She was brought manacled into the courtroom in Foley Square as though she would grab the nearest Tiffany object and run if she wasn't restrained. He had spent those awful days looking at the court personnel. The huge Hispanic usher with the streaming nose who sat for four days with her head cast down so as to speed the flow of mucus towards the avocado-coloured Kleenex; the Assistant Federal Attorney, who twitched his shoulders when he spoke, a gesture somewhere between a Mafia hit man and a camper plagued by mosquitoes, and the judge, a bony, heavy-browed woman with a voice so harsh it had a mineral texture. Sometimes Ju-Ju looked back towards him and he smiled encouragement. But from the beginning it was clear to him that it was not going according to plan. Here in Foley Square, Juliet Judd from the Upper East Side, from another planet, a woman with every privilege, was being given a lesson in the way the world worked. Up on Fifth Avenue, or even in Oxford, England, said the prosecutor, the defendant may have been able to convince people she was doing the world a favour, saving some art from the crazy people who live over in the jungle, but we take a less sophisticated view. We don't say, Thou shalt steal objects of great beauty. No, we say, Thou shalt not steal, period. And strangely enough, the laws of the United States of America also forbid stealing. They don't say there's acceptable stealing and bad stealing. No, I repeat, the law is kinda old-fashioned: Thou shalt not steal. The judge smiled, an experienced, hairy, wised-up, darkly complicit smile. The game was up. It was his helplessness that got to Charlie: I'm sitting here, I know the human truths, but there is nothing I can do. The court is not here to understand, only to corral the facts, if they are facts, in a certain direction. And the last thing they want is to hear from me. People can stand there and lie and lie and boast and still leave the court free, but if I stand up and tell the truth, I will be arrested. The helplessness oppressed Ju-Ju too. Her life was being turned into a travesty. It was a cartoon with distorted joke voices and comic characters – loony toons – giving evidence.

*   *   *

He passes Lake Oshkosh; all around the Indian names have survived: Lackawanna, Lake Cuyahoga, The Genessee River – although the departed Indians have long ago submitted to the inevitable. He remembers Ju-Ju when the jury appeared to give its verdict. She stood, her eyes now ringed by a darkness, a sort of liver stain, to hear the forewoman of the jury say she was guilty on both counts, and the judge tidying up her bench as she spoke, saying that sentence would be passed on such and such a day, and until then a bond in the amount of one hundred thousand dollars must be posted. His sister stood there, utterly alone, although her lawyer, a boxy man with an expensive reputation for getting people off, stood next to her. There were thirty British journalists in court.

Charlie pulls over at a diner. He is well ahead of schedule. He tries to call Ana, but he gets their message service, which sounds quaint. All the customers in the diner are wearing baseball caps at a rural angle. He orders a piece of cherry pie with coffee. He particularly likes the glazed cherries, bright, unnatural, cloying. He likes it in the way he likes lots of Americana – clapboard houses, old gas guzzlers, movies starring Henry Fonda, rockers on porches. *Ana and Charlie are not here at the moment, but do leave a message, or you can try Ana's or Charlie's mobile . . .* He sounds quite prissy. He made Ana promise not to tell anyone she was pregnant until he'd told Ju-Ju. Why not?

I don't want her sitting there all alone thinking the world's going on without me. I'll tell her when I go to pick her up.

Ana is beginning to swell up, the bump demanding an explanation. Charlie has inspected the bump and run his hand over it. He never told Ana that it made him feel queasy to see her navel pushing out. This area from the rib bones downwards, which was once sexual territory, is turning into something domestic. It has just been waiting for its opportunity to rise like bread. He remembered his mother saying someone had a bun in the oven. Ana's breasts are becoming bigger and that, too, makes him uneasy. He has seen girls turn surprisingly quickly into capacious, cheerful, straggly-haired mothers in sensible clothes. He didn't really want a child at all, but powerful currents are rushing downriver, taking him along. He has been told – everybody says it – that he will love being a father, that his life will change, that nothing else will seem important – all that banal bullshit. In a way he believes it, but he still can't shake his unease. Maybe when he has got Ju-Ju out and told her the news, and she is happy, then he will be able to put away his reservations. They are unworthy, anyway.

The place is called Lake Keuka Diner and Restaurant. He wondered who or what Keuka was. Out back – in the US he can't stop himself thinking idiomatically – he can see the lake, simply a large ring of snow with no trees on it. A jetty gives an indication of where the water begins and ends. *Thou shalt not steal*, the judge said. Will Charlie be teaching his child not to steal? Probably not. By the time you understand the word 'steal', wrongness is inherent in the concept. Dad has – Charlie knows – wondered how someone he loved so much could have done something dishonest. As a father he used occasionally to say to them, Aren't you ashamed of yourself? Or, How would you like it if . . . ? The paradigm case. And since he imagined Simpson-Gore betraying him at Fox and Jewell, he had become very high-minded on matters of ethics. It's a comfort for him to believe he was too honest in a crooked world.

Thou shalt not steal, or else. The difference between then and now was the warning implicit in the Ten Commandments, namely the certainty of divine retribution. As the Assistant Federal Attorney knew all too well, in these times retribution was not sure at all. It was only by a fluke that Ju-Ju was caught. It was only by a little legal juggling and plea-bargaining that she was cast as the defendant. Somebody had to fill the role. The professional thieves gave evidence against her. She had to suffer more, because, unlike them – people who did thieving for an honest living – she knew how wrong it was. The way the trial was arranged she was given the role, familiar from the funny papers, of evil genius. It helped that she had a hoity-toity accent, in American movies usually an indication of duplicity.

No, it will never go away. At some deep level the family was responsible for Ju-Ju's crime, and we know it.

He pays the bill and sets off again. Ju-Ju will be ready. She's probably been ready since five in the morning. They won't let her out a minute before time. At Otisville, she told him, the women screamed and moaned at night. Many of them, perhaps most of them, were crazy. There was one woman who night after night screamed that she was giving birth through her anus. Others cut themselves. This was the sort of thing his sister had had to live with. And maybe other things that she had spared him. She once said to him that she was probably the only criminal in the whole place, because she was the only one who could have done something else. But could she? For all her success and determination, Richie had found a way below her radar. Although she denied it she had been trying to help Richie. And for that she had suffered the hell of Otisville for eleven months. Love may have blinded Ju-Ju, but he saw Richie for what he was from day one. Everybody said he was charming, but it was the charm of the weak, a kind of bogus otherworldliness that appealed to Americans as being typically British. And his sister fell for it: they became a moderately glittering couple in Manhattan. They talked about big social issues, and art of course, but they were also prey to infantilism, chowing down on especially good muffins and wearing Yankee uniforms to games and power-walking around the reservoir in lurid clothes. Once when he visited them, Ju-Ju was going jogging, carrying some little dumb-bells that were supposed to exercise the arms.

'What are you doing, Ju-Ju?'

'I'm making good on the promise of happiness, little Charles.'

'And you need toned upper arms for that?'

'Oh yes. Charlie, in Manhattan being in good shape is the only manifestation of class.'

She said 'class' in the American way. And Richie was toning himself up too as well as driving his old Jaguar out to the Hamptons and talking about those happy days studying fine art at the Fitzwilliam – *It's in Cambridge. When I was at Cambridge* – et cetera. At that time his gallery appeared to be doing very well. Certainly many lavish books – oh, about lost tribes, and rock art, and impressionists – had been launched there. The art-money-lit-artefacts complex came to his gallery to celebrate not so much art or literature but the richness of life in Manhattan. So Charlie thought. He was young then, although that was just a few years back.

Now I am driving through the landscape to fetch my sister from jail.

And he tries to trace Ju-Ju's progress from Islington, via St Paul's, Oxford, the Courtauld, the Upper East Side, to this remote corner of New York State, a place so rural that there are bears in the woods. He tries to see if there are any clues in her early life, a sort of DNA to indicate that this could happen to her. There is no meaning to it. There is no causal law involved. Hume called causation the cement of the universe. When Charlie was sitting in that courtroom he saw that the cement of the universe was not holding. Now he thinks that there must be some comforting lesson in this, closure, but he can't imagine what it could be.

Ju-Ju never once claimed – it might have saved her – that she did it for love: *It's a loser's excuse, Charlie.* But Charlie, like all the family, cannot believe she did it out of greed.

The forests are deep in snow as he turns off for Loon Lake. French fur traders travelled the rivers and lakes for a hundred and fifty years and they left their language behind: Belleville, Chaumont, Belmont, Portageville. But the topography is also named after Dutch settlers, early presidents, and classical writers as well as Indian tribes and chiefs. It's an American patchwork all right: it's a Heinz mutt of names. He remembers his father sounding off about the sentimentality of the AIDS patchwork quilts: *More people die of prostate cancer, but that's not sexy, of course, Charlie.* Then at Westminster, Charlie had thought it was a powerful symbol. His father was a closet homophobe: *Sentimentality, Charlie. AIDS is a reminder that there are consequences. In life no actions are free of consequences.*

As we have discovered, Dad.

Charlie feels his stomach tightening. The last few miles to Loon Lake are forbidding. Here you have left the American mainstream and are entering its blind appendix. Ju-Ju had told him that Loon Lake was once a little place of fishing cabins and one general store, which sold bait, but when the Federal Government built the Loon Lake facility, as they called it, a small town grew up, providing houses for the guards and a school for their children and a few stores and workshops where the prisoners are entrusted to work and to spend their allowances. Ju-Ju has given talks on art history at the library, which has an adult education programme. Her audience started at five and peeked at seven. They are all women. Out here in the boondocks, art, and the place called *Yurp* where art originated, are still the province of women. Men support the Bills and shoot things, so Charlie believes, although he has no hard evidence. Ju-Ju also told him that this is an *isogloss*, a region of distinct accents and dialects. She has been noting them and trying to find out if they have French and Indian or Canadian influences. She has also written an essay on the art and artefacts of the Cuyahoga, a local tribe who were once part of the great Algonquin Federation. As always, even in a place like this, people have warmed to Ju-Ju. The library went to great lengths to order a book she specially wanted, Hans Kurath: *A Word Geography of the Eastern United States*.

He approaches the town – low-rise mall, some greeny pastel civic buildings, the Junior High with its snowy football and baseball meadow and, all along the edge of the lake, past the gimcrack original fishing cabins. The centre of the town is indicated by a post office, a coffee shop – the Linga Longa – a few stores, two churches and the fire station. The churches, so recently built, are supplicating recruits in an informal manner, with catchy slogans and warehouse architecture. The prison itself – the facility – is set a mile away in the woods. You can see its laundry chimney from here. It's the highest thing in the landscape, much bigger than the concrete triangle containing a crucifix on the RC church across the way from where he pulls in. At Auschwitz when the newly

38

arrived asked the kapos where they were going, they were told 'up
the chimneys'. Charlie is nervous and his thoughts are disordered.
He's got half an hour to kill before the moment that all the family
have been waiting for. He enters the Linga Longa.

'Good morning, young feller. What can I do you for?'

She's from the battered-old-broad school of waitressing, but she
has a girlish manner.

When she hears his accent, she asks, 'Are you Juliet's family?'

And he says, 'Yes.'

'Wunnerful gal. Real shame.'

'Yes, it is.'

'She said you was comin' to take her away. We'll miss her, I can
tell you. I was in her class about Yurpean art. My late husband, he
was in the Sheriff's Department, and he and I was going to go to
Yurp, but in the end we never did make it. He developed a toomer.
Have some coffee on the house, I just put on a fresh one.'

'Thanks.'

'You gonna take her home?'

'I am.'

'I dunno, but that gal should never of bin here. She's an angel.'

'I agree.'

'She done it for some feller, leastways that's what I think.'

'Me too.'

'You look like her. Yes you do. Yessiree, I can see it plain. Same
eyes and nice smile.'

So they have a communion and he begins to calm down. She
tells him exactly where to park and what to do for the pick-up. She
gives him a free refill.

She asks him to bring Ju-Ju in to say goodbye.

'But, hey, I wouldn't blameya if you wanted to lay tracks outta
here.'

Now he is driving the mile or so to the prison itself. It lies very
flat in the woods, apart from the chimney that gleams. There is no
gate, simply a parking lot with a small reception building, loosely
attached to the other low buildings behind. He buzzes to be
admitted. The room is quiet. The receptionist, a very skinny

woman dressed in blue uniform, greets him, and checks his name and confirms that release will take place in five minutes. A bus pulls up outside, presumably to take other released prisoners to the nearest bus station.

He waits with two other relatives on the moulded airport chairs. One of the relatives is a very small black woman whose face has darkly pitted marks, like the shot you find sometimes when you cook a pheasant. An elderly white woman, a country person, Charlie guesses, sits with two sullen girls of about ten and twelve. They have startled European faces, like Sissy Spacek.

Charlie can hear the receptionist's intercom.

'OK, there they go.'

The receptionist leans forward to speak into a microphone on a stalk.

'Release. Here they come, folks.'

And behind her somewhere Charlie hears a lock open quietly.

Chapter Four

S he's all packed up.
As she waits to be released from her cell – her bedroom, as it's called – Juliet reads her father's letter.

From the moment you were born, you have been the light of my life. But it must be recorded that you were very long and red and scrawny when you were delivered. You were still the most beautiful thing I had ever seen. It seemed so heroic, so utterly implausible that you should emerge (looking alarmingly like wet liver) in this way. What you suddenly realise when you have children is that you have been reborn. A large part of yourself, body and soul, has miraculously been recreated.

It's self-centred of course, but I freely acknowledge that my love for you is selfish. You have made me happy from the moment you were born. And you have had the quality of grace, and the quality of understanding, far more developed than your years would suggest was possible. Everyone has always adored you and I have sometimes been jealous that other people could see you as I did. I would have liked you to have a secret self, visible only to me. (Excuse my literary style: I'm only a bean counter after all.)

I love you so much, Ju-Ju, that I have sometimes woken at night, worrying about you. I haven't worried about the obvious things that fathers are supposed to worry about like boyfriends and drugs and so on, but about your collision with life: your lovely innocence and intelligence coming into contact with what is known as 'the real world'. Of course it isn't the real world. The real world is what you make within yourself. I know this sounds trite – *Reader's Digest* wisdom – but I believe it's true: you make your own world. As you go out into the world, try to remember what I have said. Although of course I have not been true to my own precepts. But I find the thought that you, like all of us, may be ground down by 'the real world' unbearable. Forgive me for this, but it's permissible for doting fathers to write to their daughters like this just once in their lives.

And a last thought, you are much more dear to me than my own life.

Fondest love, Dad.

She saw now what her father had been getting at. She saw that he had feared the decay of beauty, the loss of innocence and the death of hope. He was saying you are born innocent and the whole fucking thing begins to go wrong immediately. Children are born not into desert – she had read – but into a living world. But Dad feared the living world. He was very sensitive to its injuries.

For instance, when Charlie's hair began to thin at a young age, Dad suffered. His own hair, still thick, reproached him, so he had it cut short to remove any impression that he gloried in its flourishes. Only she knows why he cut his hair one day. Now Charlie has his hair very short and he has kept fit so that he looks fine, more than fine.

Charlie has visited her four times in the past two years. He seems, on the surface anyway, to be the least affected. Both times Mum came she composed her face into a rictus of concern; she had great difficulty stopping herself from saying how they were suffering. But Charlie hadn't tried too hard. When she was moved up here last summer he had appeared on the first possible day as if it was the most natural thing on earth. His smooth handsome young head was throbbing with messages of good will.

He looked around the meeting room, all pale colours and soft edges, and deep silence.

'Worse things happen at sea.'

'Like what?'

'I can't think of any at the moment.'

And he laughed.

'You look great, Charlie.'

He was wearing a green linen suit and a grey T-shirt. She was wearing the orange scrubs, and the contrast was almost too great to bear.

'Not too gay?'

'Is Dad still worried about you?'

'I don't think so. Not since I teamed up with Ana. But he doesn't talk much these days.'

When Charlie was seventeen, Dad had once asked her if she thought he was gay, because he loved clothes and wasn't interested in playing football in Vincent Square.

'Also,' he said, 'I know this isn't unheard of, but he hasn't had a girlfriend.'

'He's a straight shooter, Dad, don't worry. He's snogged loads of girls.'

'How do you know?'

'Sophie told me. He's got off with half her class.'

'That's a relief.'

'Dad, it's not a race.'

'It was in my day. You had to lay in stores against a drought.'

'All changed. The caravan has passed.'

'The dogs have barked.'

It became a family joke.

On that first visit to Loon Lake, Charlie had helped her forget where she was, for a few minutes anyway. Each morning in the long months she has woken up to a blissful moment of contentment until she remembers. And then she feels as if something has been thrust crudely into her thorax. Sometimes she begins to shake with grief. But, she discovered, she had what French intellectuals called 'cultural capital'. For a start she could read and write; she could fill in applications; she quickly understood the system. She began to help some of the other women, whose lives seemed at first anarchic. She wrote letters, she drafted appeals, she listened patiently to the tales of confusion, mistreatment and addiction. She discovered that these lives were not in fact anarchic; all of them were subject to iron laws of existence that they had no control over. Questions of causality and choice didn't apply in their worlds. They were doomed, almost from birth. And if that was the case, she wondered why they were kept locked up. She saw that Otisville was a reservoir of misery, a sort of parking lot of derelict women. There were courses available and plenty of religious instruction, but few of the women could see any point. They watched television: World Wrestling Association and shows with dysfunctional people shouting at each other – which probably reminded them warmly of home – were their favourites. But still she began to take some satisfaction in trying to help them in their doomed struggles with the world.

Even Sophie had come to visit once. Dad had never come. Last summer she asked Charlie why not.

'Who knows? He's stopped playing golf, he hardly ever gets on his little tractor and he goes for long walks all the time. He talks about getting another dog, but he never does. He feels guilty, but he can't quite understand where he went wrong. The truth is he is clinically depressed.'

'When I was twenty-one he wrote me a letter saying he worried about me at night. Perhaps he was always a depressive.'

'He never wrote to me.'

'To be honest, his letter made me feel a tad queasy at the time. But, Charlie, you know, it's fathers and daughters. It's a kind of a love affair.'

'Everyone always loved you, Ju-Ju.'

'I don't like the past tense.'

'You know what I mean. But you should also know that it got like right up our noses that everybody thought the sun shone out of your arse.'

'Jesus, Charlie, what kind of language is that?'

'I mean it in the nicest possible way.'

'Do you think anybody will ever like me again?'

He paused before he answered. She had time to look at the surprising topography of his head. There was a ridge running around from ear to ear, as though a small piece of twine was lodged under the skin. The eyes, the grey, rather bright eyes, were a family thing.

'The problem, Ju-Ju, is that most people may feel inhibited. Like when someone's died, you put off like speaking to the relatives. You don't want to say anything trite, and then time goes by and you avoid them because you've like left it too long. Mum thinks we must have a get-together, a sort of coming-out party. She wants us to be seen shoulder to shoulder. Your friends will get over it, I'm sure. The tricky question, I guess, is like how you are going to see yourself. That's the thing. I mean because you are my sister and I know the circumstances, I don't think of you as dishonest, maybe just . . .'

'Just what, Charlie?'

As Charlie pondered this, his motile scalp seemed to respond to the question first, as if it was privy to the brain forces within. When she went to live in America six years ago, what her mother called cockneys had already begun to shave their heads, so that a new species of small, pot-bellied, close-cropped men had appeared on the streets. The short hair on the short people seemed to indicate a mood of defiance: *We don't give a toss how we look*. On Charlie, who was six foot two and thin, it looked good, ascetic and purposeful.

I'm like Dad, I don't want my family to decay or suffer.

'Just out of your depth. Emotionally perhaps. Caught up in something.'

'I fenced a nine-foot Tiffany window, stolen from a cemetery in Queens, Charlie.'

'Did you do it for the money?'

'No, not really.'

'I can't understand one thing, which is why you don't say you did it to help Richie.'

'Maybe I did, but it's far from the whole story.'

'Maybe you did. Has he written to you?'

'Yes, a couple of times.'

'And?'

'Charlie, he's finding it hard.'

'I can believe it. The guilt must be unbearable. Two hundred hours of community service and a small fine for not reporting a stolen object. Ju-Ju, he's a bastard.'

'It's not that simple.'

'I think it is. He let you take the fall.'

'No, Charlie. I signed the cheques. And I found the buyer.'

'You only did it because Richie was like going down the pan and he needed your endorsement otherwise there would have been no deal. You were the expert, you worked for Christie's.'

'Is that really true? Excuse me but I don't think so. What I did was wrong, regardless of what Richie did or didn't do. Inexcusable. Most of the people in here and every one of the two or three hundred in Otisville had no choice at all, unlike me.'

'Ju-Ju. Let's not get theoretical. Don't talk philosophy. You let Richie walk away. That's what really happened.'

'No, Charlie, it's true I could have involved Richie, I could have plea-bargained, but the fact was my lawyer said I would just get a fine. He said that if I dragged Richie into it he would get ten years. I couldn't do it.'

'So you got two years, and he got the fine. Wonderful.'

'I don't want to spend the rest of my life being bitter about it. Even though, by the way, the whole case was a show trial, the first time any of over three hundred cemetery robberies in New York alone has ever come to trial. I had a strange feeling in court: you remember how Dad always used to say, "Stop it walking, then stop it flying," as he carved the chicken on Sundays? You always wanted the drumstick: "Drumstick for Charlie, Dad," Mum would say week after effing week. In court, I thought, that's me, neatly sliced off. Is she still taking cooking classes?'

'She's been at Rick Stein's. God knows why she keeps on.'

'Don't be harsh. She used to do a nice apple crumble.'

'And for a while she made a quiche with tinned clams.'

'Until you said the clams looked like little bits of snot. Your words, Charlie. After that Sophie couldn't eat it.'

'I said bogeys, actually. "How much of the liquor from the can must I reserve, Ju-Ju? I haven't got my reading glasses, I've left them by the bed, I think. Is it half a can of reserved liquor?" Reserved liquor, what a lot of crap recipes talk.'

How exactly Charlie captured her tone.

'Charlie, is Dad going to be OK when I come out?'

The thinking cranial geology, the smooth, almost lustrous skin of his face, the bold eyes. In prison everyone's eyes are defensive. They have taken a beating and are expecting another. Many of the women are mad, one or two are defiant, but all of them are bruised and beaten by life. Her own eyes, she knows, have become highly sensitive, ready to close like a wary mollusc.

'Dad's a special case. He's lost his confidence. You know how Mum has her routines and her fixed ideas, it's like he's lost his bearings. Look, it's not easy for him with the light of his life banged up. He's trying to blame nine-eleven or whatever he can: all foreigners were suspect; the dragnet caught my Ju-Ju. He wrote to Tony Blair: "Dear Prime Minister, while you were canoodling with President Bush, the FBI, in response to the national mood of paranoia which you helped encourage, arrested and charged my daughter with a major felony on the suspect and unreliable evidence of a small-time known criminal. Incidentally, I was once a near neighbour of yours in Islington, before you took over the world." Something like that.'

'No, Charlie. Did he really write the letter? You're joking, I hope.'

'He read it to me and I started to laugh. Then I advised him to hold on to it for a while. He filed it for later use.'

'Oh Jesus, he's flipped.'

They were silent for a moment. Charlie took her hands in his.

'Ju, what has happened to you is completely unfair. You're not a criminal, and you're not responsible for Dad's problems.'

'I am a criminal. I have accepted it. And we will all have to accept it, even Dad.'

'Ju, the point is, you will be out quite soon, even if it doesn't like feel that way, but for us you're not a different person.'

'You're floundering, Charlie. It may be that one day I will be less ashamed of myself, and less angry, but I will always be a criminal.'

'Bollocks, Ju-Ju. You did something extremely foolish in order to help Richie. The fact that Richie like turned out to be a cunt doesn't make you a criminal.'

'Charlie, Charlie. It does, it does. I want to talk about you. I have been longing to talk about you. How's your business going?'

'It's going pretty well. Everybody wants to buy it, but I am not ready yet.'

'It's going to be hard to accept that my young brother is a millionaire.'

She was thinking, particularly as I am broke. She's had to borrow to pay the $300,000 fine and legal costs of almost as much. Her co-op wanted her out as soon as she was charged and she had been unable to sell, so it was rented for two years at less than the monthly payments. The self-righteous haste with which the committee acted was shocking. She saw that life is not solid or well-intentioned. Instead it seems to be improvised, and temporary, and knocked together to attract money.

'Do Mum and Dad know you are a tycoon?'

'I'm not exactly a tycoon, but no, they don't. They don't understand the Internet. And Dad thinks clothes are gay, as we know. Can you guess what our best line is? Dark socks. We sell like black socks to City types. They place an order and we send them socks every month. They throw the dirty ones away. And underpants are big and designer T-shirts are also good. It's not very glamorous.'

'Charlie, you're a genius. I always knew you were the cleverest of us all.'

'The trouble with having you as a sister is that you cast a pretty deep shade.'

'And Sophie? How's she?'

'She's got a job in advertising films. She's shagging the director, who's about forty, and taking too much up the nose, so more or less no change there.'

'She'll be fine. She's got whatever it takes.'

She's in her own clothes sitting on her bed for the last time, translucent with suffering. Loon Lake is very quiet. Occasionally she can hear a susurration, like the noise of a distant seashore, but it is just the higher frequencies of the industrial cleaners that move down the halls. In Otisville the screams and moans of her fellow prisoners had kept her awake. Criminality seemed to be inseparable from this harsh, anguished screaming. And another aspect of criminality, which she couldn't discuss even with Charlie, is a fierce, destructive sexuality. Here the silence is supposed to induce calm in the disturbed, but somehow it feels as if life is being smothered.

She is in her own clothes, which have been in a storeroom, some folded, some on hangers, for seven months. They have the smell of confinement. Before that, at Otisville, they were bundled into a plastic bag. She's used some make-up: the duty warder, Gaynor La Motte, who came to explain the release procedure, said, *My oh my, you scrub up pretty good.* Charlie has booked a quiet inn on the Finger Lakes east of here. On the way – she's never coming by here again – she wants to see the Tiffany Prodigal Son windows at the Second Congregational Church, Buffalo. They are based on the rose windows of Chartres and it was Chartres that, in a way, landed her in prison: Gothic windows were the subject of her dissertation at the Courtauld. When she went to work for Christie's she discovered that Louis Comfort Tiffany had been so taken with the colours of Chartres that he had tried to recreate them. He had made a number of Prodigal Son windows. But first he had to learn how to make stained glass again, an art that reached its apogee in the early thirteenth century when it was, André Malraux pronounced, the acme of Europe's painting before Giotto. By the nineteenth century, the art of stained glass was entirely lost. And a strange thing: studying the dialects of this area, she found that the word 'comfort' was used for a rug, a comforter. If you followed

49

the immigration records, it was clear that the word had come straight from the West Country. At the Hudson Valley, where the Dutch had settled, there was no trace of it.

Louis Comfort Tiffany's story was an American story: with energy and capital, he had succeeded, although for nearly ten years he had made little progress and had suffered – like Dad – depression. Juliet became one of the world's leading experts on Tiffany windows, all in the space of a few years, and published her lavish book. The launch party was held at Richie's gallery on West 22nd, and was a great success. They were a couple and were mentioned in *Talk of the Town*: she was described as 'alluring, proof that brains and beauty can happily reside in the same form'.

She sits on the bed, knees together, her possessions in a bag provided by the Federal Government, Department of Correctional Services. She is Whistler's Mother trapped in a moment that might last for ever. The ability of great art to take one moment, one pose, one fleeting expression, and turn it into something universal, something that becomes the culture, fascinated her once, in another life.

In Louis Tiffany's windows she saw America. Not all of these windows were good and the designs seldom matched the technique, but the best of them – the landscapes, the magnolias and wisteria, and a few of the religious works – seemed to her to rival the paintings of Frederick Church and Winslow Homer in their distillation of the unique American sensibility. It did her no harm of course to say these things. Americans, as much as any people, are happy to hear their national genius, their uniqueness, extolled. She wasn't the first European to have cottoned on.

She sits on the bed waiting for the signal, enclosed in this stifling silence. Stained-glass windows have a characteristic that sets them apart: they exclude the outside world. They are windows that do not allow a view; instead they invite introspection, an examination of moral virtues. Among the thirty quatrefoils of the Prodigal Son window in Chartres is one in which the son receives a kiss, suggesting that on his travels he has been up to hanky-panky.

Nobody had noticed until she pointed it out. Sitting or kneeling in Chartres, the thirteenth-century communicant was enclosed by the cathedral's own moral universe, in contrast to the chaotic and arbitrary world outside, which the windows pointedly exclude. Tiffany windows, particularly the decorative windows, don't invite introspection so much as self-congratulation. They are more Protestant, too: Look, we are saved, we are the Elect, we have shaken off fear and superstition and subjugation.

Her thesis had been called *Gothic Windows: the Narrative*. Her book, launched chez Richie, was called *The Glorious Windows of Louis Comfort Tiffany: America in the Ascendant*. The cover, which wrapped right around, was a reproduction of the William Nel Strong and Sarah Adelaide Knox Strong memorial in the First Presbyterian Church, Albany. It contrasted lustrous colour with dark, twisted trees, all subtly lit with patches of sunlight that suggested election. Technically and aesthetically it was a masterpiece of Tiffany's style, without the lurid vulgarity of some of his less successful windows. The glass itself was infiltrated with the express promise of happiness.

I am the prodigal daughter, she thinks, as the minutes shamble reluctantly by.

Now there is an announcement, in the significant and confidential tones they use, that release is in five minutes.

She is sitting facing the door which, all being well, will soon open quietly, as discreetly as a fridge door, with a reluctant parting hiss. The crazy thing is, her door is usually only locked at night, but perhaps a release must be formalised. Kimberley Mayberry, who kidnapped her baby, and went on the run before killing it, is being released today. Joyce Biehl, who held up general stores in three states with a borrowed shotgun, is also being released.

And I, the piece of wet liver released into the world thirty-two years ago, am about to be released again.

I am young, and already I have lived too many lives.

I have seen the screaming pinkness of black women's mouths.

I have lost sight of the beating wings of art.

I have betrayed, and I have been betrayed.

I have broken my father's spirit.

As the door opens, almost without sound, two fish kissing, the prodigal daughter lies down on the bed and pulls the rough blanket up over her head.

Chapter Five

Almost three years before

Daphne is alone in the house. Outside the rabbits are approaching the edible things, as they always do when darkness begins to fall. Actually darkness in Cornwall – she is learning – seems to come in waves, sometimes almost literally, as the sea mist, half water, comes in, deadening the landscape, so that she can imagine highwaymen on Bodmin Moor and wreckers putting out lights at Cadgewith. Darkness seems at other times to rest only in patches, so that the sea might be silvery while the gorse along the golf course and the back of Bray Hill are utterly blank. Sometimes the hay field beneath the house seems to give off its own light. Ju-Ju has got her sensitivity to light and colour from her. It is in her family – on her side of the family as she sees it – sort of lined up with its banners. Families harbour distinct and sometimes warring genes. Her side are aesthetic, Charles's side more pedantic, especially about words. Charles doesn't like new words or words he calls 'collective nouns' used in the plural. When one day Charlie said, *A gang of boys were trying to mug a kid on the tube*, Charles said, **Was** *trying to mug a kid. And did it succeed?* And Charlie said, *No, Dad, it did not succeed, one prevented it. You know what, Dad, you're a sad sack. Get a life*. Charlie was fifteen at the time.

Actually Ju-Ju seems to have had the pick of both sides of the family: word skills and artistic ability. And she can play the piano.

It is almost unfair on the others. That's something she never anticipated, that you could wish your own daughter was not so talented. Or rather that the other children shouldn't suffer by comparison.

The rabbits are advancing into the open. They take comfort from each other, so each rabbit goes a little further than the next one in a game of grandmother's footsteps. Charles is playing golf. He plays twice a week. And sometimes he lingers in the bar, the nineteenth hole, as her father used to say with a little emphasis, as if he was saying something witty: *The nineteenth hole*. Another of his favourites was, *All's fair in love and war*. As a little girl she never understood what that meant. How could you be unfair in love?

Her father used to refer to the people above him – perhaps better organised people – as box wallahs. He was sustained by the idea that he was born too late. Men of action, simple fighting men like him, were no longer required. Pen pushers, grammar-school grey men, boffins, all seemed to be favoured ahead of him. When he had finished his stint as instructor, the promotion to Colonel never came. He had run up Sword Beach in 1944, pistol in hand, when she was just five. It didn't help his career; perhaps, like those officers who took part in the last cavalry charge of the British Army at Omdurman, he was thought to be an embarrassment. By the time of the Gulf War, the idea seemed to be that you just pressed buttons, and stayed as far away as possible.

The rabbit invasion is now complete. They have crossed the dangerous open space and are approaching the shrubs and vegetables. The dog is on the golf course with Charles, or perhaps waiting anxiously in the car, peering out hopefully, while Charles has a few drinks with Paul Fairbairn and Clem Thomas. Paul is a retired City man and Clem is a retired engineer, but it is important for all three of them to maintain the fiction that they have business – small directorships, some family trusts, a consultancy, a charitable board – to look after. They each have a computer in their houses and they have more or less mastered e-mail. They talk about it a lot, and the fact that it enables you to stay in touch from anywhere in the world. All three see some redemption in mastering golf: getting the handicap down is their mission. Everyone has goals these days. Even companies, good old firms, have mission statements. Charles says that Paul cheats. None of them wants to admit that this is the end of the line. They're taking time off from the real business of life although Daphne is not sure what that could be. Clem is something of a lady's man and despite herself she finds him amusing and a little risqué. He says the sort of thing Charles never could, which women like to hear, even when they know it is utterly bogus. For instance he once said she had bedroom eyes. Her father used to describe men like Clem, a trim sixty-six, as ageing Lotharios. A Lothario was a greaseball of some denomination. In those days, foreigners were prey to many weaknesses. The weaknesses seem to have crossed the Channel and taken hold here. Or perhaps, and this is more likely, we were a little smug.

If the dog was here she would have sent him out to disperse the advancing rabbits. Instead she takes a wooden spoon and a saucepan and trots out bludgeoning the saucepan. She sends the bunny shapes bounding for cover. But they'll soon be back: rabbits seem to have short memories. But then, to be a rabbit at all must demand a fairly limited understanding of the dangers.

When she gets back into the house, the phone is ringing.

It is Charlie.

'Mum, is Dad there?'

'No, darling, he's playing golf. He should be back soon.'

'Mum, I have got something to tell you.'

She starts in fear.

'What? What is it?'

'Ju-Ju has been arrested.'

'What are you talking about? What do you mean, arrested?'

'A lawyer rang. She's being questioned about an art theft. I don't know the details. The lawyer says it's a mistake. And he's like posted a bond – bail – so she should be out soon.'

'Why didn't she ring me? Charlie?'

'I don't know, Mum. I'm not sure if she's allowed to make any calls. She like gave the lawyer my mobile number.'

'Ring the golf club. Your father's probably in the bar. What's it all about, Charlie?'

'I'm not sure, Mum. I hope it's a mistake. OK, sit tight. I'll call the club.'

'Don't ring off, Charlie. Please.'

'I'll just speak to Dad and then I'll call right back.'

'Please, darling.'

'Don't worry, Mum, we'll straighten it out.'

She thinks of him as a boy, cheerful, eager enough to please, but also quick and independent. He will sort this mess out. She tries to remember exactly what he has said. Ju-Ju is being questioned. Maybe she hasn't been arrested, just summoned to give evidence, as an expert. Over there they issue writs at the drop of a hat. But Charlie said that she is being bailed, which means she has been arrested. Why? Why?

It doesn't occur to her that Juliet could have committed a crime. She waits by the phone, but Charlie doesn't ring. When the car finally comes down the lane and turns into the gate, she runs out to Charles.

'Charles, what's happened?'

But Charles does not do what he should do. Instead he strides past her into the house. He almost – she thinks about it for days – pushes her out of the way. The dog tries to make restitution by jumping up and scratching her knees.

'She's been involved in a theft. Has Charlie rung again?'

'No, he said he would. Charles, what do you think has happened? Is it a mistake? It must be a mistake.'

Charles's forward-angled face is damp and flushed. He is wearing his new golf windcheater, in claret. On his head he wears a tweed cap, although he also has a baseball cap in the club's livery. The moment is to return to torture her: Charles becoming angry, and, in his golf clothes, looking confused and even a little ridiculous.

'It doesn't sound like a mistake to me. Where's my address book?'

'Where it usually is, darling. I'll get it.'

Still wearing the rustic cap, he fumbles with his address book. He starts flicking through it.

'Why are you watching me like that?' he asks.

'I'm not watching you like anything, darling. I'm just very, very concerned. Are you trying to ring Charlie? I know his number.'

'No. I am not.'

She sees that he is drowning again. He takes his reading glasses off, wipes them with his sleeve and puts them on again. One arm of the glasses is pointing upwards, above his ear, minutely semaphoring a message of disorder.

'This house is gloomy. It's always dark.'

Outside the bunnies are advancing boldly with the night, or perhaps in anticipation of the collapse of order. Charles is trying to find someone to ring, somebody important, who can sort this out. He dials a number hastily and she can hear the error signal. He dials again: *Our office hours are between 9 a.m. and . . .* He fumbles with the phone and puts it down. She feels intensely sorry for him, but they are saved by Charlie's call. She picks up.

'Sorry I took so long to get back to you. It's not good news. She has been arrested, apparently for like selling a Tiffany window which had been stolen. The question is whether she knew it had been stolen.'

'What's he saying?'

'She has been arrested. But it's probably nothing to do with her.'

'Let me speak.'

He pulls the phone away from her. The phone is all they have.

'Who rang you, Charlie? Who? Get me a pen, Daphne.'

And so they stumble into the darkness, which is the news that their beloved daughter may have stolen a valuable window and sold it to a collector in Japan. More than two years of hell are starting, although Daphne cannot believe, she will never believe, that Ju-Ju is guilty.

*   *   *

That night they discover, if there was any doubt, that they are minor people, somewhat adrift in the world. And more shocking for Daphne than this impotence is the realisation that she and Charles share nothing of substance except the children. Their good qualities, few enough, have somehow accumulated in the children. And now people are saying that Ju-Ju is a thief.

'What are you going to do, Charles?'

'For God's sake, Daphne.'

'It's a perfectly reasonable question.'

'All our damned lives you have known exactly when to reproach me.'

'I'm not reproaching you. I'm worried. We need to do something.'

'I'm trying to do something. If you would only shut up for a moment.'

'Why don't you ring Simon? He's in with the Americans.'

'Daphne, Simon is a shit. An A-1 shit. And the sort of Americans he is in with, as you so quaintly put it, are accountants. What Ju-Ju needs is some hotshot New York lawyer, preferably Jewish. Maybe she has one, I don't know. Charlie just said she has a lawyer. I'll ring Charlie again.'

'What about Richie? Can Richie help?'

'I don't know.'

He tries, unsuccessfully, to ring Charlie.

Later, as they sit miserably, Charlie rings again to say that it looks as though Richie has left town. But at least Ju-Ju has been bailed. An hour later Ju-Ju rings from her apartment, a co-op, as she calls it.

'You didn't do it, did you, darling?'

'I can't talk, Mum. All I can tell you is I am out of the FBI's custody, and I may be charged. If I am, I will be tried in a few months.'

'The FBI. Ju-Ju.'

'Mum, try not to worry too much. When I know exactly where I stand, tomorrow anyway, I'll call back. I must go to bed. I'm so sorry, God knows what time it is with you. Can I speak to Dad quickly?'

'Yes, please do, he's got some questions for you.'

Charles takes the phone. She studies him closely. Under his bottom lip, the pores are bunching and puckering, and above his nose where his eyebrows, increasingly bushy, just avoid each other, is a small floe of skin, backed up. Where has it come from? Could it be possible that she hasn't noticed this before? The pores are open and slightly oily. Ju-Ju is doing the talking; Charles seems calmer. Occasionally he says yes, OK, uh-huh, understood. He doesn't ask any of the right questions, such as would she like them to come to New York. She, Daphne, has some money in the post office for a rainy day and this is that day.

'Get another pen, Daphne, this one's running out.'

He begins to write down some numbers. And while he's writing and making businesslike hooting noises, she thinks in her panic about a million things. She thinks about New York and the co-op, which has a lift right into the front hall – this is apparently important – and something she had never seen before, large tubs of flowers, narcissi and tulips, which we would think belonged in the garden under a tree, but which are available here, eleven storeys up, to bring perfect spring into your co-op. They even come in baskets, the soil hidden by moss. And she remembers putting Ju-Ju to bed, how she would suddenly go from fully awake to unconscious with just one roll of her eyeballs as a warning. There would usually be a brief sighting of those little quails'-eggs whites and she would be gone. And now Ju-Ju must sleep; nothing's changed. She remembers Charles carrying her to bed. He was young then, in his thirties, and so sure of himself.

She's crying. Charles turns away. How long does this conversation last? When it's finished, she can't even make a guess.

'What did she say, darling?'

'She gave me some numbers. She's going to need money. And she wants me to ring some people. Also she wants me to see if Richie's mother knows where he is. She gave me the number.'

'Is that all? Does she want to see us?'

'I didn't ask.'

'Why not?'

'She's been in FBI cells for twelve hours, since 5 a.m. her time.'

Her time. Her universe.

'I'm going to go in the morning. Don't worry, I'll pay for myself.'

'Don't be so damn silly.'

Why does she make this stupid declaration of independence? A few plane tickets to New York – they're all so cheap nowadays with the Internet and so on – are not going to break the bank. As Charles has no doubt registered, she is claiming the high ground. They have always fought, at a low level, for Ju-Ju's approval.

Charles starts to get ready for bed. He locks the French windows, although this may be the last place in England to experience the new realities, and then he takes the dog, which has been lying puzzled on a needlepoint rug by the fireplace, out of the kitchen door. *Rabbits, get them. Rabbits*. The dog has become sanguine about rabbits. It trots, swaying, towards the door, its claws clattering on the Amtico tiles.

Daphne wishes they were back in their old house. This bunny-haven, these wind-battered, sheep-cropped, gorse-spiked fields, the freezing implacable booming sea down there, the wretched bungalows with their slate patios, the relentless wind trying to get in under every tile, the sense that they are all just holding here for departure, all this makes her long to be home in their Victorian terraced house where the children grew up. The children's lives filled the house. She had a – she struggles with the word, but she can't find a better – she had a focus. And now she sees that maybe that's why she wants to rush off to New York, to regain this lost sense of purpose. Although she doesn't believe all of it, she sees that the health and family pages of the newspapers are right when they say that people – mainly women – should have a focus. Everybody is doing a lot of focusing these days. It's only a word, however much Charles hates it, but it contains a truth: you need some purpose. Her work at the church, only partly religious, doesn't quite do it. She has a feeling that leaving their narrow house near the canal was reckless, almost sacrilege. She's crying again. Leaving that house has led to this: Ju-Ju being arrested. She remembers Ju-Ju staring at the television, opening her mouth like a blackbird for each spoonful; even then her concentration was fierce. Her eyes never moved, but her little mouth gaped wide. Sarah-next-door's boy wouldn't eat a thing, however lavishly he was bribed. Charles was never there at meal times, always at some do or other, or some client golf match, arriving home tipsy, saying he was never going to do these damn things again: total waste of time. And of course, going to them. All partners have to do these things, part of the game, unfortunately.

The dog doesn't want another walk. It follows Charles unwillingly, creeping along. Charles feels bitterly angry that he doesn't know how to help his daughter. He hopes a walk will clear his head. It's typical of Daphne to suggest that he get in touch with Simon, that two-faced crook. Daphne doesn't really think he ever engaged fully with the world, when he was a partner and hosing the cakes of deodorant and screwing trainees. And secretaries before that. Deep down, Daphne's suspicions are well founded. He has never at any time felt that the world he was in was the right one.

He has to stop himself blurting things out these days. A few weeks ago outside his club in St James's Square, he heard a young man say to a woman, 'Look, there are issues about marketing, you must take them up with Mel and discuss them.' And he had said 'Bollocks' audibly as he passed. All these companies with all these people scrabbling for something: recognition, self-esteem, sales targets, promotion, mortgages, share options, pay rises. All complete and utter bollocks. Don't they know they will be dead? He wished many times that he had been as bold as Ju-Ju. Bold and blithe.

The wind off the estuary is cold and wet. Ju-Ju had once said to him that beauty was redemption, and he had said arty nonsense, but he understood what she meant. Consider the lilies of the field.

He is feeling sick, as though what has welled up inside him is a physical thing, a tumour or a foetus growing out of control. He also feels angry: his only justification for the boredom and humiliation of life at Fox and Jewell, and latterly Brown, Kaplan and Desoto, was the belief – instilled in him by school, post-war dreariness and by his father – that drudgery was noble. It was necessary for country and family. My God, what a deception. He took accountancy because – his father's dictum – there will always be work for accountants. And it turned out not to be one hundred per cent true. Ju-Ju had been in no doubt that she would live in a world of beauty. He remembers her coming into his office in the City, only fourteen, and sitting behind the Moroccan leather-covered desk with the repro Directoire lamps and the eighteenth-century lithographs or engravings or whatever they were of Cheapside and the Mansion House, and the dark-green velvety carpet.

Dad, this crap is not really you, is it?

Darling, I'm an accountant.

You're just playing at being an accountant.

After Oxford she went to the Courtauld for her MA and wrote her prize essay on Gothic stained glass and she was happy. He used to visit her sometimes at lunchtime; they would eat a sandwich from Pret a Manger, watching the new fountains splashing merrily on the cobbles. Then accountancy disgorged him on to the pavement.

The dog is increasingly reluctant to walk. Charles feels inside himself the tumour growing; he must walk or it will burst. Man and beast, they head along the side of the estuary towards Greenaway. The rabbits, their ears flattened by the wind, are nibbling away. Despite the wind, the sea is only moderately angry; it's slopping against the rocks, slopping and sucking and gurgling. He feels he has to walk on, past Greenaway, past the empty caravan site. It's one-thirty, maybe two. He knows he's being unfair to

Daphne. She'll be worrying. She'll be seeing again all his wilful-
ness, what she calls his destructive streak. But he can't bear to be in
the house with her. He can't bear the knowledge that his daughter
has been manhandled into a police car, that she has been searched,
and photographed front and profile, and that she has been charged
with a crime. And he can't bear his certainty that Daphne, in some
way, blames him. He remembers Ju-Ju putting her legs up on his
green-topped desk and he remembers seeing her panties and
feeling pain that somebody would be removing her panties soon
and that the animal–human business would begin.

We are all subject to its tyranny, but somehow women come off
worse.

He walks down on to Polzeath beach. Conditioning kicks in:
the dog, thinking it must be playtime, seizes a piece of seaweed and
frolics ponderously. The tide is out, and the grey sand is firm
beneath his feet. It's a long walk across the sand to Baby Bay,
which was where they – and other desperately upbeat parents –
brought their children when they were small. There you could see
the English at play: soft-fleshed, nesting women, small chubby
men, spindly inept children, ranged against a backdrop of striped
windbreaks and Kelly Whip ice-cream vans. It was a kind of
undemanding infantile heaven, when it wasn't raining. Later they
had moved to more isolated coves that required, in that congra-
tulatory English way, a hike carrying all the ancillary equipment,
the frisbees and the buckets and the green tennis balls and the
travel rug and the crab sandwiches. The unspoken reason was that,
on these remote beaches, you would not meet the working class
who could not bear to stray too far from the deep fryer, something
Betjeman had observed forty years earlier. There was a chance,
almost worse in Charles's mind, of meeting someone from London N1.

And later still they took holidays in Portugal and Mauritius. As
he walks, he feels the swelling inside him subside. Ju-Ju had
wanted to live in a world of beauty, but look where it has got
her. That's his crude reaction. He knows it's crude and unfair. He
is walking up a steep path on the National Trust headland.

Something terrible is happening to him: his personality is fragmenting so that he can be insensitive and crude and guilty all at the same time. He's experiencing the pain of being one of those Englishmen who knows he is out of time. Only with Ju-Ju does he have a sense of what he really is. And now that she needs him, there is nothing he can do. Perhaps he should ring Simon. Perhaps Simon will feel obliged to help him, because of his treachery at the time of the fishy merger, and the threats he made, off the record, to him during the hearing, which forced him in the end to give up and practically bankrupt himself. He had never told Daphne the nature of the threats. How could he? And this is the person Daphne wants to ask for help. He has a yacht in Palm Beach and he's probably skiing in Aspen, ergo he's in with the Americans. But if there was the remotest chance it would help, he would even ring Aspen or the ship-to-shore satellite phone number.

The dog won't walk. It's sitting now, only its ears responding to his urging. The dog knows that this walk is folly. Charles turns for home, and miraculously it recovers its energy.

By the time he gets back to the house, it's nearly four in the morning. He fears that Daphne will be sitting waiting for him. He knows that at some deeper level, a level not accessible to the male intuition, he has failed her. And now he's been set a test at which he cannot possibly succeed. His beloved daughter is in the hands of the FBI. They – he corrects himself – *it* won't be taking any account of human weakness. Ju-Ju fell for Richie, and Richie is behind this. Richie has left New York, apparently. In the morning he will ring Richie's mother. She lives frugally near Bournemouth, sustained by monthly cheques from her only son. He must persuade Richie to go back. Even though he has no idea of the facts, he knows that Richie is to blame.

Daphne is sleeping. He waits a few moments to see if she is dissembling, but then he hears those little familiar noises and exhalations, which have become more pronounced and even deranged in recent years. She is asleep. Like Ju-Ju, she goes out immediately, no matter what. He undresses and pulls on his pyjamas, and still she gives off these minute noises, little whimpers and snorts, and he goes quietly along the corridor to what she calls the guest room, although they never have guests, and climbs in under the blankets and whispers Ju-Ju's name and hopes that he may sleep and never wake.

But he doesn't sleep.

Chapter Six

Ju-Ju is lying in the tub. Charlie is in the barn tasting wine. She lights the scented candles the inn has provided and she hopes in this way to hasten the removal of the stain that prison has left on her. It has almost certainly gone deep, like moisture on old manuscripts or like water-colour laid on wet plaster. The human stain.

Charlie booked the inn. He found it on the net. It is his idea to approach New York slowly. The tub has a view down to the lake over vineyards. She inhales the fruit odours of the candles eagerly, and gazes down towards the water, which is rippled by a wind so that it appears to be in metallic flux. Sometimes the sea in Cornwall is just this dull silver colour, beyond the beach where she and her mother used to collect sea-glass to make necklaces.

I mustn't place too much hope in Cornwall.

In Buffalo earlier they drove through the bombed-out streets where obese people in stretchy Buffalo Bills clothing wandered, eating as they went. The church was standing somewhat exposed in what had been a prosperous section of large Victorian houses. The neighbourhood looked now as if an army had moved through it: buildings were burned out, fly-screens hung on one hinge and crudely lettered signs advertised discount liquor and haircuts. Some of these haircuts were illustrated.

They found the church's caretaker, a small, furtive Ukrainian in an extra-large overcoat, who let them in a side door after taking their money carefully and folding it, maybe as a precaution against the Cossacks. There in a side chapel was the Prodigal Son, the Schoomacher memorial window, a tribute by Tiffany not only to the Dutch American family, which had made money in barges on the Great Lakes, but also to the great window of Chartres. Tiffany had taken the three-light perpendicular Gothic – the Ivanhoe look – and added lilies and magnolias for the homecoming scenes and a rich roundel – the round bit at the top, Charlie – that contained tulips and a Dutch sailing barge. The prodigal son in the central light is being clothed and fed.

'It's one of his best windows,' she told Charlie, 'it's his rendering of Chartres, but it's unmistakably American. It's glamorous.'

When she first arrived in New York to work for Christie's, she saw the Tiffany windows in the Met. They had American qualities which she quickly came to recognise: competitiveness and a lack of inhibition. The self-abnegation of Old Europe was gone. The Bible and its images were not, it turns out, admonition but congratulation for the elect. And no people were more clearly elect than New Yorkers. She saw in the next few years that this was the spirit of New York especially, a place which believed itself blessed and slapped itself on its own back with childlike pleasure. As a consequence it also had a large number of bitter, disappointed people. And she started on her researches, which resulted, two and a half years later, in her book.

Charlie was grave. Art, when it's directed your way, produces this anxious response.

'It's so fucking beautiful,' he said. 'The colours are so vibrant but so subtle.'

'Technically Tiffany was a genius. Unlike others he never painted on the glass; he used layers of glass to produce these wonderful effects. You can tell me to shut up at any time.'

She looked at Charlie's face, itself bathed by the light from the window, so that he could have been a young saint, perhaps Francis of Assisi, scanning the skies to see if his pigeons are returning safely, and she had to turn away, remembering his earnest attempts to build barriers against the water as she looked for sea-glass. Charlie was never daunted by the daily proof that his efforts were doomed. Sometimes he enlisted Sophie, but she panicked as the waves lapped over the sand fortifications. She seemed truly concerned by the evidence that some things were out of control.

And as they stood beneath the window, only six hours after her release, she tried to re-enter the world she had once inhabited, but somehow the more elemental world of confusion and anger still had a hold on her. Charlie had had to come into her cell. To be honest it didn't need much to persuade her to come out. The moment she saw him again, holding some dime-store flowers, puzzled, she got off the bed.

As they left the church, wished God-speed by the diminutive Ukrainian waving from inside his large coat – he had an earthy, root-vegetable quality – she started to explain to Charlie her reasons for not wanting to leave her cell.

'Ju-Ju, don't explain. It's like you so don't need to. Let's just head for the lakes. We're booked in for two nights with the option of staying longer. You don't have to explain anything, just get yourself back on this planet.'

'Charlie, my little Charlie, you are – I don't know – strangely mature.'

'Believe me, it's an act.'

They left grey battered weather-ravaged Buffalo and rolled on. In America you don't just travel to get somewhere, you travel in the expectation of reward and fulfilment. When Ruskin said that the railway had allowed the fools of Buxton to visit the fools of Bakewell, and vice versa, he had missed the point. Typically English and snobbish too. Although – as Dad liked to say – the English are losing the restraints that once bound them.

When you first arrive in a city you don't share the received wisdom nor do you understand the prejudices and hierarchies. You don't know why one street, only a few blocks from another, is five times more expensive. Nor why an art gallery in a warehouse in a rundown area will prosper while another, where the rich people live, will die. These understandings extend to restaurants and bookshops and stores. And it takes even longer to know the confused and scattered suburbs, with their small celebrations.

After a year in New York she knew her way around Manhattan and Long Island including Brooklyn and further afield up into the Bronx and Queens, and also some of the towns of upstate New York and of New Jersey. The Tiffany Studio's own list of commissions for windows – there were three thousand – guided her all over the city and the state. She learned that many windows had been lost or vandalised. But also she discovered that cemeteries and gardens of remembrance held mausoleums with Tiffany windows that nobody had ever seen or catalogued. She found windows in cemeteries out in the boroughs, in the Bronx and under the flight path of JFK and also in Hoboken and Newark. She could soon read the social history: it was as clear as the rings on felled trees. Usually a once grand church stood in a street of capacious houses that had been doomed to dereliction by the flight to the suburbs. Sometimes the windows had been left untouched or been protected by the new Gospel or Orthodox churches that had moved in after the spirit of Episcopalianism and Methodism and Lutheranism had followed the congregations to the burbs. More often the windows were broken or boarded up. Once in a chapel of remembrance she had found perfect pebbles of Tiffany *favrile* glass lying on the floor, in tobacco and a magnolia pink whose colour reminded her of the heather in Cornwall. The chapel was a crack den.

Starting with the Met's American Wing, which had reconstructed the façade of Tiffany's house, Laurelton Hall, she plotted New York the way radar picks up the blips that turn out to be solid objects. And all the time, of course, she was getting to know the restaurants and galleries and neighbourhoods.

'Hello, gorgeous.'

In New York Englishmen adopted the manner of Englishmen in films; there were really only two kinds, the good-looking, slightly foolish public-school boy in suede boots or the cocky hard man, short spiky hair and leather.

'*Hello, gorgeous?*' she said. 'Does that really work over here?'

'You would be surprised, it seems to. I'm Richie de Lisle, and this is my gallery. In fact I'm your host.'

'Excellent Chardonnay, Richie de Lisle. Shame about the pictures.'

'Yes, the pictures are crap, but they seem to be selling. You're at Christie's, aren't you?'

'Yes, I'm Juliet Judd. I'm pond life over there. But thanks for inviting me anyway.'

'You need a middle name or two. Juliet Sackville Judd. Sound good?'

'Sorry, I'm from Islington, we don't do middle names.'

'Never mind. Come, I would like you to meet the artist. Zachary, Zachary Birdseye, meet Juliet, Juliet Judd from Christie's. She was just saying how much she loves your work.'

Zachary Birdseye was a tall man with very dense, dark hair, which had been razed with precision by baldness, leaving the scalp between the dark, supporting hedges vulnerable to attack by any number of forces, from religious ideas to biting insects.

'Nobody's buying,' he said miserably.

'Zachary, they're buying, trust me. You stick to art, and I'll handle the commerce. Look.'

From his pocket he produced some red stickers on a roll, peeled one off and placed it in the corner of a work, which was an enlarged and silkscreened tourist postcard of the Twin Towers smothered in ivy for a ruined-Gothic look.

'This one is on its way uptown.'

Close up, Zachary Birdseye's head was lightly beaded just like the outside of Juliet's glass, caused by the cool Chardonnay's introduction to the body-warmed gallery.

'I sometimes think I have strayed into a Woody Allen film. I know that's not fantastically original or anything, but it's true,' she said after Birdseye had shuffled anxiously away.

'Life imitating art, et cetera. We don't know the difference here. Do you want to have dinner later, when the freeloaders have gone?'

'If this was a Woody Allen film, you would say, *I know a great little Italian place not far from here*, but don't you think you should be with your artist? He looks distressed.'

'Don't worry about him – the men in white coats are coming at nine-thirty. Yes or no?'

'OK.'

'Don't sound too enthusiastic, will you?'

'You don't look very reliable to me. But still, yes please, yum-yum. Oh, Richie.'

'Yes?'

'There's one condition: don't overdo the boyish charm.'

'Super,' he said, squeezing her upper arm.

She starts the motor of the jacuzzi, and tries to imagine that it is relaxing her. The water rushes around pointlessly. Some of the women in the jail said that, when they were out, when they hit the bricks, they was gonna get theirselves a hot tub, ooh-hoo, oh yeah. Richie wrote to her twice in two years. He is living in Europe somewhere. Possibly Hydra. Charlie thinks that Richie is responsible for all her troubles, from the moment the FBI came to the co-op at five in the morning. She turns off the bubbles and tries to calm herself, although the Swedish Bilberry scents are choking her. Richie's perfunctory and somewhat formal letters expressed his deep regret, his disappointment at how it all turned out, the perfidy of lawyers, et cetera. It was like getting a letter from a politician, urged to write by his secretary. Her father never visited her. Her mother said he couldn't bring himself to see her in distress.

'Is he angry with me?'

'No, definitely not angry with you. No.'

But as her mother said it, Ju-Ju knew that he was angry. He was angry that his life hadn't turned out the way it should have and that all the hope he had invested in his daughter had come to nothing. And this is worse than the humiliation of being dragged out of bed and the loneliness and terror of being locked up with mad people. And yet eventually some of the mad people had become her intimates. What she had discovered – she should have realised it from the beginning – was that these women were living in another moral universe. They were criminals only in the sense that species are classified by a zoologist. They were really a subspecies of the human race that is not able to make moral, or many other, choices.

Most of them suffered, a few were strangely untouched, yet all of them, and that includes me, had been treated in an arbitrary way.

The FBI knew that Richie had been offered the window by Anthony Agnello and that Richie had needed money desperately and that he had asked her for her help in finding a buyer. Yet on a technicality – that she had actually dealt with the Japanese buyer – she was convicted of a Federal offence, while Richie was convicted of a state offence, carrying a large fine and community service for not reporting a suspected stolen property to the police. An act of kindness on her part, because she knew how desperate Richie was, had become a major crime.

But however arbitrary the conviction, she was guilty of a crime. There was no opportunity to explain to the court the true human circumstances. Her fellow prisoners, who had murdered their children or smuggled drugs or crudely defrauded credit-card companies, were less culpable because they knew nothing else. What they did with their limited resources was known as crime, but that was not a category they recognised.

Agnello was the star witness. He was funny, a Damon Runyon figure. He had been robbing cemeteries for years, stealing urns, statuary, benches and stained-glass windows. The way he described his life of crime made the jury roar with laughter: Agnello depicted himself as just a regular guy trying to make a buck. It wasn't so funny for her, of course. He had stolen the window years before. Nobody even knew it was missing. His career was full of colourful episodes; he described stealing an urn from a cemetery, which proved to hold someone's ashes. He had felt real bad as he emptied the urn into the yard behind his house in the Bronx. He recounted how he had removed the window. He and two friends had spent half the night getting it out. He showed a picture of it to a dealer, who said he would see if he could authenticate it. This dealer – a fellow citizen of the Bronx – had contacted a British guy, a Limey, who had a gallery because his girlfriend – also a Limey – was an expert. It turned out to be the real deal. And the rest, as they say, is history. He was a born storyteller: even the judge laughed, her thin lips revealing curiously pink guinea-pig gums.

In Woodlawn Cemetery, up in the Bronx, one of the comic Agnello's favourite haunts, there is a small stream that falls down a picturesque waterfall and meanders and babbles through the three hundred acres before disappearing near the Thruway. The chuckling of the water, the artfully placed trees, the mausoleums set sufficiently far apart offer the promise that to lie here is going to be restful and also the promise of recognition of worldly success. Yet, as Juliet discovered, more than a hundred windows had been stolen from here over the years, some of them by Tiffany and his rival La Farge.

Juliet examined many of the surviving windows; some were signed by Tiffany Studios, others, unsigned, were also clearly by Tiffany. She could identify them and date them at a glance now. The glass itself contained all the clues she needed. But also she came to recognise the subject matter, more or less offered by catalogue, from the Angel of Resurrection to the landscapes, which often featured a gentle waterfall in a setting of magnolias and wisteria. She came to see something endearing about Tiffany: his windows had an unmistakably American quality; they wanted to be liked and admired. She thought, although she never talked about it, that you could understand a country and its people through art.

Her lawyer had tried, ill-advisedly, to suggest that, because of her love for Tiffany, she had wanted to save the stolen window. After all, nobody had reported it stolen and many windows had been lost to demolition or vandals. In her summing up the judge had been contemptuous of this argument. She was equally dismissive of the lawyer's argument that the defendant could not have known that the window was stolen simply because it was not on the register of stolen art. Did she make further enquiries? No, she didn't. But the clincher was the cash cheques that were produced at the trial, signed by her and cashed by Agnello. Who, the judge asked, did she imagine Agnello was, an international connoisseur? Richie had asked her to pay Agnello because he had nothing left. Agnello wanted cash, and she had had to write five separate cheques, so that he could cash them on different days to avoid money-laundering regulations, which restricted cash withdrawals to ten thousand dollars.

In a recess her lawyer had urged her to explain that she was only helping Richie.

'She's got it in for you. This is not turning out the way we wanted.'

But she couldn't do it.

America was in the ascendant; it needed its own art; it could afford its own art. Woodlawn was the final resting place of those who had made it in America. This harsh capitalist struggle with government regulation and city hall and the immense movement of lumpen raw materials, the laying of the railroads, the arrival of the immigrant masses, the fervour of work, the explosion of wealth, had a triumphant outcome for the winners: they would lie, bathed at certain times of day by the soft light of Tiffany, and soothed at all hours by nature's own voice, the babbling brook.

In America's first garden of remembrance, the people buried here formed a rough poetic roll call of America's rise. That's how Ju-Ju saw it, and that's where she found the title for her book. Some of the mausoleums are as big as the houses down below in the Bronx, certainly as big as Anthony Agnello's board-and-flypaper dog kennel. In Woodlawn the Armour meat packers lie next to the Babbit soap manufacturers. The Bearded Iceberg lies next to the inventor of barbed wire. The father of golf lies near the father of the Blues; the most hated man in America, Jay Gould, looks towards Gail Borden who gave the world condensed milk. Six mayors of New York are buried here, including Fiorello La Guardia who said that there was no Republican or Democratic way to collect garbage. Robert Woods Bliss is here, but only in spirit: he was lost on the *Titanic*. J.C. Penney, F.W. Woolworth and Samuel Cress are here, representing retail. The railroad magnate Collis P. Huntingford lies in granite and marble splendour. The body of A.T. Steward, the store magnate, was stolen from one of these tombs and was ransomed for $20,000. The handover took place on a rural Bronx road, somewhere near where the zoo now stands.

Wealth looked to the classical for a final endorsement: many of the tombs have classical themes, others biblical or Egyptian motifs, scrolls, urns, columns, inverted torches and exedra.

The unstoppable rush of American history. Juliet believed that she understood the hunger for success and beauty and Arcadia and salvation, all of which Tiffany catered for. Tiffany himself was the victim of the rushing torrent of change, falling out of favour for decades.

Charlie knocks on the door. She pulls on the white towelling robe – white towelling is luxurious – and opens the door. Charlie has a bottle of wine in his hand.

'I've brought a bottle of their finest gnat's piss. Come.'

The sun is striking the lake weakly. There are patches of snow still on the hills at the other side of the water. Charlie lights the fire. She drinks for the first time in two years. And then Charlie sits next to her and puts his arm around her.

'I'm a bit pissed,' he says. 'I don't think I spat out enough.'

He squeezes her and she feels as though he is trying to transmit something to her, perhaps the gelatinous bone marrow that they share. He begins to hum cheerfully.

'Coldplay,' he says.

'Who are they?'

'Never mind.'

She's missed a lot in two years, obviously.

'Little Charlie, who used to make dams on the beach. You were an angel.'

'Ju-Ju.'

'Yes?'

'I have a confession.'

'Oh God, what is it?'

'I used to like spy on you in the sand dunes.'

'You little pervert.'

'Snogging with that wind surfer.'

'As long as it was only snogging.'

'And sometimes a bit more. In fact a whole lot more. You're an animal.'

'Jesus, Charlie.'

Over dinner he says, 'Ju-Ju, Ana and I are going to have a baby.'

'That's wonderful.'

'We want you to be a godmother. OK?'

'Of course. But you don't have to try too hard to make me happy, Charlie.'

'Actually, Ana and I only did it because of you.'

'Duh duh.'

'Yes, we guessed you would have plenty of time to babysit.'

She's drunk now. Later they sleep in the same bed and she imagines the stealthy return of her human essences. It's not a rush, not a babbling brook, but the slow drip from a tap or a stalagmite.

Chapter Seven

In the long winter of 1381 sodomy was rife at Rievaulx Abbey.

S ophie is barely awake. These are the moments when first lines come to her. She should write them down. She's been thinking of an historical novel. She's also been thinking of a novel based on her life right here in picturesque Hoxton, near the flower market. The truth is she probably knows less about the locals than she does about the Cistercians of Rievaulx. Writing, everybody says, should be about something you know.

But the truth is I don't know anything. Not finally. I don't even understand the nature of special effects. I could possibly write a very short story based on my life in advertising films. Being snogged by Ornella Illuminati, for example. You have to find a voice, but *voice* sounds middle-aged. Mum used to drink Amontillado – most of her friends drank Fino – and *voice* is a sort of sherry word, slightly old-fashioned and clubby and self-serving. That was before Mum discovered the wines of the new world. Now Chardonnay flows like water down at Curlew's End.

So many people seem to think writing is a way of changing their own lives. And maybe I do too.

I'm late.

She dresses quickly. She tries not to worry about the mess she's forced to abandon although she can hear her mother saying, I really don't know, I just can't understand how you can live in such a tip. She leaves behind a Brit Art set, which contains lost underwear, fragments of forgotten meals and the sort of organic evidence that would send sniffer dogs into a frenzy.

Last night after she spoke to Ju-Ju she decided she must give up this life. She's had enough of Dan. She fell for him because he is the Big Cahuna of this world. All the women, from stylists to clients, recognise it. He's a tribal chief in his own compound. But she's losing interest fast. He's really a child, with his love of toys, which he calls 'kit'. Even his sexual habits are beginning to irritate her; he wants her to do things with cucumbers and belts, which she finds silly, rather than disgusting. Men's sexuality is a strange business; they are endlessly peering, tremulous, into an abyss.

When the call finally came last night, Ju-Ju sounded so tired.

'I'm fine, Soph. I'm fine. A little startled. Charlie's driving.'

'Is it great to be out?'

'It's wonderful. It's quite disorientating in a way. What are you doing?'

'I'm still at work. We're like turning Alfa Romeos into porpoises. I think. Actually I don't care that much. When are you coming home?'

'Charlie's the tour director. We're going to New York via the Finger Lakes. It's re-entry. We will be home as soon as I have sorted out my apartment and so on. I can't wait to see you, Soph.'

'Oh Ju-Ju.'

'Don't cry.'

'I'm sorry.'

'No, I'm sorry.'

'And so am I.'

She hears Charlie shouting cheerfully in the background, 'Women, Jesus, blub, blub, blub.'

'He's going to be a father.'

'Who?'

'Charlie. Oh, perhaps I wasn't supposed to tell you.'

'Is it true? I can't believe it.'

'I'll put him on. She doesn't believe you are going to be a father.'

'Sopheee, yes, I am going to be a daddeee and you are going to be an aunteee. I thought I would tell Ju-Ju first, so that she like was in the loop and not excluded. Oh look there's a moose. No, it's a horse. Here, speak to your sister. No howling.'

'Congratulations, Charlie.'

'It wasn't difficult. Here she is.'

'Christ, he's in a good mood.'

'He's a wonderful person.'

'Are you sure?'

'I'm sure.'

'OK, if you say so. Where are you?'

'We're heading for Buffalo. Why? Because I want to see a Tiffany window there. Not to steal it, no.'

So typical of Ju-Ju. The minicab is late. The driver, an African, smells strongly of beer and sweat. He fiddles with the radio. He's trying to tune a station which sounds as if it's being broadcast from underwater.

'Sorry, but I'm in a bit of a hurry.'

'Everybody in a hurry. Too much hurry.'

He has tribal scars on his cheeks. He stops tuning the radio and puts his foot flat. She hasn't had much sleep and she feels weak, but happy. Now the mad African is making her pay.

'You like to go fahst? OK. You like Michael Schumacher the famarse drivah? OK, let's go fahst.'

They lurch and screech and shudder through the early morning streets. It's still dark. In these sombre streets, the sense of being up and about before the city gets going makes her light-headed. And the way the driver is hurling her about in the back is adding to her elation, as though she was at a funfair on the Roller Ghoster, which used to come to Highbury Fields: *Roll up, roll up, Roller Ghoster, fast ride, fast ride, down the hill, Roller Ghoster*. She's going to give up coke at the same time as she gives up Dan. She won't tell him today, but as soon as she has been paid, as soon as the job's done, and the Alfas have become dolphins, that is it. She met Dan's wife the other day and that may have been a turning point. She is an ethereal blonde, once a model, wearing an expensive and exquisitely embroidered, floating dress. Spiders might have worked incessantly to produce the thread. The effect was of a pre-Raphaelite muse left out in the sun. Dan had talked of her as a sort of crackpot, so it was a surprise to meet this elegant, although etiolated, creature.

She had a strong cockney voice.

'You Sophie, darlin'?'

'Yes.'

'Good luck.'

It was cryptic, but Sophie got the point: she wasn't the first. Not that I ever imagined I was.

She holds on tight. Ju-Ju is out. For nearly two years the knowledge that Ju-Ju was locked up has sapped her strength. She remembers her mother's overgrown garden, the clematis wilt, the rose mildew, the red beetle on the lilies; they caused the plants to lose the will to live. She hasn't blamed Ju-Ju, but she was off drugs for a year before the trial. The imprisonment of her sister undermined her, as if she were suffering a kind of blight herself. But today she is free, and Charlie is having a baby!

'Michael Schumacher, weh-heh,' she shouts as the driver overtakes a Sainsbury truck.

They arrive at the studio before Dan, fortunately. She makes herself a coffee and goes down on to the floor, where everything is set up for Dan to give the signal, *Fiat lux*. The crew call her *dahlin'* and grin at her suggestively. She's well aware that she's a sort of fantasy for them, wild in bed as they believe all posh totty to be. She knows them all from various jobs; they have dirty trainers and soft bellies and they are short, good-hearted people, elves and dwarves working in this dark cave which will soon be magically lit. That is the thing about dwarves, they were little men who never grew up. And this job, playing with lights and track and cameras and cars, is perfect for the mentally arrested. Last night Ornella told her that in Italy dolphins are sex symbols. But then everything is a sex symbol in Italy.

When she rang Mum and Dad last night after speaking to Ju-Ju, Dad answered.

'I'm so happy, Daddy.'

'Yes.'

'Aren't you speaking?'

'Yes.'

'What's the matter?'

'Nothing. Why?'

'I don't know, I sort of imagined you would be celebrating.'

'I was just off to bed.'

'Oh, OK.'

She waited for him to speak. After all it was his duty.

'Sophie, I'm coming up to London on Thursday. Shall we meet?'

'Yes please. We'll be finished with this job, so I'll be free.'

'Where shall we meet? I'm a little out of touch with the flesh-pots.'

'I'll ring. Can I speak to Mum?'

She can hear them speaking briefly.

'Mum, what's wrong with him?'

'He's fine,' she says *sotto voce*, 'just tired, perhaps a little shocked. Darling, are you still working?'

'Yes, but it ends on Wednesday and then I'm going to take a break. I may come down next week.'

'I'll get your room ready. Are you eating?'

'Yes, Mum, listen, that's the sound of a bacon roll going down. Actually, sorry, it's pretty quiet. You'll have to take it on trust. It's tasty.'

'You sound different.'

'It's the bacon.'

'That's not what I mean; you sound lighter. Is it because of Ju-Ju?'

'I think it is. Lighter is just the word. I feel a weight has gone. When do you expect Ju-Ju to get back?'

'She didn't know exactly. She has things to do in New York. Something about her apartment.'

'Her condom-minion, as you so memorably described it to Clem Thomas.'

'And nobody has allowed me to forget it, least of all your father. How did Ju-Ju sound to you?'

'She sounded tired. Actually I spoke to her twice. They were like both pissed the second time.'

'Your language, Sophie, really it's out of control.'

'Mum, I'm going to break up with Dan.'

'I don't want to say I'm pleased, but I'm going to. You are so young and pretty, you don't want –'

'I know. Just be happy. I've come to the same conclusion, even if it was by another route.'

'My sister Sarah went out with a married man.'

'And? What's like the moral of the story?'

'It was years ago.'

'Oh fine. Is Dad still there?'

'No, darling, he's gone to bed. Just before you rang he said, I think I'll be able to sleep. For more than two years he hasn't slept for an hour at a time without the pills. Frances Cooper has asked us all to dinner.'

'When?'

'When we're ready. She's quite sensitive underneath the jolly-hockey-sticks exterior.'

'OK, as long as her dykie daughter's not coming.'

Whenever she speaks to her mother she feels the presence of the unspoken, hovering reproachfully.

Why did I say I was going to break up with Dan? Maybe I was trying to tell her that things are going to get better. Or maybe I am competing with Ju-Ju.

Dan arrives.

'Fucking traffic. Light 'em up.'

The lights hesitate for a moment, before they settle to full brilliance. The roller starts under the car – it's the Lusso 430 T-Spark today – so that its wheels begin to coruscate.

'Right,' says Dan, 'last night after you was all tucked up in bed, I made a little edit. If I say it meself, it's fucking brilliant. Gather round.'

He hands over a disk. And it is brilliant: the dolphins drive in and out of the waves, turning into cars and back into dolphins: it has already, in this low resolution, an irresistible rhythm and glamour.

'It's like only a short bit, low res, rough as guts, but I thought you would like to see what we are doing.'

'Ee's a genioose,' says Ornella, who has slipped in. 'The dolphin is like, 'ow you say? Like phallus. Geenioos.'

Ornella pats Dan's shoulder.

'Not far wrong, dahling,' he says.

Sophie gets Ornella some coffee and a Danish and then she asks Dan if he's got everything he needs.

'All set for a long one,' he says. 'How's your sister?'

'She's out. And happy, of course.'

'Good. Can you do dinner tonight after this is finished?'

'I can't tonight, Dan, we're all like adjusting and getting ready for her return. I need to stand by.'

'No problemo as the English say.'

'You don't do accents, remember. The film looks good, Dan. Ornella is chuffed.'

'It is good. I don't know how I do it for the money.'

'It's because you are a geenioos, with – 'ow you say? – the phaloos.'

'Enough banter. I'm glad your sis is free and clear.'

'Thanks, Dan.'

'Good gel.'

He turns back to the monitor: his hair is long and slightly grizzled and parted in the middle. He suddenly looks a little archaic in the way that the physical aspect of old rockers seems to have parted company with their calendar age. The attendant apple-shaped elves are waiting for his instructions.

She watches for a moment. She wonders how he will take it. It's a strange thing, no matter how young you are, you have in the back of your mind the idea that there is a man out there for you and that you must find him. Not anybody, but somehow the one you were supposed to mate with. It's nonsense, of course, but it must correspond to some deep instinct. It's not Dan, that's for sure. Dan, hunched over the monitor, the skin of his face becoming a sort of vellum before her eyes, the skinny arse – as she knows – a little deflated, a long grey hair or two on his chest, his hair rather defiantly upbeat, his crafty little eyes fixed on the screen, his intense childish absorption – no, it's not Dan.

Whatever it was that attracted me to Dan was too quickly explored and used up. Maybe I am too avid in my desires – not sexually really – but in my hope that I will find something, something permanent.

It seems to Sophie that everything, including Ju-Ju's arrest and Dad's humiliation and her affair with Dan, sends a message of instability. Maybe it's the drugs, which she is already cutting down.

There's something in my personality, I probably get it from Dad, which doesn't quite want to live in this world and accept it for what it is. Religious people take comfort from believing there must be something else. My problem is that I don't believe there is. I need to learn more. I need to read.

She watches Dan with his black cowboy belt and his exactly faded jeans and his Paul Smith shirt and his perky hair and she knows that this is it. Ju-Ju is out; everything is going to change. She'll never see Dan's cock again, with which she has formed an independent alliance, a small country entering an agreement with another.

Every boyfriend I have ever had – six or seven, depending on what you mean by 'boyfriend' – has left a different memory in this regard.

Sometimes she has found these bits unappealing, lacking aesthetic qualities. Sometimes she has found them mismatched, not at all what you would associate with the whole, visible person. But then it's difficult, perhaps even impossible, to guess in matters of sex. You never really know what your parents think about sex either. Dad was obviously a bit of a lad, as Mum once put it. But how much of a lad? One day a schoolfriend from St Paul's, Emily Schuster, told her that her father had a whole parallel family, living in Surrey. She had just found out; she had a sister, for Chrissakes, who was about the same age as her. They were having lunch at Yo Sushi in Poland Street, popping the empty plates back on the conveyor when nobody was looking, and Emily cried over the miso soup and then they had both laughed over the sashimi, which they were pretending to like. They had drunk saki, but Sophie was never quite clear if they were celebrating – after all it was quite intriguing, even contemporary – or mourning. You heard these kinds of story every day. Parents, it seems, can't be trusted to lead dignified, asexual, oldie lives any more. Yet, strangely enough, whatever goes on, however anarchic their own interior lives, they have strong opinions about boyfriends and girlfriends, which they can barely suppress.

Dan, oblivious, fiddles with the track and the motion control. She goes off to the production office. She longs to speak to them, but Charlie and Ju-Ju will still be asleep. They're staying at an inn by a lake. She sometimes thinks, without much hope of being proved right, that there must be a proper place to live. She rings Ana to congratulate her, but she gets their really twee message. Ana, who is two years older than her, is bearing her nephew or niece; this fact demands that they become closer. Ana intimidates her: she is lushly beautiful, different from the girls Charlie used to go out with, who were interesting-pretty rather than glamorous. She is South American, Venezuelan or Colombian, and there is just a hint of the Aztec in her basalt brow and nose, Sophie thinks, although she is a little vague about Aztecs and Incas and so on. Charlie hasn't told Mum and Dad because he wanted to tell Ju-Ju first. Family, whatever that is, must be protected; it's not a stable organisation. Also, by having a child, Charlie is opening the gates to the invaders.

Later, Ornella is doing some coke in the production office. Sophie apologises for not joining her. Suddenly, so suddenly that it's Damascene, she sees the whole thing as ridiculous – the snorting, the grimacing, the rubbing of the nose, the self-congratulatory smirking. Dan comes into the production office. He says the computer needs reprograming; he's calling it a day. It's a wrap. Still, they've done well: it's a goodun. He's off to do some more editing seeing as how she's stood him up. She rings Steve, the editor, to warn him, and orders Dan's car. Ornella gazes at Dan, rapt. She is looking at the Brunelleschi *di nostri giorni*; she asks to go to the edit to watch the maestro at work.

Next morning, over her Danish, Ornella tells Sophie she has had sex with Dan, which Sophie finds surprising under the circumstances and, despite her firm intention to drop him, hurtful. She tries, for a moment, to comfort herself with the thought that for a writer it's all material.

When Dan arrives for work he says, 'You've got a face like thunder.'

She says, 'I can't stand the sight of you for another minute. That's the problem.'

The little people draw back, mute, but looking grave. She walks out of the studio, after a momentary difficulty with the heavy doors, and catches a bus to the nearest underground station.

A train arrives immediately. Although it's the underground, they are so far out in the suburbs that it is still scuttling along the surface. She thinks it has the flustered air of a mole out of its burrow. Her phone rings: Dan says that whatever Ornella is saying it's a lie. She had done too much coke in the edit suite. She's off her trolley.

'Goodbye, Dan.'

'Sophie.'

'Dan, I'm going home. Like I won't be coming back.'

'She's seriously fucked up, Soph.'

'Dan, this is it. Good luck with the dolphins.'

'Please, Soph, not now in the middle of the shoot.'

'Dan, anybody can make tea and order cabs.'

At that moment the train dives happily underground, back into its own domain, and the phone goes dead. But she hears his voice whining, Please, Sophie, please, Soph, please, Sophie, in a metallic descant above the rails and the cables of this Götterdämmerung.

And this pleading cheers her up because it contains a note of weakness.

Chapter Eight

Daphne is laying the breakfast. She hears Charles outside. It's one of those mornings that come out of the gales and the storms at the end of February, so soft and calm and moist – tender is the word – that you almost think you imagined the wildness that went before. The vicar once said that living in Cornwall was like being at sea: Cornwall, he said, is a big liner nosing into the Atlantic. He has a good line in metaphors. His sermon usually starts with a text from the scriptures, which he then updates to encompass modern life: *Oh that I had wings like a dove, or as we say these days, Ryanair. My text today is flight. We are all in flight, but what from? What is troubling us, as our lives unfold? Why do we feel the need to get away? What are we lacking? Why do we feel restless, in a society of plenty?*

Charles is stacking wood. She can hear the logs clanking; they have a metallic sound. When they first came here he built a little lean-to for the wood, which was going to scent their life and in some way make it richer and more spiritual. Fires and woodsmoke are elemental, something the human race required to prosper: she thinks of those Eskimos and Lapps in their tents in the endless night, when they needed the comfort fire could provide. Charles has neglected his woodshed. Just before Christmas she suggested that he order some more logs, but he looked at her with a blank face.

'Logs?'

'Yes, I think a fire would be nice. It might cheer us up.'

'Do you think we need cheering up?'

'Just to make the place warm and cosy.'

'You think I am depressed.'

'Charles, I'm just saying it might be nice to have a fire as the nights get longer. Nothing else.'

'Our nights are getting longer. That part of the proposition is true.'

'What's that supposed to mean?'

'It means I can't see the point.'

'I'll do it. I'll order some tomorrow.'

'Ah, the blackmail. Coming in low under the radar. You have always been good at that.'

'Charles, please don't start this. Please don't go there.'

' "Don't go there." You've been talking to the beardy vicar again.'

She ordered the logs, which were dumped off a truck beside the garage two months ago. Now, as she burns some toast, she thinks that the clunking sharp sound of the logs being stacked is a good sign. Clunk, clunk: it's an anvil. Ju-Ju is on her way home, via the scenic route, as Charlie said, and maybe Charles will snap out of it. She goes outside to call him for breakfast; the round logs are nearly all stacked, end out, so that they look clean and orderly the way they do it in Scandinavia, almost a work of art in itself. And he's standing looking at them as if he's the curator of an outdoor exhibition.

'Breakfast, darling.'

'Yes, I could smell the burnt offerings from here.'

But he says it cheerfully and her wretched little heart gulps in hope.

The truth is women of my generation were brought up to believe that they existed through men. It doesn't matter how much you know it's nonsense and how clearly you see that men are just as fallible, more so perhaps, deep down we have been conditioned to believe that somehow men have been granted custody of the life force.

Charles stacks the last few logs.

'Do you remember when we went to Lapland?' he asks.

'I was thinking about Scandinavia too.'

'Oh good, we must be psychotic.'

'Don't you mean psychic?'

'It was a joke, Daphne. Memo to self: no more jokes.'

He is wearing his fleece and his jeans, which hang a little vacantly from his buttocks, like a flag on a windless day, but still she can see the tall, slender young man he was; the younger man has not quite left the scene. She wonders if we are the same people we were forty years ago. She doesn't really believe in reincarnation, although a lot of well-educated people do, but you can see in your own life that you change into somebody else. Once she went to a demonstration of Japanese cooking, and the food was transformed into flowers that were symbols of spiritual values, so the demonstrator said, although the translation was a little hard to understand. She didn't even begin to describe food-as-symbol to Charles. It's strange that he's become irritable and scornful, because he's actually always been very open-minded. Frances has a theory that men, as the sexual powers wane, become destructive. 'Vengeful' was the word she used for it.

Charles comes in and pours himself a large cup of coffee from the cafetière.

'What a day.'

'It's beautiful.'

'I'm playing golf.'

'Oh good.'

'What are you doing?'

'I'm doing the beds and the linen.'

'For Ju-Ju.'

'For Ju-Ju. And Sophie, and maybe even Charlie.'

'What did Sophie say?'

'She said she's broken up with Dan and left her job. She's got some money saved.'

'Poor girl. Was it difficult?'

'Apparently not. She just went up to him and said it.'

She knows that, although Charles reserves his deepest passion for Ju-Ju, he has been unhappy that Sophie is going out with a forty-something married man. She met Dan once, and he was pretty charming, although with a distinct cockney accent. Estuary English, they call it these days.

'Yes, and then this evening I'm going up to London right after golf. I've got some accounts to sign and a trustees' meeting in the evening. I'm meeting Sophie for dinner and then I'll be back on Friday.'

'Mr Dynamism.'

'You think it's because Ju-Ju is out of jail, I suppose.'

'Is it?'

'I don't know.'

'Who are you playing golf with?'

'Clem. Just Clem. I'm going to get up there early for a bucket of balls.'

In these trivialities she sees hope of a normal life returning. Although when you look at families there is no such thing as normal. She doesn't tell him that she asked Clem to invite him.

Charles eats his toast and his Weetabix and then he starts to get ready for golf. But even here, although he takes some time, things are better. Instead of accusing her of hiding his clubs and throwing away his best shoes, he ferrets them out of the garage, finds a damp cloth without asking for help, and cleans them.

When he's gone, she walks down to the bay and splashes on the wet ridged sand. The tide is rushing out so that you can see the cataract created on Doom Bar. There is no wind at all. Sometimes Bray Hill reminds her of Pieter Bruegel's *Tower of Babel*. When Ju-Ju was at the Courtauld they were forever going to galleries together. Ju-Ju was in a ferment: she wanted to see every picture in London, every installation and every exhibition. They went to Hackney to see Rachel Whiteread's inside-out house. They both thought it was wonderful. She sometimes thinks that Bray Hill may contain a town or a ziggurat or a celestial city turfed over. She wouldn't say that to Charles, because he would think it was affected. But for Ju-Ju, art and imagination were real and true.

It was different for me. In an Army family you could admire the

Colonel's wife's water-colours, but you weren't encouraged to think expansively about the truth or meaning of art. Or about anything much. It was bad form.

In my next life I will be bold and free.

She always looks out for sea-glass and today, after the tumult of the past few nights, she quickly finds a few pieces, including a large blue piece of a colour that only exists in glass, a deep, theatrical blue. She has often asked herself if their forays for sea-glass are what sparked Ju-Ju's interest in stained glass. Ju-Ju was in this way the perfect child: she was always happy to do whatever was suggested; her eagerness made life difficult for both Sophie and Charlie. Ju-Ju would do these things, collecting moths in the dunes at night or going to the Science Museum and the zoo in London, with a kind of amusement as if she was humouring her parents, so that you felt privileged to be with her. Whereas Charlie soon developed a line in moody defiance. For years he would hoot 'Boring, boring' at any suggestion, and Sophie, even at nine or ten, was irritated and sometimes embarrassed by family initiatives. Charles encouraged her subversion. At first she thought he was doing it to help her over her difficulties, but then she realised that he was using Sophie against her. He seemed thrilled when Sophie had to be taken out of St Paul's. But anyway, she's pleased he's off at the golf club. He may be on the hill above the beach even now. This is their little universe, and it's cooling fast.

Charles sighs when he sits down heavily on the train. Why do you sigh when you sit down? Are you sighing because your body is stiff – his is very stiff after the golf – or are you sighing out of world-weariness? *Weltschmerz*. He must stop himself sighing. He always starts train journeys full of hope.

What am I hoping for? Deliverance, redemption?

As you get older, you begin to see that these biblical words have a meaning, or at least a meaningful sonorousness.

On the first tee Clem said that he had read that golf was like the Catholic Church, full of rules that no one obeys, and characterised by equal amounts of devotion, shame, guilt and the firm belief that it would be ruined if women were allowed full membership.

He was standing on the first tee nervously. It was an inviting first shot, sweeping downwards towards the church tower. Although he had spent an hour on the practice ground, he was too tight and dragged the ball into the rough. *Mulligan*, said Clem, *to welcome you back*. And it had gone quite well after that.

The train moves uncertainly and then more steadily as it leaves the station. It's a funny little station, miles from anywhere, never intended for passenger use until Dr Beeching cut the train network. He can still remember Beeching: round, moustached, tweed-suited. Now, when they occasionally publish his picture, he looks as though he has come from a cartoon, like the Mr Men books he used to read to the children. Yet Beeching was a familiar figure in his youth, a sort of leftover from Edwardian times, the pork-butcher type, massive belly under the restraint of thick suiting. Mr Kettle at prep school, his housemaster, was another with those little round glasses, and a full, powerful meat face.

And now I am turning into a type. I wonder what I really look like to Charlie and Sophie. And how I am going to look to Ju-Ju after three years.

Just behind Bray Hill where the tenth hole slopes down into a surprising sheltered valley towards the beach, Clem had said, 'How's Juliet? I hear she's coming home.'

'Yes.'

'Aren't you ready yet, Charles?'

'It depends what you mean.'

'I mean, are you ready to talk about it?'

'No.'

'Well, I won't mention it again. Except to say that we all know the hell you have been through and so – no, stop, Charles, just let me say this – we all know that there's been a terrible miscarriage of justice.'

'Thanks, Clem. It has been difficult.'

Charles walked off into the wiry dune grass looking for his ball, thankful that Clem could not see that he was overcome by his own admission. He found the ball resting on a patch of sand – funny how golf focuses the mind down on to tiny bits of topography which for a moment acquire profound importance: the way the grass is bent, the way the twigs accumulate in miniature wood piles, the depressions in the surface. This is called *the lie*, a category that does not exist in nature. Sometimes the lie reminds him of those models he used to make as a child, with lead farmyard animals, fragments of mirror for lakes, twigs for trees.

He hacked the ball out and, by the time they reached the green, Clem's attempt at a sort of communion was behind them. Yet later, when they were leaving the clubhouse, Clem gave him a card on which was written: *Oriental Angels*, with a phone number and a web address.

'What's this?'

'What's it look like?'

'Jesus, Clem, what are you doing? Setting up a knocking shop in Trebetherick?'

'Charles, I came to the conclusion after two minutes of soul searching, that at my age – our age – a hundred and fifty quid once in a while is money well spent. Ask for Honey. She's Vietnamese.'

'North or South?'

'Any direction you want. Look them up on the net. Are we going to play next week?'

'I'd love to.'

'Welcome back to the world.'

As the train hustles down towards Plymouth he wonders what connection Clem sees between Ju-Ju's release and a Vietnamese hooker.

He always finds the crossing high above the Tamar exciting. You can tell from the small boats tethered down there which way the tide is moving. There's a cottage on a creek that he usually looks out for, with a dinghy pulled up on the bank and two perfectly placed swans on the water. It looks idyllic in the true meaning of that word. There's a poem they learned at school called 'The Wild Swans of Coole'. You always think the grass is greener,

Daphne has said to him, and it is true that he is hoping there's more, which has led to a little nagging discontent all his life. When he was with Fox and Jewell he had a sign behind his desk, small of course, reading: *Somos mas*, We are more than this, the cry of the Chilean pro-Allende opposition. It took some time for Simon and co to deconstruct this subversive message and no doubt it was marked in the ledger against his name. When he was doing his articles they still wrote in ledgers and he can remember the smell of the bindings and the uncertain courtship of ink and paper. The pens had nibs that couldn't be trusted, particularly first thing in the morning. Overnight they acquired an ink thrombosis.

I wonder why you never forget this kind of sensory memory?

As usual, he hasn't told Daphne the whole story. He has to sign the accounts off, but there is no hurry. He sleeps, goes to the revolting toilet, reads the paper and sleeps again. He hopes that his mouth doesn't gape when he's sleeping. He hopes that he doesn't sigh.

She lives in Norwood. As far as he knows, in forty-odd years of living in London, he hasn't ever been to Norwood. She's forty-six now. Or maybe forty-five. Still young. Not young, in the way she was, but young in his cooling universe. It's already dark, in that London fashion, a sort of gaseous twilight. In Cornwall the nights are sometimes so profound that you can barely see your own hands. But this London life is played out nightly in a miasma. When the children were young – particularly when Ju-Ju was fifteen or so – their coming home out of the gloom so cheerful and unconcerned seemed to him a minor miracle.

They are Londoners, which I will never really be. If you are sent off to boarding school at seven, as I was, as Daphne was, you never belong anywhere again.

He's come to think that his anxious, rootless feeling is a characteristic of Englishness of a certain vintage.

It's why we talk in cheerful platitudes and avoid questions. It's pre-emptive.

Also it was thought at that time – it seems so long ago – that

London was for working and for pleasure, but not for living. No matter that his father spent five days a week in the City, home was just outside Petersfield. When he and Daphne bought a house in Islington, his parents behaved as though he had moved to Timbuktu, although later his mother marvelled at how compact their house was, and speculated that it must be easy to maintain. Running large houses in the country was women's work: there were flowers to be cut, china to be laid, pressure cookers to watch over, gormless village girls to be instructed, joints of meat to be ordered. The gardener had to have tea with lethal quantities of sugar.

The underground is always full these days, but at least they aren't packed in. Hardly anybody appears to be English down here. There are tadpole clusters of young Chinese, there are two Africans asleep. There are some beefy young American backpackers, there are some black women listening to music on headphones and there are some Pakistani youths with earrings, plastered hair coming down in spikes, and wearing very large trainers.

I may be the only English person in the whole carriage.

But things change quickly down here in response to the demographics above ground: at Leicester Square a party of girls, all dressed up, soft flesh visible about the waist, come laughing into the carriage. Fatness, even rolls of it, is no longer considered unsightly.

Charlie always hated his comments about people in the street; he suspected that it was clear evidence of prejudice.

'Charlie, I have been driving down this road for twenty years. It is my experience – look, look at that BMW – that ninety per cent of the people who use the right-hand lane here to go straight ahead are black. That doesn't mean that I hate black people. As a matter of fact, I don't.'

'Oh shit, Dad, please, spare me your pop sociology.'

Is it wrong to notice that your country is changing? Do you have to pretend that multiculturalism is an unmitigated blessing, or that we were a race of grey mice until rap music and Yardies and sushi came along to cheer us up? Of course he knows exactly what Charlie is getting at: you can't make generalisations, which is what the ignorant do. Yet even Charlie makes crude assumptions about types of people, about music, about politicians, about taste, and recently about America.

As he heads, clattering and whooshing and jolting, down south of the river, he is longing to see Ju-Ju and to talk to her again: the awful thing is he needs her as his world – his self – fragments, yet he should be the one who is offering certainty and comfort. Are you ready to talk about it, Charles? There was Clem with his complicit face – what Daphne called his ageing Lothario face – cocked hopefully. How could he have told Clem that when Ju-Ju was locked up his soul (whatever that is, it certainly isn't the sort of cut-price spiritual commodity the vicar deals in) had thinned to nothing? For more than two years he has been barely alive, while Clem has been scenting and marking the masculine old-lag trails of leather and walnut-trim Jag – saggy scrotum – the Armagnac's for me waiter – carbon fibre shafts – what veg comes with the fillet? – spunk on an oriental woman child – MCC egg-and-bacon tie.

And now the Pakistani boys are trying to talk to the giggling plump girls and the train is rushing, apparently downwards, towards the centre of the earth.

Daphne is alone. She always thinks that she will enjoy being along – a little time to myself – but the truth is she becomes edgy. Often she cleans or writes letters or phones friends. But tonight she is reading a book from the travelling library about angels. The children's rooms are ready, although she doesn't know exactly when Ju-Ju is coming back. She knows that they always expect fresh linen, even if they live in squalor themselves. Fresh linen, the table properly laid, roast chicken; all three are innately conservative when it comes to family matters. In their minds family should be unchanging. She and Charles never really had a proper family life as children. She thinks now that it was conducted from a kind of script: *You must eat up; you must sit up straight; you must wash your neck; you must polish your shoes. A clear plate is a clear conscience.* It was as if moral chaos was always threatening. Charles said it was the effect of having had an empire: the unknowable was lurking beyond the firelight; the fuzzy-wuzzies were ready at any moment to reclaim the wilderness.

The book she is reading says that the high mortality rates of Victorian England caused a certain nervous watchfulness that could be mitigated by the kindliness of angels. Lots of people believe in angels these days. Sometimes when she's alone in the church doing the flowers she imagines that she is in communion with others, all of them departed but benign. They make a low noise that is compounded from bee-music, the roar of surf, and organ chords heard at a distance. She's never tried to tell this to Charles. They used to talk. Once he told her that he woke up sometimes in a sweat, hearing the noise of a boy at his school being thrashed by the prefects; there was, he said, a terrible stillness between strokes of the cane before the sharp turbulence of the air and the vicious cuttings of the flesh. These sounds will never, never leave me, he said, his hair stuck to his forehead. Maybe Charles has taken Ju-Ju's jailing so badly because he had always imagined that he could shield their children from all that had been harsh and lonely in his own childhood.

Angels are messengers. And – she admits she is surprised – they exist in Islam as well as the Old and New Testaments. Jesus himself, according to Matthew, floated the idea of a guardian angel for children. She's seen the wonderful Epstein statue of St Michael at Coventry Cathedral, but this warlike winged creature is not the kind of angel people have in mind now. Instead they think of their angel as a friend, a sort of confidant who is *always there for them.* Charles, of course, hates that phrase; he says it's mawkish.

When the phone rings in the softly creaking house, she is startled for a moment.

'Mum, hello.'

'Charlie. How are you, darling?'

'I'm fine. We're both fine.'

'Where are you?'

'We're in an area called the Finger Lakes. We're setting off for

New York in the morning. Ju-Ju's asleep. She's beginning to relax, I think.'

'I'm so pleased. You're a wonderful boy.'

'Thanks. Mum, I didn't want to tell you until I had told Ju-Ju. Mum, are you there?'

'What?'

'I wanted to tell you something.'

'Not something terrible, Charlie.'

'No, Mum. Ana and I are going to have a baby.'

'Oh Charlie.'

'You're crying. Don't cry, Mum. Everybody in this bloody family is always crying these days.'

'Oh Charlie, that's wonderful.'

'And before you ask, yes, we are planning to get married.'

'Will you do it here in the church? That would be so lovely.'

'I've got to speak to Ana, she has a family too, well, a father anyway, but yes, I would like love that. For God's sake don't take it as like set in stone, and please don't talk to the bearded one just yet.'

'No, no, I'll wait. Darling, I'm so happy. Dad's in London, but you can get him on his mobile.'

'You tell him. Do you think he's ready for this?'

'He's perked up a lot. Was Ju-Ju happy about your news?'

'I think so. I was worried that it might, you know, that it might look like a contrast thing. Like we're all happy and settled . . . you know what I mean. So I couldn't tell you until I had told her. She said have you told Mum yet, and I told her that we wanted her to be the first to know.'

'I think you were right. You're an angel.'

'Night-night, Mum.'

'Congratulations, darling. To Ana as well. I'll send her some flowers.'

'And congrats to you. A granny at last.'

She needs to speak to someone. She tries Sophie's mobile, but it's not answering. She tries Charles, but his phone is dead. It's too late to ring Frances so she puts another of the metallic logs on the fire and picks up her book. But angels seem rather remote now. She wonders if they know what sex the baby is and she wonders how many months gone Ana is.

Because we will want to book the church before she's too obviously pregnant, not that people worry much about that sort of thing these days. As my mother often said, I need something to look forward to and now I have two things, no, three, Ju-Ju's return, a wedding and a grandchild.

The empty, windswept landscape of her life is peopled again.

Chapter Nine

Her dinner with Richie did not go well at first. They were too conscious. Richie made some remarks about colour and form too obviously stolen from Ruskin, and she thought he was trying to impress her. He was also a little over-fond of the contrast between Apollonian and Dionysian. You're just an art hustler, she thought. He was trying to ride any little art wave he could catch. He had no standards and no real point of view. But later she found that his technique was to scatter opinions and smart remarks to see what stuck. He was what her father called a chameleon.

When she told him, that night, that she thought Brit Art was celebrity art, vacuous and flat and lacking in any moral or aesthetic standpoint, he said, 'You think that's me. You think I am an opportunist.'

'You are obviously an opportunist, the question, though, is whether there's anything more.'

'Very little. In fact nothing. I make a point of saying things I hardly understand. I don't want people to become uneasy around me.'

'You also have a self-deprecating manner, which is actually a front for extreme cockiness.'

'In New York, I find, they expect the English to be charming in a way that never really existed back home. This is my pathetic attempt to pander to them.'

'Can we eat? What's good here?'

'It's all good. For starters, try the carpaccio of blue-fin tuna.'

'Oh God.'

'Wha-a-t?' he said with a long Brooklyn vowel sound. (He turned out to be good at accents.)

'I don't know. It's all so New York.'

'Yes, it's sooo fun.'

She had slept with him that night, because she thought he was amiable and good-looking enough, and also because they were both away from home.

When he asked if she wanted to come back to his place, she said, 'Why not?'

'Blimey, are you always this enthusiastic?'

Her little brother is at the door.

'Ready for breakfast?'

'Yes please.'

Later in the car he tells her that he has spoken to Mum about the baby.

'And Dad?'

'He wasn't there. He is in London.'

'Was she pleased?'

'She sounded very happy. But it was like all the better that we're going to get married first. Are you OK?'

'Charlie, I'm entering the world slowly. I can't tell you what it was like to see that display of fresh fruit and granola and the flowers and so on. I'm sure to you it looks pretty average, bog standard, but it was like looking at a still life by Fantin-Latour. Everything I have eaten for the past two years looked as though it was scraped off the bottom of someone's shoe. The phoney pastel colours of Loon Lake, the deep grime of Otisville, the prison uniform, it's all, oh shit, Charlie, it's all somehow entered right into my bones. I'm not going to complain too much, I promise, but it's gone deep.'

'You didn't deserve it.'

'I love you, Charlie. I love you for apparently having faith in me. The problem is I don't really have faith in myself. Where are we going today?'

'The Hudson Valley. I have booked a few places and we can hit Manhattan at the weekend.'

'Sounds good.'

His face. The family face. She looks at him sideways as they whizz along. She's looking to see what's in the face; faces are supposed to be a sort of outcrop of the qualities beneath. Behind his face, trees – what a lot of trees – clapboard houses, vineyards, lakes fly by. His face flickers. It's a funny thing, this idea that family turns up in faces. It does, but why should it suggest that qualities of character have been passed on in the package?

Expressions suggest character too, as painters know. At the Courtauld, the sly *Adam and Eve* by Cranach and the complicit Modigliani nude, which she looked at almost daily, were too explicit, too full of suggestion; no human face can be read like that.

Charlie has something of Mum in his face. It's the way he looks up from driving, raising his chin slightly, his eyes adjusting downwards as if they are on gimbals; it's also the way he screws up his eyes a little when making a serious point. The mouth, unlike Mum's, is large.

In prison I lost faith in painting. I lost faith in the truth of art. Art seemed indulgent in there. Some of the women painted lurid fantasies involving white horses with wings, and lime-green zodiacal signs and women with serpent hair. The faces they painted were usually poor facsimiles of comic-book art. The idea that you could read character in a painting – a Vermeer or even a Stubbs – would never have occurred to them.

And she came to see that to them character was not a subtle thing, but rather a limited range of crude qualities involving violence and sentimentality and lack of restraint. Their lives and their faces were often out of control, directly connected to these categories, so that they were set to violence and screaming and crying as if these things passed along a wire from one to the other. And when she looks at Charlie, piloting her through this dappled and deceptive countryside, she sees a certain assurance, a pleasing sense that he is happy in his skin, as the French say. *Bien dans sa peau.* The ridge, apparently just under the scalp, is sometimes thrown into relief by the play of the light.

'Charlie, Charlie.'

'What?'

'You're a good-looking little devil.'

He smiles. His smile is full of warmth, but she couldn't say, if anybody asked, exactly how that manifests itself, except as an absence of those prison convulsions that find their way to the surface. All she knows is that he has an innocence which for two years she has believed she might never see again.

'What's troubling you, Ju-Ju?'

'While I was inside I began to believe that what I had known before was not real.'

'Like, like what?'

'Like you, for one, Charlie. I wasn't sure if I was going to wake up.'

'Oh Jesus, Ju-Ju, that must have been crap.'

'I felt, I still feel, that I have been dragged into something unspeakable. I mean I don't want to equate them in any way, but when you read about Holocaust survivors, they think that, they think –'

'Let's stop, Ju-Ju. We're not far from a place called Watkins Glen, famous for pancakes. I feel a pancake coming on.'

She is shaking.

'It's your face, Charlie. I see so much in it and I thought it was taken away from me. Maybe some of it –'

'There we are, pancake heaven.'

He puts his arm around her and they stumble across the parking lot to the wooden pancake house, which looks out over a lake. She feels his body under her hand, the ribs and underneath them a softer isthmus, which he of course had as a boy, a sort of endearing vulnerability.

Far out on the lake panhandling ducks are gathering. They know that pancakes are coming. The light stains the water diffidently and unevenly, the way candlelight falls on silver, not that she has seen either candlelight or silver for two years.

The waitress, unasked, brings them a special treat, Vermont Fancy Grade Maple Syrup, the top grade, and she offers them more coffee before they have finished.

'She's after your body, Charlie.'

'Do you think we're sexy, as a family?'

'I think maybe we are. Dad was always a bit of a goat, although I'm not sure if he was putting it about. But he just had that look. And now you've got it even though you and he don't look the same at all.'

'You've got it.'

'Still?'

'You're completely beautiful.'

'Tragically beautiful? You can be beautiful but not sexy, by the way.'

'Tragically sexy.'

'Oh good.'

The duck flotilla gathers. A few ducks come ashore, where they walk awkwardly, having left all their grace behind in the stained water, which is the colour of cream soda.

'My thought is that you need to do lots of ordinary things, like giving Vermont Fancy Grade Maple Syrup to ducks, before you go home.'

'It's working, Charlie.'

The maple syrup from the pancakes has produced a fancy-grade slick on the water. When they are moving again, up towards another lake, she asks him where he and Ana are going to be married.

'Mum, of course, would like it to be St Enodoc.'

'And Ana?'

'We'll have to ask.'

'What's she like?'

'She's great.'

'Is that it?'

'You'll have to meet her. You'll make up your own mind.'

'Does she mind having a jailbird for a sister-in-law?'

'No, I think she thinks it's like quite glamorous. Her father is from South America. They know about these things.'

'Have you got a picture of her?'

'No, not on me.'

'Jesus, men are hopeless.'

He seems to be reluctant to talk about Ana. And she wonders, picking up where she left off before the pancake interlude, what Ana is going to bring to the family physiognomy. Maybe the family face will take a diversion towards the dark and aquiline. She feels oddly jealous of this unknown Ana, who is entering their family and producing another Judd. The child will be an indisputable fact, even if it has that touch of Spanish-American otherworldliness, a kind of high-altitude haughtiness, as if the effort of living in this world is barely worth making.

'Are we going anywhere near Ithaca?' she asks.

'Yes, we are.'

'Cornell University is there and they've got a Tiffany window I would like to see. Is that OK with you?'

'Absolutely fine.'

'It's a memorial window, I think. It's not a religious thing, just ornamental. If I remember, it's magnolia and apple blossom.'

They spend ten or fifteen minutes looking at the window. A tracery of apple in blossom meets a magnolia tree in flower at the apex of the window, which is made to look like a gate. She tries to think if she has seen this colour before; the effect of the window is extremely subtle, as though Tiffany were deliberately reining in his enthusiasm for vibrant colour. At the bottom of the window are these words: *And with the morn those angel faces smile which we have loved long since and lost awhile*. Resurrection.

'What are we looking for?' Charlie asks.

'It's not art, really. It's a kind of applied art or craft. I am looking at the development of technique. But it is unique and very American. I think that America is still ambivalent about art. Maybe literature too, so they often have to have a flattering quality in what they buy: *I am going to get something out of this*. That's what they want. I am going to demonstrate something about myself by buying this. Do you know that the emigrating congregations believed in election? And success was the evidence of God's favour, and so the sign of election. We lost it back home after Cromwell, except perhaps for the few throwbacks to non-conformism, like Mrs Thatcher, who said that there was no such thing as society. She meant there are only the saved and the damned. I see all these things in the windows; it's almost a passport to the next world for the departing Knapp family with their angel faces. It's not art in Picasso's sense, a weapon against the enemy.'

Charlie stands silently, bathed this time in pale, spring green, apple green.

'I'm sorry, Charlie, I'm talking too much.'

'Keep talking. You're a wonder of nature. You used to scare me, you were so brainy.'

'Just an act,' she says, although they both know it's not true. 'I'll try to stop.'

As they walk back to the car, past the Big Red Stadium, which occupies the centre of the campus, she wonders how long before the old family irritations will kick in, which they surely must. She sleeps for a while as they drive onwards. She wakes to find Charlie talking on his mobile; he has a funny earpiece with a tiny microphone. He's a tycoon. He quickly chokes off the call, and removes the earpiece, to indicate that looking after her is his main concern.

'Sleep well?'

'Was I gone for long?'

'No. Half an hour or so.'

'You know, I never slept for more than twenty minutes at a time during the whole of the first year. I got migraines from waking up ten or fifteen times a night.'

'You never told me.'

'I couldn't. You had come all that way to see me and we only had an hour each time.'

'Ju-Ju, why did you do it for Richie?'

'I didn't really do it for Richie.'

'OK, you didn't do it for Richie. I won't ask again. Mum rang. She hasn't like spoken directly about our wedding in the church, but she has discussed a wedding, like in principle, with the bearded one.'

'Uh-oh. Sounds like it's a done deal. You realise, of course, that the wedding is the perfect cover.'

'Yes, it had like struck me.'

'For all sorts of things. Do you think Ana's going to be OK with it?'

'She's cool. She understands, I spoke to her.'

'Yes, but does she understand Mum?'

'No. But like who does?'

And she knows what Charlie means. Mum has a sense of something just out of reach that she's always groping for. Cookery is one thing, but also she is plagued by less tangible things such as the desire for effortless taste and accomplished friends. She spends a lot of time reading biographies of women who *lived interesting lives*. Most of them were also rich with large houses in the country and tractable dogs. In her last letter she wrote about 'the need to have a spiritual dimension to one's life'. Ju-Ju wasn't sure if the life in question was hers or her mother's. Her own experience of spirituality has a sinister aspect: not many of the women in prison were living fully in reality. Like the woman she shared with in Otisville who woke her up screaming night after night, convinced that she was giving birth to a devil. The spiritual world, as she has experienced it, seems to be the product of schizophrenia or epilepsy or abuse. It's not a lifestyle choice, as Mum suggests. But you can't deny that the irrational and the emotional have very real consequences. Charlie believes that Richie must be the reason she did something so irrational and out of character: as if your character is set in stone.

If I've learned anything it is that character is not a fixed commodity. Dad believes in character. He believes it must be cultivated like a garden or it will become derelict. He sees the whole country falling into disrepair through indulgence.

Richie was strangely without character, in her father's sense. He was, he said that first night, blotting paper.

'Meaning things leave a blurred impression on you?'

'Meaning I tend to soak up whatever is closest.'

He was trying to do what Miles Black had done with his gallery near by, to sell fashionable art while becoming a figure in the art-social landscape. When they started to go out she lent Richie some credibility. She was able to secure an exhibition by Piotr Polasky and the little gallery began to be noticed. Soon Richie wanted to take bigger and more expensive premises.

'Richie, the numbers don't add up. You can't move from here, where it's almost free, to there, where it's two hundred, without any big names.'

'And I won't get any big names without going there.'

'I don't think that follows.'

It didn't, of course. The new gallery was busy and it was fashionable, but Richie never got the really big names, Uklansky, Jeremy Diller, or any of the older crew who paid the rent at Paul Kasmin's, where the openings always featured lots of silly ties and floppy linen jackets. She saw Hockney there one evening, smiling sagely among the affluence. Success in art leads to self-parody, a process bound by convention as surely as what applies to success-ful lawyers or army officers.

It was obvious to her that Richie was quite quickly going bust, but it didn't seem to be obvious to him. It was a month after the new gallery, De Lisle's White Heat 2, opened, with espresso bar and club, that she met a writer from Louisiana who had just published his first novel, *The Boy from the Mudflats*. If anybody other than herself was the cause of her going to jail, it was the Faulkner-obsessed Davis Lyendecker. He was a soft young man, who had once had a Rhodes scholarship, and was now working on a new novel and doing some reading for Random House as he waited for success to claim him. The knowledge that they might have passed each other in the High or in the Bodleian drew them together. He had quite big thighs and in bed she shared with him a simple passion, his large, chummy gams and her lesser ones discovering a mutual ease and attraction. Also he had something that Richie lacked entirely, a belief in the transcendent power of art. Through literature, he believed, understanding is possible, although the nature of that understanding is necessarily limited.

At first he treated their relationship lightly, but it wasn't in his nature to live the unexamined life and he began to examine. She was happy not to look too closely: it was almost unbearably erotic to have two lovers. The contrasting tempos were exciting. One day she made love to both of them twice. How could you explain to any sane person the sort of ease and abandon your body could achieve? So when Charlie asked about Richie, she couldn't begin to explain. For example she could have prevented Richie from borrowing more money and she could probably have found him a backer, but it suited her to have him rushing about in a fervour of self-importance for those four or five frenzied months. She and Davis would usually meet at lunchtime and make love and talk without restraint at his small apartment. She checked in to her little cubby hole in Rockefeller Center each morning, and then the day was hers to track down Tiffany and to meet Davis. Much later she would meet Richie at some opening party or in a restaurant. He greeted her with his eager charming innocent look while she was still – she thought – lightly glazed with the animal-chemical secretions of lovemaking. She imagined that she had a kind of scent, not quite a fragrance, which her body was producing. I'm a tramp, she thought happily, aware that it couldn't last as Davis became more anxious and inquisitive: he wanted her to give up Richie. He had an endearing quality, an openness, which she loved. All the time she knew that Richie was going down the toilet and she did nothing to help him.

Charlie is steering them up into the Catskills. No, she didn't do it for Richie; she did it for herself because she wanted to carry this life on until it had run its natural course. She did it in obedience to the selfish primal call of the blood, in the face of which most people, even people of previous good character, are helpless.

Charlie tells her, which she already knows, that the Catskills were once the Jewish New Yorker's playground. He's a diligent guide. Near a wooden covered bridge they see some deer. And later they pass a huge reservoir, which supplies New York's drinking water, said to be the tastiest in the world.

By the time Richie understood the seriousness of his predicament, he owed nearly six hundred thousand dollars after just six months; there was no way out until Anthony Agnello came along with his request. She viewed the window in a small warehouse, a shed really, behind Agnello's house in the Bronx. It was unsigned, but it was genuine, from Tiffany's middle period. The angel announcing the resurrection to Mary Magdalene, and the other Mary: *Why seek ye the living among the dead. He is risen.*

'I'm not asking you to do any more,' said Richie, but she made enquiries anyway and it was not listed as stolen. It seemed Agnello had obtained the window a few years ago, from a cemetery in Flatbush. Two days later she agreed to provide the name of a collector in Japan. All she would be doing was certifying it as genuine. It was crated up and sent to Japan, and the money, four hundred and fifty thousand dollars, arrived in an account as smoothly and quietly as the flutter of angel wings that decorated the panel.

What happened – she has had plenty of time to think about it – was that, in the tumultuous sensuality of those months, she had felt herself indifferent to mundane considerations. The judge and the Federal Attorney had both painted her – 'characterized' her, as the *New York Times* reported – as arrogant, with a disdain for the law. But she never thought about the law. She wasn't trying to make money or steal anything or fence anything, simply to prolong this state of grace. When Richie asked her to write the five cheques of ten thousand dollars each to cash, because Agnello didn't have a bank account, she did it happily. And it was this insouciance which in the end made her a criminal. It was two or three months later that Agnello was arrested on a minor offence and embarked eagerly on a new phase in his life, as a licensed entertainer, which included elaborate plea-bargaining: he could reveal the big guys in the art-fraud world. And when Charlie asked her why she had let Richie get away with it, the answer – if there is a clear answer – was that she had betrayed him because of lust. She was also planning to leave him for Davis. And – a lesser consideration – the lawyer had said with legal, leather-bound, deeply creased, I've-been-around-the-block assurance that she would be fined. Nothing more.

They are descending towards the Hudson Valley through an American landscape of small towns, woods and gimcrack enterprises. Many of these enterprises, in the middle of nowhere, must have been doomed from the start: bowling alleys, a raptor flying display, discount respraying, an Indian tepee motel, a Mongolian barbecue, a chicken-wing drive-in, motels of hardboard, a dinosaur park, an historical Redcoat display, an Algonquin village and deli.

Davis wrote to her in prison. His letter was steeped in self-pity. His second novel was going badly; he was finding her duplicity hard to deal with. He didn't seem to have the novelist's ability to put himself in her position and to understand her state of mind. He was now teaching creative writing in Minnesota; he and his chunky thighs, thighs like piglets, were out there in the alien corn. But he still loved her. She didn't reply. How could she? She didn't even open his second letter.

On they roll. She's been stationary for months.

Charlie smiles.

'You OK?'

'I'm fine. I'm in motion with my little bro. I didn't appreciate how much being stuck in one place was getting to me. I don't mean prison, I mean lack of movement. I could sit here all day watching it flash by.'

In the mouth she can still taste prison, but now she sees wine-dark tulips beneath a picket fence and smells vanilla essence as they pass a Krispy Kreme and sees children selling toffee apples outside their brick school.

Why do I remember his thighs, as if the rest of him, his pinkish lips and his spoilt-boy face and his long, straight, nut-coloured hair, were bystanders in that physical drama?

'The only moments of complete happiness I have ever experienced were with you,' he wrote. *Ah ha-a-ve evah experienced wah with you-oo.*

Chapter Ten

Charles is on the train, heading back for Cornwall. He has signed off the accounts. A violin student from Leyton and a PhD student from Rochester have received the Shad Thames Apprentices annual awards. The Apprentices had their heyday in Gladstone's time, and their last hurrah during the dock strikes of the sixties, led by Jack Dash. But the money given by the soap manufacturer Sir Ephraim Smedley for the marine education of young Londoners continued to exist. It now provides an annual dinner for the trustees and two scholarships for the study of navigation, or failing that any worthwhile programme of further study, as decided by the trustees. At Fox and Jewell he was the honorary auditor and a trustee; when he was fired he kept up the roles. It was a strange, apparently pointless trust, but there was no known way of killing it off.

As always the meeting passed smoothly, semi-strangers brought together over the glass of sherry the benefactor had prescribed. Not exactly strangers, but in that English way acquaintances who never became intimate and never wanted to. Actually the benefactor had bequeathed a butt of sherry for each of the trustees annually, but they had decided that expenses were a more suitable reward.

The train is bounding towards Cornwall, gulping the fresh air. He's trying to think exactly what happened two nights ago in Norwood. In a sense he knows what happened, but the deeper significance is a mystery. Also Charlie rang to tell him that he was going to be a grandfather. And Ju-Ju came on the line saying don't you think it's wonderful? He wasn't sure, but of course he said yes, oh that is wonderful, and foolishly he asked her who the father was, imagining a prison warder or someone on a chain gang.

'Not me, Daddy, Charlie. Charlie and Ana are having a baby.'

Ju-Ju started to laugh. He could hear her saying, 'He thinks I'm pregnant,' as she handed the phone back to Charlie. The fact was he didn't want to talk about this new child.

'We're going to get married at St Enodoc. What do you think, Dad?'

'I've got to go. Congratulations, my boy.'

Someone was coming to the door of No. 43 Doggett Road. But it was a figure deep in an anorak posting leaflets, and he felt ashamed that he had choked off his son who was bringing Ju-Ju home and who was also filled with that sense of importance and the sublime that seizes new parents. All new parents. He tried to ring back, but he didn't know what code he was supposed to use. As he was struggling with the phone, standing just across the road from No. 43, he almost missed the woman unlocking the door and going in. It was nearly nine o'clock. Was it too late? He crossed the road – Jesus, what a road, the masterwork of nullity – and rang the doorbell, which was one of those cheap Perspex things with a little handwritten label – *Zwiebel*, which was her married name – underneath.

She came to the door but she didn't open it. He positioned himself a few feet away, so that she could see him through the spyhole.

'Who is it?'

Was he unrecognisable in the gloom, or had too many years passed?

'Charles.'

'Charles who?'

'Charles Judd. Jo, it's me. Charles.'

The door opened after a preliminary scrabble with bolts and double locks. You can't be too careful south of the river.

'Charles, my God, what are you doing?'

'Jo, I need to ask you something. It won't take long.'

She looks tired, not as a result of any one event, but chronically, constitutionally – existentially – exhausted. Her avid remembered face, with all the attention somehow drawn to her mouth, is fuller than it was and she seems generally to be more earth-bound.

'Charles. God. What a surprise. Come in. It's a mess; I've been at work all day.'

The place is large, semi-detached Victorian, with a coatstand and a pot on a wooden plinth in the hall. The plinth has been inexpertly painted to look like pale veined marble.

'Come in here, I've just lit the fire.'

It's a gas fire, with coal effects that are undulating evenly. She takes his coat.

She's wearing a suit, in buttercup yellow, which is curiously dispiriting. Her hair has been cut quite short, but without much of a plan beyond that. It's unfair of him to pass judgement, but she seems to have joined the army of anonymous disappointed women.

'Jo, do you remember when I sued Fox and Jewell?'

'Yes. Sit down, Charles, if you want to. I was just brewing some tea. Do you want some?'

'Yes please.'

She leaves the room. There are signs that a child has been this way: some family pictures, a school portrait, so stiff and false, a boy in a school uniform, the photograph highlighted so that he looks like a small chubby saint in a blazer, resting on the mantelpiece. Once somebody tried to cheer the place up with those Scandinavian flowery curtains, but the room is so tall and the furniture – suede and steel – so close to the ground that it seems as if the occupants are camping here.

She comes back with a tray and pours the tea.

'Charles, before we start, how are you?'

'I'm fine.'

'I heard about Juliet. I am so, so sorry.'

'She's coming home now.'

'That's good.'

'And you?'

'I separated from Tony two years ago, and I work for the local estate agents, Bearman's.'

'How many children do you have?'

'Just one, Jason. He's eleven.'

'Eleven? Goodness.'

'Sugar?'

'No. No thanks.'

'You look well.'

'You probably think I look half dead.'

'No, I don't. Honest. You look great.'

He can't bring himself to say that she looks great. Instead he says you meant so much to me. It's lame but at least it's true.

'Charles, why have you come?'

'I had your address and I wanted to see you.'

'You wanted to ask me something about the case.'

'Yes. What I'm going to ask you, Jo, is not supposed to be a criticism of you or anything . . .'

'But.'

'But I always wondered exactly what happened.'

'Meaning?'

'Why did you give them an affidavit saying that I had harassed you, harassed you sexually, and that I had a reputation for it in the office?'

'I didn't exactly say that.'

The flickering fire – he guesses that there must be a small wheel going around, diffusing the glow to add verisimilitude – is catching one side of her face.

'You did, in effect. Jo, that practically ruined me. I had to give up when my barrister read the affidavits. Not because they were true, but because I couldn't allow them to be made public.'

'But we did have sex in the office.'

'There's a big difference between having sex and being some kind of sex pest.'

She stands up. He stands up. He expects her to tell him to go, but she leaves the room. He sits down. On the wall an electronic brass clock with a decorative pendulum chimes the quarter. She comes back, holding a Kleenex.

'Sorry.'

'I haven't come to upset you. I feel bad.'

'Charles, I was in a terrible position. They knew that we had had an affair. Everyone in the office knew. So they asked me to produce an affidavit saying that you had taken advantage of me. I was a trainee, and I was only twenty-three or four, and you were a partner. Of course it wasn't like that. I loved you, or I thought I did. When the take-over came, ten years ago, and you had left, they said look, he's suing us, but we know he's got a history with female staff. If you say he harassed you, et cetera, like the others, we will pay you some compensation. It was nonsense, but they dressed it up in legal stuff. It was twelve thousand pounds. I was skint. I'm still skint as you can see. And they said don't worry, this won't come to court. Anyway, Tony and I were going out, I was pregnant, and we needed the deposit for a house. This awful house. Are you going to ask me to say I lied? I won't do it.'

'I'm not going to ask you to do anything.'

'So why did you come?'

'It's hard to understand. I don't think I really know, but with my daughter coming home I wanted to ask you if you really thought I had, I don't know, been a pig.'

As he used the phrase *been a pig*, it turned in his mouth.

'You were never a pig, Charles. I was completely knocked out by you. I had never met anybody like you. And you just loved fucking me. It made me feel so good.'

This is a little more directness than he needs at this moment.

'Yes.'

'It's twenty-three years ago, Charles.'

'And I am an old man.'

'You may be older but you look great. And anyway I'm a dumpy single mum now, living down here in this place we couldn't afford to do up properly.'

His heart – actually his innards – are melting. This too-human tale is rendering them down. He stands up again, feeling an oven-brick warmth on his face, and she stands up in her buttercup suit and puts her full arms around him.

'I'm so sorry, Charles.'

He feels with pain, selfish pain, the way her body – it must be the same one – seems to fit to his as closely as a gecko to a wall. But also he feels a great relief, a sort of emptying of the bladder, to know that she didn't think he was a sex pest, an abuser of his position.

After the minutes and account signing and the sherry drinking, he wandered around Charing Cross Road, looking at books and prints and memorabilia. A few months ago he bought a book here on ethics, which he hasn't read yet for fear of what it might tell him about his own moral failings.

He felt better than he had for months, but still he thought what's the point: I'll never buy another travel book again or an antique map, or a beautiful engraving of a duck, first seen by some explorer-naturalist in Patagonia. He read, while standing idly among some bookshelves, that Ludwig Feuerbach said that Christianity comes from man's need to imagine perfection: 'Man, by means of the imagination, involuntarily contemplates his inner nature. He represents it as out of himself. The nature of man, of the species, is God.' Who is Ludwig Feuerbach? He has no idea, but he will save the thought for the next time the beardy vicar talks about the Church's ministry, which seems to be an Anglican catchall for whatever issues the vicar wants to bang on about.

When he rang Daphne last night she said that she had already, in a general, let's-just-pencil-in-something-for-the-moment sort of way, spoken to the vicar about a church wedding for Charlie and Ana. Ana's parents are lapsed Catholics and anyway they are living apart, she in Bogota or Quito, and he in Lima and Washington. So it was down to them.

'I think we owe them this, don't you?'

'What?'

'A proper old-fashioned country wedding.'

'Do we?'

'Yes. You know what I mean. Don't be difficult.'

He did know what she meant. A family was supposed to be the repository of values and goodwill, and St Enodoc, with its interesting dunes and its golf course and Betjeman's grave and its sand-in-the-sandwiches-wasps-in-the-tea promise, was stuffed with barely suppressed symbolism. Of course it was also a neat way for Daphne to demonstrate family solidarity, with Ju-Ju home soon.

He felt – my mind is wandering – like a Jew who has cleansed the door-posts. At least he could welcome Ju-Ju home now that Jo had confirmed that what had happened twenty-some years ago was not a form of rape, a vain middle-aged man exploiting a young girl. He could welcome Ju-Ju home, cleansed of that fear. He sometimes wishes he was Jewish, with a much stronger sense of himself in the universe, even if Jews did acquire this sense under extreme circumstances.

There's something ridiculous about me these days.

He had promised to keep in touch with Jo, although he couldn't think how that was going to work.

When he met Sophie in Covent Garden, her tummy and the elastic of her pants were revealed to the restaurant as she took her coat off. Her tummy was slightly rounded, and for a moment he was transfixed.

'Just my tum, Dad. It's the style. Oh, I'm hungry.'

He wanted to ask her about her man, Dan was his name, to confirm that she was no longer seeing him. But it was too soon to pry. Dan is twenty years older that Sophie, and married.

He remembered what Jo said: 'You loved fucking me.' But he tried not to connect this Dan with his daughter's sweet body.

'Dad.'

'Yes.'

'Have you chosen?'

'Oh, no, sorry.'

A young waiter, probably from Australia or South Africa, was standing by the table with his pad.

'What are you having, darling?'

'I'm having a chimichanga.'

'I'll have one too.'

He had no idea what that was, even though he had been to Mexico years ago. As he remembered, no matter what you ordered, you ended up with brown soggy beans and some sort of stuffed pancake, with a little pile of avocado sludge beside it.

'How's work?' he tried.

'As you know, I've quit.'

'Oh yes, sorry. Are you OK for money?'

'I'm like OK for a few months.'

'And your chap?'

'My chap, Dan, forty-three and married, as you also know, is toast.'

What does she mean, 'toast'?

'He's history.'

She moved on to the subject of Ju-Ju fast. She thought the family was like energised by the prospect of her return.

'It's strange but somehow we need her. We were like in limbo while she was behind the door.'

'What do you mean, "behind the door"?'

'Banged up. In the slammer.'

'Sophie, I find that a bit harsh.'

'It was harsh. I was there.'

When the chimichangas arrived, suspiciously quickly, she ate furiously. As he had feared, there were unidentified lumps of something arranged like tumuli around a central pancake.

Suddenly Sophie stopped eating.

'We have to get out of the habit of thinking she is innocent. I've been considering it: it's true that she took the rap for that prick Richie, but that doesn't make her innocent. It's true she was like dealt with harshly, like it was a show-trial, but we are not talking Dreyfus or Nelson Mandela here. Mum tells everyone it was a miscarriage, and you wrote to Tony Blair saying it was hysteria and xenophobia by the Bush Administration.'

'Hold on. I did write the letter, but I thought better of it.'

'You know what I think?'

He looked at her, her small innocent mouth and beneath the table the small innocent tummy and – although he tries to stop himself – he imagines Dan's semen on them.

You loved fucking me.

'Dad?'

'Sorry. I was having a senior moment. Yes?'

'Dad, I don't think we know the whole story. There must be like a reason why she allowed herself to like take the fall.'

She seemed to have acquired a whole new vocabulary, maybe from *Friends*, which they all used to watch. He has watched it too, and quite liked it. Did Ju-Ju take the fall? If she did, it was a fall from grace. And now they have entered the post-lapsarian phase. But he agreed with his little daughter that nothing is ever quite what it seems, particularly in matters of the heart.

'How's the writing going, Soph?'

'Nowhere. I don't know enough.'

These kids want to be writers and paint or make music. And the London day-schools seem to have produced a lot of successful musicians, painters and so on, but his old prejudices, inculcated by his father – *someone's got to do the real work* – haven't quite died. He felt heavy as he contemplated the disappointment she would face. But that is a parent's dilemma, how to be encouraging in the face of the evidence of life.

I haven't been a good father, although on the theoretical level at least I have been open-minded and tolerant.

'Dad, Charlie says Ju-Ju is a little anxious, like anxious about you.'

'In what way?'

He felt the heaviness in the air oppressing him.

'She was hurt that you like never came to see her.'

'She never said that.'

'Well, obviously she couldn't say that while she was inside. You would have felt under pressure. I told Charlie you couldn't like bear to see her suffering. That's right, isn't it?'

He busied himself scrabbling about in the Tex-Mex mess on his plate, shoving the avocado mush behind the beans and chopping the dry pancake and eating what seemed to be a piece of chicken that he found sheltering inside it.

'Dad?'

He couldn't look at her.

'I'm sorry, Dad.'

'You're right, Sophie. Basically.'

He couldn't bear to see Ju-Ju suffer, but also he couldn't tell Sophie that he feared that the sight of Ju-Ju in prison uniform would demolish the unsteady edifice that his life has become. He has just one aim now, to remain calm, whatever it costs him, until the family is back on track. Although he is not sure how he will know – what signs will appear when this has happened. He has loved Ju-Ju too much, more than poor Sophie or Charlie, but he knows that his love for her has been selfish and a burden to her.

'Sophie darling, would you like pudding?'

'Are you OK?'

'Of course. You made me think for a moment. I desperately wanted to see her, but every time I made up my mind to go, I convinced myself it was the wrong time. We all seem to be communicating through Charlie these days, so ask him to tell Ju-Ju you are right: it would have upset me and I think that it would have distressed her. I've thought about it a lot. That's the reason.'

'Official?'

'Yes, darling. Can I tell you that I am glad you've dumped Dan?'

'If you must.'

'I must. I think at your age you don't want to be tied to someone desperate. Middle-aged men with young girls are desperate.'

He was thinking about what Jo said, and even now, down the years, he remembers that terrible sense of time running out, which sex makes so acute. And that's why Clem is paying for a Vietnamese hooker, with the body of a child, and it's probably why paedophiles are mostly fifty or more and why many older women

– women are exempt from none of the sexual madness – become obsessive about young men.

'We can never cast anchor for a single day on the ocean of the ages.'

'What's that, Dad?'

'Alphonse de Lamartine.'

'Dad.'

'Yes?'

'He's here again.'

The waiter was smirking complicitly at Sophie. He saw and felt keenly the shared understanding that the old boy needed a little time.

'Have you got a pudding that doesn't involve some little Mexican chappie pissing in a coconut?'

'That's our speshaltee as a mitter of fict, sir, but we do also hive a nice chizceck or icecrim.'

'Cheesecake,' said Sophie over-enthusiastically. 'Yes please, sounds great.'

'You're from New Ziland.'

'Yessir, I'm frim Willington.'

'I'll have the chizceck too.'

'Dad, honestly.'

'Just a little light banter. Colonials love it.'

'Pissing in a coconut? What's that all about?'

The train is crossing the Tamar. Off to the left he can see warships, strung with lights in the evening gloom. The tide is in. The swans stand out in this murk, clean, luminous. In the little house on the creek he sees a light in a window. It's the colour of cheese, almost the colour of Jo's suit. It's exactly the colour of candlelight in an Advent calendar.

When he said goodbye to Sophie he felt afraid: she vanished behind the small crowd watching a fire-eater exhale fire while juggling burning torches. She left him with an impression that her thin body was too frail to cope with the sheer mass – he was amazed the earth's crust could stand it – around them. The impression that inert physical things can threaten you – rocks, buildings, cliffs – has been growing. Seeing Sophie who he has never loved as fully as he should have (although it's a fact that love is not subject to the will), with her small belly and her soft, unlined face, her child's nose with the awful ring in it, all its surfaces rounded and unformed like that German doll his mother kept sitting loosely on a chair in her bedroom as a reminder of her own idyllic childhood, which cast some comparative gloom forwards over his, seeing Sophie disappear suddenly like that, a Dickensian urchin, into this vast city, filled him with unease. As he has discovered, as he has really always known, cities are great works of deceit.

Jo said to him, when he was leaving: One of the reasons Tony gave for separating was that he was always jealous of you. I always talked about you.

Chapter Eleven

Charlie sees that he has been elected the steady one in the family. Sophie called and said Dad wants you to tell Ju-Ju that the reason he didn't visit was because he would become so upset that he would distress her. This is always the thing about Dad: he can't bear to be seen in a bad light, so he told Sophie that the fact that he didn't visit Ju-Ju must be put down to his extreme sensitivity. He finds excuses for himself.

'Charlie, he has some special relationship with Ju-Ju.'

'So special that he couldn't visit her for two years.'

'More than two.'

'You're right.'

'He's not in very good shape. He told the waiter at Camelback that he didn't want piss in a coconut for a dessert.'

'What's that mean?'

'I think he thought he was like being witty. He's losing it. Can I speak to Ju-Ju?'

'No, she's walking around the Rockefeller Mansion. One of them, anyway. She's amazing. Too bright for me.'

'And you?'

'I'm sitting on the terrace of the Tarrytown Inn looking at the river and making phone calls.'

'Is Ana cool about the wedding?'

'It's like a tad worrying: she loves the whole idea. Why don't you go and see her and explain who Betjeman was.'

'Maybe. Don't get me wrong, I like her, but she's from another planet to me.'

'Mum says you've split with Dan?'

'News travels fast. Yes, yup, I have.'

'And the marching powder?'

'Just a little weed is my new plan.'

'Good girl. I've got work to do. Speak later.'

This is family. In the family you are a certain kind of person. Your mother, my mother in particular, piles one half-truth about your character on another until she has built up a whole structure, a fabricated person. It begins in small ways: you are untidy or reliable or good with figures or you eat too fast; you're frightened of frogs, you hold your pen in the wrong way, and then these threads are woven into the family tapestry, a sort of Bayeux which for ever commemorates this entirely imaginary scene. Now he is becoming – the myth declares – competent. But you don't tell your mother about pornography or mastur-bation or dishonesty or dope smoking at school or cheating in exams or shoplifting. Mum thinks, for example, that Sophie 'experimented' a little with drugs. She doesn't know that he paid for her to spend six weeks in a place in Bristol to get off drugs when she was nineteen. Even now, she's still not in the clear although she's apparently convinced herself that she can get by with a little weed from time to time.

And, he doesn't really love Ana. The baby has brought this home to him.

If I loved her, I would be overjoyed to be having a child.

When Mum suggested St Enodoc for the wedding, he was pleased, as if, by pushing all the right buttons, he could make up for a lack of passion.

Maybe it was Ana's exoticism that convinced him that he loved her. Now small, unavoidable facts are annoying him. He hadn't realised that she bleached the hairs on her upper lip from time to time. Somehow, finding the bottle of hydrogen peroxide in the cupboard, alongside the eyelash curlers and the scores of bottles of shampoo and conditioner and creams she collects, many containing interesting Australian and Mexican ingredients, had been depressing to his spirits. But what had he expected from a dark Latin girl? And also he found her habit of talking on the phone to her absentee mother in Lima irritating. She explained that in South America, although she was brought up in Paris and Washington where her father had some unexplained diplomatic status, endless chatter was simply a kind of background noise, comforting but meaningless.

Don't take it seriously, Carlito, she said. He doesn't like the infantile diminutive. He fears that after the baby she is going to turn into something large and moist and demanding. Already they employ a maid, a furtive little person from Dominica, who doesn't speak English. She worships Ana, and has acquired superciliousness as nanny-in-waiting. It's true his business is going well, but it's not yet going so well that they can buy a house in Notting Hill, which is what Ana wants. You have to sell a lot of socks to buy one of those stucco mansions, even down the bottom end near the poor people. Where they are looking.

But he has tried to tell himself that when you have a baby everything changes. Just as the Judds have been telling themselves that when Ju-Ju is out, everything will change.

Charlie puts in a call to a friend called Gus who has a company specialising in industrial intelligence. It's housed in his bedroom in Clerkenwell. Mostly Gus gets his information off the net. He tidies it up and writes reports. For instance, a few years ago he found a Swedish website that showed beyond a doubt that Iraq had bought equipment which could be used for the manufacture of nerve gas. This important fact was hidden away in a Norrskoping company's export application. The information was gratefully received by government.

Gus's number comes up on his phone.

'Any luck?'

'Charlie, I have found Richie de Lisle. He's running a gallery selling Native American art and artefacts in San Diego. He's called

Richard Lillie now. Actually that was his original name. His mother calls him Dickie, by the way.'

'OK, Gus, thanks.'

'When are you back?'

'Next week, maybe end of the week.'

'OK, I'll e-mail the details.'

He writes down everything in a Moleskine notebook. He spends the rest of the morning e-mailing: there is nothing to his business, really, just a willingness to be thorough. He finds that he shares his father's easiness with numbers, even though he gave up maths at school. It seems that you do inherit certain abilities. He can add up, Sophie can spell and there is no limit to Ju-Ju's talents. It turns out she's planning a dialect dictionary of Eastern America. She has a contract, negotiated from prison. This morning after breakfast – huge, lavish, pleasing to the senses – she set off to do the grand tour of Kykuit, the Rockefeller Mansion. It contains rare tapestries designed by Picasso and outside there is a sculpture garden. She's also arranged to see the nearby church where Nelson Rockefeller commissioned a window by Chagall to commemorate his mother. Ju-Ju says that it's the only church window by Chagall in America.

Ju-Ju looks, he thinks, as though she has been drained. Some essential human understanding has gone. She's finding it difficult to accept the normal, banal comforts of kinship that he is offering her, although she makes all the right noises. Maybe she's trying to rehydrate herself – he's thinking of those Japanese paper flowers – by soaking herself in beauty and art, as if the key to what she was must be there. He was deeply moved when she said that she had begun to believe that what she had known before was not real. Like what? *Like you, Charlie*. She said that *Heart of Darkness*, which he only knew as *Apocalypse Now*, was about Kurtz regressing, turning into a lesser form of evolution: *That's what I felt like, Charlie. Maybe I have somehow become something else*.

So now she's taking a ritual bath in art and he, the one who doesn't love the mother of his child, has become the competent one, with a father who is losing the plot and a family who look to him. He must hope that he finds his own salvation in fatherhood.

He's been looking closely at parents with young children. The parent who is obsessed with the children often seems to be trying to exclude the other one. And he sees young fathers on duty who might as well be wearing a fucking T-shirt saying: *I wish I was with a grown-up*. He e-mails the office: *Get a T-shirt designed that says: I'm a dad, but I'm also part human*.

Ana calls him from Bond Street. She's looking at table gifts from Tiffany. How much can she spend? Does he like berry spoons as table gifts? What are table gifts? Little mementos of the wedding for the guests in silver – cheap, or platinum – expensive. Look, Ana, it sort of depends on how many are coming. He's shorter with her than he would like to be, but manages to salvage something by saying loveya a few times in closing.

Why does she adore luxury goods? If it said Prada on it, she would buy a jock strap. It gets to him, because his own company has been built with an eye to the small independent designers, and by selling their goods cheaply. Although it's the socks – **sock-it-to-me.com** and **sockscribe.com** – that make the money. Once you've signed them up, they hardly ever cancel.

Ju-Ju has taken a beating, as they say here. Americans know that life can break you. In Britain we haven't embraced this idea: we respect weakness and human frailty; they seem to be part of a continuum, rather than two sides of a dividing line. What Ju-Ju said was right, the elect are successful, the others go to the wall. She's usually right. He watched her waiting for the bus to Rockefeller heaven this morning, clutching a cheap green rucksack (he needs to tell her a thing or two about fashion bags), ready to leave, her face unnaturally tense like someone about to go into the dentist's chair.

'Have fun, sis.'

'I wish you were coming.'

He should have gone. She waved to him forlornly from among the pastel elderlies as the bus moved away.

Richie has a lot to answer for: that glimpse of the drawn,

nervous face of his beautiful sister, refracted by the plexiglass as the bus pulled away, so that she looked for a moment as though she was going to scream, this is top of the list of his grievances against Richie, also known as Dicky. Dad sometimes calls a bow-tie a dicky bow. Dad is under the impression that phrases like that have a kind of solid yeoman ring to them, whereas anything to do with the net or young people – he says 'youf culture', a phrase he picked up from *Private Eye* a hundred years ago – is somehow trashy and impermanent. No, Dicky Lillie, even if Ju-Ju doesn't want it, is going to have to answer for his sins.

Charlie likes women. He prefers their company to men's. What he dislikes about being with men is their complicity: men smirk when they are together. He knows it's because of women. Men see themselves as outposts of honest, no-bullshit values, in a world where women are spreading a sickly and insidious miasma. You can see it, at its most basic level, with workmen in the streets, scaffolders and shopfitters particularly, and you can see it in the City pubs. They think they're winning: *We're still here, don't you worry, mate*. So he feels bad that he should have these thoughts about Ana because his reservations are of the irrational kind: she dyes her – let's put this bluntly – moustache; she likes to shop; she loves handbags; her tits are becoming heavy. When Ju-Ju asked him if he had a picture of her, he felt guilty that it had never occurred to him to keep one in his wallet. He wonders how Ana and Ju-Ju will get on.

In a way, I always wanted to end up with someone like Ju-Ju.

He's waiting, comfortably, on the terrace. Below him, some way below on the huge river, barges pass, wagon-trains of barges. From up here you get the idea that there must still be a hinterland with giant, crude mines producing ores, or vast mills producing timber that must come down the river. All major American towns seem to be on the conflux of rivers and lakes. That was the only way of getting the heavy stuff to market. He's waiting on the terrace to see if the bid from Germany, expected any day, has been received by his lawyer, who is handling the negotiations. His lawyer is also twenty-eight, another friend. Her name is Martha

Wilkes and he used to go out with her. He hasn't told Ana that he may be selling up. She would immediately pillage Bond Street and buy up Holland Park.

'Do you like Ana?' he asked Martha, just before he left for America.

'She's gorgeous.'

'That's not much of an answer.'

'We have a little history, Charlie. I find it difficult to be objective.'

'I know. But I value your opinion.'

'Charlie, girls always make comparisons when they see a new significant other.'

'That's such a crappy *Friends* kind of phrase. What do you actually mean?'

'What's she got that I haven't? That's the sort of thing. I don't mean me versus Ana, I mean that's the comparison girls make.'

'And?'

'She's very different from your other girlfriends, including me.'

'In what ways?'

'She's sort of old-fashioned feminine. Hard-core Latin glamour-puss.'

'You're like saying I'm going out with Evita Perón and she's going to go and run off with her tango instructor. I see.'

'That's the sort of thing.'

'And by the way, you dumped me.'

'I only dumped you because you shagged my friend.'

'We were too young.'

Martha sends him a text: *Still waiting for the Krauts*. He sends a reply: *The hard-core glamour-puss and I are getting married. Oh what might have been.*

Ana's father has the look of a professional member of the South American ambassadorial-entrepreneur class. For a start he has – he *sports* – a thin moustache.

It was, Charlie now thinks, a warning. He also wore his jacket on his shoulders like a cape, to indicate a readiness to tackle a maverick fighting bull or to hand the jacket to a flunky the moment he should become too warm. His face was curiously flecked with nicotine-coloured, flat moles. His hair was thin, but thicker than Charlie's and combed back over his head like the Italian Prime Minister's. He was in London for a conference on whaling. Charlie suspected he was being bribed by the Japanese, a useful source of income for diplomats from landlocked countries. Curiously enough, he was the one who seemed totally at home in London. At the Savoy he fitted right in. He spoke to Charlie with amusement as if he had met a member of that new tribe, the whacky cow-embalming English. His intensity was directed towards his second daughter, Ana, who was studying fashion at St Martin's, paid for by the United Nations. They discussed money. The family house back in the jungle was falling down. You wouldn't believe how many bad people there were, crazy, *loco*, in Ecuador. Meanwhile his sumptuous daughter seemed to be equally at ease in the elaborate, richly decorated, mirrored and faceted bar and also the Grill where the roving whale expert and diplomat appeared to have mislaid his wallet. It should, Charlie now thinks, have been seen as another sign.

At the same time he was intrigued, even impressed, by his effortless command of the Savoy. It was as if Juan-Pablo had been expected home for some time and every effort was being made to soothe him after his valiant diplomatic efforts in the recalcitrant world outside. He needed a better table and more olives and the music turned down and less vermouth in his Martini. Yes, sir, yes, Excellency.

Waiters and maîtres d'hôtel have notoriously poor judgement: they are invariably taken in by the conman-aristo look, by older men with improbably young girlfriends, by signet rings and money clips and crocodile wallets and especially by over-tipping.

God help us if he comes to the wedding.

Charlie thinks that there is the real possibility of farce on the wedding day if Ana arrives on her father's arm, a galleon under full sail blown into a small English port.

Ju-Ju doesn't want to discuss Richie. Richie – he's speculating, because he only ever met him in a cheerful, social New York rush – points to a side of Ju-Ju that she can't control. It might be sex. But Richie is that sort of Englishman to whom sex is light entertainment, on a par with owning a dog or having a wine cellar. Who knows? On the night before leaving, fucking Ana, trying to avoid any glimpse of the mown hay on her upper lip, he stared at her deep greeny grey – actually the colour of a kind of seaweed – eyes, and he felt that he saw a sort of impersonal frenzy, an episode of *petit mal*. Her eyes actually rolled and her lips worked. Maybe they were mouthing obscene words in Inca. But he wasn't sure that she was aware of his presence. Her orgasm was loud, tortured and entirely personal. Her redemption, like that of fundamentalists, a matter between her and her god.

What have nearly two years in jail done to my sister in that department? While he had criss-crossed the Atlantic to see her in Otisville and Loon Lake, Richie had never visited her. And in those places – they could not discuss it – she had been wrenched away from the two men she loved most. Dad and she – Sophie is right – have a deep and unfathomable communion. It must have been doubly painful to see Mum concerned and flustered and Sophie and me turning up dutifully in those terrible places. Without Dad. When the judge, that sneering bitch, said that Ju-Ju would have to learn that nobody was above the law, what she failed to observe was that to take Ju-Ju from her lover and her father and from art and beauty was cruel and unnatural punishment. We must get over believing she is not guilty, says Sophie. But exactly how guilty is she? Only she and Richie know.

Maybe I will never discover the truth, because in the business of sex nothing is clear or logical. Still, I must talk to Richie.

Martha calls. Nothing to report: the Krauts are keen but delaying. They will make an offer next week, she thinks.

'Charlie, I hope I didn't suggest the other day that Ana was a freak.'

'No, not really.'

'Charlie, I'm very happy for you.'

'What aspect of me?'

'Like all aspects: the glamour-puss, the nipper, the dosh, your sister coming out of jug.'

'Martha, I'm not sure about her.'

He feels the need to blurt.

'Don't be a prick, Charlie. Of course you are; you're just having a male wobble. As your lawyer, and ex-girlfriend – one of them anyway – I am advising you to take a cold shower. Remember, you're having a baby, and the baby is the thing. Freedom is the recognition of necessity. Hegel. I'm leaving the office now. Goodbye.'

She's right. He's having a baby and the baby is the thing, but Martha's voice, the shared knowledge, the London street-smarts, the language itself, has touched him directly. Ana will always be, at some level, a stranger.

When Ju-Ju comes back from her tour she is a little dishevelled. Her hair, dull chestnut – it used to pulse with expensive life – has escaped from the band she tied it in this morning and is hanging around her face. She looks beautiful and slightly crackers, her face angled distractedly away, but she's smiling. As they leave the bus, two elderly people clasp her hand, a man in his Sta-Prest golf trousers, which reach way up above his natural waist, and a woman in the kind of jeans only the elderly are able to find: elasticated and pleated.

Ju-Ju, suddenly seeing him, calls him over and introduces him.

'This is my young brother, Charlie. Charlie, Mr and Mrs Morgenfruh.'

'Pleased to meet you, young man. Your sister is a wonderful person.'

'I've been hearing that all my life.'

'She's so knowledgeable. She told us all about Chagall.'

'Was she just a little bit boring?'

'Was she heck. She's a professor in disguise.'

When they have gone into the inn, the husband shuffling as if he's walking on treacherous ice, Charlie embraces Ju-Ju.

'Did you have a good time?'

'Fantastic. And you?'

'Just business. Nothing too interesting.'

'Mr and Mrs Morgenfruh come from Montreal. He started out there cutting the salt beef in his father's deli, his father was an immigrant, and became one of the richest men in Canada. He owns Morning Fresh supermarkets.'

'And now they're getting culture.'

'That's not a bad thing.'

'Do they know about you?'

'They know all about me.'

'And?'

'They think I have been victimised.'

'We all think that.'

'So you say.'

She gathers herself so that he recognises the eager, amused, slightly pigeon-toed, bunched way she moves as they head for the terrace; he remembers that when she's happy she walks in this way, with a blithe impatience, as though there is no time to waste. Her face has drawn some colour up from the brackish depths and her eyes seem to have acquired brightness. Over tea – the inn has an ecumenical choice laid out in a wooden display case – she tells him about the house, the Rockefellers, Picasso and Chagall, the Hudson River School, and also about the moving story of the Morgenfruhs. It's typical of her to see, not the elderly, ridiculously garbed tourists, but the human story.

Down below, way down in that deep gorge, the barges and ships pass as if to remind them that in the early spring sunshine the real business of America is still going on.

'Charlie.'

He looks at her, flushed and perhaps over-stimulated by freedom.

'You look happy, Ju.'

'Charlie, Noah Morgenfruh thinks that I am in some way a celebrity. He says everyone will want to hear my story.'

'And?'
'I don't think that would be a good idea.'
'Do you mean the full story?'
'Ah Charlie.'

Chapter Twelve

Another thing about angels: they are not direct participants in life's struggle: they are above it. And that's why we like them. They are disinterested observers, impartial do-gooders. They only acquired wings in later centuries. The author thinks that they were a necessary invention, an antidote to the harshness of religion and a comfort in death.

She and Charles never speak about death, except in terms of insurance – his pension, his will. What they never discuss is how the survivor will cope. Or how the children will cope. 'Coping' is something that has gone out of fashion; even the word has a strange sound now. But coping, in her parents' list of virtues, stood near the top. Being a good coper was essential for an Army wife. It required only steadiness and adaptability: imagination or brains were not part of the job description.

Have I been a good coper? Not really, if I'm honest.

Somehow that effortless style and ease to which she aspires has escaped her.

To welcome Charles back from London, she's cooking Goan fish curry. Charles likes spicy food and she knows exactly how to make it because it was one of the dishes they learned when she was doing the Rick Stein course.

She loves taking the ferry across to Padstow to the market. Because the tide is low, the ferry has to make a loop out into the estuary so that now, on the homeward leg, she sees Bray Hill and Daymer Bay sliding away to reveal the church hunkering in the rolling green. Now the ferry has found the dark tape of the channel, and follows it up the estuary to the beach where it makes land. She is one of only three passengers. Soon, from Easter onwards, the ferry will be full, with lines of holidaymakers waiting on Rock Beach or over at Padstow. The holidaymakers – she was one – make her feel uneasy: their lives are in full swing; their children are still at school; the husbands are plumped up with purpose; everything lies ahead of them. They come down here with their Mercedes and BMW wagons. Expressly to lord it over the residents. But today she has a lot to look forward to.

As the ferry buffets its way up the arterial stream, the little church is enfolded back behind Bray Hill. Frances is doing the flowers this week. She and Frances have discussed the flowers for the wedding. Charlie has asked Ju-Ju to be his best man. This, apparently, is something that the young do now. When she said to Charlie that she wasn't sure the custom had reached Trebetherick, he said, Mum, it will give her a chance to speak. The vicar thinks it's a fine idea. The church has no official view: *if it has, nobody has told me*.

When she spoke to Ju-Ju yesterday she sounded much happier. She was always a busy child and she has been looking at modern art at the Rockefeller Museum outside New York. They are going to Manhattan – as they call New York – and Charlie has to go to California for a business meeting while Ju-Ju sorts out her flat. She wishes she was there with Ju but she knows, hard as she tries to be calm, that she tends to say the wrong thing. As she gets older she can't hide her feelings. When she told Frances about the baby, she said, perhaps to show that human misery is evenly doled out, that there is hardly a day in her life when she doesn't have a little weep about her daughter and the fact that she will never have grand-children. Although the papers have stories of lesbian couples who have babies, by some means.

She thanks the boatman, whose face is weathered to the colour and texture of a russet apple. From behind this facial gouache, created by wind and sun and salt spray, a little, suspicious, angry mind peeps out on the summer passengers. It's a pleasure to her to be treated now almost as a local: *Mind 'ow yer go now, Daphne*, he says as she steps ashore with her aromatic bag of provisions. Coriander is very important in Eastern cooking although she prefers parsley. Even parsley has entered the popularity stakes: the flat Continental parsley has ousted the curly English parsley in cookbooks. When she's in the car she can smell the cumin and coriander seeds and fenugreek. She has long-grain rice too; she finds rice difficult to get exactly right, so she has some naan bread just in case it goes wrong. She wants to demonstrate that the Judds are also in full swing again: no more fish and chips from the Codfather or pasties from Barnacles for the Judds.

Clem came round last night to drop off Charles's cap, the tweed one that smells distinctly of mackerel. He had left it at the club. He stayed for a while and they drank a bottle and a half of Chardonnay. He's very good value, full of jokes and gossip. He probably wore his wife out. They had some smoked salmon with brown bread and lemon. You can't beat it, really. It's hard to tell with Clem if there's more than meets the eye. He said that he's very fond of Charles and glad to see him back on form; when he left, finally, he kissed her on the mouth, but lightly.

'Are you all right to drive home, Clem?'

'Are you inviting me to stay?'

'Don't be silly, Clem, I mean should you drive?'

'I'm too tight to walk. I'll have to drive.'

She feels a little guilty, in case he thought she was suggesting something. And possibly the elaborate dinner – all those spices, all those chunks of cod – is a demonstration of her steadfastness. Clem has a strange habit, while sitting like a pasha in his armchair, of reaching down the front of his trousers as if to free his balls. It's a quick adjustment, more of a twitch than anything deliberate, she knows, but she found herself counting down anxiously to the next excursion, rather like the way she waits for an alarm clock to go off.

'Yes, I think Charles is much better,' she said to Clem without any wish to continue the inquest.

It's something about us English, that we don't really like to talk about anything. Or maybe it's just our generation: life, death, love, sex, that sort of thing, are all smothered over with deprecation. She and Charles never really discussed how they were coping with being the parents of someone who was in jail. Obviously they were coping very badly, Charles studying the cliffs endlessly, even the dog committing suicide, and the ghastly, tense visits she made, conspicuously unaccompanied by her husband, to those frightful prisons full of deranged, misshaped people. Of course she only glimpsed the other visitors on the way to the 'contact room', but judging from their visitors, the prisoners must have been freaks of nature. The central question, which the vicar thinks they should address, is whether or not they are plagued by guilt. They have no reason to feel guilty, he says. But Charles won't discuss it.

Back in her kitchen she lays out all the ingredients methodically on the table. It's very important to prepare. Johnny's Taxi is picking Charles up from the seven-twenty-five, which means they can eat at about eight. She's got two hours. She finds the mortar and pestle for grinding the spices after roasting. She tips them out, making a pleasing, ferrous mound. She chops the onion. Her eyes water fiercely so that the rabbit pasture begins to swim. The fish is already cut into even chunks. You can use grouper or snapper or yellow tail, but she doesn't know anything about these fish and cod is always nice. She chops the fresh coriander in a cup with a pair of scissors. She goes out of the house to get a couple of bay leaves. In the old days you just used dry bay leaves, which her mother would put in a stew, giving it a cough-medicine taste after the obligatory five hours in the Belling. Now fresh bay leaves are the thing. She chops them very fine. The recipe suggests five large red chillies for six people. You can never be sure with chillies so she carefully cuts open two chillies and discards the seeds. You do this with a teaspoon, scraping them out. The seeds are, apparently, lethal. Then she chops the chilli, holding it in cling film as they were shown. One woman on the course who wore contact lenses rubbed her eyes and was in agony. The lenses had to be removed. She didn't have her glasses, so she was led back to the hotel, her eyes swollen and angry.

On the wooden board the little pile of chopped red chilli alongside the spoil heaps of spices and the green of the bay leaves and the lighter green of the coriander produces a still life like one of those photographs in magazines. The cod is smelling a little so she covers it. She turns on the oven and spreads the spices on a piece of foil. They should be roasted for maximum effect, before grinding them into a paste with some oil. She looks at her still life and inhales the pleasing effect of the spices roasting in a hot oven. They are soon ready. She grinds them down and rubs them into the fish, and places the casserole in the oven. Then she realises that she has forgotten the limes. It's visual intelligence, a lacuna; she misses the baize green of the limes in this miniature souk. She heads up the lane to the shop, which has one lime, two lemons, a grapefruit and a dozen small oranges. That's it for citrus. She takes the lime and the two lemons. As she leaves the shop with her small plastic bag, Clem drives by in his Jaguar. He slams on the brakes dramatically, and backs up, practically pinning her to the pebble-dash wall of the old post office.

'Sorry I didn't take you up on your offer last night.'

'Clem. It was lovely to see you anyway.'

'You look gorgeous.'

'Steady the Buffs.'

'Quick drink at the Mariner's?'

'I'm not sure –'

'Come on, live a little.'

'Oh all right.'

She giggles, a quick violent burst, as she gets into the car. He's at home in here. He is wearing knitted driving gloves. His forearms are very brown, with some discoloured patches, from the golf exposure. He's wearing yachting trousers of a faded burgundy colour and a polo shirt in pink. He drives with a flourish, down the lane and accelerating past the garage, towards the beach.

'You must be happy.'

'About what?'

'About Juliet, of course.'

'Yes, I am. Of course I am. I'm a little nervous, because Charles hasn't seen her for three years.'

'Charles is deep.'

'Meaning?'

'I find him hard to read. I'm shallow, by the way. I have no hidden depths.'

In the summer the pub is always jammed full. Now it's almost empty. Without asking her, he orders two glasses of champagne.

'We're celebrating.'

She looks at his seasoned, almost jaundiced, old-smoothie face and wonders if it is true that he has women in London. *I'm shallow*. Deliberately shallow, more likely. Camouflage.

When he drops her back at the house they are both a little drunk. As he says, you don't celebrate your daughter's safe return every day. She moves fast, to avoid a kiss.

Before she has reached the front door, she can smell the burning. The kitchen is fogged and highly scented. The lights won't come on. When she opens the oven door, dense black smoke rolls out. The oven has fused the lights. She rushes to open the back door, but the whole house smells of burning spices and fish. This must be how Goa smells at mealtimes. The chilli in the smoke is catching in her lungs. She looks at the kitchen clock, through the fog. It's seven-forty-five. She takes the casserole out of the oven. Apart from the limes, which she has left in Clem's car, she has followed the recipe exactly. She feels the weight of matter pressing hard. The fish and the spices have fused. Something chemical has occurred. A small flame flickers as the last of the cod burns itself out, like that doomed spacecraft entering the earth's atmosphere. That was terrible. She could imagine their last few minutes. She sees car lights approaching. She runs awkwardly out of the back door with the casserole and puts it under the garden tap, causing geysers of steam to rise. But it's not Charles's taxi, it's Clem.

'Daphne. Are you in there somewhere?'

He comes into the gloomy kitchen with the pathetic bag of limes and lemons.

'You left these.'

'I don't suppose we'll be needing them.'

'Doesn't look like it. Where's the fuse box?'

He helps her restore order of a sort. It seems she had the oven on the grill setting.

'What were you, if I may use the term, cooking?'

'It was supposed to be Goan fish curry . . .'

'I didn't realise they still practised cremation in Goa.'

'What am I, the widow who throws herself on the fire?'

'You've got to look on the bright side.'

'What's that?'

'Well, the stately home might have burned down. No harm done, apart from the fact that your house is going to smell of incinerated fish for ever. When Charles arrives we can explain that the oven malfunctioned and that we are going to go to the Blue Banana at Polzeath, on me.'

'I don't think he will want to go there.'

'It's fine, trust me. I'll tell them to turn the music down.'

The Blue Banana has just opened. She's paused, half turned non-committally away, to read the menu, which is mostly funny sandwiches or pasta and the coffees with silly names that the young like. Sophie would love it: maybe she should get a summer job there when the surfers arrive.

Johnny's Taxi is waiting. Charles has never quite got over the feeling that this station is a temporary arrangement. One day they will realise that you can't put a station in a forest miles from anywhere. It's like a scene from *Dr Zhivago*: he's the only passenger getting out. Still, there's Johnny, climbing with difficulty out of the old Nissan, his hips moving as though each one is waging its own campaign; he yaws. He smokes all the time and eats pasties; the car usually smells of both despite the pine-tree deodorant hanging from the mirror, but he's a good man with a severely rationed stock of rural wisdom. Ignoring the state of his hips, he insists on carrying the small case to the car. Charles would prefer to sit in the front, but the front seat is cluttered with maps, receipt pads, tabloid newspapers and large flakes of pasty.

The back is cramped and the seat is worn. Johnny holds the back door open for him, and then takes a deep drag on the cigarette, before flicking the butt into the brambles.

'I don't suppose the weather was as mild as this uppin Lunnin.'

'It wasn't too bad.'

'Still, you'll be glad to be home.'

When Johnny sits down, the car's chassis squeaks and then settles with a sharp noise.

'Shocks,' says Johnny. 'She's done two hundred thou.'

They set off into the night.

Charles has a deep feeling of loneliness: he's heading home, but he is thinking of Jo and her dreary house. And the sadness of seeing her so plump and ordinary in her cheap yellow suit. And the last glimpse of Sophie slipping away into London, leaving him in the heedless crowd among the weeping buildings. Perhaps he embarrassed her. So he tries, as they enter the deep lanes beneath the hedgerows that is Johnny's secret route, randomly accompanied by the musique concrète of the clapped-out shocks, to imagine the face, the presence, of his daughter Ju-Ju. He can't. At least he can only remember her as a little girl or receiving one of the bushel of prizes at St Paul's or on holiday holding a crab by one leg.

Because I didn't go to see her for nearly three years her image has been erased; I am being punished for my cowardice. What he wants is to get near to her. He tries instead to make an inventory of those of her things that remain in the house; they are items preserved because they have what Daphne calls 'sentimental value': some pious crap from St Bartholomew's about her christening, a childish letter proclaiming the virtues of the tomato museum on Guernsey, a photograph of the whole family in ski clothes, a tiny Brownie costume, some certificates for swimming a length in an overcoat. Actually, as he remembers it, the tomato letter makes him laugh: *I know more about tomatoes than I want to.*

'You're in a good mood, Mr Judd.'

'Not bad, Johnny. How are the horses?'

145

'Now that's what I call bad. One of mine is probably still running at Chepstow. He started Satterdee, mind you.'

Johnny has a betting problem.

I mustn't laugh out loud or say things in public.

On the tube to Paddington he said shut up to two young women who were screeching with laughter about a friend who had thrown up in the back of a car. Fuck off, mind your own business.

What is the essence of another person? That's what I want, not the remembered bits, the discarded insect wings and insect bodies of memory, but the living person.

He hums.

'Cliff Richard. One of the greats, Mr Judd. Say whatya like. Livvin Doll. Absolutely fucking brilliant. Excuse my French.'

When they reach the house he sees Clem's Jag outside. He gives Johnny a big tip to make up for humming and for laughing inappropriately.

'Crikey, it's not Christmas for another nine months, Mr Judd.'

'For the shocks.'

The car lurches away, Daphne comes out to meet him.

'Hello, darling. The oven went mad and luckily I ran into Clem. He's taking us out for a snack. No, he's insisting. You know how he is. He would be hurt. Come in, come in.'

Her breath smells of green grapes that have recently soured. He remembers a place called Rüdesheim where he met a girl, a waitress. Just opposite Bingen where the King of Prussia (titular only) committed suicide.

'Welcome home to the gypsy rover,' says Clem offering him a glass of his own Chardonnay. 'Nice suit.'

'Thanks, Clem. What happened here?'

'The oven blew up while I was cooking. Clem came by to deliver your hat, which you left at the club.'

'It fused itself, luckily. Not the hat, the stove.'

Charles can't quite follow the sequence of events. Clem and Daphne are facing him, complicit in some way. The place smells like a tandoori restaurant, yet heavily infused with fish. He sees something he has been groping for, a true piece of Ju-Ju, in the way Daphne has her head alertly cocked, and again as she walks forward eagerly, almost pigeon-toed, as if suddenly aware that they are arranged in the wrong order.

When I was a boy we were often told where to stand and when to stand up and so on. Invisible spaces were well understood. Now nobody cares. But why should they?

The Blue Banana is almost empty. A girl, who Clem apparently knows, welcomes them: they can sit anywhere, obviously. They sit near the window. Across the beach they can see the disorderly surf in the semi-dark. A local man of about fifty – he runs a surf-hire shop in season – sits at the bar, exchanging jokey confidences with the barman who is very young. The locals go in for this kind of banter.

'Our specials today are on the blackboard, otherwise it's what's on the menu.'

'I recognise her, Clem. Who is she?'

'She's a little cracker, isn't she? She's the daughter of the family who take the big house above Daymer every summer.'

'I remember. The Talbots. She's going to Exeter University. She's having a gap year. She's called Phoebe.'

Charles is always amazed by Daphne's knowledge of other people's children. This Phoebe has a tattoo of a surfer who appears to be riding a breaker so that if the wave broke the surfer would disappear from view beneath the gentle swell of her buttocks, which her shirt – her crop top – doesn't quite hide.

'Is that a real tattoo, Phoebe?'

'Charles, really. Sorry. You're Phoebe Talbot.'

'Yes, I am. How is Juliet?'

'She'll be home soon. In a week or so.'

'Oh that's great. And no, Mr Judd, it's a like stick-on tattoo. Are you ready to order?'

Her T-shirt reads: *fallen angel*.

'The first thing we need, Phoebe, is a good bottle of New Zealand Chardonnay. OK with you, Charles, Daphne?'

As Phoebe goes off to order the wine, Charles finds it difficult to avoid following the gently undulating progress of the surfer pictogram. He wonders what this Phoebe is indicating. He envies the young. Who doesn't?

'Sophie's broken up with Dan,' he says.

'She said. Is she all right?'

'She seems to be.'

'Is she eating?'

'Sorry, Clem. Yes, at least she was eating some Mexican muck with me. Voraciously.'

'She doesn't eat,' says Daphne to Clem. Daphne thinks that if Sophie starts to eat it will indicate that her experiments with drugs are over, although they don't discuss drugs.

'She's quite plump actually. They're all wearing nothing around their tummies like that Phoebe.'

'You don't know where to look sometimes with these young girls,' says Clem.

'You seem to know,' says Daphne cheerily.

Charles is happy that Daphne is so relaxed. It directs some of the pressure he feels, atmospheric pressure, away from him.

'You have to make a choice. Either you stare fixedly at their faces like a madman, or you try to behave naturally. I belong to the act-natural school.'

And you have a Vietnamese prostitute in London.

'What did you say, Charles?'

'Sorry. Nothing. I was just muttering.'

'Sometimes he hums.'

'He's always done that,' says Clem. 'He hums on the golf course, in the rough.'

'My father did it. He used to know songs from the twenties. Now I hum songs from the fifties.'

'It's the same with jokes. I can't remember any jokes after about 1960,' says Daphne, perhaps conscious of her disloyalty a few moments earlier.

'Women can't tell jokes,' says Clem. 'I don't know why.'

Clem is gradually colonising the whole table and his reach is extending outwards towards the bar and Phoebe.

'You breathe a hell of a lot of air,' says Charles.

'Oh, lighten up, Charles. Phoebe, Mr Judd needs something to drink. Another bottle of Chardonnay, pronto. His house nearly burned down.'

And Charles sees himself being cast adrift by Clem's generosity of spirit, if that's what it is.

Chapter Thirteen

Perhaps it's because they are going to be sisters-in-law. Or because Charlie is away: Ana has called her twice. Sophie has agreed to meet her for a drink at a place in Walton Street. Ana wants to talk.

Sophie sees London, she has to admit it, in a peculiar way: certain areas have certain colours. She sees Chelsea and the whole of the area between the river and Harrods as a dense maroon. Of course she goes there from time to time, but mostly she prefers the thinned-out green colours of places like Shoreditch, Clerkenwell, Camden, Soho and Brixton. Then there are other areas that she hardly knows, like Battersea, Finchley and Waterloo. These are mustard yellow. She tries to avoid Hammersmith, where she was at school; it has no colour. It is like the unexplained clear liquid you find cohabiting with your blood. Walton Street, with its excessive polish, its flower boxes, expensive curtain and tassel shops, its expressive door knockers on white front doors, its general air of self-congratulation, is deep in maroon territory.

She's headed that way. Once you cross into a maroon area you are in a world of confident voices and expensive accessories. And chaps. Chaps are usually dressed – still – in loafers and they favour long-sleeved shirts, sometimes loosely rolled to the wrist. Chaps have longish hair, with uncontrollable bits. In winter they favour dark overcoats over pressed jeans. Richie is a chap, although he said that it was what was expected of him in New York. She had sex with him one night when Ju-Ju was at a reception. She was off her face a lot of the time then, and she was only nineteen.

She lives in a part of town that's supposed to be more interesting, more lively, more varied, but that's not why she lives there. Although she's been thinking of a comic novel set in a bagel shop called *The Betjemans' Kosher Kitchen*: *Not many people realised that the poet laureate loved lox and bagels. As a break from the drudgery of writing royal poetry, in 1958 he opened a bagel shop in Bacon Street. The first Betj Bagel contained home-smoked salmon with Gentleman's Relish and Stilton. It was not an instant hit with the market traders.*

The maroon of Kensington and Chelsea is exactly the colour of the lining of Daddy's last good suit, made by Gieves and Hawkes. He wears it for his charity meetings. She's not feeling confident about meeting Ana, so she had a few quick tokes before setting out. (Weed only, from now on.) What's to come? Ana is pregnant. Ana is dark and voluptuous. Ana – Mum said – has smouldering beauty, as if beauty on this scale can only mean trouble. Sophie feels pale, drained of colour, when she is near Ana.

Compared with the pubs where she lives, which have a kind of utilitarian, train-station feel, with green tiles and deeply ringed and soiled wood, this place is a bordello in grey and pistachio with swags and textured seats, which, at the King of Bohemia, would be expertly appraised for a car-boot sale. There's a cappuccino machine, a huge vase of regal lilies and some tables laid with linen and chunky silver. A man in a spotless floor-length apron asks if she has a booking. A booking, in a pub? For lunch? I don't think so. I am meeting someone, she says. Any name? Sophie gives Ana's name, and the man says. Ah, you're in the corner by the fireplace. He brings her a Bellini and some fancy nibbles, obese olives and fish-shaped chilli crackers. She should buy some for Mum.

As she waits for Ana, the place begins to fill with regulars. But these are not regulars as she understands them – one daft old lady in support stockings, a Bangladeshi drunk called Ali and two plasterers who leave a fine layer of dust when they move. No, these are estate agents and jewellers and women who have nothing to do all day except to buy handbags and eat lunch, while their ex-husbands eat lunch down the river somewhere, in the shade of the Gherkin. This is a part of town where Englishness still survives, but in pantomime costume.

Daddy said the other night, about nothing in particular, *How fast things change*, probably meaning values and standards of behaviour. At his school they had had a daily inspection of the back of the neck, the place where dirt finally came to rest, and they had to take cold showers even in winter, little frozen boys with their snail willies – Guylian chocolates – were lined up under Matron's gaze every morning at seven. *Now*, said Dad, *it would be called child abuse: the point I am making is that the older I get the more I see how everything we believe in is temporary and shabby. How clean is the back of your neck, for example?*

Ana has not shown. Sophie orders another Bellini: the effect of the weed and the Bellini seem to be complementary; perhaps it's the natural ingredients. Whatever, she feels strangely well disposed to this forgotten English tribe, living in these remote creeks, all of whom are now in full cheerful voice. She hears odd phrases – *five hundred k minimum – hunt-ball – first fifteen captain – absolutely adores Ludgrove – four point five fuel injected – gone lame behind – New Zealand nannie – Val do Lobo – half his age – Cobbler's Cove – loves being with his chums – four hundred k top whack* – she hears these phrases and she doubts if Dad is right. Maybe what is happening is simply a reshuffling of the cards. What if there are categories that have to be filled – greed, snobbery, idealism, et cetera – and these categories are constant, but the content of them is what changes with fashion? She has made a resolution to carry a notebook; indeed she has bought a Moleskine like Charlie's, but she hasn't brought it, and anyway so far she hasn't made any notes. All the good ideas come to her at the wrong time.

I need to get these thoughts down, particularly if I'm going to university.

More and more girls keep little diaries, travel diaries. Although there's a whiff of pretentiousness about recording your thoughts in public.

Just as she is about to order her third Bellini, Ana arrives; she stands in the doorway for a moment for maximum effect. Good God, she is carrying a green Birkin bag! These bags cost four thousand pounds! For a fucking handbag! Ana sees her, shucks off her coat, which has a rich fur collar, into unregarded hands, and waves and shrugs. Her hair tumbles, cascades, blackly over her shoulders. There may be such a thing as having too much hair. She probably has dark aureoles around her nipples.

'Sophie, I'm so sorry. The cab went to Randolph Road, can you believe it?'

'No problemo. I'm quite pissed.'

'I'll have the same,' she says to the waiter.

'New bag?'

'Yes, lovely, isn't it? I got it from a PR who used it on a shoot. Cheapo cheapo. I could get you one.'

Sophie looks at her closely as she details the horrors of her ten-minute journey which became thirty minutes.

Ju-Ju asked her to describe Ana, because apparently Charlie doesn't have a picture of her. *Hiya, Ju-Ju, I am looking at her now and this is what I have to report: Ana is beautiful, in a Latin way. Her hair is almost indecently thick. It glows: it seems to have taken electric energy from the universe. Her eyebrows are solid, perhaps she should thin them, and her eyes are enormous. I am looking closely at them to see if she has enhanced the effect, but alas no, she does have VERY BIG GREENY-GREY EYES. Her lips are ribbed, like those extra-sensation condoms – they are camellia pink today – and her cheekbones are high. The most extraordinary thing about her is the sort of noble, forward-thrusting look of her forehead. It's quite odd once you notice. She definitely has some Indian blood. Perhaps she's an Inca. Her teeth are fantastically white. There is a slight shadow on her upper lip. She looks like an extravagantly healthy animal, like one of those racehorses you see at Ascot – glowing. Mum says she's smouldering: I would say it's more animal, more primal. Maybe that's the attraction for Charlie.*

Maybe, like a tropical plant, she will go off quickly. We can only live in hope. And she has a Birkin bag: four grand, the price of a low-mileage VW Polo.

Sophie thinks that as you look closely at a face you have to make a conscious effort to see it properly and to try to get in balance the face and what you know about the person. The relationship between your self and the face in front of you, which is a painting or unreliable guide to what's behind, is not fixed; you bring your own prejudices to the evaluation. You adjust the relationship constantly every time you meet someone. You're running a kind of Dow Jones. Dan's face gradually fell in her evaluation: the attractive aspects seemed to change as she got to know him; the middle-aged boyishness became a little sinister, a sort of perversion. Ju-Ju will want to know what the essence of Ana is, but I don't know what to compare her to.

Ana has her drink. She is in a family mood. Sophie feels a warmth directed towards her, the sort of warmth you get from an animal with a noticeably higher body temperature. In her mind we are already related; she's swapping the family particles. She's drawing DNA from me.

'Have you spoken to Charlie?'

'A couple of times,' says Sophie.

'He seems to be very busy with Yew-Yew.'

'It can't be easy.'

'No. I'm looking so forward to meet her.'

Her English, American-accented, occasionally stumbles, as if her first language remains embedded, a rocky outcrop.

'She's had a rough time.'

'Very bad. Charlie says she is like devastated.'

'She has a lot of resources.'

'How you mean?'

'She's clever and talented. She's like always interested in something. Even a little like obsessive. She'll be fine in the end.'

'I hope she likes me.'

Sophie sees now why they are meeting: Ana is wondering if Ju-Ju is competition for Charlie's affection.

She's lining me up on her team.

'Ana, I'm sure she will like you.'

'I'm not like intellectual.'

'Who is? It's so like old school.'

'You know what I mean. I maybe won't be able to speak with her.'

'Oh don't worry, she speaks like normal people. Most of the time.'

'Charlie loves her.'

'Dad loves her. I love her. Everybody loves Ju-Ju. It may be a curse, but I don't think it's anything for you to like worry about.'

They drink another Bellini each. Sophie wonders how many Bellinis her nephew/niece should be ingesting, but she says nothing. They move on to less quaggy ground, the question of houses. Ana thinks that a nice big house in Notting Hill would be perfect, and Sophie sees that she hasn't quite grasped English life with the presumption, the entitlement, of that remark.

I'm a bit like Dad sometimes; my reaction is that you can't just walk in, you have to pay your dues.

'I think Notting Hill is really totally cool,' says Ana.

'How's Charlie's sock business doing?'

'Good, I think. He plays his cards close to his chest. Like he only told me last night he has to go to California.'

It cheers Sophie to see that this green-eyed panther is as prey to insecurity as the next person.

'He's always been like that,' she says, still feeling the *Freude* of this revelation of *Schaden*. 'The funny thing about Charlie is that he is the competent, well-organised person my father never was, although he was supposed to be the accountant, my father I mean.'

Ana is still troubled:

'He's always kinda busy.'

'I'm, like, not saying he's boring,' says Sophie. 'Not at all. Charlie's like got a sort of self-sufficiency, that's all. I find it quite surprising how he's turned out.'

'You know he never wanted a baby. I mean like it just happened. I didn't plan it or decide, hey, I'm gonna have a baby.'

'He'll love being a daddy.'

She knows that there is no direct evidence for this, but she also knows that most new fathers are so overcome by the unique wonder of what they have created, for a while anyway, that they become entranced with their own newly discovered spiritual qualities. They see themselves not, for example, in a flat in Fulham, but in the universe, in solidarity with the generations that have gone before and the generations to come. Very few people – she thinks – are immune to this licensed sentimentality.

'I want to have my own life. You know what I'm saying. I don't want to be like sitting at home like turning into a vegetable. Talking about like nothing except babies.'

Sophie feels sleepy.

'I don't want Charlie to find me like boring all of a sudden.'

'No. That definitely won't happen.'

'I've alway been like active. Like real busy. Will you do things with me?'

'Of course. What sort of things?'

'Like normal things. Like going to shows and like galleries and whatever. Like lunch.'

'Talking of lunch, shall we like order? I'm like losing it.'

She's also wondering if it's a good thing for Ana to order another Bellini on an empty stomach. As they wait for the food and Ana unloads what has been on her mind, Sophie sees from the window on to Walton Street that it is raining. She hates books where weather is used for literary effect: rain when it's intense or emotional; sun going down for romance; dark nights for added significance. Instead you should allow weather its place: it's raining, it often rains, it will rain again. Weather is interesting, but weather is not a cheap metaphor. The restaurant, oddly, seems brighter and more alive as the gloom settles outside. And possibly this is the thing with life, to look for a certain truth in small details.

Christ, I must be drunker than I thought.

Ana is saying that Charlie wanted the traditional church wedding and that Charlie suggested Juliet as best man. Sophie has spoken to Mum about this already: the vicar doesn't mind the best man being a woman. Ana had envisioned being married at Chelsea Town Hall with a few close friends for drinks and lunch. Her father, the roving ambassador, wants to give her away, if his commitments permit. Charlie says he's a crook. The food arrives, the familiar upscale mishmash, sprinkled and daubed with colour and texture around the rim of the plate, as if Jackson Pollock was moonlighting in the kitchen.

There are tiny beads of sweat on her upper lip, Ju-Ju. Charlie is marrying someone with big, active pores, like a sea anemone. Her brow is shining. The child is going to be a greaseball.

God, we are a terrible family. We're clannish and critical. Even Mum believes that we are from some natural aristocracy. And Dad is pulling up the drawbridge against the barbarians. She has a sudden vision of her mother walking across the golf course to the church, stooped against the rain, carrying that plastic bucket. There's something heroically instinctive about her, battling on. The Good Woman of Trebetherick.

The restaurant-pub has arrived at a certain lassitude now: not everybody is concentrating. A low-level drunkenness, and perhaps a little doubt, is evident. The coffee ritual, the oily leering glasses of port over there, signal the end. There's some sadness. But Ana is swimming happily against the tide. She is discussing her wedding dress: a designer friend of theirs has some great ideas. Sophie feels her own spirits, nudged downwards by drink and dope, sink further. She tries to explain to Ana how perfect the little church in the sand dunes is, the walk across the tenth fairway, the excavation myth, the poet laureate's grave . . . but she loses heart before she gets to the nub of it, which is the message of return and redemption that the wedding sends out: look, Charlie Judd and his Jennifer Lopez have come to old England for a blessing; look, Juliet Judd, so cruelly treated, has returned for atonement; look, the Judds are where they belong, after a few glitches. Englishness has healed them all! Jerusalem!

I am pissed. I am turning into a discount William Blake.

And now she's tired of Ana, who hasn't asked her a single question about her life.

Later, back across the border in Hoxton, she feels as though somehow she has landed up in Romania or Bulgaria, such is the comparative filth and dreariness and colour deprivation. Her flat looks like a cell in an interrogation block in Tirana.

If I don't get into university, I'm going to Barcelona.

It was OK living here when she was working sixteen hours a day, but she can't stay here.

She calls Charlie: he's paying; he has tri-band, of course.

'Hi, Charlie.'

'Both the sisters in stereo. The other one's sitting next to me. By the way, thanks for talking to Ana.'

'It was fun.'

'She said you were great, although she couldn't get a word in edgeways.'

'Oh fuck off. She like never drew breath. And you've got to stop her drinking or you will be the father of a freak. Let me speak to Ju-Ju.'

'Hi, Soph.'

'Where are you? In Manhattan yet?'

'We're just approaching the Bronx. I spoke to Ana too; don't listen to Charlie: she said she unloaded on you and that you are an angel. What's she like?'

'She's majorly glamorous.'

'Everybody says that. Is she nice? Ow, Charlie's hitting me. Stop earwigging and keep your eyes on the road, Charlie.'

'He's always been a bully. It's hard to tell. She never stops talking. She's like worried that you are going to find her stupid. I told her that you are very tolerant of dumbos. And, Ju-Ju, you probably won't have heard of them, but she's got a Birkin bag.'

'What's that?'

'It's a leather bag with a lock on it. Hermés. It costs like FOUR THOUSAND POUNDS.'

'Oh my God. Does Charlie know?'

'Ask him. He's sitting right next to you.'

She can hear Ju-Ju speaking to Charlie.

'Yes, he knows. He didn't pay for it. That's the important fact. I think he's lying. Ouch. He's hitting me again.'

'Do you know when you are coming back?'

'It won't be long.'

'Are you OK, Ju?'

'I'm getting back to myself, I think. Sophie, sweetheart, it's not going to be quick. I've got to take my time.'

'Please come home, Ju-Ju.'

'As soon as everything is sorted here, Soph. Promise.'

Sophie finds herself alone. She shouldn't have begged Ju-Ju to come home. But they're all waiting for her. It's fine for Charlie and her in their own little road movie.

Later Dan rings, and she agrees to go to the Lahore with him, but it's just a temporary concession because she's lonely.

'Nice one,' he says, 'nothing like a good Ruby Murray when you're down, as me old dad used to say.'

'Who says I'm down?'

'I know your voice.'

'How are the Alfas?'

'Done and dusted. Sophie gel, I want to tell you something.'

'Yes?'

'I've left Patsy.'

Her spirits dive. Like one of those fucking dolphins in fact. To prepare herself for meeting Dan she rolls a joint and draws deeply.

Chapter Fourteen

In prison she had begun to think about the theft itself. Up until the trial, the theft had belonged to another world. In fact she did not discover all the details until Agnello gave evidence. But during the tortured sleepless nights that followed, she found herself dreaming about these details. The dreams formed into a narrative: three Italian-Americans from the Bronx drove a pickup to the cemetery in Flatbush. One of them, Anthony Agnello, opened the gates with the keys he had copied. The lock was rusty. There was a scare when a patrol car passed. The gates creaked; the overgrown cemetery was spooky. They drove the pickup right to the mausoleum, which stood conveniently hidden behind some locust trees. Agnello and his friends were not competent. They dropped the wooden crate as they unloaded it from the truck. It made a loud crash, and they ran to hide behind the mausoleum. The judge asked why they had done something so foolish when the truck was still standing there. *We was not, how can I say this, your honor, we was not one hundred per cent sober. Dutch courage, that's a Bronx expression, your honor. It means . . . I know what it means, Mr Agnello.* Then Agnello had opened the mausoleum. It needed the best part of a can of WD 40 to loosen the lock. Nobody had visited these dead persons for fifty years. Then it was Marcel Mostarda's turn: he began to loosen the window from the inside without breaking the lead tracery or the glass. It took two hours. Jimmy Fusco meanwhile laid the crate he had made outside the back window of the mausoleum and lined it with blankets. Fusco was shitting himself – *beg pardon, your honor, Jimmy was noiviss.* He wanted to go home when an owl hooted. Finally they lowered the nine-foot window down on to the crate and Jimmy nailed it up before they loaded it on to the pickup.

In prison she sees herself as supervising this operation, actually present at the heist as the three wise guys hack out the Uma Stimhouse Memorial Window. In her waking hours she wonders, although she has no interest in dream theory, why she is constantly replaying the evidence in her sleep. The feeling that she is in a cheap crime novel – an owl hooting, a police siren sounding on Flatbush Avenue, the damp cold of the mausoleum – is stronger than her rational mind can accept. Dreams seem to choose this mode, the simple narrative. And when she plays the events again, if play is the word, events which took place two years before she arrived in New York, when the grave-robber and budding comic, Anthony Agnello, with two of his friends, stole a nine-foot Tiffany window depicting the discovery of Christ's empty tomb, she is always there in the damp, overgrown grass and nettles and seedlings, standing to one side as the three clowns get to work on the window, which bears the legend: *Why seek ye the living among the dead. He is risen.*

It is part of her defence to emphasise that this window was not unique. It was stolen – as we now know – like so much else from cemeteries in the boroughs of New York, and even as far as Westchester and Newark. Everyone in the art world knew that the windows were being stolen. Mr Agnello himself admits to stealing all sorts of artefacts. The authorities did nothing. The real crime was committed two years before Ms Judd arrived in our country. What Ms Judd did was simply to acknowledge the fact that this window existed. Ms Judd was asked to authenticate it. She did this. She may have suspected it was stolen. After all, what was it doing in a shed in the Bronx? But it wasn't on any report of stolen goods. It was likely to be sold or broken up anyway. Later she was asked if she knew any collectors. Of course she did. She has a list of them; that is her business. Ladies and gentlemen of the jury, is this the same thing as going to the Flatbush Pond Cemetery in the dead of night with a pickup truck and a box of tools and a large crate?

The jury concluded, when they heard about the cheques she had paid to Agnello, that it was the same thing, in fact worse. And, with two years to think about it, she saw how misjudged her defence was. She might as well have been standing there that night. As it happens Agnello and his chums would have continued to steal urns and marble ornaments with just as much enthusiasm if people like her had not created a market for certain artefacts such as stained-glass windows. It was a highly subjective process, one opinion upon another, one sale on another, until a commercial consensus was achieved. Her book had helped send prices for Tiffany rocketing.

Now she thinks she understands the nature of that recurring scene at the cemetery. Americans, and not only Americans, are increasingly prone to see events in the real world through the infantile syllogisms of television and film. In this case three lovable wise guys from Queens (one of whom actually wears a gold medallion over his shirt as he gives evidence), just goodfellas, minor criminals in a long and honourable tradition, knock off a cemetery in Flatbush. They have no idea what they are stealing, until a highly educated Upper East Side broad, from Old England, from Oxford no less, where ole Bill Clinton was a student, where another slippery customer, Jay Gatsby, claimed to have studied, makes the honest endeavours of these chumps into a major crime. That's how it plays. And the judge understands her part: it's payback. Her words, addressed to the fidgety, obese, absurd jury, crudely suggest whose side they should be on. She offers them the opportunity to strike a blow for the little guy. And they do. They place Juliet Judd at the centre of the crime. They have, with a little help, turned the events from something complex into something familiar: A STORY. And she is led away in manacles because a story needs a recognisable ending.

She sits now in her apartment. The doorman, an Irishman called Sean Costello, who left Cork forty years ago, is the only one who knows she is in the apartment. She's furtive, although it is her apartment for a few more weeks. She is perfectly able to do the sums, but before leaving for California, Charlie offered to take her through her options. Charlie is, in that brotherly way, beginning to irritate her: in his desire to protect her he is treating her as though she has picked up some affliction in prison, which needs constant vigilance. He also told Mum that he thought she was agoraphobic.

'Charlie,' she said, 'I've got to do things myself.'

'I'm only trying to help.'

'You've been great. In fact you've been more than great. But while you are gone I'm going to have to grapple with the realtor and the bank and so on.'

But now that he has gone, she wishes he was still here. She feels overwhelmed. In prison she was strangely protected. Perhaps she is suffering from agoraphobia. When the apartment is finally sold next week, with the committee's blessing, she will still owe the lawyers a hundred thousand and the bank about a hundred and fifty. The bank has accepted her proposal of stepped repayments, but in return it wants all kinds of deeds drawn up, for which it will be charging. It also wants a list of her potential earnings and a sworn declaration that she has no undeclared assets. Charlie offered to go to the bank with her, but she can't wait until he gets back. She wants everything settled as soon as possible.

She's sitting on the floor in the empty apartment surrounded by paper. Just here Mum met Richie for the first time. Mum was impressed by Richie: you could always tell when this happened because her voice took on a false, cheery tone, and from nowhere she produced a tinkling girly laugh. This laugh is like a downpour on a clear day. Of course to people who haven't heard its sudden onset before it sounds spontaneous. It may be something bred in the daughters of Army officers: always trying anxiously to impress men, always trying to be a good sport.

'And what exactly do you do here in the Big Apple, Richie?'

'I'm an art dealer.'

'What sort of pictures do you deal in?'

'Mum, I did tell you, Richie does modern pictures and installations.'

'Do you paint, Mrs Judd?'

'Please call me Daphne. I daub. I know my limits. But I love it. I do water-colours mostly.'

She giggled flirtatiously.

'Terrifically underrated, I think.'

'Oh you don't have to say that. I know that water-colours are on a par with golf and bridge as a hobby.'

Mum was very impressed with the separate hallway where the elevator came up. And she was soon asking Sean Costello's advice on everything from cabs to exhibitions, even things that they had already discussed, as though requiring a second opinion.

She's sitting on the floor: the woodblock has been stained by other human lives while she has been in jail, losing money on the forced rental. The new owners have plans, Sean says, to impress their own personalities on the place. It is universally accepted that decoration has become an important form of self-expression. Tiffany did houses for the design conscious and tombs for the aesthetic elderly.

In jail she sometimes wondered about her own love of beauty. It wasn't that she actually wanted things, but she was in thrall to the idea that art is different from the rest of life, something pure and more authentic, what Hugo Von Hofmannsthal said was the true deep inner form that penetrates matter. A religious person would say something closer to God. In jail where a picture torn from a magazine of some cute puppies or a waxy postcard of a tropical sunset passed for beauty, she found herself at a loss to say what beauty was or what it could possibly signify, or to what great truth it testified. Sitting here with all these bits of paper, she knows that she can never return to a time when she found such pleasure – sometimes even ecstasy – in art.

I remember instead the night Lavelle Brown committed suicide with a kitchen knife, and the day I was forced to become a keester bunny.

The entrance-hall phone rings, just as she is trying to estimate how much her clothes and personal effects are worth: *List all effects, including diamond, gold and platinum jewellery. List all antiques, carpets and works of art, with approximate value.* The phone is harsh in the empty apartment.

It's Sean.

'Ms Judd.'

'Yes, Sean.'

'I've got a gentleman here who says he's a friend of yours.'

'What's his name, Sean, could you ask him?'

She can hear him say sharply, 'What's your name, bud?'

'Ms Judd, he says his name is Davis Lydendocker, sumthin like that.'

'Let me speak to him.'

'Sure thing, Ms Judd. The lady wants to speaktcha.'

'Davis?'

'Hi, Juliet.'

'What exactly do you want?'

'I want to see you.'

'I can't see you, Davis. This is not a good time.'

'Just for a minute.'

'No.'

'Please. I have to see you.'

'OK, put the doorman on, Sean. You can let him come up.'

'You sure about this, Ms Judd?'

'Thanks. I'm sure, Sean.'

'You said don't show nobody up. Stand back, buster.'

He whispers, 'He's been hanging about here for days. I seen him.'

'You can show him up.'

'OK, whatever you say.'

She waits, standing by the elevator door where once she had a huge vase of flowers; her feeling – so absurd – about flowers then was that you should have plenty of the same thing, fifty tulips or twenty-five peonies, or a hundred daffodils. As she's waiting, she sees her mother arranging half a dozen carnations and some greenery in those little cut-glass vases in the church, as dead as funerary wreaths. Why is Davis coming to see her? Why is he in New York? Why has he been hanging around the apartment building?

She hears the elevator approaching. In the medium-security prison there were distant, and not so distant, metallic sounds, like a shunting yard, which spoke harshly and eloquently of lockdown and confinement; these sounds always caused her stomach, and the adjacent organs, to re-arrange themselves violently. She has that feeling now as the elevator bangs and bumps its way upwards. The door hesitates before opening. She knows precisely how long it will take. Clunk. The door opens. He is wearing a linen suit, which has progressed some way beyond fashionably crumpled. He stands in the doorway, his hands by his side, the palms facing her, like a Southern Baptist conversing with his Lord. There he is, grown fat, the rest of him having caught up with his porcine thighs.

'There is nothing to do in Minnesota, only eat,' he says.

She knows that he has been rehearsing this.

'Oh Davis. Come in. There's no furniture, but come in.'

He's never been here before. He walks slowly.

'How are you, Davis?' she asks in the silence.

'Only a negro can tell if a mule is awake or asleep.'

'What does that mean?'

'It means I am not sure.'

'The doorman says you have been hanging around.'

'I read that you were coming out and I wanted to see you. I kept on looking for signs of life.'

'I would say sit down, but there's nowhere to sit, except the floor.'

'Let's sit on the floor.'

She sees that Davis has had problems: his hair has been cut very short, but roughly, and his features have migrated in some way, so that they are out of alignment. His eyes, in particular, seem to have taken a beating: they are cloudy.

Yet I am the one who spent two years in jail.

'What do you have to say, Davis?'

She had once attended a wedding conducted by a Lakota shaman (in reality she was a Jewish Australian from Crouch End), and they had sat on the floor to wish the bride and groom long life and happiness and any other extempore wisdom they could summon, while passing a peace pipe around. It was daunting.

'Speak, Davis.'

'I don't have anything to say. I just kind of felt it was right and proper that I should come and see you.'

'You could have come at any time. The visiting regulations are all on the net.'

'I was in Minnesota. I wrote.'

'You wrote a pathetic letter. About yourself.'

'And you wrote back saying I should get out of your life.'

'No, Davis. I wrote back saying it was too late. You weren't there when I needed you. I found it insulting that you should write me some mawkish letters, full of Faulkner folksiness – I assume the mules and the negroes is Faulkner? Yes? – about your state of mind. But the moment I was arrested, you disappeared. And do you know what, I couldn't tell the truth at my trial, that I had been sleeping with you, because you had gone. If I could have said, as we discussed, look, I was in a terrible position, I was two-timing Richie, I was falling in love with another man, this man here, this poet from Mississippi, and look, when Richie asked me to help him, I felt I had to out of guilt, because in my distraction I had allowed him to bankrupt himself, because I was so in love with you. The jury would have believed me, because it was true. I had no intention of committing a crime or any interest in it. I only ever intended to keep things going until Richie got his money. But you vanished. What was I supposed to do, subpoena you? Or say I loved him but he turned out to be a prick? So we had to opt for the other strategy: we didn't think the piece was stolen, and in a sense we were trying to conserve it. Two years. Two fucking years, Davis, while you were out in fucking Minnesota teaching lame-brains creative fucking writing.'

She is crying. Tears come in many forms; these are deep-mined, of elemental origin: they come out of her eyes, her nose and then, mysteriously, out of her mouth. She is vomiting tears and bile and mucus and stones. Davis begins to cry too, his fat body shaking almost soundlessly. He tries to put his arms around her. Perhaps she would have accepted the gesture if it wasn't so timid, so weak, so conventional.

'Fuck off. Don't touch me. You piece of shit. You phoney piece of Mississippi mud pie. You fat, sickening cunt. You disgusting selfish creepy fuck.'

'Stop, please stop,' he chokes. 'Nothing is that simple.'

'It's simple enough. You went to teach co-eds showing-not-telling, characterisation and plotting, the importance of fucking beginnings and endings, the meaning of style, the use of dialogue, the thirteen voices of the novel, the omniscient narrator, the introduction of dialect, with reference to that fat faggot, Faulkner –'

'He wasn't so fat or –'

'But you are.' (She's choking on chemical effluvia.) 'You went off to Minnesota while I was locked up in Otisville for a year. Where women rape one another and mutilate themselves and scream all night and steal Tampax and shoot up straight into their stomachs, and keep drugs in their rectums. Or somebody else's. That's a keester bunny, in case you are interested. And you suffered out there in the snowy wastes, because – don't tell me – you found the more you talked about literature, the more your imagination dried up; and you couldn't write and you wondered if we aren't just stones and crippled apple trees and frogs, with a brain, and then you thought maybe Juliet and I were really meant for each other, but unfortunately Juliet is not here to listen to me, so I'll bang a few co-eds to ease the pain, until she comes out; and then you took some drugs and Southern Comfort and then you thought maybe if I hook up with Juliet again, I can somehow use my experience. I can get my life back on track. I can be the author of my own narrative again, or some such crap. I can show instead of telling. I can hitch my wagon to this fallen star, I can acquire some notoriety chic, I can –'

'I love you, Juliet.'

'Oh fuck, now I have heard it all. That's taken the fucking biscuit. Do you know that black women have pubic hair like Brillo pads? Do you know that women in prison shoot heroin, smack, hop, right into their stomachs? Oh, I said that. Do you know that women fuck their visitors in the contact room and the warders make home videos and sell them? Do you know that most of the women are mad, fucking insanely demented' – she's screaming herself, just like one of them – 'so fucking crazy that they have killed their own children or stabbed themselves in the cunt with kitchen knives?'

'Juliet, stop. Please stop.'

She hears the long afternoon vowels of the way he says 'stop' and she pauses.

'I had a breakdown, Juliet.'

'Oh dear. I feel so fucking sorry. What hell for you. Writer's block. Over-abundant, but utterly meaningless sex. Early promise trickling away. Davis, you are totally and utterly pathetic. I am not the same person. I may never be, but I can tell you one thing for sure, I loathe you now, and I will loathe you for ever. Have you got that?'

'You were so –'

'Whatever it is you're trying to say, whatever I was, I don't want to hear it. You can go now. If I were you I would find a good gym and a job involving manual labour. Maybe shelling peanuts. Oh no, it's cotton where you come from, isn't it? King Cotton. Get back to Jefferson and start again, lard-ass. Tote that barge, lift that bale.'

'Juliet, I always loved you. I just couldn't bear the idea that you were fucking Richie.'

'And I couldn't bear being . . .'

But she can't speak any more. She feels – how true clichés can be – utterly drained. Even as he wipes his chubby, battered face and gets heavily to his feet, she wonders if this speaking in tongues will have cleansed her. She gets wearily to her feet too. Davis paddles over her papers on his way to the door.

'Juliet.'

She doesn't answer.

'I have been asked to write about you.'

'And?'

'I thought I should tell you. I've done it.'

She picks up the phone in the hall.

'Sean, I need some help.'

'I'm going. I'm going,' says Davis.

'No, Sean, it's all right, he's going. Just see him out of the front door.'

In Otisville when the officers threatened to lock up a prisoner they said, 'I'll gas you up.' For prisoners, 'gassing' had another meaning: it meant throwing shit on another person, sometimes while holding her down. A few prisoners called this 'dressing out'. The mental ward was the 'ding-wing' where people 'bugged out'. A feminine lesbian was a 'fluff'. And she, Ju-Ju, was a 'keester bunny'.

But there was no term for writer's block, as far as I know.

A few minutes later, Sean comes up.

'He's gone. He looked like a crazy person to me.'

'He's got problems.'

'Who ain't got problems?'

'True.'

'You OK, Ms Judd?'

'I'm OK.'

'You've had a bum deal. Everyone knows it. I'm real sorry you're going.'

'Thanks, Sean. I appreciate it.'

Chapter Fifteen

Today the Germans may offer for **sockscribe.com** and **sock-it-to-me.com**. In a sense it is true that the Internet is making things more global. But it's also passing around a lot of junk, not to mention porn. Of course, control was slipping away from the rational long before the Internet, but now it's flooding away. Charlie doesn't see the Internet as a goal in itself. One day Dad asked him if he worried that he was putting shops out of business. He was probably thinking of those creepy places in Jermyn Street.

'No, Dad. I'm not worried about that. I'm not doing that. The net is not doing that. It's neutral. All the net does is to provide the means. It's like blaming the car for putting horses out of business. Or blaming the car for drunk drivers. You can't say let's have no cars.'

'Facile.'

'OK, mow your lawn by hand then. Or go back to rabbit power.'

'Something sinister is going on. I think you know what I mean.'

'What, exactly? Like what do you mean, precisely?'

'People saying "like" all the time, for a start.'

'Oh shit.'

What the net has undoubtedly done is to encourage the loony-tunes to have a voice. There is no moral, educational or documentary standard on the net. It is truly the moronic inferno, with spelling mistakes. Everywhere, people are trying to find some meaning in the thinned-out air; they believe that by writing their banal thoughts they are investing them with gravitas; they are proclaiming their destiny.

In the San Diego neighbourhood where Richie's gallery is said to be, he sees a tarot specialist, an underwear shop, and a warehouse church, almost side by side. The gallery, when he finds it, has a makeshift look. In a few hours it could easily be a car showroom or a kitchen shop. In the window is a huge painting of a Western scene, after Frederic Remington: Indians mimicking buffalo. In another, an Indian on a painted pony rides home through the snow. He may be the only survivor of a battle; the pony's head hangs low, depressed. Other pictures, too, demonstrate the poignancy and fragility of Native American life and the lost innocence of bronco busting or cattle roundups. There is a display of George Caitlin posters. All of them have a certain message for the metaphysically questing citizen: it's not a message about fact or history but about the importance of personal and emotional development. And it's this dumb exculpation, this infantilism, that his father sees coming down the pike.

I just sell socks, Dad. It's not my fault.

In the reception a bright cheery thirtyish woman sits at a trestle table in front of a computer terminal. Her breasts are appropriately optimistic in an art T-shirt. Behind her, Navajo silver-and-turquoise jewellery and porcupine-quill necklaces are ranged in a display case.

'Good morning, sir. How may I help you?'

'Could I speak to Mr Lillie?'

'I'll just see if he's available. Who may I say wants him?'

Her face creases with sincerity; the lines are as faint but as distinct as the folds left on paper. They are created by squinting at bright sun.

'Charlie Judd.'

'You're British.'

'I am.'

'Dick, there's a Mr Charles Judd here from England.'

Richie comes out of a back office. He's wearing a chunky

Navajo bracelet and a neck drawstring in silver and turquoise. He hasn't aged so much as frayed.

'Jesus, Charlie. Charlie my boy. Come into my office. Do you want something to drink? Kynance darling, run round to the deli and get some Chai and something to eat. A croissant, or whatever. I'm starving. I'm hung-over, actually. What about you? Charlie, what do you want?'

'Latte. Skinny.'

In the back office, Richie looks starled, his Anglo-suavity all gone.

'What's happened, Charlie?'

'I was in town and I thought we could have a chat.'

'Don't piss about, Charlie. Tell me what you are here for. And how you found me.'

In New York Richie wore Paul Smith and Boateng suits. As Charlie remembers, he favoured broad chalk stripes. Here he seems to have gone more informal, yet provincial, in his Indian jewellery and faded jeans. Only the suede loafers have survived from his earlier life. They could be moccasins, of course.

'Does she know who you are?'

He nods to the street, where Kynance has headed.

'She knows I am Richard Lillie, as you obviously do too.'

'I mean, Richie, does she know your history?'

'No. And I would be pleased it you didn't blurt it out.'

'Ju-Ju's out of prison.'

'I know. It's in the paper. Did she tell you that she wrote to me telling me never to contact her again?'

'I'm not surprised.'

'Why do you say that?'

'Well, it could be because she did two years and you got a rap over the knuckles.'

'Oh Jesus.'

Richie is tanned. He looks fit. He may have taken up running or in-line skating. His eyes, however, are holding out against the upbeat regime. They are wary and tired.

'How is she?'

'She's in a terrible state.'

'Oh Jesus. Can I help, do you think?'

'I don't think so. Unless you like want to turn yourself in for perjury.'

'Charlie, there are –'

But at that moment Kynance comes back with the supplies.

'Hi, guys. They didn't have the croissants you like, Dick, so I got some Danish.'

'Fine. We're going to be some time, honey-bunch, so don't put any calls through. Charlie and I have a lot of catching up to do.'

Richie takes some plates from a cupboard.

'I like a proper china plate, don't you? Out here they eat everything off cardboard. The coffee will taste of polystyrene. But I try, in my small way, to keep up standards.'

He transfers the pastry on to the plates. A hint of comedy attaches to him: he is trading his last few assets cheaply, out here in suburban San Diego. His nose has a fine capillary tracery, as though he has been rubbing it.

'You were going to say?'

'I was going to say that it wasn't quite like that. It's complicated. I wanted to go to the FBI and say look, I didn't know the window was stolen, I only asked Juliet Judd, well-known expert, to check it out, and she said as far as she could tell it was genuine and clean. The lawyer said she might not even be fined, whereas I could get ten years if I knew it was stolen and exported it.'

'But you both knew it was stolen.'

'There's stolen and stolen, Charlie. We never discussed it; it was obvious really. They're all stolen, as the FBI knows. And Ju-Ju wasn't interested anyway. It was strange. In the end the problem was with the exporting. Our legal tactics were wrong. When the cheques were produced in court, it looked as though it was all her doing. Up until that point she wasn't linked directly to Agnello. But they kept that information back until the trial. Even then I offered to take all the blame – and at that stage I would definitely have got ten years, or more, but she wouldn't let me. I offered to say that I never told her what the cheques were for.'

'You've had more than two years to polish this little story, Richie.'

'Charlie, don't get heavy with me. Please. I have been through hell. Not, obviously, anything like what your sister has suffered, but hell all the same. Look at me: selling Navajo tat and crap prints of Native fucking Americans as they never were, and I'm living in this shit hole. I can't go to New York. I can't go back to London. In fact I'm just existing. I still owe huge amounts of money.'

'I don't know why, but I don't like feel that sorry for you.'

'I don't expect you to feel sorry for me. I'm sure you're upset about your sister. I know where you're coming from. I just want you to know that I didn't run out on her. On the contrary. I loved her. I probably still do. I got her into it, and I was prepared to take the rap. You can ask her yourself.'

He has torn his pastry into bits, but he hasn't eaten it. His teeth have been bleached. The whiteness of them sits in the golden tan, making him look unreliable. Which, of course, he is. He is also certainly banging the woman with the perky tits. What else have they got to do, sitting in this warehouse all day waiting to sell an amulet or a print of the first Americans behaving ecologically?

'Charlie, did Ju-Ju ask you to see me?'

'No. She has no idea where you are. You were last seen in Montreal.'

'How did you find me?'

'It wasn't that difficult. Two clicks on the net, according to my man.'

'Ah, the net. You were setting up a clothing company when I saw you last. Is that working?'

'Looks like it.'

'And your parents?'

'They're in Cornwall. They're bumbling along.'

'I loved your mother. I remember her laugh. She's got a great laugh. How are they taking all this?'

'Not well. Richie, sorry to be blunt: I want to believe you, but it would be a good idea if you like told me everything now. None of us can handle any more shocks or publicity.'

'There's nothing more to tell. I swear on my life.'

'OK.'

They sit for a moment, becalmed.

'Where is she?'

'I can't tell you that.'

'Well, you can tell her that I want to see her again, if possible.'

'I can't tell her that either. She doesn't know I'm talking to you.'

Charlie feels a sort of hardening within him. Richie is probably lying. But whatever the truth of his story, by whatever routes he has come to believe it, Richie is the cause of Ju-Ju's misery and the family's disaster. Sophie was off drugs for a year until the arrest. Dad was coming to terms with his banishment and Mum was trying so hard, through cookery and the flower roster and so on, to keep the ship afloat. Dad, of course, belittled her efforts. In his mind he is way above fish and flowers and socks; he's Ovid on the Black Sea, dreaming of a return to Rome. Charlie feels his anger against Richie, in his ridiculous country-and-western get-up, rising dangerously.

'Richie, I have to go. I just hope you have been telling me the truth.'

'I have. Don't threaten me, Charlie. It's pointless. Look at me.'

While he's waiting at LAX for his flight, Martha calls to say the Germans have made an offer.

'How much?'

'Wait for it, Charlie. Are you sitting down?'

'Come on.'

'Three million.'

'Deutschmarks?'

'Pounds, Charlie, proper English dosh. I can get them up a little.'

'Try: I'll call you when I get to New York.'

'Call me in the morning.'

On the flight he wonders what it is going to be like to be rich. At twenty-eight he is going to be far richer than his parents ever were; he is going to enter a different country. He wonders how Ana is going to take it and how the baby will grow up, being rich, although that only means something in relation to the absence of money. And wealth has lost its mystery. All kinds of people are rich.

I've done very little to deserve it: I haven't studied accounting or painted a picture or toiled physically. I have simply understood that there are lots of people out there who want certain things, without having to go shopping or sign a cheque or think. And I know what those things are. For that I am getting three or four million. Maybe Dad is right, the old certainties and eternal verities mean nothing. Zilch. Nada.

For some reason, airports cause him to become reflective, even melancholy. He feels none of the elation other people report when they enter the airy up-up-and-away precincts of flight. He sees Ana settling into Notting Hill; he sees himself walking the baby; he sees the baby being entered at birth for one of those expensive kindergartens; he sees Ana lunching. The lunches seem to stretch like a sushi conveyor belt into eternity. When he first met Ana she was at St Martin's and doing some part-time modelling. She was running around with interesting people. But 'interesting' turned out to be vacuous, people who wanted to make videos about the mysteries of primates or to persuade all the world leaders to renounce violence, at a specially convened festival, where Radiohead had agreed to headline. Some of the things they said, while drinking his drink, were way beyond laughable. And yet Ana seemed perfectly happy in their company. One boy, a Croatian model, spent half a lunchtime speaking on his mobile to a friend in Mykonos. He was telling him what they were eating: *Now I'm going to have the combination salad. Combo. Bombo. Ya. Comba la Bomba. Cool. How are the Greek chicky-chicks? Nice booty, yah? Ana is having the Singapore noodles, right Ana? Singapore worms. Right. Cool. And cool Charlie, is having the pig's cojones. I'm making a joke, it's dumpling. Dumplings, you say, no, Charlie? Dumplings. Whatever.*

Charlie had to leave suddenly. Ana was angry: he had offended her High Andes sense of propriety. Later that day she told him she was pregnant: it's the connection between the row and the annunciation that has been worrying him. And also the fact that the wedding is being loaded with significance.

He rings Ju-Ju, but she's not in the apartment. They may already have cut off the phone. She's the only person he wants to tell about the money. He's realised how much he missed being able to chat to her. In prison she had a phone card, but she was only allowed one a month and each card allowed her to call home for one and a half minutes. She may let him help her financially. He boards the plane. Ju-Ju is probably at the bank, handing in her miserable forms and statements. As the plane lifts off, he feels the weight of his disloyalty to Ana pressing on his inner ears as if the plane is not properly pressurised.

It doesn't take long before they are flying over nothingness; the lights of the suburbs, which are endless when you are on the ground, prove to be paste jewellery, loosely strung along the edge of the continent. And this thought reminds him of the contract he has entered into, via Ana, with life.

What did Ju-Ju see in Richie? What is the attraction that causes people to throw their lives together and then, as if they haven't thought about it at all, become subject to arbitrary rules? Why did Ju-Ju risk so much for Richie? When he saw them together – admittedly in good and frivolous times – Ju-Ju gave the impression that she thought of Richie as an amiable halfwit, barely fit company for an intelligent woman. Yet Richie says she wasn't interested in the stolen window. She knew it was stolen, but in the way the Elgin marbles are stolen. He sees now what happened: Richie cast himself as the innocent, foolish but harmless, while he set her up as the mastermind. He wasn't so stupid: the pay-offs to Agnello were made from her account. Unless there is some other explanation. If there is, it may be one of those things that is not susceptible to reason. In sex, in family, there are deep pools of unreason. His expectation of finding the truth from Richie was naive.

The other night Ju-Ju said to him, 'Charlie, I like the idea of you as a tycoon. The only thing is, you must never believe that making

178

money proves you are a superior person. Nor does poverty, by the way.'

'Thanks for this. I'll treasure it.'

'What I mean is, Charlie, that I have seen rich people come to believe that they have talents in other fields like art. Big things. Big concepts. Collecting, as I know, is a way of suggesting that your wealth indicates some deep cosmic understanding.'

And already he has seen the truth of what she said: as the self-appointed Mr Fixit of the ragged Judd family, he had allowed himself to think he could resolve the moral issue in Ju-Ju's favour. It was a delusion: his first sight of Richie, essential oils leached out, showed that. Richie's account of the events was so well rehearsed that he probably believed it. But how different is he from the rest of us in this respect? He is now consoling himself with Kynance: he has moved down a couple of leagues in romance as well as in art.

Ju-Ju was subtly trying to reproach me for a tendency to manage the unmanageable.

He sleeps from time to time as the plane flies in a flat arc back to New York and his beloved sister, who is loved also by Richie. He wonders if it is dangerous to attract too much love in this avid world.

Chapter Sixteen

Frances says that her daughter Pip has been seeing a man. She doesn't, of course, use the word lesbian, but it is clear that Daphne should take on board the significance of this news. The young couple are thinking of moving in together. Daphne wonders if lesbianism can just be a phase in someone's life. She's never been attracted sexually to women, but she thinks that it's possible that in extremis some women confuse the companionship that exists between women with sexual love.

'What sort of chap is he?' she asks.

'I haven't met him yet. "Bit early, Mum," she said. "Don't want to frighten him off too soon."'

They are cleaning out the vestry and making lists and drawing up the new roster. The church, unusually, is unscented: during Lent they don't have flowers. She wonders if Frances has invented this new relationship as a response to the fact that there is going to be a wedding and a grandchild in the Judd family.

'We need some more Oasis foam, don't you think?' Frances says.

'Yes. I'll order some. Let's go mad and order a dozen. What about secateurs? Do you think we can afford a new pair? I've been using my own. They're also completely clapped out.'

The vestry is tiny. The odd thing is, it seems to Daphne more redolent of religion than the church itself. Here they have the old cupboard containing the religious apparatus which nowadays has to be locked, and the flower-arranging cupboard, which houses twine, floral foam, florist's wire and the crystal vases, and also they keep the kneelers and the prayer books that need work here. The stitching on the kneelers has been done for a hundred years by parishioners. It's a very broad stitch, but intricate enough. Over the years it begins to fray and come loose. Then there's the shabby but serviceable period, before the kneelers come back to the vestry for repair. There are still women in the area who do the kneelers happily. The flower stalks, the wear on the cupboard doors, the mouse-squeaking secateurs, the worn wooden knobs, the cracked tiles on the floor, all tell of generations of women performing small, unregarded services. Now women get out into the world, women like Ju-Ju and Pip, the reformed lesbian, to make their mark, which she applauds, although, as she and Frances know, it is not easy.

'I hear that Ana is incredibly glamorous.'

'Yes, I've only met her twice, but she's definitely got what I call smouldering beauty.'

'Do you want me to help with the flowers?'

'Frances, that would be so kind of you.'

'Is that a yes?'

'Of course. I'm going to order them in London from an acquaintance.'

'Not from Bodmin? They may be hurt.'

'No, I've had some pretty far-out thoughts that I was going to consult you on. I'm not sure Bodmin is up to it.'

She can't tell Frances yet that she is going to Stella Stevens' Flowerhouse to draw up a plan so lavish, so wonderful, that the church will be a bower: she's thinking of angels and the Pre-Raphaelites and into this garden of enchantment her beautiful daughter, her handsome son with his smouldering bride stepping proudly and defiantly. She's had a preliminary chat with Ana, who says it sounds totally, mega cool, which she takes to be the green light. Ana is having the dresses designed by somebody who is incredibly fashionable, and they are going to keep in touch on colour. She hasn't told Charles, of course. He would be horrified at the cost – which she is paying – because he would say don't be so bloody silly, Daphne, this is Trebetherick, not Beverly Hills. But she sees something that Charles doesn't, namely that the Judds are drinking in the last-chance saloon.

As they are packing up, pinning the new roster to the board, Frances says, 'Daphne, how is Charles?'

'He's a lot happier. Why?'

'I don't know. I saw him in the churchyard the other night.'

'And?'

'And he was peeing on Betjeman's grave.'

'Are you sure?'

'Yes. It's actually the second time. I don't know if it's some sort of literary criticism. And of course, I don't care, but some people might.'

'I'll try to talk to him. Don't mention it, please.'

'I won't.'

'Oh God, I suppose we're all headed in the same direction.'

Frances begins to laugh. They both laugh.

And then Frances says, 'It's not all bad news, my daughter seems to be going straight.'

'Frances!'

'Everybody knew. It was a torment. You knew.'

'Everybody always knows everything.'

'Let's go and have a drink.'

'Let's drink the communion wine and run naked up the thirteenth fairway.'

'Let's just go to the Mariner's, with our clothes on.'

'Brilliant idea.'

Charles is looking for his coat. She can hear scrabbling noises, the noise the hamsters used to make in their sleeping compartment.

'Charles,' she says.

'Yes?'

'I've got to go up to London in the morning.'

'Why?'

'Ana and I have to talk. I'll be away for a few days.'

'Ana? Who is Ana?'

'Ana is your daughter-in-law to be.'

'Oh yes, that Ana. What are you going to talk about?'

'The wedding. That sort of thing.'

'It's always puzzled me why women –'

'I know what you're going to say. The answer is someone has to. We keep the show on the road.'

He appears in the doorway. He is trying to zip up his National Trust fleece.

'Where are you off to?'

'Just the usual little walk. My walk. Is that all right? Permission granted?'

'Darling, of course. May I ask you a question?'

'I don't suppose I can stop you.'

'Have you been weeing in the churchyard?'

'What are you talking about?'

'Apparently, so Frances says, you peed on John Betjeman's grave.'

She giggles.

'Are you tight?'

'No.'

But she is quite drunk. She and Frances drank a bottle of Cloudy Bay.

'Goodbye, Daphne. I'm off.'

His departure is, as usual, delayed as he looks for his stick and does up his shoes. He sits down for the shoes; he leans forward. It may be the light, but his teeth seem to have become the colour of his old ivory-handled hairbrushes. His hair, so abundant, flops lifelessly forward. It is the colour of what's in a cuspidor. The bunch of flesh gathering above his nose like cattle herded towards a gate is thickening visibly.

'Charles, it's not serious.'

'What are you talking about, the wedding?'

'No, peeing in the churchyard.'

When he leaves the house, she regrets having mentioned the churchyard. She wouldn't have done it if she and Frances, newly complicit, hadn't drunk so much. In the spirit of glasnost, she told

Frances about her first love, Jerome, who she ran into again when she was thirty-five or six. In those days Charles was always at the office or away on business. She and Jerome would meet at lunchtime. He would pick her up round the corner on his motorbike. The au pair, Kaylene, would give Charlie his nap, and then watch television. The wonderful thing, she tells Frances, is that it couldn't possibly go anywhere. He was married and loved his children, and Charlie was only ten months old at the time. When it ended, as all affairs are doomed to do, she was very unhappy, but she knew that, if Jerome had wanted to leave his children and set up with her, she would not have done it. Frances told her that her daughter's gay phase, which has lasted seven years, was a result of Eric's philandering. Perhaps because of the wine, she couldn't follow the logic of this. It sounded quite Freudian. Charles is fond of quoting one line of Freud: 'After forty years of dealing with women, I still don't know what it is they want.' It was unfair of her to tackle Charles. But as you get older, you become impatient with the other's frailties, perhaps because you can see what's in store. When my father was ill after a stroke I was impatient. His slowness irritated me. The way he ate disgusted me. She feels shame even now.

Charles likes fish pie. She was planning to do it for tomorrow, but now she's going, she thinks that if she greets him with a fish pie when he returns from his wanderings he will see that she is atoning. After all these years they both know how to send up smoke signals, offering a pow-wow. This kind of fish – a few chunks of cod, some smoked haddock and some cooked prawns – is from an earlier age of fish cookery. You don't have to chop anything; you never see a scale or a glassy eye. Before applying the roof of mashed potato, you poach the fish in milk, which gives the dish its reassuring Anglo-Saxon blandness. She finds the blades of mace, small, dry, inoffensive; even though you can't taste mace, it must go in. She puts the milk on low. She remembers Jerome's legs. They were slim and hairy, like a faun's.

Charles by-passes the church. He walks quickly across the path, looking straight ahead, towards the tenth green. There's a valley here that you must avoid at all costs when you are driving from the tee way above. Because it's sheltered by Bray Hill, the valley is full of trees. It's a jungle. He looks around and climbs down from the path and approaches the stream. You can often find good golf balls down here. He decides to have a pee. In fact it's decided for him: there's a Pavlovian response in the bladder to the noise of the stream. He can't afford to be seen: he seizes a branch of a tree and starts his step across the stream towards the shelter of the trees, but the branch snaps and he falls, shoulder first, into the water. He wonders where the water comes from; it's very cold. He tries to pull himself out of the stream, but there's nothing to hold on to and his legs are splayed out painfully, one foot still on dry land, the other underneath him in the water.

I'm going to drown; the last time was a rehearsal. I won't be able to hold my head up for long.

But the solution comes to him: he must submerge himself. If he pulls himself into the stream, using his hands rather than trying to stand upright from his awkward, contorted position, he should be able to get out. The National Trust jacket, although it repels light showers effectively, soaks up water eagerly when submerged. He slithers downstream, his head underwater for a few feet, and then he pulls on a branch and surfaces. Now he is able to get his legs under him and stand up. The bank is quite steep and muddy. His phone is wet. His plan was to walk up around Bray Hill to call Jo and suggest they meet again. Still standing in the stream, he tries to call her, but the phone is dead.

What was I going to say to her? I was going to suggest we meet for sex.

But now, wet, cold, and standing in a stream, he knows it was ridiculous.

I am ridiculous. Ju-Ju is coming home. My duty is to her: to keep myself, my dignity, together until she is settled, whatever that means.

How will he explain to Daphne why he fell in the stream?

I can't say I fell in because I can't pee beside the lychgate any more. Once Ju-Ju is back, I will go to a doctor.

He clambers out of the stream. Two walkers come by: he crouches in the low ground so that they don't see him. They have a dog, which runs right across the green. Dogs are supposed to be on a lead. Jo said he looked fine: 'Yes, you look older, sure, but just the same.' When Ju-Ju comes back he will tell her everything: he will tell her why he couldn't go to America to see her locked up: it would have pushed him over the edge. He takes some comfort from the idea that he couldn't go because it would have been irresponsible to add to her worries.

He decides, although he is freezing, to walk in order to dry himself. He follows the path around the hill; out to sea, not far from where he nearly drowned the first time, he sees the sails of windsurfers, the wings of insects, racing away across the estuary.

I'll never learn to windsurf. I'll never fuck Jo. I'll never fuck anybody. Except Daphne.

His shoes are full of water and mud. He sits down on a bank of thyme and thrift to empty them. He thinks of those comics he read as a boy: anybody who fell into water always found a fish in his pocket when he got out. It was a convention. The fish always had sort of exclamation marks around them, to suggest wiggling motion. They had full round lips. The papers are always talking about Botox and collagen. Those fish had collagen lips. He's shivering like a dog. *Except Daphne*. Why does that not count? Why does he have a sense of death in their occasional sex? Maybe because there is no biological chance of producing children with Daphne, as if the act has been deprived of its only justification. Although Daphne is still – he fails to find a warmer word – attractive. Clem clearly thinks so. But Clem takes his pleasure with a Vietnamese doll at £150 an hour. What do you say to yourself when you're fucking a whore? *I'm a stud, she really loves me?* Or: *I've paid my money and I'll get my money's worth?* His cock stirs – it's duty-bound – in the freezing depths of his trousers. As he stands up, here on the hill above the wrinkled sea, looking towards the far shore, he sees that other worlds were once beyond the imagination. Now you are free to fall in a stream or fuck a Vietnamese hooker or steal a Tiffany window. This is the age of possibility.

But I still belong, some of me still belongs, to another time.

Daphne once said that she thought of Bray Hill as a ziggurat. It was a beautiful idea, and he hopes, as he follows the curling path directly above the sea, that he wasn't dismissive or cruel when she said it.

Why was Frances telling her that I take a pee in the churchyard? She must think there is something wrong with *al fresco* urination. Yet nothing could be more natural. It's not going to do any harm either: there are no flowers in the churchyard; it is just a sand dune lightly grassed. I never aimed at Betjeman, milord. I had no evil intent.

But because of Frances's tale-telling, he has fallen in the stream.

As he comes down off the hill towards the wooden bridge over the mouth of the stream, the same stream in which he was recently immersing himself, he feels the wind coming from the south across the saddle of the golf course. His fingers are numb now, even painful.

Daphne will run a bath for me. I will try to make amends for saying – if only to myself – *except Daphne*.

Daphne has a photograph of herself with her sister in her bedroom. They are about eleven and twelve, aware, in that pre-pubertal fashion, of their emerging womanhood. It's the fifties, or maybe the last squeak of the forties. Daphne thinks it's charming. Behind them are officers' quarters somewhere, and, at an odd angle, the head of a horse. The girls are wearing tweed jackets and Pony Club ties. When he and Daphne make love he tries not to look at the sisters, because their youth heightens his sense that they are at some distance from the true meaning of sex. This sex has become a form of incest.

Daphne has the poached fish laid out on a large dish. The trick with a béchamel is to make sure that the initial roux is made carefully: her mother decreed an ounce of butter to an ounce of flour. You let the flour burst in the hot butter, then you add the milk slowly, and the sauce forms. There's nothing to it, but it's one of those little miracles of cookery. Her mother used to put béchamel on all sorts of things: cauliflower, carrots, chicken –

with added curry powder – even on cold tongue with chopped parsley. The curly sort.

She hears Charles coming in from his walk. He pushes open the kitchen door.

'Daphne, I'm wet.'

'Good God, what happened?'

'Oh I was trying to reach a golf ball, a new Dunlop 65, and I slipped into the stream.'

She holds his hands.

'You're freezing. Quick, I'll run a bath. Get your clothes off.'

She rushes to the bathroom. When she gets back, he hasn't got very far; she helps him peel off the sodden clothes. He stands in his underpants, which are red with pictures of dachshunds on them, and she wraps a towel around him. His lips are drained and she thinks she can see a blueness – Reckitts Blue – appearing on the margins of his mouth. She towels his hair and leads him to the bath. She sees only his buttocks as he removes the shorts – a present from Charlie who sells novelty underpants – and holds on to the edge of the bath. But as he lowers himself into the water, she catches sight of his scrotum, very high and tentative with the cold, so that it is profoundly wrinkled.

'Daphne,' he says sharply, 'something's burning.'

The béchamel is still pale on top, but it is sending up brown ripples from the depths. From the bathroom she hears him singing mournfully, although it is hard to tell what the tune is. He never could sing. Somehow this little incident is typical of him: she won't be able to go to London as planned, because he's certain to run a temperature, and she has ruined the sauce because he has fallen in a stream in pursuit of a Dunlop 65. Golf things are fetish objects for men: even these old chaps converse about graphite and Kevlar and other nonsense as if they have spiritual qualities. He calls for shampoo, but she tells him to wait while she makes the sauce again, pours it over the fish, covers the whole thing with mashed potato, and scores it with a fork to make parallel lines, which will look like an autumn field when she takes it out of the oven again.

When she gets back to the bathroom, he is sweating heavily as if he were in a Turkish hammam.

'Daphne,' he says, 'I love you. I'm sorry you think I'm a shit.'

'You're delirious.'

But she feels a wave of tenderness.

'Oh Charles. You're such a fool.'

'For God's sake don't cry.'

His penis is floating palely on the water, although moored.

'I've made fish pie.'

'I love fish pie.'

Chapter Seventeen

A day in the life of young, single Sophie Judd,
unemployed writer, in London's Hoxton.
Her mother is coming to stay. She is super-stressed.
She has to clean the flat and have her nose ring removed.

Getting the nose ring out was, in the end, quite easy, although the flesh had grown around the tiny wing nut. You are supposed to take them out once in a while and clean them. Her eyes watered and she was left with a bloody hole.

Deciding to take the ring out, she knows, is a small but significant thing. She can see that, every time you comply with your parents' wishes, you are somehow surrendering yourself to their camp, to their world-view. Her mother's attempts to be reasonable – *We've all been through these phases in our time, darling* – made it harder still. Yet when she looked at herself in the mirror last night, after an evening with Dan, she saw what her mother's sudden, panicky stare indicated: a druggie.

When she had the ring put in, just after she was thrown out of St Paul's, she had also shaved her head up the sides. So that she was left with a horse's mane extending from her forehead to her shoulders. She dyed the mane red. There is something about too much dope, about all hallucinogenic substances in fact, that makes you believe that the alternative world is more real. You could argue that there is no 'real', but what druggies see – what I saw – exists mostly in distinction to what straight people see.

Now, the last reminder of that delusion (or more exalted state, depending on your POV) has gone, leaving only the minor excavation in her nose.

Dad is in bed with a cold. Frances is making him some soup, while Mum is away. He has always been a sort of potentate, commanding attention. It is inconceivable that he could climb out of bed and heat up a can of something for himself. Sophie is cleaning the flat.

I am not doing it because she is coming to stay, I'm doing it because it needs doing *and* she is coming to stay.

'Why do you want to stay here, Mum?' she asked.

'I just thought if you would have me I would love to see your flat. But I can stay at Basil Street.'

'It's like, well it's like a major dump. Big time.'

'I am sure it's not. Everyone is saying that Hoxton is the new Notting Hill.'

'Not round here they're not.'

'I'm coming up on the three-thirty. I had to get Dad settled. He fell in a stream. What tube do I take?'

Sophie explains to her how to get to the flat. Mum seems to be treating it as a dangerous expedition up country, for which she should be given credit.

'I'll be fine. Out of the tube, left past the market, right at the New Karachi Kebab restaurant, two doors past that, ring the second bell – no name – on the green door. I've got it all down.'

'That's it, Mum. Second bell from the bottom. We'll go out for a nice Thai curry.'

'Sounds jolly exciting.'

Sophie can't make up her mind whether her mother is deeply irritating or sweet, to use one of her mother's favourite words. Round here the word means something very different. Now that she looks closely at the flat, she sees with her mother's eyes that it is revolting. She starts on the stove, which has the caramelised remains of many rushed and poorly thought-out snacks attached to it.

I am actually living in a chick-lit novel: my mother's coming and

I'm cleaning my flat. Outside the colourful world of London's historic East End passes, unremarked.

She gives up on the stove, where a fusion has taken place, and inspects the lavatory. She hides the bowl under a thick, aromatic, viscous coating of Toilet Duck. But she can see that, long before her mother gets here, it will have slid gently into the water, revealing the sepia horrors below. At least it will smell better. In fact she's used so much Toilet Duck that she is choking. The bath, about three feet long, has lime deposits, nascent stalactites, all around the plughole and underneath the taps. As she cleans, like a picture restorer removing historic overlays, she suddenly thinks, I took my nose ring out for Ju-Ju. Not that Ju-Ju would mind, but because I don't want us to look like a family of weirdos. I don't want people thinking, what do you expect, the youngest daughter's into drugs – they always say 'into drugs' to lend themselves some verisimilitude – and the father is going bonkers?

Deep down, perhaps not so deep, she has a feeling that a family has certain expectations of you. The family demands mutely that you rally around Ju-Ju, and taking out your nose ring is a small price to pay. She breaks off from cleaning to look at herself in the mirror. The hole in her nose is suppurating minutely, a small drop of clear liquid sits on the rim of the crater. When she was about sixteen or seventeen she would spend hours trying to manipulate or decapitate spots that arrived without warning, hoping to make them invisible or at least inoffensive. The result was invariably disastrous: they became beacons of highly coloured flesh, signalling to the world. She would try to paste over them with make-up. When she met up with her friends, in their over-elaborate sexy clothes selected after long agonising, they all had the same eruptions along with the braced teeth. And then they were girls again, collectively suffering nothing more than faintly comical zits, not the stigmata that they saw in front of the mirror. She dabs her nose with toilet paper. For the first time she sees that the lino around the toilet is curling up. It's the duty of mothers to notice potential sources of infection, and her mother won't fail, although she won't don a pair of Marigolds and a pinny, as chick-lit would demand.

One of Mum's unstated reasons for visiting is because she is not going out with Dan any longer. She is coming to assist with the last rites. Dan picked her up in his car. His wife, Patsy, has not fully accepted Dan's declaration. Or could it be that he has not fully declared himself?

'I hope you didn't say I'm leaving you for Sophie?'

'No. No.'

'So you said look, I'm sort of fed up with you, let's have a bit of a, I dunno, like a bit of a rest?'

'Jesus, Sophie, what do you want? Watch my lips: I – have – left – Patsy.'

'I don't want anything. Like I just don't believe you've split from her, and I don't think it would be a good idea anyway, if I am part of the equation.'

'Let's play it by ear. I'm starving.'

'I will eat with you, but I won't sleep with you.'

'No? Well, I'll take a chance. Anyway, who said anything about sleeping?'

'Hah fucking hah.'

On the journey he utters a continuous commentary on other drivers. It's almost a stream of consciousness: *Fuck will ya look at that, now I've seen it all, silly cunt, white-van-man lives, get back under your fucking stone.* While they are stuck in the traffic with all the cheaper cars, she wonders how she could ever have loved him. On a film set, turning Alfa Romeos into dolphins, for instance, like an actor enclosed by a stage, he is the centre of attention, but away from a film set he seems to be out of time, even embarrassing. At the restaurant he has some matey chat with the woman in a saree who greets them, and then he grins at the owner who has a plaster cast on his arm: 'Ow's tricks? Fell off yer wallet?' Dan carries his world-view around with him. Wherever he goes, he brings his own banality, like a hermit crab.

Why has it taken me so long to see it?

The evening ended sadly; it ended broken-backed.

Dan tried to kiss her as they pulled up outside her flat, and she said, 'Sorry, if I let you in, I will be in some way like encouraging your split from Patsy. Which I am not.'

'You're a little cunt. Don't fucking mention Patsy again. You're not fit to polish her fucking shoes.'

She scrambled from the car. As she hurried over the littered, orange-suffused yards to the front door – the lights gave the pavement the colour of a Moroccan drink – she could still see his angry hurt face; she could still smell the leather and cumin in the car. He knew that he had lost her: he can see himself through her eyes. She took no pleasure in his unhappiness although she felt a lightening within her on her own account. Dan, just as her mother had hinted, had been a drag on her spirits; they weren't making the world new together, as young lovers do.

Back in the flat she wiped her mouth; it seemed to be smeared with an oily film, perhaps the curry, perhaps Dan's saliva, perhaps just the secretion of human folly.

We Judds expect too much of other people. Or maybe we are just naive.

While she was still in bed this morning, Dan rang up to say he was sorry, he didn't mean it, he's been under pressure. She can have her own space if she wants it. She can call him any time. Meanwhile, he's going to be away on a big job in Milan. The Eyeties have gone mad for him. The mention of the job in Milan is a sort of mantra to remind her, and perhaps himself, of his powers. But as she tries to stick down the lino with some Superglue, originally used in a failed attempt to glue a teapot together, she tries to remember any single thing Dan said to her outside his own sealed world that made an impression on her. She can't think of one. He can't even explain his understanding of special effects. Perhaps he's autistic. Perhaps we are all hard-wired. *Hard-Wired* would be a good title for a novel, about people who believe they have some choice, but are in fact programed: *Hard-Wired in Hoxton*, Jane Austen re-written.

The phone rings, but before she can answer it she has to free her fingers, which have become bonded to the lino, although the lino has not become bonded to the floorboards underneath. By the time she has got rid of the caller, who is selling insurance, and done it as politely as she can, she finds that the narrow spout of the Superglue has closed for ever. As advertised, it is very tenacious. She goes back to cleaning.

At eight-thirty the doorbell rings. She rushes down two flights, conscious of the meanness of the shared areas and the fatigued smell that will soon be inhaled by her mother. She opens the door.

'What an interesting area,' says her mother, hurrying in. 'Lovely smell of spices.'

'Hello, Mum, welcome to the new Notting Hill.'

'Oh this is charming.'

'I'll carry your bag up.'

They kiss.

'It's gone. Your ring has gone.'

'Yes, I took it out last night.'

'I'm glad.'

'I thought you would be.'

'Have you put something on the wound?'

'Yes.'

Her mother looks smaller; she can't actually have become smaller, but she is crouching defensively as she mounts the stairs.

'Oxygen?'

'Not just yet.'

'Oh this is sweet.'

'It's not the word I would have chosen, but thanks.'

'No, darling. It's full of character. It's the sort of place we've all lived in at one time or another. Although I must say, the view is not so hot.'

'No. It would be better if we had like Kilimanjaro and a galloping herd of wildebeest rushing by the window, rather than a view of the back of the housing department.'

'Fawlty Towers.'

'Bas – il!'

Her mother is wearing a print skirt, a sort of blazer jacket and very shiny shoes. The shoes mark her out as a provincial. Shoes speak distinctive dialects; these ones have a West Country accent.

'I've brought you a present.'

'You shouldn't have.'

'Open it.'

'*Summoned by Bells*. John Betjeman, 1960.'

'It's a first edition.'

The book is pulsing. Sophie, like a bat, can pick up the sonar message: all roads lead to Cornwall.

'It will be valuable one day. I found it in an antique shop.'

'It's beautiful. What did I like do to deserve it?'

'We just want you to think of us, occasionally.'

'That's so kind. Although I do think of you. All the time, as it happens. How is Dad?'

'Oh, he's having a jolly good wallow.'

'What happened exactly?'

'He fell in the stream in mysterious circumstances.'

'Is he losing it? Charlie thinks so.'

'There's always been a little horn-locking between them. Particularly since Charlie saved him. How was Ana?'

'She's like a little too much for me. A bit too lush. To be honest, she intimidates me. She's like from another planet. Is her father coming?'

'We haven't heard. He's on some mission in the East. He's very high up in the UN or one of those organisations.'

'Charlie says he's a crook. Is Dad ready for Ju-Ju's return?'

'It's hard to tell. He's cheered up a lot. I asked Clem to talk to him, to sort of say that people understood, but I don't think he got very far. I'm sure the wedding will help. The main thing is that Ju-Ju understands.'

'Ju-Ju always understands. Charlie says even the prison officers at Loon Lake adored her. But she told him she's not sure she'll ever be the same person again.'

'I am sure she will be. She will be. Why do you think she got involved in this in the first place? That's what I will never understand.'

'Mum, I don't know. I've tried to find some explanation but the only one I can think of is so cheesy that like I can't believe it.'

'What's cheesy?'

'Corny. Crass.'

'What is it, what's your explanation?'

'Love, in a word. Ready for the Thai taste experience?'

'Come on then.'

'Keep your head down.'

They exit into the hustle, arm in arm.

Mum thinks it's a bazaar or a souk, which is why she's holding my arm so firmly.

'This is very exotic.'

'It's the new Notting Hill. You said it.'

She feels a rush of affection for her mother, who sat in the court dutifully and visited that hell-hole of a prison, and suffered as she waited in the contact reception with people so strange to her they might really have come from another universe. Their bodies were twisted with agony. And now she's planning the wedding. The flowers are going to perfume what has gone before.

When she wakes, her mother has already gone to meet someone at New Covent Garden flower market. She feels guilty that she didn't get up and prepare breakfast. As her mother has done for her all those years.

She puts her fingers to her nose before she remembers that the ring has gone. The absence of the ring is disturbing, like the sensation of loss after having a wisdom tooth out. By her bed is the Betjeman. It's funny how women like Mum are always interested in painters and writers, particularly if they were adulterous, like cuddly little Betjeman. Betjeman was also a raging snob, who spoke in a sort of code that made him the authentic voice of middle England. She looks at her nose in a mirror. It has stopped weeping and the hole has closed.

Over the green Thai curry, which her mother said was scrummy, not too hot, not really, they talked, of course, about Ju-Ju. The waiters seemed to recognise something English in Mum that had been lost for ever in Hoxton – if it ever existed – and they were very attentive to her. It may have been the neat jacket and the scarf decorated with snaffle bits that stood out in this swamp of informality; informality being the new way of conforming.

'Sophie, there is something I have to tell you. I know you think, and Charlie thinks, that Daddy and I favoured Ju-Ju. We don't have favourites, I promise. But before Ju-Ju arrived, we had a baby, a girl, who was still-born. And when Ju-Ju came along we were so relieved that we may have rather overdone it. The affection and so on. By the time you and Charlie appeared, we had forgotten the angst. We could behave normally.'

'You never mentioned it.'

'No, we didn't. We decided not to because we didn't want Ju-Ju to think she was just a replacement. I thought I should tell you. Perhaps I shouldn't have. Too much Tiger Beer.'

'It's fine. I'm glad you told me.'

The truth is that Dad had a kind of love affair with Ju-Ju that excluded the two of them. It was in some ways a relief when she went to live in New York. A child psychologist would probably say that was why they both got into so much trouble at school. Mum drank two Tiger Beers. She had three.

She feels unsettled by the story of the still-born baby. You don't want your parents to have withheld secrets. It may be hypocrisy, but it's a necessary hypocrisy. Parents should keep up a front at all times.

She had slept on the sofa, with Mum in her bed, and they were happy and contented, like children in a tree house, congratulating themselves: Mum said that it was such fun. She had brought her white nightie, with the minute roses embroidered around the neck, and her rosewater, which she used to cleanse her face. Sophie slept in a T-shirt that read Xfm, given to her by a boyfriend who had been a DJ.

'Oh Sophie,' she called through the very thin wall.

'Yes, Mum.'

'There may be a job for you this summer at the Blue Banana.

Phoebe Talbot, her family takes that big house, Sheepfold, the one with the tennis court, is working there. She's going to talk to the owner.'

'I'll think about it.'

'Only if you want her to. I thought it might help, for a bit.'

'In what way, Mum?'

'If you want a break from London.'

'Mum, I don't think we are all going to settle in Cornwall, if that's what you are hoping.'

'No, but if you – '

'No, Mum. It's not going to happen.'

'Goodnight, darling.'

'Goodnight.'

'Sophie, you don't mind me asking Phoebe, do you? She's a sweet girl. Nothing's fixed.'

'No, Mum, it was like good of you to think of me.'

'I just thought it would give you an extra option. It's just an idea.'

'Night-night.'

Her mother has no way of hiding her thought processes.

She thinks I need a break because of Dan and drugs. She thinks there will be a sort of Betjemanesque innocence by the seaside, and she hopes the family can be together in some way. She's obviously finding Dad heavy duty: Ju-Ju will calm him down, if he isn't beyond help. It's typical of him and this is really what annoys Charlie, that it's always about Dad: his health, his pride, his sensitivity, his humiliation at that awful accountancy firm.

At school she had said he was in investment banking although she had no idea what that was, because she couldn't bear to say he was an accountant. And now Ju-Ju's main job, after two years of being banged up in a Federal Prison – I beg its fucking pardon, *correctional facility* – is to get the magnificent wreck that is Charles Judd back afloat.

She makes herself some tea and picks up the Betjeman. Mum's idea – the book is supposed to provide the inspiration – is that every table at the reception will have a verse or two from Betjeman inscribed on it (Frances's daughter, who is officially no longer a dyke, does calligraphy) and be decorated appropriately.

'What, sand in the sandwiches, wasps in the tea?'

'No, darling, don't be silly. Themes. Churches, coves, wild flowers, places.'

'Deep fryers?'

'No, darling.'

'Miss Joan Hunter Dunn springing out of the cake, burnished by Aldershot sun? Ju-Ju with a tennis racquet saying, "Hi, folks, I'm back. Shoot, I can't tell you how much I've missed you."'

'Now you're really being silly.'

Chapter Eighteen

C harlie looks at Ju-Ju sideways. He's trying to catch her off
guard as if this will give him a better reading of her mental
state. But there are no clues. She's intent, her ferocious absorption
on display, taking in this New York hinterland for the last time. 'I
won't be coming back,' she said. They are driving on a spring
morning through Brooklyn because she wants to see Flatbush
Pond Cemetery, the scene of the crime, which she says she has
visited in her mind so often. He doesn't ask her why. He knows
there's a vogue for resolution, closure, a sort of final ritual, and if
Ju-Ju thinks it can help, he's more than happy to spend their last
full day in New York driving her.

Yesterday they went to the Met and Ju-Ju took him to the
American Wing to see the display of Laurelton Hall and the
Tiffany windows that, four or five years ago, had started it all. And
today we are going to Queens. But the connection between the
two places is imagined: at the time Agnello stole the window, Ju-Ju
had not yet arrived in Manhattan, not yet seen the Tiffany display
in the Met. The connection has been made artificially. The events
of the story have been assembled in court, to make a narrative.
That is how Ju-Ju sees it. She said the other day that the facts could
have been ordered in a completely different way.

If there are any facts. The more he gets to know about this affair,
the harder he's finding it to say what the facts are.

The air out here is coarse, the buildings crouching, as if the flight
path to JFK above them has caused some stunting. Back behind

them the skyline of Manhattan, that great reef of capitalism, which the sons of the desert believe is a deliberate provocation, rises into the clear sky. It could easily be seen from here, as they turn at Flatbush Avenue into the anonymous grey streets with their packing-crate houses, as a provocation to the little people, or a testament to their optimism, even to their credulity: they can live huddled here in flypaper houses, while back there, outlined against the blue air, which has not yet lost its wintry harshness, great palaces of limestone and granite and rare marble – half of the Apennines have been exported to build them – aim for heaven. Cities – London is no different – always demonstrate in their contrasts the realities that lie behind the cultural-tourist-capitalist-enterprise bullshit.

'We turn left, Charlie, and then second right, by that deli place.'

Next to the deli is a used car lot, backed by some crumbling buildings which have been boarded up. Bunting proclaims: *Spring Specials*. The cars are of the sort favoured by the poor, large and sway-backed.

Ju-Ju, closely observed for a week, is a better colour. And this colour suggests, perhaps falsely, a return of animal health. She always had a kind of sexual stain; it was in her skin and even in her laugh, unmistakable. Her hair is hanging down rather limp as she looks at the map; it's lost vitality, but he thinks he can see the return of this vitality to her skin. He hopes so. *I'll never be the same person again, Charlie.* One day she may tell him what happened to her, but the knowledge that she has suffered so badly, suffered at a level far deeper than most people ever have to experience, is haunting him. It leaves him anxious, almost queasy, although he tries hard to be cheerful. And it worries him that he should be more concerned with his sister than with Ana or the baby.

The Germans are stalling, as they consider if they can make a better offer. They have asked for a week. Martha is certain they will go higher.

They turn down a boulevard of large houses, some derelict, many of them hung with wires and bearing the scars of cheap and ill-advised improvements, schist panelled exteriors, and colonial carports and carriage lamps.

'You're taking me on a tour of the derelict burbs.'

'Tiffany windows stayed when the rich folk moved on. We must be nearly there.'

The gates of the cemetery are generously made of thick, fluted columns of cast iron; but the gates are padlocked and rarely opened, to judge by the brown undergrowth. They enter by a side door in the wall and pass through turnstiles.

Sitting inside a small office looking at a television set is a security guard.

She glances through the window at them and says, 'Closing four-thirty, sharp.'

They walk past the crematorium, which has a drive-in look, a curved approach and a crudely made portico where the hearse unloads the coffin. It doesn't look as though it is still functioning. There's some spray tagging on the main doors.

'I never came here. In reality.'

'You said.'

Ju-Ju knows exactly where the mausoleum is. They walk hand in hand like lovers, or like a brother and sister come to pay their respects. The place is enormous, acres spreading out towards JFK, which is the magnet for the planes circling overhead. He can see a control tower's lights and a rising oily haze. The mausoleum faces a grove of trees and is deep in a sickly jungle of saplings, just coming into leaf among last season's broken and dispirited growth. The rear window of the tomb is boarded up, as it must have been for the last six years or so. Other tombs are open shells.

The first day of the week cometh Mary Magdalene early, when it was yet dark, unto the sepulchre, and seeth the stone taken away from the sepulchre. John 20, verse 1. Mary Magdalene gazing at the empty sepulchre in fear. The Uma Stimhouse Memorial Window. Two angels are in the tomb reassuring Uma's family that there is life after death: *Why seek ye the living among the dead. He is risen*.

They stand for a while: the air is heavy and cold, depleted.

'Ju-Ju, why have we come, really?'

'I wanted to see it.'

'I know that. Why did you want to see it?'

'I can't really say.'

'Try.'

'Charlie, there are some things you can't explain. But when I was inside I thought about the actual robbery. I began to think I was there. Perhaps I was rationalising the fact that Agnello and his pals got off. Or possibly, and this is more likely, I just didn't see myself committing a crime. You asked if – actually you stated it as a matter of fact – if I had done it for Richie. In a way I wish I could say yes. It just wasn't real. That is the simple answer. I just did it. In fact all I did was look at the window up there a way, and then I wrote some cheques. But during the trial I began to wonder how I could have been so blind. I wondered if the judge wasn't right, if I was arrogant, and did think I was above the law. And then in prison I went over the whole sequence of events, thousands of times, Agnello and his chums stealing it, Richie being offered the window, because, as it turned out, one of them had seen my picture with Richie at his gallery, and the two, actually three, things I did, including giving my Fed Ex account number, tied me to the crime. I began to believe that I was going mad. Every night unspeakable things happened in Otisville, and every night for nearly six months I lay awake – I don't think I ever slept for more than twenty minutes – going over the whole thing. And I re-membered the evidence – you remember – an owl hooted, the mausoleum was damp and spooky, the carpenter guy panicked, and I began to believe that I was actually there. I began to remember all the details. At night, fully awake, I believed it. During the day, I knew it couldn't be true.'

'Jesus, Ju-Ju. You don't deserve this.'

He puts his arm around his sister.

'I don't know about that. But I'm glad we came. Thank you.'

'And now?'

'And now I can see there couldn't have been any owls. These trees are far too small for owls.'

Is she joking? He doesn't know. She's shaking. At first he thinks she is crying, but when he holds her he finds that she is trembling. She's like someone who has been in a motor crash.

'Somebody said everything in France – weddings, christenings, duels, burials, swindles – everything is a pretext for a good dinner. We seem to come into almost every category,' she says.

'So you did it for a good dinner.'

'I must have.'

They are sitting in an Italian restaurant in Brooklyn Heights, a family restaurant that she and Richie favoured. The proprietor not only remembers her, but calls out his mother from the back and looks on happily as his mother embraces her. Ju-Ju introduces Charlie first to Aldo Donadio and then to la Signora Donadio.

Aldo says to Charlie, with great gravity, 'She was badly treated. These people are the scum of the earth. You're always gonna be welcome here.'

Throughout dinner la Signora fusses around them and Aldo breaks off from his meeting and greeting to make culinary suggestions.

'You know the strange thing is they think you are a celebrity.'

'It's deep in the Italian-American psyche: if you're in trouble with the law you must be doing something right.'

At the end of the meal, Aldo brings out an almond cake and insists on being photographed with Ju-Ju and his mother and the chef. 'It's going on the wall, right next to Giuliani.' Giuliani has written on the photograph: *The finest tagliatelle I ever ate.* Even the Yankee's star Derek Jeter has eaten here: *Great meatballs. Good as a home run, bases loaded.*

'God, I love New York.'

'New York still seems to love you.'

'But I can't come back.'

'Never say never.'

'I'm not sure if I will stay in England either.'

'Don't torture yourself. Just take it step by step.'

When they finally leave the restaurant, Aldo sees them off. A photographer takes a picture of them. Aldo tries to grab the camera, but the photographer moves smartly off.

'Pigs,' says Aldo, 'fuckin' pigs.'

As they drive back over the Brooklyn Bridge, in the iron-work high above the river, Charlie thinks of his sister alone, terrified, trying to put her story into some sort of order, the way children put coloured bricks into a box. It's painful to him.

'Ju-Ju, when I was in California I went to see Richie.'

'What are you saying?'

'He's living in San Diego and I went to see him.'

'What is he doing there?'

'It's a bit pathetic. He runs a sort of gallery, selling prints, Indian – Native-American – knick-knacks.'

'Why didn't you tell me before?'

'I wanted to talk to him. I didn't want to upset you. I didn't get any answers.'

'What answers were you looking for, Charlie?'

'I just thought, now it seems naive, that he could tell me what happened. I thought that there must be an explanation. Like a different explanation. But what you said in the cemetery may be true: there isn't always an answer.'

'You know what happened, Charlie.'

'To be honest, I don't. It doesn't make sense. You weren't fantastically in love with Richie, yet you ruined your life. For a while, anyway. He says he offered to take the rap.'

'I did ruin my life, you were right, but I didn't do it for Richie. I just didn't think about it.'

'Why not, Ju-Ju? You are the most intelligent person I know. How could you not have seen what could happen? I just like find it impossible to understand.'

'You sound like you did when you were a little boy, slightly petulant, but lovable.'

'For fuck's sake, Ju, this whole business has practically de-stroyed the . . .'

'I know. I know, Charlie. For two years and more I've been

feeling guilty about what I've done to people. Dad, Mum, even to you and Sophie.'

'Richie said something to me, which I didn't understand: he said that when the cheque business came out he offered to go to the Federal Attorney and admit perjury and to take the rap. Is that true?'

'It was discussed.'

'But is it true?'

'No. I don't believe at that stage he meant it. He was phoning from Canada, by the way, did he mention that? It wasn't anyway clear that it would have helped me. What else did he say?'

Charlie edits his account. He doesn't mention Kynance – he doesn't know anything for sure – but he describes Richie's Indian-scout look and his new circumstances.

'Ju-Ju, do you think that it's possible that he set you up? I mean that he took precautions, covered his arse?'

'That's what you think, obviously. I've thought about it a lot. But I don't see how he could have. We knew the window must have been stolen, but there was no record of it, no possibility of being caught if nobody else knew. Not until Agnello was arrested for a minor burglary. Richie would have had to get me to arrange shipment and to pay those cheques deliberately. But the only reason that he did it was that he had no money.'

'And then he ran.'

'He ran. A lot of people ran, Charlie.'

Ju-Ju is staying at the apartment. She says she wants to sleep there, even though the place is empty. Charlie is at the Westbury, near the Frick Collection. In Manhattan proximity to art is reassuring.

'Sure you won't come and stay at the hotel?'

'No, Charlie. I am going to leave town quietly. The apartment's still mine, legally anyway, mine and the bank's, for a little bit longer.'

'I may have some money soon. If you need any, let me know.'

'I'm fine at the moment.'

'So English. Still so English.'

'I'm fine. Really.'

He pulls up outside her building.

'I'll come in, to see you safely tucked up.'

In her mailbox there is a thick manilla envelope. There is a yellow Post-it Note on the cover.

'This parcel was delivered to you by the nutcase. He said I should give it to you. I wanted to say no, but he says it was important. I hope I did right. Sean Costello, Doorman.'

'Who's that from?'

'Some slightly deranged guy who read about the case.'

'Has he been before?'

'Yes. But he's harmless.'

'Ju, please stay at the hotel.'

'No. It's fine.'

She's holding the envelope close.

'Ju-Ju, do you know him?'

'No, Charlie. Look, I don't think this whole business is going to be put to rest in a hurry. There have been a lot of strange letters and things. I've just got to keep my head down. It will go away in its own time.'

'OK.'

At the elevator she kisses him.

'Bye-bye.'

'No, I'm coming up to see you safe.'

They ride up in the panelled elevator. They stand side by side. He glances at her and sees her frowning at the floor-indicator lights, which are round buttons, like marshmallows. A dozen marshmallows flash into life before they stop.

She opens the apartment and turns on the lights: the emptiness, the telephone resting on the parquet floor, the mattress in the bedroom, her clothes lying on the floor suggest a wilful desolation, bordering on madness.

'I'm staying with you, Ju-Ju. Or you can come to the Westbury.'

'We'll have to share the bed.'

As they undress she says, 'Charlie, let me hold you.'

He holds her close. She is soon asleep. Her grip on him loosens and tightens as her thin body twitches; sometimes she appears to start, as if the unbearable memories are assailing her. For hours he lies, holding her.

I owe her some peace.

Finally – how many hours later? – he sleeps too.

Chapter Nineteen

RETURN TO SENDER
Davis Lyendecker

For more than two years I have been unable to write. The reason is the one that Phillip Roth uses as an epigraph in one of his books, *The Facts*:

> *And as he spoke I was thinking, the kind of stories that people turn life into, the kind of lives that people turn stories into.*

My own life has turned into a story. The woman I loved had her life turned into a story. So acute were my feelings of helplessness and guilt that I have been unable until now to approach my desk, let alone write a word. I was able, just, to read the work of my students at the University of Minnesota and to discuss it with them. But I had lost myself. I had the feeling that my life had been taken away, unfairly, and turned into a fiction. It was a sort of robbery. The more fervently I strove, the more my self disintegrated. I was cracking up.

To seek some comfort I tried to think about other writers who had broken down – Roth, Styron, Fitzgerald, Waugh. But they were all older than me and they had all published good, even great work. All I had was one small novel, *The Boy from the Mudflats*, to my name. I couldn't write, but I couldn't write for my own specific reason: I had lost my humanity.

This is how it happened: these are THE FACTS in as far as I am able to describe them. They seem to come, nonetheless, from a fiction. I was in love with a young English woman, called Juliet Judd. She was living in New York with a British art dealer named Richard de Lisle. We began to meet while he was working, promoting his artists, setting up exhibitions, attending parties – all the things that people in the art world do. I had fallen hopelessly in love, long before we were lovers. Each day I could barely wait to leave my small apartment and meet her at a café on Bleecker. On special days we would meet at Grammercy Tavern. Usually we would go back to my apartment.

She never talked about Richard (Richie) de Lisle: although I read about him occasionally, and I had been to his gallery, White Heat 2. Juliet, I believed, still loved him and she gave no indication of wanting to break it off with him. I began to brood about what they did when they were together. Once or twice I waited outside White Heat, to see if I could observe them together. What I didn't know was that de Lisle's gallery was going bankrupt. He covered his financial tracks in a blizzard of publicity.

One day Juliet said to me, 'Richie is in deep trouble. I want to leave him, if you will have me, but I can't do it just yet while he is in dire straits, and I can't do it without knowing that you love me.'

I was happy, even ecstatic. She asked me to wait a few weeks.

But then, as all the world knows, Juliet Judd was arrested, charged with a Federal offence, the selling of a stolen Tiffany window to a collector in Japan. She was bailed.

She called me from a payphone. She said to me, 'I helped Richie, because I love you. I had no other interest in the window. Please meet me and I'll explain.'

We arranged to meet at a café, not the usual one. She said to me – and the words are burned on my soul – 'I can only do what I have to do if you love me.' I told her that I would go through fire for her. Those were my exact, melodramatic words. 'If you can stand by me,' she said, 'I will explain that out of guilt I gave Richie the names of some collectors and that I authenticated the window. I had no intention of committing a crime. I was simply trying to help him in his hour of need because I had betrayed him. I tried not to think about the window itself. You and I were caught up in a force bigger than ourselves. That is my only excuse.'

The next day I took a plane to Minnesota, where I had been offered a job teaching creative writing. From a distance, I followed the trial. I remembered her words: You and I were caught up in a force bigger than ourselves. And I remembered that I had run as far as I could run from the person who needed me, the person I loved. This was not fiction.

Soon I couldn't face my students without a drink: I was the great fraud, preaching artistic truth, while living an enormous, unbearable, lie. I hoped that if I could start my new book I might begin to recover my humanity. But fiction seemed completely useless. My life had become a fiction, involving a strange character who shared my name. I began to take Halcion Triazolan to sleep. Then I heard from New York that the trial had taken a very ugly turn: the Federal Prosecutor revealed that Juliet Judd had paid off the grave robber, Anthony Agnello, with personal cash cheques. I knew it was true when she said, 'I did it because Richie de Lisle had no money. Agnello had no bank account. I gave five separate cheques, because I was not allowed to draw more than ten thousand dollars in cash at any one time.'

And then the judge made remarks that seemed to support the Federal Attorney in his claim that Juliet was the brains behind the whole thing. She was, in addition, guilty of a money-laundering offence.

The Halcion was now giving me paranoid delusions. I believed the prosecution was after me, that I would, at best, be subpoenaed. A doctor advised me to come off it. I tried, but I was addicted: although the drug was no longer helping me sleep, I couldn't get off it. When Juliet Judd was sentenced, I attempted to kill myself. I took two dozen Halcions: I finished my prescription. I had betrayed the woman I loved, I had betrayed my calling, I had betrayed my students.

But one of my students found me; my stomach was pumped and I spent six weeks in rehab. When I came out, Juliet Judd was in Otisville Medium Security Correctional Facility. I wrote to her trying to explain the crisis in my life and my true feelings. My letters were mawkish and full of self-pity. I can only plead impairment: the drugs, self-administered and prescribed, had dulled me. The conversations in the hospital encouraged me, and all the patients, to think about themselves as the way forward. What a delusion! I wrote again but the letter came back unopened, labelled: *Return to sender*. As I write this I have the letter in front of me. The Federal Correctional Services stamp on it is unbearable. I can do no better than quote it:

Dearest Juliet

I wrote to you some weeks ago. It was a grave mistake. I was still under the effects of medication. What I should have said, and what I am saying now, is that I betrayed you by running to Minnesota.

I can't explain my failure of resolve. When I left you at the café that day, I was in no doubt that I would give evidence, that you would be acquitted, or maybe fined on a technicality, and that we would live together, perhaps even be married. But by nightfall I began to think of Richie, about whether you had been sleeping with him, about whether I was strong enough to stand by you. I thought that my work, my precious work, would become less interesting than my life, if I showed up on the witness stand.

But worse, and I can hardly bear to write this, I wondered if you saw me as some sort of defence, a defence of the heart, bound to play well in court.

This was my final betrayal and it has led to my breakdown. You would be justified in thinking that talking of love under these circumstances is an abomination. But I must tell you that I loved you then and I love you now.

Davis.

What I wrote then, more than a year ago, is still true. I have finished teaching now and I will be going to Mississippi to try to restart my novel, which, when *Mudflats* was published, was a burning beacon. I am grotesquely fat, the effect of the drugs, I am unable to concentrate, I am easily discouraged and I still find it difficult to sleep. These sentences should not be seen as a plea in mitigation or as punishment: they are simply facts.

If I can draw any lesson from this as a one-time writer, it is from William Faulkner's Nobel acceptance speech: *No man can write who is not a humanitarian*. I hope to be back when I have found my humanity.

Juliet reads this, sitting on the floor in the living room, with the expensive view, the slice of the park, now darkened but outlined by the mazy course of lamps through the bare trees. Actually, in the daylight it can be seen that the trees have new life, close and lichen green, like the mysterious growth on a deer's antlers.

She sees that this manuscript is the proof copy of a contribution to a small literary magazine, published in Minneapolis. Davis has stuck a note on the manuscript: *Juliet, these are my true feelings.*

She reads the words again, his true feelings, the facts. True feelings and facts are rarely the same thing. And true feelings, written down, are not the same thing as true feelings, felt.

When she gets back on to the mattress with Charlie, in the pregnant dark, he says: 'Are you all right?'

'Charlie, this is the happiest I have been for two years.'

They know that they have arcane knowledge. They lie silent in the dark for a while.

Chapter Twenty

There are fifteen women and one man gathered at New Covent Garden. Two of the women are, like her, wearing green puffa jackets. The others are wearing jeans and sweatshirts or denim skirts and parkas. They seem deliberately chosen to represent the assorted shapes of womanhood. One young girl, who turns out to be from Adelaide, is wearing a miniskirt and thick green-and-white leggings. There are also two Koreans, strangely poised. The solitary man is probably, she decides, a homosexual. She's not quite sure in her own mind if you should say 'a homosexual' or just 'homosexual'. Charles once said that homosexuals are like flies trapped in a bottle. This man is tall and lean, with short cropped hair and an anxious but energetic look, which she thinks is typical.

Stella Stevens arrives, and gathers them round. She remembers Daphne, and makes a point of welcoming her. In that ridiculous schoolgirl fashion, she feels she has scored some points. Stella explains where the flowers come from, mostly from the huge auctions in Holland, and how she chooses them. It's important to be here early. They follow her as she takes them on a tour. The two Korean women have small DVD cameras. The market is run by cockneys. You don't hear the word much these days, but these are the real article, jokey, short-legged, tubby. Women are a sort of necessary nuisance to these men: they all have copies of the *Sun* on their makeshift desks amid the ocean of flowers. In this feminine world of flowers, this great scented cavern of colour, these unreconstructed dwarves mark and patrol their Nibelung, with a friendly-aggressive mien.

Stella explains how the market works, and how she buys. One stand has all the flowers colour co-ordinated. Another specialises in tropical plants, another does dried flowers and another nothing but foliage. In a corner is a huge store selling vases and candelabras and coloured wire and bamboo torches and lanterns and six-foot-high champagne flutes, and the wire skeletons of wreaths and arches and every known floral sundry, as they call them. She buys a few things for the church, a floral knife, twine that contains wire, some Blu-tack for holding the flower spikes in position, and some floral wire.

After the tour of New Covent Garden they go back to the Flowerhouse to learn to tie bouquets. Hand-tying is the secret. Back in Trebetherick she has always set up the vase with its floral foam or pin-holder, and then poked the flowers into it, ending up with something that looks symmetrical and coordinated. Hand-tying involves holding the flowers and foliage in your left hand, adding the stems one by one, and rolling the bunch as you build it up. For Stella it appears to be instinctive. She has in front of her flowers and foliage sorted into piles. She quickly picks up something from each pile, a rose, some ivy, a lily, cotinus, and a bouquet emerges.

Stella is now demonstrating the making of the bridal posies. The Flowerhouse is large, light and airy. It's the modern way of living, without too many small fussy rooms or objects.

Too late for me to go minimalist with glass blocks and banana trees and large blond tables. Too late for me to go backwards in time, or to skip forwards.

She's here to learn how to make a wedding into something transcendent, to welcome her daughter back, to proclaim the continued existence of the Judds, and the arrival of a grandchild. Even if the flower course has cost her a thousand pounds and even if the flowers will have to be brought in by the Flying Dutchmen, or driven down in a hired van from New Covent Garden. The Flying Dutchmen travel the country, their vans stuffed with twenty or thirty thousand pounds of flowers.

As Stella shows them how to make a posy of pale-yellow and white roses, mixed with astilbe and rounded off with dark camellia leaves, and as she shows them how to tie off the end of the bouquet and cover it with a kind of carpet tape and – very popular – with ribbons of the same material as the bridesmaids' dresses, Daphne can see the bridesmaids holding their posies and passing through the lychgate, which is swagged with flowers, reaching right to the ground, and she can see an arch around the porch of the church itself.

The bridesmaids' posies repeat the bride's theme, but in a minor key. With posies there is a variety of tricks to keep them fresh and intact. She writes it all down in her notebook. She sees that weddings should reflect the seasons. Even though she is a celebrity florist, providing exotic flowers and arrangements for the famous, Stella suggests that seasonal themes are more genuine for a country wedding. Everything works better if there is a strong theme; the bouquets, the posies, the church decorations, the table decorations for the reception, even the best man's buttonhole. But it should not be too slavish: rogue elements add excitement and avoid the corporate look.

The man she has thought is gay turns out to be recently divorced, a City person who has been made redundant. He plans to set up a chain of chic mobile flower stalls with his pay-off. All morning they make bouquets. Ana's dress has two panels of a deep red and a dramatic veil flecked with the same red. So the bouquet might, for instance, contain spray roses like Tamango and Red Velvet, mixed with orange peonies. Alternatively, how about burnt-orange arum lilies and Maggie Oei orchids, which are green with red centres, the whole thing rounded off with very tropical-looking galax leaves? She writes it down. The Korean women record everything with their tiny cameras.

After lunch – they all sit matily around the scrubbed, no-nonsense, tables – they make the most beautiful thing, a cushion of moss edged with silver cord: in the middle of it is a heart made of chincherinchee flowerheads. The ring rests in the middle of this heart.

By the time they break for coffee, she discovers, in case she has forgotten, the pleasure of being part of a group with a common purpose. Some of them have already trained, and know how to tie flowers and wire stems and shape the foam. Others simply want to know how to make their houses look lovely or to do the flowers in church. But they all understand that flowers have a meaning and a language. Above all flowers speak of the briefness of life: 'the pensive monitor of fleeting years' is how Wordsworth describes snowdrops. And Shakespeare says that daisies 'figure innocence'. Shakespeare was deeply interested in the symbolism of flowers and his good opinion, Daphne feels, is in some way a validation of her own feeling. She sees too that flowers have a poignant quality, as the funeral service suggests: *Man that is born of a woman hath but a short time to live, and is full of misery. He cometh up, and is cut down, like a flower; he fleeth as it were a shadow, and never continueth in one stay.*

Before they break, they learn how to make bridesmaids' circlets and tomorrow they will be doing pew ends for the church and table decorations for the reception. It's important to have low decorations on the table so that you can see over them to the other guests, or very high decorations so that you can see under them.

She's walking down to King's Cross; rising above the sprawl, the London muddle, is the tower of St Pancras Station: in the soft, hazy, unconvincing evening light, it looks like Mad Ludwig's Castle. It must have been cleaned since we left Islington: it is now a rich unfamiliar terracotta.

The underground is busy. Yet she ploughs gamely into the crowd, conscious that her puffa and pleated skirt mark her out. It was just here that the fire broke out, killing thirty people. She was on her way to a parent–teacher meeting, and she remembers the smoke pouring up to the surface and the screaming fire engines and ambulances. Standing, holding on to one of the uprights in the carriage with her fingertips, swaying with the train's motion, a surprisingly primitive motion, she thinks: out on the periphery, in Cornwall, my human qualities have thinned out, so that I have become a pressed flower rather than something living. And I could have told this to Meg from Devon when she asked why I was doing Stella's four-day course, I could have said, Meg – new friend up from dairy country – I am fading away and my husband, a former accountant, is drowning, and one of my daughters was in jail, and my son is getting married to a tropical beauty and my other daughter, who used to experiment with drugs, has been going out with a married man twenty years older than she is. The Judd family is disintegrating. Or perhaps it is just going through a cycle of change, like the flowers mentioned in the funeral service. Whatever the truth, whichever way you look at it, I have decided that an act of witness – my beardy vicar's phrase – is needed, Meg. Because we can't speak about such things, I am using the language of flowers to speak for us.

Sophie is waiting for her. She has a bottle of Chardonnay ready and some Bombay Mix on a saucer. The flat smells strongly of cleaner.

'Good day, Mum?'

'Very interesting. It was wonderful, really. And you, darling?'

'Not bad. You just missed Ju-Ju.'

'How is she?'

'She sounds happy, like really happy.'

'Can I speak to her?'

'She's going to call later.'

'I'm so glad she's happy. I worry that this thing may hang over her for a long time.'

'Mum, Ju says she would like to stay for a while, if that's OK. Until she can find her feet.'

'Of course, darling. That's wonderful.'

'She was worried.'

'What about?'

'I don't know, like loading you and Dad with her problems.'

'That's mad. We've been longing to see her. I can't think of anything better than having her at home.'

On top of the happiness that the long, busy, sensual day has given birth to – she is sprinkled with saffron-coloured lily pollen and her clothes are scented – she has been giving a blessing: the prodigal daughter is coming home to stay.

'And maybe you could come and work at the Blue Banana during the summer.'

'And maybe Charlie and the smouldering beauty can take a cottage.'

'Now I think you're being ironic.'

'Who knows? More Chardonnay?'

'Yes please.'

'I've got an idea. Let's get off our faces. I'll go out and get some chicken tikka.'

'Sounds good to me.'

They raise their glasses – Sophie's has had another life as a Dijon mustard container – and they are full of hope, she and her pale, skinny, lovely daughter. She looks so much better without that ring, though of course you can't say it.

'What's a daphne in the language of flowers, Mum?'

'Immortality.'

'I'm up for that. Definitely. Here's to immortality.'

'And I'm loving being here with you.'

She's probably gone too far. Sophie doesn't answer for a while. She hopes she's not going to explode.

'You and Dad have been through hell, haven't you?'

'It has been bad. It has. Particularly seeing Dad not really coping. But I have a new sense of optimism. The flowers have been speaking to me.'

'Can I help with the flowers? I'll just obey orders, honestly.'

'Oh Soph, that would be lovely. You could drive a vanful down from New Covent Garden. I've realised we are going to need a huge amount. And some chicken wire and a floral arch.'

'Is that all? No problem. Have we got like a date for this flower festival, sorry, I mean wedding?'

'I'm talking to Ana about dates. She doesn't want to be too big, obviously.'

'Are you sure she's pregnant? I couldn't like see anything.'

'She's twelve or thirteen weeks.'

The blood spot on Sophie's nose has gone completely, although there is still some discolouration. She has a strange feeling that she is seeing Sophie for the first time. When she was experimenting with drugs – the young always say 'doing drugs' – she could be coldly withdrawn and truculent. Their meetings almost always ended in vicious rows. Although she knew it was hopeless, she would try to tell Sophie something about eating sensibly or getting some help, and it would quickly become a hateful round of accusation. She couldn't control herself any more effectively than Sophie could. One day a friend of Sophie's called to say Sophie was feeling sick and she rushed to an address off the Holloway Road and found her lying on the floor, her thin body smelling of excrement and her breath of decomposition. Even now the carrion foulness of that day comes back to her. The young doctor at UCH was eloquently mute as he put in a drip.

After that Sophie seemed to improve until Ju-Ju was arrested. The most terrifying thing about her was that she changed into someone else: the sweet girl who only a few years before played on the beach, assisting Charlie with his irrigation projects, became a snarling, pompous stranger. That was what hurt her most: the hatred. You can't explain to children that you are owed something because you have carried them around the room for hours in the deep unease of the night, holding them to your shoulder, pressing their small, contorted, plaintive unhappiness as close to your bloodstream as you could. You hoped that the susurration of your blood would calm them. You hoped that their deep unfathomable misery would subside – it was almost unbearable; above all, you wanted to spare them unhappiness. Instead of gratitude, or even understanding, you get the bland, repellent stare, that awful reptile loathing.

Charlie often said, Don't worry, Mum, she's going to be fine. And it seems that Charlie was right. The strange thing is that Charlie, even though he is so young, is a better judge of people than Charles – or me. He seems to understand exactly what it is that other people feel, and what they need. It's a gift.

'I'll go and get the chicken tikka now, Mum. With chapattis. Is that OK?'

'It sounds lovely. Anything you decide.'

'I won't be long. Don't like let any strange men in.'

'I might.'

The small flat, two floors up above a dingy street, seems to her heroic. From here this thin, pale young creature has been setting out in the early dawn to work. Here, presumably, she has been having sex with Dan. There is something sickening about the idea of a middle-aged man and her child running through the range of sexual follies together. She must come down to Cornwall for the summer. A family doesn't have to be in one place together all the time, but it must gather or the bonds dissolve. Charles – of course – thinks this is self-serving nonsense. But then men don't think about family in the same way: they see a sort of hierarchy, with themselves at the head of the table. Her own father used to make an enormous fuss about sharpening the carving knife, as though everything that went before, cleaning the sprouts, peeling the potatoes, making the gravy (with Bisto and cornflour), and cremating the roast, had been a preparation, mere scene-setting for this wonderful moment when the knife, newly keen from the sharpener, which had a bone handle that matched the carvers, sliced into the roast beef of Old England. Since then beef, like so much else, has taken a few knocks in the public esteem.

Down below in the tumultuous street, there is probably not a single person who would know what I was talking about if I tried to conjure up the Sunday lunch of fifty and more years ago, the dutiful, slightly fearful, but also self-congratulatory heaviness of Sunday. You were eating beef and the Royal Tour of South Africa and Winston Churchill: it was a sacrament and Daddy was distributing the host, cooked some way beyond the point of no return.

And she remembers that she hasn't rung to see how Charles is getting on. From here, he seems to be very far away. And no doubt Frances is finding every opportunity to pander to him. She should ring him, but before she can, she hears Sophie on the stairs and as the door opens she smells the chicken tikka.

'Mum, I forgot to tell you. I've looked at some lines from *Summoned by Bells* for you. It's a lovely book. Thank you. Do you want to hear my ideas?'

Sophie explains her ideas for the tables as they eat chicken tikka with plastic forks.

'For the top table, we should have these lines:

> As winds about
> The burnished path, through lady's finger, thyme
> And bright varieties of saxifrage,
> So grows the tinny tenor faint or loud
> And all things draw towards St Enodoc.'

She still has a little of that unrelenting druggie insistence, but she is so, so much better.

'I think that's charming, Sophie. Perfect.'

Chapter Twenty-One

For the last ten years of her life, his mother took to her bed. Strange phrase, defiant, a sort of feminism. Even then people knew about depression: she may have been depressed, but if she was, she hid it behind a ready truculence. She would retire after lunch, with a brief levee for tea or a stroll around the garden, and then back to the billowy comforts of her bed. She read indiscriminately, or listened to the radio, sometimes laughing loudly and harshly.

Now I am in bed. The house is completely quiet, although it is whistling and groaning a little under the effects of the wind off the estuary.

He has his meals prepared and instructions about how to heat them, in Frances's neat handwriting. It's not that difficult, but he pretended to be grateful. Women seem to need to infantilise men: men must be seen as incompetent and not fully grown up.

They want us to be ill.

I will be up tomorrow. I feel better already. Yes I do.

Being in bed under orders, or at least with permission, is liberating. Also, although he's feeling cold and shaky, he has a strong sense of order returning. Ju-Ju rang to say that she has sold the apartment finally and that she is gradually getting back into the world. That's how she put it.

'Mum says you're in bed?'

'Yes, I am a silly bugger. I slipped and fell into a stream on the golf course, and caught a bit of a cold.'

'Dad, when I come back, I want us to go on a major walk. Will you take me along the coast path?'

'Of course I will, darling.'

'In prison I often thought about the walk, particularly from Lundynant to Porth Quin. I tried sometimes to remember every rock, every gate, every hill, every view, high tide or low. Do you know near Epphaven when you go left along the cliff or straight over, I would debate which way to go, the low, scratchy way, or the schlepp over the top? Do you remember the day we found shaggy parasol mushrooms?'

'Yes. There were hundreds.'

'Have they ever come back?'

'I've never seen them again.'

'I have a feeling they will be there. Look after yourself. And, Dad, Charlie sends his love.'

'When are you back?'

'Charlie's coming tomorrow. I'll be a few days. I've got a few things to do. I'm longing to see you. Get better, Daddy.'

He has been out of the world for three years himself; now, like Ju-Ju, he is on the comeback trail. The comeback kid. He lies in bed with all the pleasure of a seal on a spit of sand.

The world is my medium; these three years have been a temporary beaching.

He gets out of bed to look for a book he bought in London ages ago. It's called something like *Morality, an Introduction* by a Bernard Williams. He hid it, but he can't remember where. And his reason for hiding it reveals a certain ethical weakness of his own: he wanted to hide his concern that there may be some defect in the family make-up. Daphne has tried to talk to him about the ethics involved; although he has no answers, he certainly doesn't want any of the solutions on offer, courtesy of the bearded one. He doesn't want atonement or witness or celebration or even acknowledgement of having paid a debt to society. There is, anyway, no such thing as society: it's all gone to hell. The world is full of hypocrisy going by the name of politics and journalism and counselling.

But he's put off reading the book because he is scared of what it might say.

He wanders about the house in his dressing gown. He knows it will come to him. He looks at the bookshelves and behind the dictionary and in his filing cabinet, and then he looks out of the window towards the back garden where the trees are heaving gently like mourners at a funeral, and he sees the rabbits, emboldened by the perception of abandonment, foraging all over the lawn, and he remembers: the book is in the toolshed underneath the manual that came with the mower. He pushes open the back door, sending the rabbit maquisards back into the undergrowth. At that moment Frances appears from the lane carrying something, which, even from this distance, he knows is going to be a sponge cake.

'Aren't you supposed to be in bed?' she shouts. She is wearing the long waxed coat.

'Yes. But I'm allowing myself a certain latitude.'

'I've brought you a cake.'

'That is very kind of you. Thank you.'

'Are you going far?'

'No, just to the shed.'

'Can it wait, while I make us some tea?'

'Of course.'

They head back to the house, he in his striped dressing gown, she carrying her sponge cake in a tin decorated with pictures of wild flowers. We're stuck in a fucking pantomime, he thinks.

Later, again routing the uppity rabbits, he retrieves the book and takes it to the bedroom. He feels that he needs to know the order of the moral universe, if there is one. Before opening it, he has another slice of orange sponge. Frances also makes damson jam and preserves. Like the rabbits, she forages widely. This cake has her bitter orange marmalade between its two layers. Frances let on that Daphne has gone to London to learn about wedding flowers. Daphne has a habit of telling slightly different stories to different people. Horses for courses. He wonders what there is to know about wedding flowers; there's something sickening about weddings, with all that pastel and arrangements on pedestals and gold-sprayed chairs and virginal posies. For a moment, quite a long moment, he finds himself trying to remember who Ju-Ju is marrying. But he sees what has happened: Charlie's wedding is actually Ju-Ju's re-entry; Charlie and his Brazilian girl are providing the cover. Frances certainly sees the significance. Her own daughter, according to Daphne, is making a return from the wilder shores of Sapphism.

And in my own way, I am making a comeback.

He opens the book at random. When he was a child he often used to do this; sometimes he would read the last paragraph of a story first. He reads: *The trouble with religious morality comes not from morality's being inescapably pure, but from religion's being incurably unintelligible.* So how do we acquire an ethical sense that means anything? When Charlie accused him of being intolerant, or when Ju-Ju stole the window, or when he fucked Jo on his desk, or when Fox and Jewell altered the partnership deeds, or when he failed his daughter, what was the justification for moral outrage? Where does the justification come from? He can't really imagine the answer, unless there is just a sort of morality that most people understand. But why should they accept it? He reads on: *Why is there anything that I should, ought, to do? It is very unclear that we can in fact give the man who asks it a reason . . . Of course it is true that if he stays alive he will be doing something, rather than something else.*

So that is all that is left to me: to stay alive. There are no absolute standards; I have beliefs but I don't believe in them.

He goes down to the kitchen; his face is hot, whether from the tortuous nature of philosophical discourse, or from the fact that he hasn't taken his paracetamol, he can't decide. If there are no standards, why do I feel guilt? If there are no standards, why should Ju-Ju feel shame about spending two years in jail? If there are no standards, why have I felt diminished by what Fox and Jewell did to me?

His cheeks are prickling, like tonic in a gin, quinine tonic.

Nobody knows any more why it's called tonic. Nobody cares. What has happened – this must be the answer – is that accepted ideas of morality have fragmented. The suicide bombers have a sense of morality. The vicar probably has a sense of morality. But for the bearded one and his suicidal co-believers, the justification for morality – religion – is easy. For the rest of us it's unintelligible. It's *incurably unintelligible*, Kevin, my bearded friend. He feels better: there may be no intelligible explanation for belief, but there's an incurably intelligible explanation for lack of belief. He has another slice of cake, swallows his paracetamols, and returns to bed to the pursuit of higher reasoning. And then he thinks of his daughter trying to imagine every detail of the coast path, and he remembers that she has never reproached him for failing to visit her, and he feels – despite his new knowledge – shame and guilt again.

Perhaps what we have to do is to try to avoid causing unhappiness: I have caused a lot in my time, although probably not more than most.

If he remembers, this is called utilitarianism. And as if by magic he finds a chapter on the subject: *I think there are major attractions of the utilitarian outlook for moral thought. First, that it is non-transcendental, and makes no appeal outside human life, in particular not to religious considerations. Second, its basic good, happiness, seems minimally problematical: however much people differ, surely they at least all want to be happy. Its attraction is that moral issues can, in principle, be determined by empirical calculations of consequence. Fourth, utilitarianism provides a common currency of moral thought: the different concerns of different parties can all be cashed in terms of happiness.*

This is good stuff: do your best, taking other people into account. But then Professor Williams goes on to show that the whole idea is problematic after all: it depends on measuring the nature of the happiness against the value of some proposed action. The utilitarian answer could conflict with the morally right answer: for instance, where the execution of an innocent man is necessary to avoid great harm. He sees now that what happened to Ju-Ju was a form of utilitarianism: they locked her up for reasons that had nothing to do with right or wrong. And he also understands Professor Williams's objection to utilitarianism: the greater satisfaction of the Federal authorities was bought at the price of the misery of the lesser Judds. It seems so clear. He wants to speak to someone to explain the uses of philosophy. The book, he sees, has some oil on it and the blue traces of a pulverised slug pellet.

If you are looking for an example of the problems of utilitarianism, the dog's death provides a good one:

It's an August morning, one and a half years ago. He has been neglecting the garden because of his worries about Ju-Ju. In the garden centre at Trelights, he buys some slug pellets, as the slugs are devastating the hostas, which are supposed to form a natural-looking clump in the shady area against one of the lichen-covered stone walls. The lichen is a close-growing fur, flecked in grey, green and mustard. He shakes the pellets out generously around the plants. Later, when he's ready for his walk, he calls the dog. There is no response; but then he hears quiet whimpering, and there is the dog lying in a flowerbed producing blue bubbles of foam at the mouth. He picks it up and runs for the car, placing it on the front seat next to him. But before he can reach the vet in Wadebridge, the dog dies; the ghastly blue foam has stopped bubbling and frothing. He continues on to Porth Quin and turns into the National Trust car park and carries the body of the dog towards the coast path, even nodding a greeting to a walker, while propping up the dog's head, and then he throws the body of the dog into the old mineshaft, where it bounces once on the way down. He goes for a short, dogless, walk before going home. He tells Daphne that the dog, in mad pursuit of a rabbit, has fallen off the cliff. She is shocked and concerned for him, because she thinks his mental state is not good. He is concerned to protect her from the truth, that he poisoned the dog. They are able to comfort themselves with the thought that wire-haired dachshunds are impulsive animals, following their noses recklessly, even over a cliff. This is utilitarianism in action.

Or is it moral laxness?

Also he wonders if they ever send someone down the slate mines to check for missing persons or stolen property. If they do, they will find a small canine corpse with their phone number attached, and it will be very difficult to explain why the dog, after falling off a cliff, clambered up a hundred feet of sheer rock, and then threw itself down a mineshaft.

An empty house is eloquent. This one is turning into an old person's house. He himself is contributing to this state, with the newspapers he puts away to read later and the fussy coats and hats he has by the door and the excuses he makes for keeping things that should be thrown away. Also, now that he sleeps alone, he finds his room has a peculiar, elderly smell. It's hard to say what its components are, but it is unmistakable. The kitchen, which started out bright and clean, has gradually become greasy, the oven ingrained, the worktops burned in rings, the glasses as grimy as a morning in Gdansk. Even the house plants – weak cyclamens in a trough and an etiolated ficus – speak of a lack of vigour. The rabbits, always on the offensive with their lop-eared fundamentalism, are only a larger version of what is happening minutely all around him inside the house. Charlie thinks the roof should be fixed and the exterior paintwork renewed.

There's something of the fanatic about Charlie. He doesn't understand utilitarianism, but then neither did I until ten minutes and two slices of cake ago.

Frances was quite skittish. She's a solid woman. He can't imagine having sex with her. It seems to him unfair that middle-aged women can't get men, can't even buy them. It's a taboo, he thinks, rather than a physical thing.

Yet Clem is screwing an economic migrant, and Jo back in Norwood is keen to see me again. There is more than a hint of desperation about her, but still, it's not fair.

'You look great,' she said. Her breath had coarsened and grown thicker.

*   *   *

The house is sighing. When Daphne is away he feels more calm. He is able to think. It's as though the years together have produced a fine mist of resentment which neither of them can quite dispel. It's like the atmosphere when you step off the plane in the tropics, a pressing sense that the air is burdened. And yet he misses her. She didn't phone last night, and this has left him faintly uneasy, as though she is able to exercise influence over him from a distance, by not doing the things that irritate him, like making pointless conversation. He could ring her, but it would be a minute defeat.

I've never had any of this low-level tension with Ju-Ju. It's because you are one flesh with your children. One flesh: another strange phrase.

More and more he finds himself stopping and thinking about phrases, in case he won't hear them again. One flesh must be religious, but also we now know about DNA. DNA is literally the explanation of life. He and Ju-Ju are one flesh.

But I don't quite have this feeling for Charlie or Sophie.

Daphne thinks it's something to do with their first, still-born, baby, but he wasn't deeply affected by that.

When you're young, you are resilient, even callous. I was.

Ju-Ju wants to go on a walk: he feels blessed. They'll go when the tide is out to Epphaven. She's always had the ability to know exactly what to say to him. On holiday she would follow him gamely until she could walk no more: she was passionately attached for two summers to some shorts with blue spots and the remembrance of her thin legs, the small shorts, the hillsides of sheep and gorse, the deep disturbed sea, the indifferent gulls, the eager little face, above all the little face; he struggles to think what it was about her that grips his heart so painfully. The remembrance of the little face turned trustingly to him is unbearable. He finds himself weeping.

I have to explain to her why I couldn't come to see her in the prison. I have to tell her. I have to beg forgiveness.

Down below there is a banging on the front door. He wipes his face on the candlewick, pulls on his dressing gown, which has managed to turn itself inside out, something he only discovers when he finds the cord on the inside.

'Coming, coming.'

Clem is at the back door with a bottle of wine.

'You want to do something about those fucking rabbits,' he says. 'I've come to cheer you up. You look as miserable as sin.'

'I've been sneezing.'

'And I just went round in fifteen over.'

'Nine holes?'

'Hah bloody hah. Give me a corkscrew.'

'How did you know I was ill?'

'Word gets around.'

'Did Daphne put you up to this?'

'All you need is a nightcap on your head and you would be Scrooge. No, Daphne did not send me. This is a bottle of the club's finest claret, guaranteed to cure anything from the pox to schizophrenia.'

He's wearing yellow moleskin trousers and the club's V-necked sweater. He pours the wine, which fills the smudged crystal glasses with a warm terracotta.

'I feel like getting tight as a tick. Rat-arsed,' says Clem.

'I'm ill.'

'That's absolutely no excuse. The court does not accept your defence. Now tell me, why were you scuba-diving at the tenth?'

'I was trying to fish a ball out of the stream, one of yours probably, when I slipped. Belly flop, right into the water.'

'Jesus, I wish I had seen that.'

Clem is laughing. He is laughing without restraint, perhaps with malice.

'How long were you under for?' he gasps.

'I had to sort of crawl a few yards, I had to wriggle to get out. I thought I was drowning at one point.'

'Sorry I am laughing, but you have to admit, it's hilarious.'

'It wasn't hilarious at the time.'

'Damned difficult to laugh underwater, I find.'

Now they are both laughing.

'I tried to make a phone call from under the water.'

'Oh my God.'

Clem's eyes are full of tears; they laugh like schoolboys. They become weak, helpless. Eventually they wheeze to a halt.

'Charles, stop. I'm starving. Got any nuts?'

'No, they dropped off.'

And they start to laugh again.

'Golf: Mastering the Underwater Game, by Charles Judd.'

They microwave a cottage pie and eat in the kitchen. Clem eats in a curious way, with his lips projecting forwards at the last moment to meet the fork. His face is strangely preserved: you can see the boyish outlines, despite the thin hair that he keeps securely attached in some way, and the bushy eyebrows that have a source of energy denied to the hair on his head. This boyishness, Charles thinks, is faintly ghoulish, as if the application of aftershave and lotions – Clem is always scented – has acted like formaldehyde. He thinks of those rows of specimens kept in bottles at school, the indistinct shapes of small mammals and foetuses and frogs in a murky liquid. On this evidence, the boy Clem was a chirpy little fellow.

'Clem, I want to ask you something.'

'Shoot.'

'What's it like fucking that Vietnamese totty?'

'You must be pissed.'

'Am I embarrassing you?'

'No. Not at all. To tell the truth, Charles, it's not the real thing.'

What is the real thing? Lying in bed again, after Clem has stumbled away into the softly complaining night, shouting, 'Fuck off, rabbits,' he wonders what Clem means. Paid sex is providing him with a measure of happiness, because the real thing is no longer in reach. And this seems to Charles – I'm a little drunk – a cruel deception, perhaps the cruellest, that when you need the real thing most, when you need unmediated passion and blitheness and ecstasy, it is only available in its simulacrum.

Chapter Twenty-Two

When Charlie had gone, she didn't feel lonely.

On a grey spring day in a New York diminished by the surfacing detritus of winter, she allows herself to hope that her dark night may be lifting. Shower time at Otisville lasted exactly four minutes for each group of women. On her second night there she was seized by a *clicka*, the Bull Daggers, and dragged into the showers where darkness fell. *En una noche oscura.* Such a beautiful phrase.

At the door, his keys in hand, Charlie asked, 'How was I, by the way, on a scale of one to ten?'

He was trying to lighten the moment of departure.

'We'll never know, Charlie. There is no scale for holy mysteries.'

'I'll take that as an A-star then.'

They kiss, conscious of the chaste placement of the lips, just below the cheekbones.

'Give my love to Ana.'

'I will.'

And he was gone.

'You go bumpin' your gums to the badge and you gonna wake up dead.'

That's what they said to her that night in Otisville. Afterwards a guard asked her how the water was.

'OK.'

'Welcome to the world.'

*   *   *

Davis is sitting reading in the window of the café on Bleecker Street. The light from the outside is weakening – she can see it happening – so that the yellowish glow of a cone-shaped lamp hanging above the table is becoming stronger, giving his features a dairy-produce look. He is still wearing the plantation-owner suit, which, if possible, is even more creased.

He jumps up when he catches sight of her in the street; his fat thighs tip the table and his coffee spills over the book. When she reaches him he is mopping the table with a bundle of paper napkins.

'I'm nervous,' he says.

'Don't be nervous.'

She helps him clean up.

'Why did you call?'

'I read what you wrote.'

'Were you angry?'

'No.'

They order coffee.

'I'm going to Mississippi on Sunday.'

'And I'm going to London. Yuh, I read what you wrote. The facts, as you call them. To be honest, after I read it I felt bad about some of the things I said to you.'

'You don't have a single thing to apologise for. What you had to endure was beyond comprehension. Way beyond. And me? Shit, I can hardly bear to think, to remember, to, uh, to uh . . .'

She reaches out her hand and places it over the back of his for a moment. His hand is moist. He stops trying to speak.

'Davis, you said you didn't come through for me in the end because you thought maybe I was using you as a sort of alibi. You used a fancy phrase, a defence of the heart, you said.'

'I did. I can't deny it. No I can't.'

She thinks that she can see how he would have been on the witness stand, a grave emphatic young Southern gentleman: 'Ah cain't deny it.'

His face is damp too.

'Davis, I was sleeping with Richie at the same time. It was

unavoidable. So in a way you were right about me. But I want you to know, seeing we're trying to be honest, that I was in love with you, not Richie. What you wrote, what you said I had said, that we were caught up in something bigger than ourselves, is true. We've paid for it, my God, we've paid.'

She looks at him, drug-bloated, damp, shabby with his chopped hair and his realigned features. She wonders what he sees: a stringy broad with a hunted, pallid, share-cropper face? A face of accusation?

'You didn't deserve what happened to you, Juliet. I did. I betrayed you.'

In the past he used to speak in an orotund, measured fashion, perhaps like Faulkner himself, but now he has a thin note to his voice and an uncertain wavering cadence, begging for confirmation.

'I did deserve it under the law. I fenced a Tiffany window that I knew was stolen. At the time, I just didn't see it as a crime. It became a crime.'

'How bad was it in prison?'

'It was very bad, Davis. I didn't think I would survive. And you, has it been terrible?'

'I don't want to compare what happened to me. It would be a category mistake. My parents have kinda tried to ignore me but I can't imagine what yours have been through.'

'That's a question that I can't fully answer. There were times when I asked myself if it would be better for them if I killed myself. My father never visited me once.'

'Oh God.'

He gulps half a mug of coffee.

'Davis, I don't want to pretend it was a mystic St John of the Cross thing, but last night I suddenly, absolutely unannounced, I felt that there was some hope. I thought – you remember what Jung said? – "This is me." I realised that I did still exist, which I had honestly doubted. I couldn't really talk to anyone else like this, Davis. We've got to put it behind us. It wasn't fair of me to blame you.'

'You called me a phoney piece of Mississippi mud pie.'

'I'm sorry.'

'You were very generous in my estimation.'

He laughs. His face suddenly breaks open like a pomegranate. She sees now some vestigial reminder of what she loved, a sort of boyish eagerness.

'Oh Davis.'

'You called me lard-ass.'

'I was angry.'

'Lard-ass is from Mordechai Richler. He used it first. It's in Lighter's dictionary.'

'You always loved slang. I read some dictionaries of dialect up there in the boondocks.'

'Are you going to be OK with your father? I know how much you adored him.'

'Who knows? Charlie, my brother, says that he wanted to come and see me but thought he would be so broken up it would make things worse.'

'Are you going to work?'

'I should think I'm unemployable. But I have some projects. And you, are you going to write again?'

'That's my hope. My only hope.'

'You have talent, Davis. *Mudflats* is a brilliant book. You once said to me, sitting right here, two tables from here actually, that it is our duty to pursue a kind of truth. While I was in jail I lost all faith in truth. You probably need to go to jail to understand just how fragile our beliefs are. But I see that you can't give up. There isn't anything else.'

'We used to talk. I miss it. Juliet, do you truly forgive me?'

'I do. If it's in my gift, yes, I do.'

'Thank God.'

The café has a picture of Allen Ginsberg just before the *Howl* trial. New York likes to think of itself as having a questing, awkward spirit. Small things – the smell of arabica, the gurgling preceding the throttled scream of the milk for the cappuccino, the aroma of prosciutto and provolone for the famous toasted sandwiches, the sight of two people kissing sumptuously, the long white aprons of the waiters and waitresses, the pyramids of pastries, the salsa music – they all fall on her fresh, paint on damp plaster. The Italian cups, red-rimmed and small, are a miracle of delicacy, in each one a puddle of espresso, rimmed with *crema*. Up in Loon Lake everything was large and crude and brutal.

The large contorted face of Davis Lyendecker is looking at her. It's hard to read the expression because of the surface upheavals, but she feels a surprising warmth rising in her.

'Do you think we will ever meet again?'

Somehow the voice is nothing to do with the location from which it emanates; it sounds like the voice in Grandma's teddy, which Mum keeps in the bedroom. When you pull a string it squeaks the first line of 'The Teddy Bear's Picnic'.

'We will.'

The teddy-bear voice is really asking if they can ever love again.

'Davis, the question is, will we be the same people again?'

'You cannot step twice into the same river. I don't know if that really means anything, by the way.'

She remembers the fevered conversations in the café before they went to his flat. That was during the age of innocence.

'You like rivers and tides. I remember you saying that your favourite line in all literature – apart from Faulkner, of course – is the final line of Gatsby.'

'I am from a flat, wet place. Swamps and rivers is all I know.'

'You know a lot more than that. I must go now, Davis. I've got your e-mail address. As soon as I have one of my own, I'll e-mail you.'

He's struggling to speak; the anarchic face is trying to locate and arrange the words.

'Juliet, are you still in touch with Richie?' Squeak.

'No, Davis.'

'Any plans to see him?' Squeak.

'None.'

* * *

239

After the ground-hugging lowness of Loon Lake, the city is too tall, teetering dangerously and presumptuously above her cab. It was her lies to Davis and Richie that led her to Loon Lake. In a curious way the Tiffany window had nothing to do with it. If her story went horribly wrong, it was at least following one literary tradition faithfully: scarlet women have to pay in the end.

A city is a physical fact, but really a city is an accumulation of human longings and folly and ambitions and failures. These streets, bright under an indigo urban sky, are routinely described as canyons. But they are not canyons, they are living things like coral reefs or anthills, the improbable product of all that longing and folly. It presses on her, the sense of the dead, the deceived, the noble, the crazy, who have contributed to this ziggurat of unreason. And now her own deceit has been added to the heap.

I could take comfort from realising that in this monument to absurdity it will count for little or nothing.

Sean pops out from the side door to the store room. He has news for her: a journalist from the *New York Times*, Lloyd Hirschman, wants to speak to her. He has come over especially by cab.

'Did you tell him I was leaving Saturday?'

'I didn't tell him nothing. He left his cell number. He said to tell you, he has some very important information for you. He left his card with the number, here, and he wants you to call him at any time.'

'Thanks, Sean.'

'That's OK, Ms Judd.'

He calls the elevator for her, and reaches his hand in to prevent the door doing anything unexpected.

She sits in the empty apartment on the mattress. She dials.

'Lloyd Hirschman.'

'Hi. It's Juliet Judd here. I just want to tell you, I am sure you will understand that I am not going to give an interview.'

'Ms Judd, what I have to tell you is far more important than any interview. I need to speak to you in person.'

'Nothing will be published, not a word, without my written consent?'

'Nothing.'

'Can you come over now?'

Chapter Twenty-Three

It seems that the wedding, which he has too hastily franchised to his mother, is gathering unstoppable momentum. He called Sophie from a cab on his way from Heathrow and she said that Mum is in London doing a flower-arranging course, wedding flowers, to be precise.

'Whose wedding is this?'

'Ah Charlie, that's not an easy question. I am like in charge of literary inspiration and flower transport. What's your job?'

'Fuck knows. Ana's bought up most of Bond Street. She still hasn't been able to explain to me why people need berry spoons. I actually planned to get married one day in a registry office. I only agreed to Trebetherick for Ju-Ju.'

'You offered. Mum told me. How is Ju?'

'Everybody asks that all the time, as if she's ill. But she's definitely much better. It is all incredibly confusing for her, even overwhelming, coming out of prison. Sophie, can we keep this under control, this wedding?'

'It's a runaway train, Charlie.'

'Oh God. Will you come over for dinner?'

'Don't you and the glamour-puss want to be alone?'

'Sophie, we are going to be alone for a long time. Will Mum come?'

'Sure. She would love to. She's kicking up her heels. I can safely speak for her. You're a funny boy, Charlie.'

'Bye-bye. Nine o'clock.'

'That's way past her bedtime.'

'Nine o'clock.'

He wonders if she's clean. He'll know as soon as he sees her. Martha's office is above a shop selling coins, opposite the British Museum. It's amazing that you can still buy coins from the time of Constantine the Great or Vespasian. They rest in little Perspex display cases.

The receptionist says go straight in. Martha is sitting at a vast table, which she uses as a desk. Not for her chased leather and looming shelves of unread law books. He kisses her.

'No tongues, Charlie, I'm your lawyer. Papers are all ready.'

The papers are marked with red tabs where he should sign.

'What's it feel like to be rich?'

'For God's sake don't tell Ana.'

At that moment the receptionist comes in with a bottle of champagne.

'Martha,' he says, 'will you marry me?'

'All right.' She opens the bottle. 'Here's to us.'

They drink.

'You look troubled, Charlie. You're supposed to be happy.'

'I am happy. But I want a prenuptial agreement.'

'Jesus, Charlie. Don't you think that's going to sound a little brutal at this stage? There are other ways. You can get the money offshore as fast as possible.'

'Is that legal?'

'Yes, for the moment. I can put it out of reach and you just draw what you need. Charlie, what's your problem? In ten minutes.'

'You should never have someone you've had sex with as a lawyer. Ten minutes may not be enough. I only agreed to this marriage, actually I volunteered myself, because of my sister. I wanted something simple or like just to carry on as before. This is getting out of hand.'

'Whoa, Charlie. You can't carry on as before when you've got a baby.'

'Whose side are you on?'

'I'm on your side, but babies are legal matters. They come with moral responsibilities too. What you are really saying is that you don't want a baby. Or is it like you don't want to feel as though you are committed for ever? Or even less than for ever?'

'I wasn't consulted on the baby and I felt pressured into agreeing to a wedding down in Cornwall. Now it's turning into a flower festival, a fucking orgy of flowers, with lists, favours – do you know what berry spoons are? I didn't think so. And poems by John Betjeman. I hate John Betjeman. My Dad hates him. My Dad will probably expose himself at the reception. We're all atheists and the effing vicar, who is a touchy-feely creep with a beard like a goat's scrotum, has been lined up to marry us. Jesus, the whole thing is a nightmare. Ju-Ju is going to be paraded like the prodigal daughter.'

'It sounds so fun. The perfect English wedding. How is your beloved sister?'

'Oh God. That again. She has had some re-entry problems, but she's definitely getting to grips with things. She never told me when I visited her, but prison was hell. Total hell. I don't even want to talk about it. She nearly killed herself when Dad refused to visit her. It cracked me up when she told me.'

'What is it exactly that Juliet has? What is the hold she has on everybody?'

'I'm quite pissed on one glass of champagne, but all I can say is there are some holy mysteries, things not quite accessible to reason. Ju-Ju has like a kind of innocence. She's a believer. Yes, I know I'm being cheesy.'

'You're saying you love her, I think.'

Yes. I love her and I've always loved her. And now I don't love my wife-to-be.

'Of course I love her. But what it is, I think – seeing you asked – is that she believes in beauty and happiness. She's not selling anything.'

'Apart from a Tiffany window.'

'Don't be a twat, Martha. Nobody likes a smart-arse.'

'Lighten up, Charlie. You're rich, you're about to marry the most beautiful girl the world has ever seen, you're going to be a father and your sister's out of jail and heading for mega-celebrity.'

'I don't think she'll write about it or give interviews.'

'In my experience, people feel the urge to explain themselves.'

'You're twenty-eight. You don't have any experience, even though you are a shit-hot little lawyer. You look sexy in that suit, by the way. Is it Dior, by any chance?'

'Yes it is Dior. It cost me a month's pay and I bought it to celebrate this deal. And now I'll wear it to the wedding of the year.'

'Why did you dump me, Martha?'

'We've been here before. You shagged my best friend. Charlie, what's this about?'

'Nothing. I'm just howling at the moon.'

> *So grows the tinny tenor faint or loud*
> *And all things draw towards St Enodoc.*

Why did I say that I hate Betjeman? I don't hate Betjeman or even his poetry. What I hate is Betjeman as part of the code: Betj and sea bathing and sand in the sandwiches and looking at churches and not owning a television and believing abroad is too hot and valuing ineptitude and plain cooking.

He remembers how it was with Martha. Your past relationships seem to fall into categories: Martha was in the category where everything is fine, but there is no mystery. At some cellular level there is a failure of attraction, which happens despite friendship and admiration and even shared interests. With Ana he must have been deceived, dazzled by her glamour. He couldn't help thinking when they were lying in bed that he had received some sort of sexual windfall, and that he should nurture it. But now that all things are drawing towards St Enodoc, he sees that after a year he had already begun to lose interest in her, although he still felt flattered and exalted that they made such a striking couple. In truth he is happiest when they are in company, a double act. She gives off a sort of glamour, which adheres to him, but what his friends don't know is that this glamour has a mineral quality, like the radiation from Cornish granite. She is beautiful, but it signifies nothing.

He calls Ana, finally, but the nanny-elect says she has gone shopping. He tries her mobile: it rings for a while and then cuts out. He calls the nanny again and tells her that he will be home about eight, eight-thirty latest, and to alert Ana to the fact that Sophie and Mrs Judd are coming to dinner. She should book a restaurant if there's nothing to eat. The conditional clauses are causing a problem. He re-phrases: 'I come home eight o'clock, my mama and my seester she come too, we go eat restaurant.'

'Hokay.' The 'hokay' is pregnant with reproach: Why you no say so first time?

He sees a future of being cast as a domestic chump, a sort of obscurantist delaying the important business of life. He takes another cab to the one and a half rooms that are **sock-it-to-me.com**, a minor success of the New Internal Enabled Web-Architected Economy.

I feel guilty because I am utterly disloyal to the mother of my child and the child itself.

He can't really grasp the full meaning of a child: at the moment Ana and the child are the same thing. The child is a small lump, but one that will grow quickly in that tropical lushness. Ju-Ju next to him was painfully (as they say) thin. Holding her to his own body he felt an overwhelming poignancy: she had turned into a young girl again. So thin, so bony, so frail: he felt as plump and sleek as a seal by comparison. In the night she said, 'One flesh, Charlie.' People say strange things when they are asleep – they speak in tongues and they express dark or spiritual longings – but Ju-Ju spoke the words calmly. What did she mean? It wasn't a question he could ask when he woke.

The office in Beak Street is small. He has two full-time employees, Jason and Stephanie, who are at their screens. No product other than samples ever enters this office: everything is packed and dispatched in various parts of the country and places abroad. Jason and Stephanie spend all day receiving and processing orders. Over the past three years Charlie has acquired the addresses and the credit details of nearly thirty thousand people and it is this information that the Germans have bought. Jason and Stephanie are a new kind of person, who have no education of any sort, and no curiosity beyond computers. They understand computers, and live through them. Jason, who always wears an Arsenal shirt, has devised complicated programs designed to encourage the customers to commit to more payments, but he probably thinks that Canaletto is an Italian striker. Stephanie loves heavy metal bands like Napalm and Marduk 4; she only wears crêpe platform shoes. Her hair could be a haven for small birds and her lipstick is the colour of Queen of the Night tulips.

Charlie loves these two: they live fully in the cyber world. He thinks of them as exotic pets. They are devoted to the task of keeping the business running. They don't see the whole enterprise as an illusion. Far from it: they see stores and window displays and posters and advertising as old school. In fact, Charlie believes, they see the material world as the illusion. He delays telling them that he has sold the company: it won't make any difference to them anyway, as he is staying on. He asks them what response there has been to the new cufflinks: not bad, T-shirts mega. It gives him great pleasure that this business, devised entirely by him, should work so smoothly. The building was once a milliner's workshop and house, built by Huguenots in 1715. Now all the work, the making of socks and underwear and T-shirts, is done in poor countries he has never visited. The manufacture has nothing to do with it. In half an hour he can order twenty thousand pairs of socks or change his supplier. All the payments, inwards and outwards, take place without a scrap of paper. And no customer ever calls here.

'Did you miss me?' he asks.

'Nah, not really.'

'I did,' says Stephanie. Her face is pale and her eyes are lined with kohl. She is demonstrating loyalty to another reality. She has a vampire-bat screensaver and is wearing mittens.

He goes into his small office behind some glass bricks and fires up his Power Macs. When Dad started they had ledgers and dip pens. He calls Cornwall to see how the one-time bean-counter, who allegedly spent his youth chained to a Dickensian clerk's desk, is getting on.

'Dad.'

'Who's that?'

'How many sons do you have?'

'Charlie?'

'Yes, Dad, Charlie. I'm back.'

'It's a bad line. Welcome back.'

'I hear you have been ill.'

'A bit of a cold. I got wet on the golf course.'

No mention of the fall or the ducking; perhaps they bring back painful memories of being saved from drowning.

'You sound a little weak, Dad.'

'Bad line.'

'It's all right at this end.'

'I'm fine, Charlie.'

'Has the doctor been?'

'You may not have noticed, but doctors don't come out for colds any more. Is Ju-Ju with you?'

'No, she gets back on Monday. She's getting better. Did Mum tell you, she's coming to stay with you?'

'I haven't heard from your mother for a while.'

'She's with Sophie in London. Dad, Ju's coming to stay with you.'

'Jolly good.'

'Jolly good? Is that it? She's been in jail for two years.'

'I am aware of that, Charlie. I'm reading a book and I must get on. Welcome home.'

Charlie stares at his screens. There's often this locking of horns, as Mum calls it, when he and Dad speak. Now he's ill and he won't call the doctor; he's always thought that consulting doctors is a sign of weakness. Yet Charlie feels bad, because he knows that the brief conversation, his implied accusation, will have upset him. In the Hudson Valley Ju-Ju told him that when his hair began to thin – he was only twenty at the time – Dad had gone out and had his cut short, to reduce any possible contrast.

'How do you know, Ju?'

'He told me. He said, "It's so unfair that I have all this hair, this mop, and Charlie's going bald." He was worried.'

'He never told me.'

He was moved by this revelation.

And now I have been unkind. Dad has always found it easier to talk to Ju-Ju. What is it that rises up between me and him? Maybe it's Ju-Ju, the contest for her soul.

Ana keeps him waiting. Impending motherhood has given her licence: it seems to be understood. Also they had sex: impending motherhood is wreaking havoc with her hormones.

By the time they get to the restaurant, Mum and Sophie have had two drinks each and eaten a bowl of olives. Ana, it must be said, looks wonderful. By comparison, Mum and Sophie, sitting side by side on a banquette, look like the larval stages of womanhood. Ana's face is charged with health; she is carrying her Kelly bag and she wears jeans over black boots. Her breasts – he's probably imagining this – are reaching upwards avidly under her silk blouse. She has a gold chain-link belt, which is so Latina.

'Hello, Mum.'

They kiss briefly. Ana hugs his mother. Sophie stands to one side. He gestures to her nose. Sophie shrugs happily, and then, inclining towards the nuptial conspirators, sticks her finger down her throat.

'Sophie,' he says, 'you look good. You look great.'

Mum is a little over-dressed. You can't blame her; when she was young people knew exactly what to wear. It's not so clear now, but whatever it is, it's not this cruisewear look of white shoes and blue striped jumper with a white neckerchief – perhaps a homage to the Newlyn School of painting – over tailored trousers in dark blue. Sophie is wearing a frayed and aged denim skirt and a tight pink camisole top. Her breasts, he sees, are barely disturbing the fabric.

Mum thinks she's going to have fish: she loves monkfish, she says. He remembers the horror on her face when she saw the head of a monkfish at a market in Portugal. So they go through the English rigmarole of ordering. Sophie orders chips before she's decided on anything else. Mum says she's been eating Danish pastries at the Flowerhouse: she's stuffed. And she and Sophie have been eating olives and bread. But he prevails on her to have a first course of rocket and parmesan at least. When you have the older generation around, the whole restaurant process becomes stilted. Dad always acts up, trying to impress the waiters with his bonhomie, and Mum adopts a false humility: 'Just a little portion, not too much, heavens, that looks rich. I don't like my food mucked about with.'

Now she repeats the information that she is stuffed to the waiter, and cites Danish pastries as the culprit, which she evidently thinks are rather raffish. Ana asks for something vegetarian, although she is not a vegetarian.

Charlie is tired but he can't sleep. He's been awake for twenty-one hours. Next to him Ana is out. She breathes quietly, but when she turns towards him he can feel a warm scented breeze on his chest. He moves himself away minutely. He wants to speak to Ju-Ju. Beside him Ana's lustrous hair – the lustre has to be imagined in the semi-dark – has spread all over the pillows. Tendrils are reaching towards him.

During dinner he felt the urge to strike a glass with the handle of a fork and to announce that he had sold his business. But prudence tells him to play down the deal, to let Martha hide the money and then perhaps say that new investors have come in. As he lies next to Ana, gorgeous even in sleep, he tries to imagine how it is going to be to wake up next to her for years on end. His imagination fails. Although he has made his money out of clothes, he can't see a future that is validated entirely by handbags, kitchens, home improvements and obedience to the arbitrary demands of fashion. He knows that there is a long waiting list for the Kelly bag. He has stopped wondering how Ana paid for it. The talk at the table was about the wedding arrangements; it would have been churlish to ask. Mum, flushed, happy, tipsy, explained what she and Sophie had in mind for the reception: each table will have a theme from Betjeman, thrift, tamarind, slate, and Cornish granite arrangements, with a few spectacular flowers rising from them. It's important, apparently, to have table arrangements that are either very low so that you can see over them to the people on the other side of the table, or very high, so that you can see under them. Ana and Mum have discussed the wedding dress and the posies; they must be coordinated. Their cousin's two little girls will be enlisted as bridesmaids. Sophie is going to be the principal bridesmaid. There will be rose-petal confetti, both more classy and more ecologically sound. Ana's favourite flower is the orchid, which is good news, because the flower guru believes that orchids are very versatile. Would you believe she even submerges them in water in a tall glass vase? But it's early days: nothing's set in stone yet.

He gets out of bed carefully and goes down to the kitchen. He rings Ju-Ju from his mobile.

'Hi, Ju-Ju.'

'What time is it with you?'

'Late. I've been out with Mum and Sophie and Ana.'

'Was it fun?'

'A little scary. Wedding talk.'

'Uh-oh. Did you ring for a particular reason, Charlie?'

'No, just to see if you were OK.'

'I'm fine, Charlie. Are you good at keeping secrets?'

'Yes, of course. Do you think I have been blabbing?'

'I had a visit from a *Times* journalist, Lloyd Hirschman. He says that he has evidence that the crime never happened. The window, Charlie, was not stolen.'

'It was stolen.'

'Apparently not. The agent in charge of art-theft investigation when they did the deal with Agnello, the plea-bargaining, encouraged him to say the window was stolen. In fact a relation of the family, the Stimhouse family, had taken it out of the cemetery years before and stored it in his garage. His daughter sold it to Agnello for five thousand dollars.'

'How did it come to light?'

'It seems the relative tried to get a cut of the money from Agnello when she read about the case; he wouldn't give her any. Her local police weren't interested, so she contacted the *Times*, who investigated for six months. The agent has admitted it to them, saying he was under pressure to deliver results. He needed promotion.'

'Why didn't you call me?'

'Charlie, Hirschman only left an hour ago. I've been longing to call, but I didn't want to disturb you. I thought you would be tucked up with Ana.'

'Why does everybody think I'm always tucked up with Ana?'

'Because she's a glamour-puss. Why did you really call me, Charlie?'

'No reason. Nothing special. I miss you. I enjoyed our trip. What are you going to do? This is incredible.'

'I don't know. I'm totally confused. Keep it to yourself, please. The worst thing would be to find out it's all nonsense or just some rumour. Can we speak in the morning?'

'Sure, and I'm coming to the airport for you on Sunday.'

'Night-night, little bro.'

When he creeps back to bed, Ana wakes and says, 'We love you, Carlito.'

At first he thinks she must be speaking for Ju-Ju too, but then he realises that she is speaking for the unborn baby. She wants to make love. He tries not to think of his sister's pale body on the mattress island.

Chapter Twenty-Four

They changed the partnership deeds. In a room, the new people got together with a lawyer and re-wrote the deeds, so that partners of twenty years' standing, like me, were now partners of a lesser entity, which had no entitlement in the new organisation. And to make sure that I would never get to court, to make sure that Simon Simpson-Gore had his villa and his yacht and his vineyard with his name on the bottles of paint-stripper that it produced, they forced Jo to lie about me. It was immoral and unethical.

If those words *immoral* and *unethical* have any absolute meaning, which Professor Williams doubts.

His cheeks are burning. His chest is painful. His lungs feel as though they have been scoured. They thought that happiness, particularly their own, could be served by cutting out my entitlement. My mistake – it's taken me years to work this out – was to imagine that the ethical issue was the main thing: not so, it was simply a pragmatic negotiation. I could have got a very big payout, by deploying the argument of utilitarianism: Look, chaps, I can see the way this is going. Let's say I could be very helpful, everyone will be a lot happier, but I need to see the way ahead more clearly, financially speaking.

Instead he jumped on the high horse of principle, which proved to be knackered. They were sharper than he was; they knew that you can fight legal battles endlessly without risk of disgrace, but you cannot hold out against an affidavit that says that you forced yourself on an innocent young girl who had no means of resisting. Could you say, Look, hold on, she had some pretty racy sexual tricks, which I had never even heard of? You couldn't, because however much Simpson-Gore and chums were twisting the truth, they were paragons compared with an exploiter of young, vulnerable women. They could tear up the partnership deeds and flush them down the pine-scented toilet and argue for years that the legal advice, given in chambers, was that the new entity, registered in Grand Cayman, superseded the older, archaic partnership. But you couldn't admit that you had had sex on your desk (and elsewhere) with a woman who was supposed to be in your pastoral care in some sense. Nor could you risk Daphne finding out.

When Charlie rang last night, he asked me how many sons I have. What did he mean? He said Ju-Ju was coming to live with us.

Of course, if it's true that if a man stays alive he will be doing something, rather than something else.

I must stay alive. I must forget all about Fox and Jewell, and Jo, and Clem's Vietnamese tart, and stay alive.

I am hot. I need air.

He gets out of bed and walks out of the back gate towards the church. It's raining, but it's the fine sea-mist rain, soft on his fiery cheeks and making little impression on the flannel dressing gown with the wide vertical stripes in royal blue and crimson.

I am an exotic zebra.

The golf course, stretching up past the dreaded stream and Bray Hill, is blurred by the rain, so that it is anonymous and apparently endless, like the tundra. On a holiday in Sweden he had gone walking in a mist and found that after a few miles every clump of trees, every little rounded lake, seemed to be repeated endlessly. A fortuitous Lapp on a quad bike showed him the way back to the lodge.

Professor Williams gives an example of a man called Jim who finds himself in the central square of a small South American town. Twenty Indians are bound and tied. The commandant, who has crushed the Indian rebellion, suggests that Jim, an honoured foreigner, should kill one of them. If he does this, the others will be allowed to go free. If he does not, they will all be killed, as planned. Jim has a problem: the greater good demands that he kill one man, but this would rob him of all that makes life worthwhile. Buoyed up with this interesting conundrum – I have a bit of a talent for philosophy – Charles approaches the church. He shelters under the lychgate as it's coming down more strongly.

In Jim's shoes I would have asked the Indians who they nominated, or if they would all rather die together.

He is about to have a pee, when he hears a voice.

'Charles.'

'Hello, Frances.'

'What are you doing? You're soaked.'

'I was a bit hot.'

'Let's get you home.'

He knows from the fact that she is using the first person plural that she thinks he's in need of help. So many women offering help and counselling and caring. What they don't realise is that they are mainly helping themselves, finding – they believe – the moral centre and stationing themselves there. She has him by the arm, and he realises how absurd, even pathetic, he must look in his damp – actually sodden – dressing gown. She is armoured against the rain in her long waxed coat and her head is protected by an Australian rain hat. The rain, now granular, bounces off it. Driza-Bone. She's carrying a plastic bucket. He tries to remember where he was going on his moral/ethical ramble.

My face is hot, but the rest of me is freezing. Morality, according to the Professor, entails a certain amount of luck: Jim the wandering gringo was unlucky. Ju-Ju was obviously unlucky. The rest of us live our lives in a penumbra of moral ambiguity.

'You've got a fever,' says Frances.

Back in the house she wraps him in towels, runs the bath and orders him to get in it while she calls the doctor.

In the bath he is heating up fast, just like those lobsters that made a run for it when they tried the heat-them-up-gently-they-don't-feel-a-thing method of execution. He laughs. The lobsters bounded out of the pot and scampered stiff and sliding and furious, creaking like knights in armour, across the stove before plunging to the floor. There's a Woody Allen movie where something like this happens. He can't remember the name of it.

Instead of kindly Dr Williams, the ambulance arrives just as he's thinking of eating some more of Frances's cake, to feed a fever. Frances rides in the back with him, and a woman in green sits next to him holding a drip.

I must really be ill.

And as he sinks like a weak winter sun below the horizon, he thinks: I should have gone to see Ju-Ju in America. He feels no fear, nor the reported onset of deep peace. I'm dying, he thinks, matter-of-factly.

But he doesn't die. When he wakes – if he's been asleep – he sees Daphne by his bed. For some time he lies absolutely still. He watches her; he seems to be able to do this without opening his eyes. She is reading a magazine, with a picture of a bride on the cover. In these drab surroundings, the magazine cover radiates wealth, prosperity and a peach-coloured happiness. The bride is holding her posy. Daphne's lips move, not slavishly, but in broad sympathy with the words. His arm is attached to a white plank and a drip is taped to the vulnerable underside of his forearm. It's an area of the body that doesn't come into play much, mostly concealed from view, like the plumbing behind the bath. But it's obviously the way in for these doctors. As a boy he once had blood poisoning from swinging on a lamp-post; the rusted paint entered through this unprotected area. He has two plastic tubes leading to his nose, where something is attached. His exposed veins are blue and apprehensive.

He wonders how long Daphne has been sitting by his bedside, on the traditional devoted-spouse model. Her reading glasses have pinpricks of a medical green reflection in them as she reads, but he can't work out what it is they are reflecting.

'Hello, Daphne.'

'Charles. Oh, Charles. How are you?'

'I don't know. I don't seem to be entirely present.'

'You've been asleep for fifteen hours. You've got pneumonia.'

'My goodness.'

'Yes, you had a fantastically high temperature but they've managed to bring it down. Frances found you wandering, delirious.'

'I'm so sorry. You were busy in London.'

'I came down last night. You've got to stay here for a few days, but you're going to be fine.'

'Is Ju-Ju home yet?'

'No, darling. She comes back tomorrow. Charlie's going to get her from the airport and then she'll be another day or two in London.'

'I thought I was going to die.'

'You're not the only one.'

'One day before my daughter came home.'

'Charlie says you are always trying to create a diversion.'

'Ah, Charlie. The man of the moment.'

'He has been truly wonderful with Ju.'

But he can't concentrate on this conversation. He falls asleep again, and when he wakes Daphne has gone. She has left his spare dressing gown and some fresh pyjamas. At the moment he is wearing a hospital shift, which leaves his bottom exposed to draughts when he turns. He tries to get out of bed, but then he realises he is attached to the plank and by the nose to some apparatus. He rings a bell, and a nurse arrives. She pulls the curtains around his bed, and helps him dress in his fresh pyjamas. When he asks if he can go to the bathroom, she brings a bedpan. She takes it away again when he's done, and he feels dispirited by his weakness.

He hasn't even got enough energy to look at the wedding magazine, which Daphne, typically, has left carelessly. The nurse brings him some tea, and he sleeps. He dreams of being resurrected. It's pretty straightforward: he's dead one minute and raised up the next. When he wakes again – he seems to be hovering stateless on the border between wakefulness and sleep – he sees that there is probably less difference between being alive and being dead than you imagine. A doctor comes in to see him. The V of his scrubs exposes some tightly coiled black hairs.

My chest hairs are sparse, now growing long and grey around the nipples.

The doctor checks the charts: he is apparently having antibiotics by drip.

'How am I?'

'You're doing fine. I need to take a blood sample.'

The doctor sits next to him on the bed, quickly finds one of his abused veins, and slips the needle in. The blood he draws seems dark.

'My wife says I nearly died.'

The doctor looks at the charts.

'I don't think so. Anyway, your temperature is right down now.'

He picks up *Martha Stewart's Weddings*.

'Who's getting married?'

'My daughter.'

'That's nice.'

He's run out of small talk. He leaves, having made his mark on the notes. It must be difficult to be upbeat all the time.

It's my son, Charles remembers too late. I wonder if I smell. I should have a shower before Ju-Ju comes home. I must ask Daphne not to bring her here. I must be up and about to greet her; families are personal alliances, but shifting.

With his own mother and father and brother there was a constant renegotiation of the terms. You never picked up where you left off. His father always seemed to be surprised when he came home for the holidays, as though he hadn't been in his thoughts for ten weeks.

Ju-Ju and Charlie and Sophie have never been out of my thoughts. I have been selfish and foolish, but if anybody asked I could honestly say that I have never passed a single day without thinking about them. Not in relation to myself, but hoping that they would be happy. It hasn't quite worked out, but now we are all going to be together again.

It's probably the effect of the drugs, but he feels warmly affectionate towards his absent children.

But even drugged and only half-conscious he was irritated by Daphne, sitting reading the wedding magazine.

Who am I to judge? I'm nobody, a failed accountant with antique dealer's hair, who couldn't stand by his own daughter when she needed him. In a way it would be better if I wasn't aware of my shifting standards, if I was an out-and-out shit like Simon Simpson-Gore. I have values, but they seem to be impermanent. I'm not sure I believe in them. If, like the Professor, I had studied philosophy instead of bean-counting, I might have understood things better. Is there anything I should, ought, to do? *It is very unclear that we can in fact give the man who asks it a reason.* But there are things, Professor, like Ju-Ju wanting to walk with me on the coast path, which may mean nothing in the absolute, philosophical sense, but which mean everything in reality. And how do you explain the fact that, like the piece of grit in the oyster shell, but without the prospect of producing a pearl, Daphne has been working on me, causing me, for thirty-six years, to feel a real discontent with the life I have led. That's a reality. I do need reasons. What's wrong with me? Why do I feel this impatience, even when she's innocently reading a magazine? And why do I resent the fact that she's brought me clean pyjamas and a clean dressing gown?

She doesn't have the family face. It's a strange thing: you meet someone, you marry and have children, but that person is never, at a deep level, your family. The family face is yourself, made new. Your children are you in a way your wife can never be.

He sees a bunch of flowers in a vase. How long have they been there? They are blue, perhaps irises, loosely tied and mixed with deep-green foliage and some apple blossom.

Chapter Twenty-Five

T he plane is rising into the sky, almost directly above the scene of the crime. Where, says Lloyd Hirschman, no crime took place. The grid system of roads and city blocks, outlined in lights, runs to the soft-edged bays and swamps, so that it looks as though the town-planners' charts have been torn carelessly. Hirschman is a serious person. He is motivated by his fierce belief that in a wilderness of hicks and conmen and religious hypocrites, New York and the *New York Times* represent the last redoubt of American tolerance and worldly understanding. Many New Yorkers share this belief.

The plane swings north out over the tip of Long Island where she once attended George Plimpton's fireworks party, and heads for Labrador. All transatlantic planes pass Labrador, which is a lot further east than you would guess.

Hirschman explained to her that the fourth and fifth amendments on due process did not apply, according to the conservative judges of the Supreme Court down in DC, to the investigative process, only to the trial itself. This has meant, and it is a particular obsession of his, that there is a growing tendency on the part of investigators to manufacture evidence, because, unless they do so, almost every case that relies on witness statements and identification by eye-witnesses and confessions under interrogation can be challenged successfully on the grounds of due process. So prosecutors, and that includes Federal prosecutors, come to court more and more often with plea-bargains – I'm guilty, but making a deal

– and this is unbreakable police evidence. In the case of Mr Agnello, although he may have given the impression that the window was stolen, it was not. But when he was arrested on another, relatively minor charge, he decided to bargain. It now turns out that the FBI investigator assigned to the case discovered almost immediately that the window was not stolen, but he saw that, with Agnello's plea-bargain, he had an open and shut case. The clear-up rate of art theft is not good, and he would achieve praise and promotion. Two bumps, in fact.

She and Hirschman sat on the floor. He had a tape-recorder with him, but for the moment he did not ask if he could turn it on.

'I don't need to tell you, Ms Judd, that if the window was not stolen there was no crime.'

'But there was punishment.'

Hirschman has a tight, greying beard. He has distinct fleshy pouches to protect his eyeballs: you feel they could shut effectively. It's a Jewish look that lends him gravity, wisdom acquired painfully over centuries.

'I can't really imagine how you feel.'

'This was my apartment. It is sold. I am bankrupt.'

'It's a terrible miscarriage and a human tragedy.'

He looks at his notes.

'What do you want me to do?' she asked.

'Six months before you were released, I knew that this case stank. But I had to stand it up. We couldn't say anything to anybody until we had it all completely watertight. I thought of you in jail. I wanted to write to you, but I resisted. There is another issue here, maybe even bigger than the miscarriage, and that is the trustworthiness of great government agencies. We are going to break the story soon, probably within a couple of months, but in the meanwhile I don't think you should talk to anybody else. You should maybe take a little time out to think through the implications. The appeal process, the pardon, any civil action you may take – it's all going to be stressful and time-consuming. There may be some attempt to say, OK, she got off on a technicality, but she was still prepared to commit a crime. This smear would be part of the bargaining process, which I guess will begin immediately. Looking at your testimony, I don't think you ever said you knew the window was stolen.'

'No, I didn't. But, as you know, plenty of these kinds of windows have been stolen. A hundred or more from Woodlawn alone, so it would have been foolish to assume that it was legitimate, unless it came from a private house, which it didn't. Can I ask you something? My career has gone, my family has been damaged, friends have suffered, and I have spent two years in jail. What's that worth in terms of dollars?'

'It would be huge. Twenty, thirty million, maybe more.'

'How many weeks before you go to print?'

'Ten minimum. The legal department needs time.'

'Will you wait until I am ready? In return I promise not to speak to anybody, or go into print.'

'No book deals, no leaks?'

'Nothing.'

'We want your side of the story, exclusively, and of course we will pay.'

'I'll think about it.'

'Can we meet tomorrow for some detailed discussions?'

'No. I'm sorry, we can't. I am deeply grateful to you, but I must get home and see my family. My brother's getting married, and then, after that, you can come and see me. Have you ever been to Cornwall?'

'I can't say as I have. It's down the bottom there somewhere, isn't it?'

'Yes.'

'Ms Judd, you should give us your lawyer's details, and we will send him or her all the material. Not too long from now everything will be in the public record anyway. Including our transcript of the agent's confession. Can we talk now, just in general, over dinner?'

'All right.'

'I know a great little Italian place not far from here.'

＊　　＊　　＊

She finds the sense of being absolutely nowhere liberating. There's nothing outside the windows, except the poignant signalling into the void of the light on the wing. The plane itself is free of associations; it is the product of industrial design, without art or individuality. Its blandness is deliberate: look, this is just a thing that functions efficiently. It doesn't invite meditations on death or terrorism or catastrophic mechanical failure or the human predicament. *Beef or chicken?* is about as philosophical as it gets.

Going home. Three and a half years have gone by; for nearly two of those I was in jail. Now Hirschman is telling me I did not commit a crime.

This knowledge fits perfectly with her sense at the time that there was no crime and that the narrative had somehow changed. Yet in prison she had acknowledged her crime fully. It hadn't been difficult: it required no conversion or repentance, simply an acceptance of the inescapable, that the law was within its rights to lock her up. And this is the problem: the fact that the window was not stolen does not mean that there was no crime. And she sees another thing: if Davis had stood by her, she would have been acknowledging that she knew the window was stolen, because that's what a defence of the heart entailed. Up here in the void, nothing is certain.

If I didn't commit a crime, not the one I was charged with anyway, it is still true that Davis betrayed me. Richie, it seems, didn't commit a crime either, but I did betray him. And if I didn't commit a crime, my family have certainly been betrayed. There seems to be no end to the possible syllogisms.

But, by the time the fish-shaped pretzels arrive, she has hardened her heart: a crime against me, a crime of cruel and unusual punishment, was committed on the false testimony of a government agent. As Hirschman says, this is the big issue, and justification enough for accepting my innocence.

She mentioned Cornwall to Hirschman as if it was home. It was never home, but it has a precious memory: teenage sexual desire. The great revelation, the discovery of her own humanity, happened in Cornwall.

And I think that art and sexual awakening are in some ways the same thing, the world made new.

Cornwall wasn't home, it was an escape. Most years they rented a house a little higher up the lane for four weeks at a time. It belonged to an old lady who, until she died, left for Australia to stay with her daughter every summer. The house was full of her knick-knacks and ill-assorted furniture, including a heavy dining-room suite from Maples and collections of butterflies and seashells and Coronation mugs. There was a wooden rack for drying clothes, which hung in the kitchen and could be lowered with a rope. The damp clothes hung up there above the Aga like bunting. There was no washing machine for years.

She remembers her mother: 'Why are we less comfortable here than at home, Charles?'

'Because, unless you are roughing it, you aren't really on holiday. That's the English way. That's what made us what we are today.'

Home was the thin house in Islington, really just a rectangular box of brick, with some Georgian fireplaces and cornices and fancy door furniture. For her parents' friends, the Georgian age seems to have been the high-water mark of civilisation. All the barristers and accountants and City folk favoured the Georgian; it was clean and upstanding. Over every fireplace was a gilt mirror; in every hallway an umbrella stand; in every study an engraving of an Oxford or Cambridge college; on every mantelpiece embossed, dutiful invitations; and on either side of them a pair of brass candlesticks. But the house of a friend from school had roughly painted walls, and huge colourful canvases by Howard Hodgkin and Bridget Riley and Frank Auerbach and bare floorboards and open fires; when she saw it, it was as if she had known all along how things were supposed to be. She felt a little guilt at her disloyalty.

Chicken and saffron rice, a mixed bean salad and miniature summer pudding with new season's raspberries are put in front of her.

I may be the only person on the whole plane who thinks this is outstandingly fine fare for a Saturday.

On a Saturday night at Loon Lake they would be having goulash with sticky macaroni and jello. Some of the women complained that once they were given two desserts; that was before the budget cuts. Most of them were obsessed with meals. She hopes never to hear the word 'chow' again. The Federal Government had to provide chow three times a day. Chow was one of the few things that the women were united on. The word was spoken plaintively from the outraged mad desperate mouths of her fellow prisoners.

As she sinks back, not quite sleeping, she has the sensation conveyed to her by the steady turbine hum and suppressed roaring of the plane (interrupted by the sharp choking of the lavatory being flushed) that time has been rushing since she came out. In prison time was slow. Fear made it worse in the early days: she was always waiting to be jumped or threatened and those fearful hours barely moved. But since Charlie picked her up, barely a week ago, time has been hurtling along. In a week she has travelled across New York State, she has bathed herself in rich oils, and she has, apparently, been absolved of a crime. And in some way she has been renewed. The impulse to religion is nothing to do with God: it's the urge to renew ourselves. The categories seem blurred. You need to have been in prison to see that there is less than a paper between reality and illusion. She remembers a lecture at the Courtauld about the illusion of paint on canvas. The point the lecturer, a disciple of Ernst Gombrich, was making is that what happens in our heads when we receive optical signals is itself an illusion. The ancient trick of painting was to create with crocus and egg yolk and rose madder something that fooled the brain.

It seems that in the material world there isn't as much of a distinction between the real and the imagined either. Agnello said the owl hooted. And she heard it. The cemetery where the robbery never happened had become a reality to her in those nights in prison. When she took Charlie there, it was all familiar. And this is something about America too, that your first sight of it is familiar, a country you have travelled before you ever arrived there. And maybe this is to the disadvantage of Americans, that they have never experienced other countries in this way, their own culture having prevailed.

She tries to slow herself down, to profit by these hours of nullity, by thinking of the coast path where she will walk with her father, just as she used to re-run it in Otisville and Loon Lake. She starts out at Porth Quin, and up the steep hill from the fishermen's cottages, over the stile, then swooping downwards through the meadow full of wild flowers, and onwards, past the pineapple folly on its kopje, to the narrow shaft of the old slate mine above the crashing sea, where the dog died, and through the small wooden gate to the meadow where they found the mushrooms that day, and then up, up to the top of the hill, looking down towards Epphaven and across to the Rumps. And now, because there is, as she has discovered, only a light mist settled between the real and the imagined, she is free at last. She's wearing her spotted shorts, and it's this sentimental detail that is so convincing.

> *I'm free! I'm free! The open air was warm*
> *And heavy with the scent of flowering mint*
> *And beetles waved on the bending leaves of grass*
> *And all the baking countryside was kind.*

Chapter Twenty-Six

Sophie Judd hasn't had much sleep.
She's tired after a one-night stand.

And she's nervous. The feeling is a sort of aching hunger. You long to still it in some way. It's dark outside or at least dark in that London way, the darkness not so much penetrated by the light of street-lamps and offices and passing minicabs, as suffused, a stain suspended in liquid. She's used to getting up early. But when she woke this morning she missed her mother. The consciousness of her outline, weathered into soft shapes, just through the wall, had comforted her. There is something defenceless about her mother asleep, her nose thrust upwards at a slight angle, as if to catch any passing current of air.

I'm sure that's how she saw us as children, defenceless.

She looks in a mirror. The aureole has gone from her nose; there is no reminder of the hole. The main room is graced by an arrangement of white and pink roses, a posy which her mother left for her in a glass cube. It is edged with dark-green, fan-shaped leaves, almost oriental. In this shabby room it looks like an unexpected visitor from another, more elegant world. Mum left it with a note, saying she was going back to Cornwall to see Dad who has developed pneumonia. 'Developed' is an interesting word, as though he had somehow deliberately cultivated pneumonia. Mum has childish writing: *I'm so sorry I won't be there to meet Ju-Ju. Much love, Mum. PS What do you think of this for the bridesmaids' posies, tied with red ribbon?*

Although it's Sunday, the street below is already quite busy. Ashier Fruiterers is open, with mangoes, limes and bananas lording it over the more anaemic European produce. The leather shop, which sells the kinds of lumpy leather jackets only Asian men wear, is beginning to hang out its wares on racks. Some of the jackets have inlaid red-and-white stripes, for added glamour. A van full of plants for Columbia Row has paused outside New Era Café. The minicab is ready. The driver is a serious young Bangladeshi who is studying his map: oh God, he's one of those drivers who has never been west of Commercial Street. But no, he's thoroughly prepared: time spent in reconnaissance is never wasted, he says, although he accents the word 'reconnaissance' in a novel way.

Last night she had sex with a boy she knew only slightly. They met in a bar in Islington, and somehow they both saw where this chance reunion was going. He said they had once snogged at a party when they were sixteen. Why not finish the job? OK. She was conscious of how thin she was when she took off her clothes. She could see herself from his point of view, her pale, insubstantial limbs. He was layered with fat, not much, but enough to hide any muscle or hard edges. He said she was beautiful.

In my way, I am. I have the family look, bold and slightly strange.

His name was Eddie Abbott, uncircumcised. She remembers everybody she's ever slept with, and it's quite a number, by the way they reacted to her, not by how she reacted to them. In Dan she produced a sort of desperation; with Eddie there was a simple unmediated pleasure. She felt he might have reacted the same way to eating something tasty. They are going to meet again.

'Not that a one-night stand isn't like a perfectly legitimate form of engagement in itself, Eddie, no excuses needed, but it would be nice to see you again.'

'Tomorrow?'

'Can't, my sister's coming back from the States.'

'Oh yeah, I heard about that business. Is she OK?'

'We'll see.'

'When I first met you, you had a ring in your nose. I thought it was like very daring.'

'We all go through phases, Eddie.'

She got back to the flat very late. She's only had two hours' sleep. Everyone knows about Ju-Ju: the family scandal, a jailbird for a sister. Charlie said that journalists wanted her story. And this is the strange thing, nobody blames her. Down in Cornwall they may be fretting, but up here in the Smoke, what happened was not a crime but strangely glamorous. It's as if her friends and the journalists think she was just a little unlucky. There may be some prurience too: how did a tall, slim English girl, something of an intellectual, fare in a Federal prison? These prisons are not designed for people with degrees from Oxford and the Courtauld; they are holding pens for drug traffickers and child murderers and the generally whacked. It was better in Loon Lake, but God knows what Ju-Ju went through in Otisville. That first time she visited Ju-Ju she was deeply disturbed by what she saw: Ju-Ju in orange overalls, her face unnaturally puffy, with a sac under her left eye, and her pale eyes, the family legacy, blind, blind with shock.

I thought she would kill herself. She said she was fine, she wasn't too bad, I'll be OK, don't worry, try not to worry, I've just got to get through it.

As the minicab speeds unerringly through the pre-dawn morning streets, down towards the tower of St Pancras, she remembers the leaden certainty: Ju-Ju will die here. When Eddie, smoking a Marlboro, said he had heard about Ju-Ju, she could have said, Look, Eddie, from here in jolly old ironic London, it might be a little riffle on the waters, a bit of fun, but out in the sticks there is a hell where the prisoners keep drugs up their rectums and beat up the weak and gang rape the defenceless, and that's where my sister spent one whole year.

You heard nothing, Eduardo.

Ju-Ju never told her what happened to her, but in her heart

Sophie believes she knows. And it was all the fault of that piece of shit, Richie. She's shivering now, as the light of morning seeps through, like damp coming through a wall. You wouldn't be able to say when dawn broke precisely. She's shivering because she's tired, and because she's frightened of meeting Ju-Ju.

Charlie's up and ready. He has the Pavoni, the classic chrome model of course, all fired up. He gives her a croissant and a cappuccino to wake the dead.

'You look a little wasted.'

'I didn't get much sleep. No. Don't ask.'

'You're a slapper.'

'Thanks. Charlie, I'm effing nervous.'

'Don't be. She's the same person.'

'Is that like possible?'

'It's too early for philosophy. Let's hit the road.'

Now they are standing together outside Arrivals, a democratic space. Charlie holds her hand. His phone rings.

'No, Mum, not yet. Good. OK. As soon as we have her in the car. Bye. Soph, Mum says to tell you Dad's much better. He'll be home in a couple of days.'

Charlie seems to be the dependable one these days. Everything must be routed through him. He has a look of competence: he's always casually elegant, but you also have the feeling he's seeing something you don't as if he is faintly amused by his family and also by the crude simplicities of life. She waits, anxiously.

'Soph, when I went to pick her up she wouldn't come out of her cell.'

'What are you saying?'

'I just hope she's not cowering in the plane.'

Charlie's hint that Ju-Ju is unbalanced unsettles her. The flight landed nearly an hour ago.

'What are we going to do, Charlie?'

'We'll give it a few more minutes.'

Then she sees Ju-Ju, her beloved sister, towing a large suitcase and carrying a small black rucksack on her back. She runs – she can't stop herself – pushing through a group of Pakistanis who are standing round large, over-stuffed cardboard boxes. She runs right around the crush barrier and seizes Ju-Ju. She's sobbing. Ju-Ju holds her very close. She's crying too. Their sobs are resonating in the other's body.

'Oh Ju-Ju, thank God you're back. Welcome home, Ju.'

'Sophie, Sophie, little Sophie.'

She strokes Sophie's hair. Charlie comes over and takes them both in his arms. He's smiling; he's reassuring. Ju-Ju is sombrely dressed, in a long straight skirt and a black cashmere roll-neck. On her feet she has white sneakers.

'Stop sniffing, girls. Let's go.'

A photographer appears and takes a picture of them. And then there are five photographers, from nowhere.

'Let's go,' says Charlie.

A reporter pushes his microphone towards Ju-Ju.

'What's it like to be home?'

'It's wonderful, thank you.'

Her face is very pale; she has unmistakably aged and fined down, but she has a kind of presence. How can you say this of your own sister: she has the look of someone made in heaven?

The photographers follow them all the way to the car, snapping away. A man with a television camera intercepts them. He films them getting into the car.

'We were worried about you, you took so long to come out.'

'My baggage was late, nothing more dramatic.'

She turns to the back seat.

'How are you, little Sophie? I used to like the nose ring, by the way.'

'I took it out for you, Ju.'

'For me? Why?'

'Yes. I didn't want them to think we were all flaky. Imagine if the snappers had got a picture of it.'

'That's so sweet of you. You look just great. And Charlie here has been a wonder boy.'

Don't try too hard, Ju-Ju; let us shoulder some of the burden. Even if the burden is unimaginable.

'Here, speak to Mum. Just press go.'

'Hello, Mum. Yes. Charlie and Sophie. Oh, and a small gang of photographers. God knows. Yes. I'm feeling better by the minute. I slept a bit on the plane. Now, we're in the car. How's Dad? Oh, OK. Probably Tuesday or Wednesday. I have to have some meetings. Flowers? Sure. Sounds fun. No, Charlie's place. No. I'm going to meet her now. It's wonderful to be back. No, I'm sorry too, but don't worry, we'll have plenty of time.'

Sophie knows that you can piece together the conversation very easily when her mother is on the other end. Everything that interests her is related to the familiar. That's what many women seem to do, try to bring a domestic scale to events. When Dad opens *The Times* in the morning he immediately sees himself in relation to the world; from Cornwall he is in some way vital to the Palestinian peace process or the election of a new leader of the Labour Party. Mum heads straight for the family, social or health sections: she's equipping herself for survival.

'What did she say?' asks Charlie.

'Dad's coming out tomorrow or Tuesday. He's been more ill than he realises. And she wondered if I had met Ana.'

Sophie knows all this already.

'Ana's dying to meet you,' says Charlie.

'I can't wait.'

'She's not like what you would call an early-riser. I hope she's up.'

'What did Mum say about flowers? What was that about?'

'She wants me to help with the flowers for the wedding.'

'Me too. Now you're back, I'll like be an afterthought, a dogsbody, a gopher.'

'I don't think so. When is the wedding, Charlie?'

'In about a month. Mum's got two possible dates out of the vicar.'

'And Ana?'

'Whatever, is what she said when I asked her. Time is elastic for Ana. But Mum thinks she shouldn't have too big a bump. "It is Cornwall, not Soho," she said.'

'And Dad, Soph? I don't mean just his fall in the stream, but, you know, my coming back?'

'He's been hard to read. But he's been counting the days.'

Counting the days. Has he been counting the days? The other night, lying not far from her, Mum said she wasn't sure he hadn't tried to drown himself.

'Nobody could drown themself in a foot of water, except Ophelia perhaps. All he would have to do is like step off the cliff path at Doyden if he wanted to kill himself. He's in a strange mood.'

'How do you mean?'

'I think he thinks he's disintegrating. He just doesn't seem able to decide what's what. What's real and so on. The problem is that he thinks he let Ju-Ju down.'

'He did.'

'Do you think so?'

'Absolutely. And I don't forgive him.'

Sophie was startled. Mum's body was hunched under the cover of darkness.

Eddie sends her a text: *Loveya. Eduardo.* Charlie and Ju-Ju are talking quietly. They always had an intimacy, and the past week has probably made them closer. Everyone always wants to be close to Ju-Ju, even to this slightly worn, faded version of her sister. She looks a little as if she's been freed from a cult, smiling rather pointlessly, nodding encouragement, as though making a presentation before a group of fellow escapees. But still she has this presence.

And now Eddie says he loves me. Or perhaps he's being youthful and ironic; too long with Dan has cut me off from my peers. That's what Dad had tried to tell me the other night.

'I'm going to work at the Blue Banana,' she says suddenly.

'Where's that?'

'Polzeath. It's a funky, OK, moderately funky, new restaurant. I'm going to chill this summer. I'm going to be a waitress.'

'Do you think I'm too old? I'm looking for work,' says Ju-Ju.

'No, Ju, just like perhaps a tad over-qualified.'

'What are you going to do after that?'

'I've applied for university.'

'Which ones?'

'A few.'

'Why didn't you tell me?' says Charlie.

'Charlie, I like so don't think it's going to happen. I haven't got any A levels.'

'So why did you blab to Ju-Ju?'

'Because Ju-Ju needs to know. She's an intellectual, not a sock vendor.'

'It's true. I'm just a sock vendor. I know nothing.'

She doesn't tell them that she's applied for Oxford, and has been asked to write a long essay on her reading. She's also applied to Sussex where they have asked her to sit a special test for those over twenty-one who have no qualifications.

I need more time. I need to read, to be told what to read. I believe there is some truth in literature.

By the time they have pulled up outside Charlie's place, she feels that a sort of normalcy has crept over them again, as though nothing is proof against family habits.

Ana opens the door. She has confounded Charlie's doubts by being dressed and fully made up, and wearing a short-sleeved blouse, Capri pants and flat black pumps. She's also wearing a pale-pink Hermès scarf over her hair, tied under the chin in the Audrey Hepburn look. She seizes Ju-Ju, who seems to vanish for a moment.

'Come in, come in. Charlie, will you take your sister's bags to her room. Sophie darling, will you squeeze some oranges. Sorry, my hair's like such a mess under this.'

Charlie winks at Sophie. If Ana is intimidated by being en-circled, she shows no sign of it. The occasion demands eggs Benedict, bloody Marys, muffins, fruit and pastries. In her *Roman Holiday* outfit she loads up the table. Sophie is her willing assistant, and Charlie makes coffee in his Pavoni with loud hissing and clouds of steam: toys for boys. Ju-Ju is not allowed to help, as though she has been ill. She sits at the table, the centre of attention, but at the same time looking, Sophie thinks, lonely.

'How does it feel to be pitched into this?' Ana asks as she spoons thick hollandaise on to the eggs.

'Wonderful. Truly wonderful.'

But she looks miserable and Sophie feels rich emotion, almost like indigestion, welling deep down in her chest.

'Come, Ju,' says Charlie. 'You are home.'

'I'm fine. Trust me, I'm happy really. In fact I am overcome.'

Charlie gives her some orange juice and puts his arm around her. Sophie watches Ana, who is – just for a moment – cut adrift.

Families are like sea anemones, quick to close.

Chapter Twenty-Seven

T he young doctor says there is some cause for concern. Sister reported a little blood in his urine. Nothing is certain, but some more tests should be done. The bloods he took show raised PSA. He's made an appointment with urology.

'My daughter's coming home soon.'

'She's the one who is getting married?'

'It's my son. I can't do the tests for a bit.'

'You should take them right away. Now, sister's prepared all your pills. You must take the antibiotics right to the end, and you mustn't go outside or get cold.'

'I'm not going to die immediately, am I?'

'Raised PSA levels are very common in men of your age. We just want to be sure it's nothing serious. Have you been having trouble passing water?'

'A little. I find it easier to pee outdoors. Is that a bad thing?'

'It depends what you are peeing on. Look, most men, more than sixty per cent, will experience some difficulty in that department in later life. Don't worry about it. I've got to go and see some sick people.'

'Doctor, one thing, don't tell my wife about the tests. I'll tell her after the wedding.'

'I won't. I would like you to come in in the morning, if possible at nine.'

Charles thinks he looks tired. He's been on duty for three days, although he must sleep sometimes. And being the bearer of bad news must be depressing: daily confirmation that life can be revoked casually. Most of us are able to forget about mortality most of the time, but these young doctors – boys, just like Charlie – have to face it every day. Does it put a blight on their friendships, their families, their girlfriends? Do they look at them and see signs of death?

Charles is sitting in the visitor's chair, which is covered with easy-wipe green dimpled plastic. He's dressed in the clothes she brought him yesterday. He has a few boxes of pills, antibiotics, and his toilet bag ready. His pyjamas and dressing gown are in a bag with Bodmin NHS Trust Hospital written on it, and someone has wrapped the flowers in paper.

'Are you ready?'

'I have been ready for twenty minutes.'

'Sorry, I had to do some shopping.'

Charles stands up. He moves a little too quickly, probably to demonstrate that he's fine, and he has to pause for a moment and hold on to the table on wheels that supports the meals above the bed. She gathers his things.

'You look so much better this morning.'

'I'm completely recovered. I'm as right as rain.'

He does the twist for a moment, with his right heel on the ground and his hands pumping: '"Let's twist again, like we did last summer . . ."'

'You are an ass.'

When she finds the car, he insists on driving.

'You don't have to prove anything, Charles.'

'I'm not. I would just like to drive, comme toujours.'

She glances at him as he drives. Unlike Clem, who sees driving as a chance to demonstrate his masculinity – admittedly of a rather outmoded sort – Charles drives carefully, leaning forward as if he's expecting a tractor or a badger to emerge suddenly from the hedgerows. His hair flaps forward.

'I love this view,' he says as they approach the old stone bridge and the estuary comes into sight.

'You always say that.'

'That's because I realise I love it every time I see it.'

'Ju-Ju and Sophie are both coming down. Sophie's going to work at the Blue Banana. She's going for an interview.'

'They will probably only want to see her tummy-button.'

The tide is in, so that there's a stream of mercury, like the mercury dentists used to give you in phials, running down through the sedge to the estuary itself, where it broadens out. Swans are cruising pensively: you never see them feeding except when people throw bread into the water.

'Charles, Ju-Ju is coming home tomorrow.'

'So you said.'

'How do you feel?'

'Are you speaking medically?'

'No, about Ju-Ju.'

'How should I feel?'

'I don't know. I just thought you would say something. That you're pleased or something.'

He doesn't reply. His face is inclined slightly away from her so that he appears to be looking at the road with his left eye leading, like someone aiming a shotgun. He hasn't mentioned her flowers. His one visible ear is leathery; he seems to be putting on skin. By the time they pull in at the house, the tops of his cheeks have become a russet colour.

'Into bed with you.'

He climbs into his bed and subsides backwards. He sighs.

'I don't think I'm quite as well as I thought I was. It comes in waves.'

'You need to rest.'

'I want to go to the station to meet Ju-Ju.'

'We'll see how you feel in the morning.'

'All right.'

'I'll get you some tea. And a piece of Frances's cake.'

'Daphne?'

'Yes?'

She pauses by the door. She feels like those women in those

forties films, who always pause at the door for bad news, looking back over their shoulders.

'Daphne, I know I've let Ju-Ju down. I can't justify it. I can't even explain it.'

'Don't fret yourself.'

She wonders why she used that phrase. Her mother used it sometimes; the ponies were often thought to be fretting.

'Don't worry, darling. This is a time to celebrate,' she says.

'I just hope she forgives me.'

As she brings up the tea, she hears him scuffling about. He has a large jar of coins and he is sorting them into piles by nationality.

'There's quite a bit of money here. We should take it to the bank.'

'Not now, darling. You've got to take an antibiotic with the tea.'

He swallows the pill.

'I'd better go,' she says. 'I've a lot to do.'

'Don't go. Sit on the bed for a while.'

She sees that he is troubled.

'I know you're concerned about Ju-Ju, Charles. I'm sorry if I was bullying you.'

He looks at her. His high colour, his lifeless hair, his greying teeth, his congesting skin don't quite disguise the young man he was. He was a magnificent specimen. Her mother tried to warn her: men like him are too attractive to women, they can't help themselves. It was just about the only thing her mother said to her that was true: he couldn't help himself. Although he is diminished, she can see the bold, amused look embedded in the features, like those insects in amber brooches that were once popular.

'When we're settled, Charles, let's take a trip to Kenya or go on a cruise. I've got a little money tucked away.'

'All right.'

'Now sleep and I'll bring you up some supper. What would you like?'

'Anything except mackerel.'

'Charles, I think Ju-Ju understands.'

Even as she says it she knows, with familiar dread, that she has gone too far.

'Do you think so?'

'Yes.'

'What does she understand?'

'She understands that it wasn't easy for you because you loved her too much.'

'Is that the official line now?'

'Shall we have scrambled eggs?'

He doesn't answer.

'Rest if you can,' she says. 'I'll bring up supper at seven.'

'You know the problem with you, you reduce every fucking thing to some banal platitude.'

He picks up the book which, for some reason, he was hiding in the shed for months and now has chemical stains on it as a result.

In the morning he gets up very early. He dresses carefully – I can't afford to be seen *al fresco* in my pyjamas – and leaves the house as quickly as he can, causing a panic on the rabbit prairie. He walks up the lane to the public phone. He phones Johnny's Taxi.

'Whirr, you're up early, Mr Judd.'

'Yes, I have to go into the hospital in Bodmin.'

'Right away?'

'Yes please, Johnny. I'm at the top of the lane.'

He hides behind the stone wall of a tumbledown farm, now a mysterious boneyard of water tanks and iron wheels, until he sees the taxi. There's something endearing about the clapped-out car, bucketing and swaying towards him.

'Morning, Mr Judd. I'm still having trouble with the suspension.'

'I hear that.'

'It's a bugger.'

They lurch away.

'Mr Judd, you're a bit of a financial whizz, I was wondering –'

'Past tense.'

'I'm not sure I really believe you, Mr Judd. I was wondering if you would advise me on investments? My wife's mother has left her some money. Eight hundred pound. What are equities? Are they good?'

'I wouldn't advise anybody. But if you want to invest the money ask the bank about an ISA.'

'I don't have a bank account.'

'You can go into any bank.'

'I've heard about them icers. Are they tax free, them icers?'

Charles can't concentrate on what he's saying.

'Johnny, I don't know much about investments, I was mainly concerned with tax. For big companies.'

They dip and sway and clank towards the hospital.

'I shouldn't be more than forty minutes, Johnny.'

'Right-o. Icers are the idea, are they?'

'They may be.'

When they arrive at the hospital, Johnny struggles out to open the door.

'I'll be right here, Mr Judd. I'm not going anywhere.'

Daphne wakes, and takes a cup of tea to his room. He's not there. She finds his dressing gown and pyjamas lying on the floor. He must have gone for a walk, against express orders. Mind you, she's up late. She lays the table for breakfast. The good thing is, he must be feeling better. She drinks her tea. Half an hour later Charles comes in.

'Where have you been?'

'I went for a walk. I felt I had to take a little exercise.'

'You aren't supposed to. And you didn't take a coat.'

'It's lovely out.'

'I've made breakfast.'

'I'm starving,' he says, but he doesn't eat much.

'I've decided we should have a marquee, out there, Charles.'

'A marquee?'

She thinks they should do things properly and Stella says marquees offer great scope for decoration.

'Ana and Charlie want you to say a few words.'

'Daphne, why do you think Ju-Ju did it?'

'Something went on with Richie. He must have had some hold over her. But we have to put it behind us. I know you think it's superficial, but I think we have to do it properly. That's why we're having a marquee.'

In an hour or so, Ju-Ju is leaving Paddington. Charles hasn't quite taken it in.

'Charles, I've drawn up a list of things, who's doing what for the wedding. You're going to make a short speech, but could you also order the wine? And perhaps be in charge of the parking arrangements? Clem says he'll be your number two.'

'Parking? How many people are coming?'

'A hundred at least.'

'A hundred. Well, bugger me.'

'Charles, honestly.'

'Do we know one hundred people?'

'You have to remember that Charlie and Ana have lots of friends. Sophie has friends. We have friends and relatives, and then there are the people you have to invite.'

'And Ju-Ju?'

'Ju-Ju has friends.'

While Daphne tells him about the arrangements – she's obviously put a lot of work into this – he calms himself by thinking of Ju-Ju as a little girl in her spotted shorts. Her legs are thin, without any sign of muscle, yet when she falls behind and he waits for her she comes trotting bravely towards him, the stick legs flying out at strange angles. That's a truth for you, Professor. It's a truth at the cellular level.

'I'm ordering all the flowers from New Covent Garden wholesale, and Sophie's going to drive them down. Frances, Sophie, Ju-Ju and I are going to do them ourselves.'

Professor Williams says that the idea of a good father is problematic. We know what a father is, he says, but the rest of the proposition is entirely subjective.

'Do you think I've been a good father, Daphne?'

'Yes, I think you have.'

'I always thought I was a good father. But, as Charlie says, I have a tendency to put myself in the middle of the drama. When it came to the real test, I somehow wasn't there.'

'It's over. She's coming home.'

Is there anything I should, ought, to do? Absolutely, Williams the Prof, absolutely, boyo.

Chapter Twenty-Eight

England is unrolling outside the window of the train. Although everyone complains that it's all being concreted over, the train seems to have found a quiet, untouched back route of its own. Sophie is asleep. She's got a new boyfriend, who is tiring her out. Sophie has told her everything about Dan and commercials and drugs. She wants help with her university applications.

What should I say? I mean what have I done, like nothing, since leaving St Paul's?

They'll love you. They're dying to find interesting people. Academics suffer guilt; they live among reasonable, comfortable people. The fact that you want to come to their world will flatter them.

She's offered to help a little with the Oxford essay, just to read it, if needed.

Behind the sleeping Sophie, in the spring sunshine, are the Wiltshire Downs. There is no wildness left here, just a honeyed, aged calm. The villages and farmhouses are of warm stone. The clumps of wood are decorative only. In America, even close to big towns, there are still wild woods and in them wild bears. She and Charlie, dear Charlie, saw deer in the Catskills. In America small-town strips look as though they were laid out yesterday; they peter out into nothingness. You feel that America is still hacking out bits of wilderness for car lots and drive-ins. It's unfinished business. Here – the downs sliding by – it's as if the picture was hung on the wall years ago and it can only be lightly dusted.

Charlie's lawyer, Martha, who she remembers as a teenager and briefly as his girlfriend, took her to see another lawyer, Jeff Kulick, who explained the process of recognising a miscarriage. Both of them seemed very disappointed when she said she was not going to sue the Justice Department.

'You didn't commit a crime, that's the bottom line,' said Kulick.

'I know. But I don't want things to drag on for years. Let's just get a settlement.'

'And two years in jail? That's worth, God knows, almost anything?'

'I know this isn't legal-speak, but I thought the window was stolen. And I didn't care. I don't want huge amounts of debate and muckraking. Just strike a deal.'

'In your evidence you never said that you knew the window was stolen. Am I right?'

'That's true. I never said it, because I couldn't ultimately know. It wasn't on any register, but that's not enough.'

She instructed them formally to ask for her loss of earnings, her loss on the apartment and her legal expenses.

'That's the deal. Nothing more.'

'And your suffering?'

'I'm not going there. I don't want the family to know before I'm ready. And I don't want Charlie to know what I am asking for. OK, Martha? Not even Charlie. By the time the story comes out, Charlie will be married and we'll all be back to normal.'

'But then all hell will break loose when the *New York Times* publishes,' said Jeff.

These two found it exciting. They wanted to be in the thick of it.

'It may, but if we have a settlement, if I just make a statement in *The Times*, and if we have agreed an undisclosed settlement, the storm – if there is one – will die down. If we are involved in a long, protracted process, who knows what might come out of the woodwork? I don't want to spoil your fun, but I couldn't stand that. And the family couldn't either. You can't believe how much it's worth to me to try to end this once and for all. Now I'm going to the hairdresser.'

At the hairdresser she thought of exactly what could come out of the woodwork: Richie, prison officers with videos, Anthony Agnello going on the stand again to exercise his well-known talent for narrative; cell mates who knew the meaning of the term keester bunny. And betrayal.

Before she left New York she told Davis the story. He couldn't quite take it in.

'Davis, my brother is getting married in four weeks. Can you come to the wedding?'

'Ah'm working out. Day two. In three weeks Ah will be a new man.'

'That would be great.'

'This is one hell of a thing.'

'It's almost worse that we've been through it for nothing.'

'Do you think it was for nothing?'

'I hope not.'

And so this is life. It is arbitrary; its narrative is erratic.

I have been given a harsh understanding of the human condition. I didn't ask for it, or seek it. André Malraux said that art is a revolt against fate: *l'art est un anti-destin*. That's what I believed, but somehow fate got me by the throat anyway. Art was no help.

What she couldn't tell the eager little lawyers was that she didn't want to tempt fate again. How could you say this to Martha in her snappy Dior suit and Jeff Kulick in his abundant stripes? How could she tell them that, having seen mad people scream and weep and fuck, she believes that the law is a kind of phoney order resting on a maelstrom of disorder. It is a thin structure, which not only disguises the realities, but distorts them. It was absolutely no surprise to her to hear that some ambitious FBI hotshot had decided to create his own story because the raw material was so unreliable. And she's had a few nights now to think about what happened, the wise guy giving his authentically flavoured, Bronx Fancy Grade evidence: the owl hooted, the patrol car passed, et cetera. And still she can't quite shake off the sense, fermented in the crazed air of Otisville – that she was there.

I was going mad: I was present at a fictional heist.

The whole thing turns out to be random. She is jailed because a minor hoodlum is blackmailed; the blackmailer is uncovered because the hood won't pay off some down-at-heel relative who sold the window too cheap. What next? Who would want to find out?

There's a certain smugness about the privileged – I was one – who like the idea of law and rationality. Particularly because law and rationality were both dreamed up by the privileged. One night when there had been a terrible, pointless fight between two *clickas* she lay on her cot and understood something for the first time: rational behaviour and rationality are luxuries, what they call in New York big-ticket items.

What you see as rational depends on where you are standing.

All these things crowd towards her. She's overwhelmed by the belief that she must get hold of something solid, whatever that is. She sees herself, as the train heads into Somerset, which has an apple countenance, on the cliff path with her father. She may be investing this walk with too much hope. Freud is nonsense, but it would be a trip back to a time of happiness. It may be good for Dad too: in his late middle age his courage has failed him.

She looks at Sophie, carelessly asleep on the other side of the table. She can see something of both parents there, in Dad's large pale eyes, as if the wrong size had been fitted, and in Mum's quite small mouth, which seems always to be bunching reflexively, even now as she sleeps. It's a mouth like a baby's, always questing. She and Charlie have bigger, less neat mouths.

Sophie wakes, as people do when they are being studied.

'What do you see?'

'Hello, sweetheart. I was studying your loveliness.'

'Any conclusions?'

'Sex on a stick.'

'What's that supposed to mean?'

'You have the look of, how shall I put this delicately, of sexual contentment.'

'You and Charlie both think I'm a slut.'

'Did I say that?'

'You don't need to. Ju, do you think Charlie loves Ana?'

'He had better.'

'I get the feeling he doesn't.'

'Did he say anything?'

'No. But he gives me a look whenever the glamourpuss says something, I don't know, like something not very us. Do you know what I mean? If she mentions table gifts once more, he's going to go like bananas.'

'She's gorgeous.'

'She's too gorgeous. It's sort of tacky. Although she's got quite big ears, I noticed. Luckily.'

'She's having his baby.'

'Yes, I know that. But Charlie's like looking to you all the time for approval. He like needs you to give her the seal of approval.'

'Which I do.'

'While you were banged up, we were all waiting for you. I can't quite describe it, but like nothing seemed real. We couldn't make any decisions.'

'You had a bad time. Even you had problems.'

'Ju-Ju, my problems were nothing, zilch, compared with yours. I just couldn't go out or do anything without thinking of you, so for nearly a year I just like got off my face. That was the only way I could forget that shit-hole you were in.'

'Sophie, I'm so sorry.'

Sophie leans forward and whispers, 'Did you do it because you were in love?'

'I was in love, but it wasn't with Richie.'

'Who was it?'

'Soph, this story isn't quite finished. But yes, I was in love, and he is a writer, like you.'

'I knew it. There could be no other explanation.'

There are plenty, perhaps even limitless explanations. It is all a question of how the material is arranged. And supposing she told Sophie that the sexual excitement of sleeping with two men had been intoxicating, and supposing she told Sophie that, by holding her tight all night long, Charlie had restored her to life, or supposing she told Sophie what happened to her in the shower facility, and supposing she told Sophie what a keester bunny was? And then, supposing she surprised her with the happy ending? It's far easier to attribute it all to love.

Outside the train window there are apple trees in neat rows. Nothing like this grows in nature: these trees are tied, their height controlled for easy picking. They are just beginning to come into leaf, so that the branches and spurs are stippled with green.

The train heads down to Cornwall – Cornwall is indisputably down near the bottom – and now she sleeps for a while. When she wakes, they are crossing the Tamar.

Cornwall. The train is racing downhill now.

'Oh God, I hope it's not too much for Dad,' says Sophie.

'You're making me nervous. I'm just going to the loo.'

In the toilet she looks at herself: the light comes in a flashing chiaroscuro, which makes it difficult to form a strong opinion on how she looks. But her hair is better, fuller and more lively. She puts on a little lipstick, just enough to avoid looking tragic, and outlines her eyes lightly. What's he going to see? And what's Mum going to see?

As the train approaches Bodmin, Sophie squeezes her hand. They wait by the door and they peer out of the window when the train slows.

'There they are.'

She sees them, standing quite close together, under the bridge that crosses the platform. He's wearing a dark-blue fleece and a cap, and she, a head lower, is in a green puffa jacket. Ju-Ju and Sophie wave, but it takes a few moments before Mum sees them.

They open the door and they descend to the platform. Mum runs and hops forward to embrace her. Dad waits. She looks towards him. He comes forward. She is still in her mother's arms; her mother is crying.

'Who are you?' he says.

'No, Dad, no,' says Sophie, 'don't say that, Dad, please.'
'It's OK, Sophie. Dad, it's me. It's Ju-Ju.'
'He hasn't got over the pneumonia. Charles!'
'It's Ju-Ju, Dad.'
'Ju-Ju? You have ruined our fucking lives.'

Chapter Twenty-Nine

T hey are using the vestry as their headquarters. The plan is to have a garland over the lychgate and an arch over the door of the church. Chicken wire has been bought and measured; it will be tied into a sausage shape which will be bent around the gate. Then it will be stuffed with sphagnum moss and all the flowers that Sophie is going to bring down will be stuck into the moss. The arrangement over the door will be made with a cheap garden arch, from the garden centre in Trelights, smothered in ivy and pale moss roses, tied on with floral wire. In the church the pew ends will be simple, pink and white roses and ivy, and there will be two tall pedestals on either side of the altar; so far she hasn't decided what will be in them.

Frances is good at the planning. She's drawn up one of her charts: arrival of the flowers, names of flowers, time of arrangement, setting up time. On the right hand of the chart she has written the names of the helpers: Frances, Juliet, Sophie and her own daughter, Phillipa (Pip).

When she told Frances what had happened at the station, she laughed.

'I know I shouldn't laugh, but you have to really. He knows who she is now, I hope?'

'Yes. The doctor said the pneumonia often causes confusion. He's getting better.'

'And Ju-Ju?'

'She's a little quiet. I think it's been quite overwhelming.'

'It would be.'

'But she's walking a lot and reading.'

'Brains is her middle name. Even when she was little.'

'Ana's sending some of the material for the bridesmaids' dresses to us. Apparently that's what they do these days. It's got deep red in it and we should try to match that for the posies and also make ribbons for the handles of the same material.'

Clem is helping with the parking and the drinks. In fact he's taken over. Charles doesn't seem to mind. Sophie starts at the Blue Banana at Easter. She's been almost unbelievably helpful. It's probably something to do with her new boyfriend, who is more her age. Going out with Dan was destructive, although of course she could never say that. She's back in London now, but she's coming down again at the weekend with Eddie. The vicar's coming by for a discussion. He's insisting on a chat with Ana and Charlie – instruction – before the wedding although he's agreed to combine it with the rehearsal as Ana and Charlie are both very busy.

'I'm stressed,' says Daphne.

'But happy.'

'I think women need to be busy. Men can slump in front of the television in their own world, but we have to feel connected.'

'Connected. Yes, I suppose that's it. Alive might be another word.'

When Frances leaves, the battle plan updated, she sits for a while on a pew. There's so much to organise, but Frances is right, she's happy. She loves the church and now she can see how it's going to look laden with flowers. Flowers are more important than the wedding vows. Flowers are beauty for its own sake. Surely that's all there is? You can't see the exotic Ana and clever, stylish Charlie being married for ever. In fact you can't see any of the young being married for ever. Let alone Frances's daughter, Pip.

I will look after the grandchild happily, if there are problems. All the areas of agreement, all the conventions that most people shared when we were young, have shrunk.

Flowers used to have a language. Ophelia's wreath – Sophie mentioned Ophelia just the other day – contained crow-flowers, nettles, daisies and long purples. Shakespeare chose them deliberately for their message: the crow-flower was known as the Fayre Maide, the nettles indicate stinging, the daisies virginity. The long purples were also known as dead men's fingers. So, according to *Language of Flowers*, 1835, the wreath means: *A fair maid stung to the quick, her virgin bloom under the cold hand of death.*

What flowers are saying now is less specific. They seem to have left the world of symbols and moved instead into the realm of personal statement. And that's what we are doing, let's be honest. The flowers, their lavishness and beauty, are our family statement: here's our son Charlie, entering the church through a lush archway of flowers; and next to him, welcomed by flowers, is his best man, who is also his sister, the prodigal daughter; here's Charlie's beautiful bride, holding her bouquet, probably of Tamango roses and orchids; and here are the bridesmaids with their pale-pink and white posies, tied with red ribbons, and look here, bags of rose petals, at twenty-five pounds a go, are being thrown about the churchyard with abandon; and there is my husband, his good hair brushed, his face amused, his worries past.

The family message is of redemption.

After that awful scene at the station platform, he drove them home erratically. He seemed to be entombed in a furious silence. At the familar bridge, he turned the wrong way down a narrow farm lane. He reversed the car over a rock, which must have punched a hole in something, because the car was thumping loudly like an old-fashioned motorcycle, like Jerome's Norton.

She did not dare ask him to stop or to hand over the driving. She talked to Ju-Ju, half turned to the back seat where the two girls clung together, trying to fill the screaming emptiness. Charlie has been telling her that Charles is cracking up, but she couldn't acknowledge it until now. Now she sees that Ju-Ju's return has been too much for him; instead of freeing him, it's pushed him over the edge. Mental states are always described in this way, as though we are all walking along a cliff-top. But even now she tells Ju-Ju that he was fine until he went into hospital. The young doctor said, *he said it unmistakably, Ju*, that these pneumonia drugs can cause confusion. Ju-Ju looks so sad, utterly desolate at times, but she won't say a word against him. For two days he's lain in his bed reading from the slug-pellet-stained book. Twice Ju-Ju had gone up to the room and knocked; both times he has refused to let her in.

Today at lunchtime they decided that Ju-Ju would take his lunch up to him. She hung behind.

'Dad, I've got your lunch here.'

'Your mother should do it.'

'Dad, I would like to give you your lunch.'

'Your mother should do it.'

'Dad, I want to talk to you.'

'Your mother does the meals.'

'How are you feeling, Dad?'

'Call your mother.'

Daphne couldn't stop herself. She rushed in.

He looked up calmly from his book.

'What the hell's the matter with you, Charles? You're behaving like a baby. Ju-Ju is here, you haven't seen her for three years, and we know the reason why.'

'Do you have my lunch?'

'You are a shit, an A-1 shit.'

'If you don't want to give me my lunch, you can bugger off.'

Ju-Ju was standing outside the door. She took the tray from her and threw it on the floor.

'Here's your lunch, you shit.'

Down in the kitchen, Ju-Ju said, 'Don't shout at him, Mum.'

'Why not?'

'I don't think it's going to help.'

'He's a selfish, arrogant shit. He always has been.'

'That's not true, Mum. He's been a good father.'

'You don't know the half of it. I have had to live with him for thirty-six years. You would think he's the one who has been in jail. I find it completely, utterly selfish. And childish.'

'Mum, he'll be fine.'

'I'm going to the church.'

'Can I help?'

'We're still in the planning stage. Frances thinks she's General Montgomery.'

Now Ju-Ju walks over the golf course down to Daymer and right along the beach to the end where the stream crosses the sand and Betjeman wrote that there were water irises. She climbs to the top of the hill. Two fishing boats are coming home across Doom Bar. It's calm; the little boats are butting gently against the water. Seagulls follow. She remembers some of the names of the boats: *The Maid of Padstow*, *The Cornish Princess* and *Padstow Belle*. When she was a child, she thought that there was something primitive about fishing: it was dangerous and crude and always ended in blood and piles of fish corpses. Nothing is as innocent as a fish corpse. The fishermen had received direct knowledge of an earlier world.

She watches the boats make harbour. She wants to see them safe before she runs down the hill, which is thyme-scented underfoot even though it's early in the season. She jumps down the dune at the bottom and walks back along the edge of the golf course, a tussocky no man's land between the golfers and the bathers, where a boy called Timmy inserted his finger tentatively under her pants when she was fifteen.

She wrote a poem, in her head only, which began:

> Sand in the cider, wasps in the pasty
> Sand in my knickers, just Timmy and me.

Back in the house she finds the tray where Mum threw it and she clears up quietly. She rings Charlie, but his mobile (she's remembering to say mobile instead of cell) is diverted: *Charlie, will you call me when you can? I think you are right, he may need some help. But don't panic. Give my love to Ana.*

You have ruined our fucking lives.

* * *

She reads a book, picked off the shelves. It's called *A Town Like Alice*, by Nevil Shute. Her parents' books all seem to date from about 1955. All these novels, once popular presumably, which are now never read. And there's a special leather-bound edition of Winston Churchill's *History of the English-Speaking Peoples*, and a book called *Forever Amber*, and another called *The Blue Nile*. They're all familiar, more for their covers and their smell and the way the end papers are glued, than for their contents.

The phone rings. She feels, despite herself, a little tumult in the blood.

'Charlie?'

'Hello.'

'Oh, sorry, I was expecting a call. Who is this?'

'It's Bodmin Hospital here. Could I speak to Mr Judd?'

'I'll go and call him.'

But he's not in his room.

'Sorry, he seems to have gone out for a walk.'

'Are you Mrs Judd?'

'No, I'm his daughter, Juliet.'

'He was supposed to be ringing in this morning for some test results. Look, I know he was worried, but as you are his daughter, could you just tell him everything's fine. Nothing to worry about. He should come in for some tablets, but there's no hurry. All right, love?'

'What was the problem?'

'I'm afraid I can't discuss that, love, but anyway, the main thing is everything's clear.'

'He was supposed to ring this morning?'

'Yes.'

'All right, I'll tell him.'

The car has gone. She rings Clem.

'Clem, sorry to bother you, can you take me out to Porth Quin. Dad's gone wandering and I need to speak to him.'

'For you, Juliet, I would ride a porcupine bareback.'

'Thanks, Clem, I'll start walking up the lane.'

* * *

Charles is walking down the path towards Epphaven.

There is something I should, ought, to do, Professor. I have the answer to your charming conundrum: I bet, when you wrote that, you sat back in your garden in North Oxford with a cup of tea. Or maybe a beer. You sound like a beer man, full of common sense, which points up your fierce and famous intelligence. Yes, there is something I should do.

The bracken is beginning to unfurl from its winter hibernation. You can almost see it happening, like those time-lapse documentaries. He stops to pee into the undergrowth, the same impenetrable jungle of blackberries, bracken and gorse that provides a refuge for his own rabbit guerrillas. He pees weakly.

They put a needle up my arse, Herr Professor. How does that square with your reluctance to take a moral stand?

The path splits here. It bifurcates. He takes the lower route, towards the cove. Once, when he was a mogul of bean-counting, when he was peeing strongly, when he was fucking Jo on his desk, her legs bifurcated eagerly, he tried to buy the house up in the bracken, which has its own path to the cove. This little piece of heaven was not available even to a partner of the old and respected firm of Fox and Jewell. He remembers with shame the conversation with the owner, an elderly lady: *Why do people like you imagine you can buy anything? This house has belonged to my family since 1926 and I hope my grandchildren will pass it on to their children.*

I was a prick. As Daphne says, an arrogant shit. But I always kept something back, and that's why they threw me out; people don't like doubters; they don't like ironists. Why should they? And now I have come to this, a needle up my arse, looking for the proof, if it's needed, that I am dying. Everything is connected. My beloved daughter has come home and I can't speak to her. I can't find the words. I wanted to tell her when I saw her on the station platform that I haven't passed an hour in the last three years without thinking of her, yet when she was there, right in front of me, I uttered horrible, horrible words. It's already spread to my brain.

There is something I should, ought, to do.

He pauses at the top of the green slippery ledges that lead down to the cove. At high tide there is no beach at all, but every rock is familiar. I wonder why we take in these holiday landscapes so deeply? Why do we love that rock where we picnicked, or that rock where we dived, or that rock that we used to swim to? When we are gone, this place is unmoved by our absence. That blind cave, where rock pigeons roost, will still reverberate meaninglessly on the high tide.

I'll walk around the hill, the scenic route that Ju-Ju loved, which leads to the pasture where we found the mushrooms that day.

He brushes through the brown, hard stems of last year's brambles. Ju-Ju's legs as she followed were scored by the brambles, leaving what looked like chalk marks; one or two scratches produced tiny bubbles of blood, which never quite needed an Elastoplast. Elastoplast was a badge of honour.

And here's another thing I will never know the answer to: why do children cherish an injury? When I tore a cartilage at school, I hopped around on crutches proudly for weeks.

Now he's more than halfway around the hill. There isn't a building in sight. It's as though you have entered pre-Saxon Britain; there are miles of coastline, some of it softly folded, some torn into jagged edges. As he rises up to the mushroom pasture, he sees the gate and the duckboard that leads past the mine through to Doyden; he can see the house and the pineapple folly in front of it on the cliff top. A lot of seagulls live here; they shun domestic comforts. He can see them on the steep grassy bank above the cliff. If birds can be rated in this way, seagulls truly are bastards: cold, ruthless, unlovable.

Just then he hears a voice floating on the uncertain air currents, floating fitfully. Below the big house, running towards him down the steep path, is a girl. This is the cruel sort of trick that is traditionally played. He turns away to look at the roosting bastard gulls. He hears someone calling, *Dad, Dad, Dad*. It's a girl's voice. He looks again and sees Ju-Ju running in her ungainly but quite effective way, her lower legs rising sideways off the true. She is running towards him waving. From here he can't see if she is wearing her spotted shorts.

She waves as she opens the gate. Now she's walking fast across the pasture.

'Dad, Dad. Here you are.'

'I'm having a walk.'

'I found you. The hospital rang to say your tests are clear. Can I walk with you?'

'Clear?'

'Yes, completely clear. Nothing to worry about.'

Her face is pink and dewed and her hair is stuck down. She's run all the way from the car park.

'How did you know I would be here?'

'It's our walk.'

He sits down, his back against a stone wall, on a soft mound of thrift, and she sits next to him and takes his hand.

'They put a needle up my bottom.'

It's all he can think of saying.

But she is more eloquent.

'Every minute of every day I was in jail, I thought of you. Don't cry, Dad.'

But they are both crying solvent tears.

This must be the sort of thing the beardy vicar was thinking of.

As Daphne walks along the familiar path across the fairway, not far from where Charles tried to drown himself in the stream, she thinks that, when this is all over, when everybody's settled again, she'll open a small flower shop.

I am going to buy from the Flying Dutchmen, and I'm going to go into the shop early every morning and tie beautiful bunches of flowers. Charles can take himself to the Codfather or buy himself a Scotch egg at the pub or play golf with Clem, or do just what he likes. I am not going to live as though I am only here to make his life easy.

When Simon Gore-Simpson came to see her, nearly ten years ago now, and told her that there were complaints against Charles from clients, and from young women trainees, she never mentioned the conversation to anyone. Charles said that he was not carrying on his action against the firm: he couldn't run the risk of bankruptcy. She didn't say that she knew the real reasons. As Simon had advised her, she backed his decision and – as they say – she stood by him. For the sake of the children; that's the phrase they always use, the little women who are wronged.

I am a little woman: a little, drab Englishwoman.

She walks down to the beach still miraculously deserted although soon the Easter crowds will be here. The tide is going out and she walks to the water's edge. From here she can see the buoy where Charlie saved Charles. The bell on it is clanking unceasingly.

Charles's life has been a series of incidents. I will never forgive him for the latest, for what he said at the station. I'll never forgive him for failing Ju-Ju. There's something rotten at his core, and for all these years I've tried to pretend that it isn't so.

Out beyond Doom Bar a fishing boat has anchored. It's missed the tide. It will have to come in about midnight. She walks with foreboding up the lane. The lights are on in the house as she approaches; then, through the window from the garden, she sees Ju-Ju and Charles sitting side by side on the blue sofa that is going to be re-covered before the wedding. In front of them is a green bottle of Chardonnay. Ju-Ju is laughing, and Charles pours himself another glass of wine. *The other half*, as her father used to say.

Chapter Thirty

Almost everybody has accepted the invitation, despite the short notice. Perhaps it's the hint of scandal, or celebrity, that is attractive. Perhaps it's the glamour of the young couple. It could even be the location. The little church, looking as though it is still only half-excavated from the landscape, and the unrivalled view down to the sea, past the mysterious green mound of Bray Hill, the bay gleaming after the rain, the walk up to the church across the fairway and past the stream where Charles Judd almost drowned – again – and on towards the lychgate, richly swagged with ivy and lilies and pale viburnum – all this has a powerful appeal to those who can read the signals. The appeal is to some lost sense of rightness, just as Daphne Judd imagined it.

Most of the guests have set off for the walk from the car park, a field near the beach. Clem Thomas is in charge of parking. He has a walkie-talkie and two teenaged boys as assistants. Those who don't know the way to the church are guided by wicker baskets on poles; each basket is full of lilac and rosemary and dried hydrangea heads, and tied with ribbons in red and white. The baskets – Sophie Judd's idea – stretch down the lane and – with kind permission of the club secretary – across the golf course and up the grassy hill towards the church. The effect is of small maypoles. At the lychgates most guests have stopped to chat and look at the grave of John Betjeman. The poet laureate is buried right here: his grave buzzes with significance, as though bees are swarming down below. The message is one of Englishness, although as a boy Betjeman was terrorised because of his German-sounding name.

From the church comes the sound of a string quartet, playing, most people think, a Haydn selection. The three girls in glasses and a boy with a pronounced Adam's apple who make up the quartet have travelled down from north London in a hired van and are staying at the Sea View Guest House not far away. It is cheap, because the view of the sea is limited and there are only two bathrooms for the eight bedrooms.

Although the generations are blurred at the margins, two distinct age-groups can be made out straggling up the scented spring turf: these are the crocked and battered relatives and friends of the parents, and the young and careless friends of the bride and groom. The older group walk in a way that suggests they know they are on borrowed time. They have passed just beyond middle age. One or two move awkwardly about the hips. They suspect that their hips or their stiff fingers are never going to operate freely again. One man uses a stick. Even those showing no outward signs give clues to their state: the women's dresses – mainly silk – are loudly defiant, as if by cramming into one space many floral images you can distract the attention and then – the final camouflage – you can wear a large hat burdened with silk flowers. The men kiss the women they know in jokey, self-deprecating style: let's not forget we were once young flesh too. Although three of the men are in morning suits, having interpreted Charlie Judd's 'elegantly informal' in this way, all the others are in suits of the old sort, which hide their insubstantial thighs and melanin-spotted forearms. Those women who are not on HRT are solid from shoulder to hip, conforming to an ancient and pre-ordained pattern. An agnostic might see this as evidence that God – if there is one – has a cruel sense of humour, although God's sense of humour is a very old literary chestnut.

This group, wandering across the fairway, are like the prisoners on the River Kwai, held in place, however, not by an enemy, but by Englishness, which makes them proud, ironic and ridiculous all at once.

The younger group are unconstrained. They rest lighly on the earth. For a start some of them, mainly Ana Moreno's friends, bring an exoticism with them. Who knows if they are charmed by this little place? Probably not. Compared with the coves of Croatia or the ponds of Martha's Vineyard or the Bay Islands of Honduras, it lacks obvious glamour. It has a sort of dull, almost monochrome greenness and the sea itself is like pewter. What it has, which some of them possibly miss, is an eloquence, but one that speaks in a lost language.

The younger group are polite to the older group when their paths cross. They adopt encouraging expressions as though they should be concerned but cheerful. But for the most part they walk with their peers, although the older group would feel blessed to be allowed to mingle with them and share their jokes and their fresh knowledge of the world.

At the door of the church, outlined by a wonderful arch of ivy and moss relieved by silver willow branches (sprayed with Clem Thomas's spray gun), the ushers wait to show the guests in. Three of them are friends of Charlie Judd, and one is Eddie Abbott, who is Sophie Judd's new boyfriend. Apart from Eddie, they have just reached that age when unconditional youth is leaving them: two of them have lost a little hair, revealing in the dull but insistent light some surprised areas of scalp. One of them, Jonathan Blisset, has a newly plump and soft face that seems to prefigure middle age.

Ana's father, His Excellency Juan-Pablo Moreno, has been able at the last minute to make the journey from Lima to give away his daughter. Daphne Judd has made him a buttonhole, although she has had to use a yellow rose, which she has attached to his lustrous blue suit whose threads contain their own source of light. She finds him utterly charming: he says that although he would have been delighted to sleep on a sofa, the Sea View is perfect in every way, and who knows who you could meet on the long march to the bathroom? He speaks Spanish to Ana, although she answers in English.

Ana's dress, made by the friends who design for celebrities, is almost ivory, with two triangular panels of tropical red near the ground, as though curtains are being pulled back to give a glimpse of her true nature. Daphne thinks the red is the colour of a macaw's flight feathers. Over her face Ana has a veil, flecked with the same dark red. Her bouquet is of green Maggi Oei orchids, which have dark centres, and the deep red Tamango roses. The whole thing is edged with trailing ivy. The two bridesmaids, Emma and Diana Fleet, headed by their second cousin, Sophie Judd, who is the principal bridesmaid, carry posies of pale yellow and white roses trimmed with camellia leaves. The two little girls also wear circlets on their heads of orchids and peonies.

Juliet Judd, the best man, wears a softer version of the bride-groom's buttonhole: it has two white roses and ivy berries, and two more camellia leaves. It is generally more bosky. She is wearing a pale-green trouser suit, chosen for her by her brother. Charlie Judd is wearing a light-grey suit, with a high collar. His father said that he looked like Jawaharlal Nehru in it. Charlie didn't ask who he was.

On a signal from Clem Thomas, relayed by one of the boy assistants – the guests are all settled – Daphne and Charles Judd set off towards the church. She is holding his arm. She has bought a new dress in pale-yellow silk. She also has a hat, light and small. The perforated brim makes her look less matronly. Charles is wearing his best suit with an elegant buttonhole like Charlie's. He has had his abundant hair washed and cut in London; the ivory colour has been rinsed out and his teeth too have lost their bathtub greyness. Daphne thinks he looks a hundred per cent better.

Davis Lyendecker is not looking a hundred per cent better. Closer to twenty. He has taken his place early near the back of the church, underneath the stained-glass window, which, he notices, depicts the same biblical incident as the stolen Tiffany window: the resurrection. The angel is speaking to the women, Mary Magdalene and the other Mary, who are kneeling in front of the empty tomb: *Be not affrighted: Ye seek Jesus of Nazareth which was crucified: he is risen.*

Davis Lyendecker thinks that stained glass must have appeared almost alive to its beholders. The glass itself, subject to the light, changes in intensity; it is like a very slow movie. And the glass itself, as Juliet wrote, appears to contain a religious quality. It is numinous.

Lyendecker, although he has lost some weight in the intervening weeks, knows that he is still too fat. When Juliet introduced him to her family, he could see the sudden, startled appraisal on their bold faces. But he's glad to be here in his jaunty buttonhole and unseasonal suit, which Mrs Judd insisted on ironing for him. He's been helping the younger sister, Sophie, with an essay. Also he feels blessed to be the only one to know the whole story including its uplifting ending, the miracle of Juliet's resurrection. And he is himself a character in a biblical miracle: he is going to be a father, Joseph to Juliet's Mary.

The bridegroom and his best man are walking across the fairway, arm in arm, towards the church.

'Ju-Ju, who exactly is Davis?'

'He's a friend of mine from New York.'

'Is he OK? He looks a little like whacked.'

'He's had a bad time in Minnesota. But he's getting better.'

'Why did you invite him?'

'Do you mind?'

'Of course not.'

'Good.'

'Do you love him?'

'Charlie, it's your wedding day.'

They approach the church through the beautiful flowers draped on the lychgate. They were all busy with flowers until two in the morning. But you can see now that it was worth it.

*   *   *

Their parents smile up at Charlie and Juliet Judd as they pass to take up their positions. Charles Judd has ordered a new dog, a chocolate Labrador, which he has incorporated into his speech. The joke is that Labradors love water. He thinks this will play well.

Author's Notes and Acknowledgements

Although I have been a frequent visitor to Trebetherick, I have imagined entirely what goes on in the church; if there is a beardy vicar, I haven't met him.

I would like to thank Rosemary Davidson, Liz Calder, Nigel Newton and many others from Bloomsbury; my Canadian publisher, Kim McArthur; my agents Michael Sissons and James Gill; and my family for their forebearance. I am increasingly aware of the self-exculpation that writers grant to themselves.

Others who helped me with specifics were Paula Pryke, Alastair Sooke, Emily Mears and Mark Potter.

The Chinese Slam the Door

came in the summer of 1979. For that was when a convoy party
of British tourists stepped down from their coaches at the Caves
of the Thousand Buddhas, blinking in the bright sunlight. The
last shred of mystery and romance had finally gone from the
Silk Road.

JUSTIN CARTWRIGHT
The Promise of Happiness

A READING GUIDE

ABOUT THE BOOK

In brief

The Promise of Happiness has been described as a re-invention of that much-maligned genre, the Aga-saga and indeed it does deal with a quintessentially middle-class English family trying to cope with crisis and strained relationships, but the novel reaches far beyond the domestic. Two years earlier, Charles and Daphne Judd were settling into a somewhat uneasy retirement in Cornwall when their world was shattered by the news of their beloved daughter Ju-Ju's conviction and imprisonment for her part in an art theft in New York.

As the novel opens they await her release and return. Charlie, their capable and successful son, is bringing Ju-Ju home and helping her to re-enter the world after her ordeal; his own life is unsettled by his glamorous girlfriend's pregnancy and his ambivalence towards it. Sophie, the youngest and most rebellious sibling, has decided to get her chaotic life under control. These five disparate yet closely bound family members are finally reunited at Charlie's Cornish wedding. With acute perception and gentle humour Justin Cartwright gradually reveals the inner struggles of the Judds as they grapple with their conflicting feelings for each other, Ju-Ju's imprisonment and the moral dilemmas that beset them.

In detail

Most of Justin Cartwright's novels are set in Africa, with the Whitbread-winning *Leading the Cheers* set in America where he lived for a year. With *The Promise of Happiness* he wanted to 'write a novel about a middle-class family, which was also about England'. As a long-term resident who still describes himself as South African, he was ideally placed: an outsider, but one with an intimate knowledge. *The Promise of Happiness* explores two Englands: the traditional, fading England of Charles and Daphne as they try to settle themselves in Betjeman's Cornwall and the new bustling, fast-changing England of Charles and Sophie with its slang, dotcom entrepreneurs and obsession with style.

Aside from his first two, which were thrillers, Cartwright's previous novels have tended to be loosely autobiographical, 'versions of myself to some degree' as he has described them. His protagonists are often men grappling with mid-life crises and its attendant disillusionment, echoed here in Charles Judd's attempts to come to terms with a troubled late middle-age. Charles turns to philosophy to find an answer, almost furtively thumbing Bernard Williams' *Truth and Truthfulness* in an attempt to put to rest his uneasiness about his forced removal from an accountancy firm and his distress about Ju-Ju's conviction.

Cartwright has said that all his books are about 'consciousness', about people struggling to find a place for themselves in the world: 'That to me is the theme of the modern novel. I write from what I take to be the realist point of view, looking at life as it really is, or the way I see it to be. John Updike said that his job as a novelist was to record the ordinary and out of that make the extraordinary. I think that's right.'

ABOUT THE AUTHOR

Justin Cartwright was born in South Africa, the son of the editor of the *Rand Daily Mail*. He was educated in the US and at Oxford University where he read politics. His *In Every Face I Meet* was shortlisted for the Booker Prize, *Leading the Cheers*, won the 1998 Whitbread Novel Award. His novels *Half in Love* and the acclaimed *White Lightning* were also shortlisted for the Whitbread Novel Award. He has won other awards including a Commonweath Writers' Prize and the South African M-Net award.

Justin Cartwright lives in north London with his wife and, occasionally, with his two sons. *The Promise of Happiness* was chosen as one of Richard and Judy's Book Club titles for 2005 and was the winner of the 2005 Hawthornden Prize and the Sunday Times of South Africa Prize. His most recent novel is *To Heaven By Water*, which was a Radio 4 Book at Bedtime.

FOR DISCUSSION

– How effective did you find the prologue as an introduction to the novel?

– Were your expectations of the Judds fulfilled? Charlie tells Sophie: 'Dad doesn't want to be happy, Soph. There are some people who don't believe in the promise of happiness' (page 22). When Charlie asks Ju-Ju why she is carrying small dumbbells she replies playfully, 'I'm making good on the promise of happiness' (page 36). Why do you think Justin Cartwright chose 'The Promise of Happiness' as the book's title? What do you think he means by it? How appropriate did you find it?

– How would you describe Charles and Daphne's marriage? How has their relationship been affected by Ju-Ju's imprisonment? How different are their reactions to her incarceration, and how do those reactions compare to those of Charlie and Sophie?

– 'At Fox and Jewell he had always been seen as urbane, with a light touch' (page 6). How do others see Charles? How would you describe him?

– 'The empty, windswept landscape of her life is peopled again' (page 100). What prompts Daphne to think this? Why does she describe her world as empty?

– Charlie carefully plans a gentle re-entry into the world for Ju-Ju. How would you describe the relationship between the two siblings? How does it compare with Charlie's relationship with his girlfriend, Ana, and with Charles' feelings for Ju-Ju?

– 'We must get over believing that she is not guilty,' says Sophie. 'But exactly how guilty is she?' (page 134). How would Ju-Ju answer this? Why has she decided to take the rap? How has her view changed by the end of the book?

– 'Professor Williams says that the idea of a good father is problematic. We know what a father is, he says, but the rest of the proposition is entirely subjective' (page 282). Do you think Charles has been a good father? How good a mother is Daphne?

– Charles struggles to make sense of his dismissal from Fox and Jewell, and of Ju-Ju's imprisonment. What conclusions does he come to? Can Ju-Ju's conviction be compared with the way in which Charles was forced out of Fox and Jewell?

– 'The Judd family is disintegrating. Or perhaps it is just going through a cycle of change ...' (page 219). What do you think? How typical would you say the Judd family is?

– Resurrection is a recurring motif in the book. It is the subject of the Tiffany window which was the cause of Ju-Ju's problems, and of the window that Davis Lyendecker finds himself under at Charlie and Ana's wedding. What do you think Cartwright means by it?

– 'In my next life I will be bold and free' (page 92). The narrative is written in the third person, switching from character to character, but very occasionally Cartwright intersperses it with first person comments. What effect does this have? Why do you think he chose this style? How well does he capture the voices of the novel's radically different characters?

BY THE SAME AUTHOR

SUGGESTED FURTHER READING

Fiction

The Crow Road by Iain Banks
The Corrections by Jonathan Franzen
Accidents in the Home by Tessa Hadley
A Map of the World by Jane Hamilton
The Way the Crow Flies by Ann-Marie MacDonald

Non-Fiction

Truth and Truthfulness: An Essay in Genealogy
   by Bernard Williams

JUSTIN CARTWRIGHT'S
FAVOURITE BOOKS

Children's book

Kenneth Grahame's *Wind in the Willows*. When I was a boy in South Africa it evoked a magical world, which was in fact Edwardian England, although I didn't realise it. Animals in children's books always stand for something, especially good qualities. So owls are always wise, dogs faithful, horses uncomplaining.

The characters of Ratty, Toad and Mole are classic examples of this.

Classic

I read Leo Tolstoy's *War and Peace* in two weeks when I was in bed aged fourteen, and it has never left me.

Contemporary book

W. G. Sebald's *Austerlitz* – a wonderful contemplation of Europe, European history and the lines of pain in history. But it is also minutely observed and very eloquently detailed.

Top 10

Rabbit at Rest by John Updike
American Pastoral by Philip Roth
Boyhood by J. M. Coetzee
A Tale of Love and Dark by Amos Oz
Le Rouge et Le Noir by Stendhal
Men at Arms by Evelyn Waugh
Pride and Prejudice by Jane Austen
The Coup by John Updike
Herzog by Saul Bellow
Humboldt's Gift by Saul Bellow

ALSO AVAILABLE BY JUSTIN CARTWRIGHT

TO HEAVEN BY WATER

A BBC Radio 4 Book at Bedtime

David Cross is surrounded by secrets. When his wife Nancy was alive he kept secrets from her and now that she is dead, he must hide his new happiness from his children, Lucy and Ed. But they too have their troubles: Ed's marriage is in trouble, Lucy is being stalked by her ex-boyfriend, and both worry that their father will find a new partner.

To Heaven by Water is a touching and hilarious portrait of a family trying to come to terms with loss in their own way.

*

'A high-class piece of literary entertainment'
SPECTATOR

'What distinguishes *To Heaven by Water* and turns it into a convincing take on the English (or rather London) early twenty-first century is the eye for detail and the sheer brio of the writing'
INDEPENDENT

'Cartwright has mastered a particular type of wry English social comedy invariably seething with black undercurrents'
EILEEN BATTERSBY, IRISH TIMES

*

ISBN 9781408801031 · PAPERBACK · £7.99

B L O O M S B U R Y

THE SONG BEFORE IT IS SUNG

On 20 July 1944, Adolf Hitler narrowly escaped an assassin's bomb. Axel vón Gottberg and his conspirators were hunted down and hanged from meat-hooks, and the executions filmed. Sixty years later, Conrad Senior is left a legacy of letters by von Gottberg's close friend, the legendary Oxford professor Elya Mendel, and becomes obsessed with what they reveal and finding the brutal film. Award-winning writer Justin Cartwright has conjured a masterwork that addresses the nature of friendship and what it means to be human, and it is a remarkable tapestry of passion, ideas, frailty and courage.

*

'A richly detailed evocation of one of the darkest periods in modern history, and an eloquent exploration of human fallibility and guilt'
THE TIMES

'Heart-stopping ... utterly accomplished'
SUNDAY TELEGRAPH

'A profound exploration of guilt, friendship, voyeurism and morality. A cracker'
INDEPENDENT ON SUNDAY

*

ISBN 9780747585947 · PAPERBACK · £7.99

BLOOMSBURY

THIS SECRET GARDEN

OXFORD REVISITED

Oxford is many things. But it has a symbolic meaning which reaches well beyond its buildings, gardens, rituals and teaching. It stands for something deep in the Anglo-Saxon mind: excellence, a kind of privilege, open-mindedness, respect for tradition.

Cartwright has spoken to many leading figures, looked at favourite places in Oxford, subjected himself to an English tutorial – he performed very poorly – attended the freshers' dinner in his old college, studied various works of art, libraries and museums, investigated the claim that dons like detective novels, and reread many Oxford classics. At the same time he has looked at some of the great debates and reforms which made Oxford what it is, as well as the most recent debate about funding reform, which ended in a resounding defeat for the reformers.

He finds that the Oxford myth, while it is at odds with reality, is as powerful as ever. This is an enchanting and intelligent look at Oxford, indispensable reading for anyone interested in the myth and reality of this famed city.

*

'A poignant meditation on youth and age'
GUARDIAN

'An attractively written book, which captures the university's mixture of the serious, the silly, the political and the picturesque … it will appeal to both armchair tourists and homesick Oxonians'
TIMES LITERARY SUPPLEMENT

*

ISBN 978074759618 · PAPERBACK · £7.99

ORDER YOUR COPY: BY PHONE +44 (0)1256 302 699; BY EMAIL: DIRECT@MACMILLAN.CO.UK

DELIVERY IS USUALLY 3–5 WORKING DAYS. FREE POSTAGE AND PACKAGING FOR ORDERS OVER £20.

ONLINE: WWW.BLOOMSBURY.COM/BOOKSHOP

PRICES AND AVAILABILITY SUBJECT TO CHANGE WITHOUT NOTICE.

WWW.BLOOMSBURY.COM/JUSTINCARTWRIGHT

BLOOMSBURY